THE FLAME BEARER

BERNARD CORNWELL

The Flame Bearer

HARPER

Harper
An imprint of HarperCollins*Publishers*
1 London Bridge Street
London SE1 9GF

www.harpercollins.co.uk

This paperback edition 2017

1

First published in Great Britain by
HarperCollins*Publishers* 2016

Copyright © Bernard Cornwell 2016

Maps © John Gilkes 2016

Bernard Cornwell asserts the moral right to
be identified as the author of this work

A catalogue record for this book is
available from the British Library

ISBN: 978-0-00-750425-1

This novel is entirely a work of fiction.
The names, characters and incidents portrayed in it,
while at times based on historical figures, are
the work of the author's imagination.

Set in Meridien LT Std by Palimpsest Book Production Limited,
Falkirk, Stirlingshire

Printed and bound in Great Britain by
Clays Ltd, St Ives plc

All rights reserved. No part of this publication may be
reproduced, stored in a retrieval system, or transmitted,
in any form or by any means, electronic, mechanical,
photocopying, recording or otherwise, without the prior
permission of the publishers.

This book is sold subject to the condition that it shall not,
by way of trade or otherwise, be lent, re-sold, hired out or
otherwise circulated without the publisher's prior consent
in any form of binding or cover other than that in which it
is published and without a similar condition including this
condition being imposed on the subsequent purchaser.

MIX
Paper from
responsible sources
FSC™ C007454

FSC™ is a non-profit international organisation established to promote
the responsible management of the world's forests. Products carrying the
FSC label are independently certified to assure consumers that they come
from forests that are managed to meet the social, economic and
ecological needs of present and future generations,
and other controlled sources.

Find out more about HarperCollins and the environment at
www.harpercollins.co.uk/green

The Flame Bearer
is for Kevin Scott Callahan,
1992–2015
Wyrd biŏ ful āræd

CONTENTS

PLACE NAMES

The spelling of place names in Anglo-Saxon England was an uncertain business, with no consistency and no agreement even about the name itself. Thus London was variously rendered as Lundonia, Lundenberg, Lundenne, Lundene, Lundenwic, Lundenceaster and Lundres. Doubtless some readers will prefer other versions of the names listed below, but I have usually employed whichever spelling is cited in either the *Oxford Dictionary of English Place-Names* or the *Cambridge Dictionary of English Place-Names* for the years nearest or contained within Alfred's reign, AD 871–899, but even that solution is not foolproof. Hayling Island, in 956, was written as both Heilincigae and Hæglingaiggæ. Nor have I been consistent myself; I have preferred the modern form Northumbria to Norðhymbralond to avoid the suggestion that the boundaries of the ancient kingdom coincide with those of the modern county. So this list, like the spellings, is capricious.

Ætgefrin	Yeavering Bell, Northumberland
Alba	A kingdom comprising much of modern Scotland

Beamfleot	Benfleet, Essex
Bebbanburg	Bamburgh, Northumberland
Beina	River Bain
Cair Ligualid	Carlisle, Cumbria
Ceaster	Chester, Cheshire
Cirrenceastre	Cirencester, Gloucestershire
Cocuedes	Coquet Island, Northumberland
Contwaraburg	Canterbury, Kent
Dumnoc	Dunwich, Suffolk (now mostly vanished beneath the sea)
Dunholm	Durham, County Durham
Eoferwic	York, Yorkshire (Danish name: Jorvik)
Ethandun	Edington, Wiltshire
The Gewasc	The Wash
Godmundcestre	Godmanchester, Cambridgeshire
Grimesbi	Grimsby, Humberside
Gyruum	Jarrow, Tyne & Wear
Hornecastre	Horncastle, Lincolnshire
Humbre	River Humber
Huntandun	Huntingdon, Cambridgeshire
Ledecestre	Leicester, Leicestershire
Lindcolne	Lincoln, Lincolnshire
Lindisfarena	Lindisfarne (Holy Island), Northumberland
Lundene	London
Mældunesburh	Malmesbury, Wiltshire
Steanford	Stamford, Lincolnshire
Strath Clota	Strathclyde
Sumorsæte	Somerset
Tinan	River Tyne
Use	River Ouse (Northumbria), also Great Ouse (East Anglia)
Wavenhe	River Waveney
Weallbyrig	Fictional name for a fort on Hadrian's Wall
Wiire	River Wear
Wiltunscir	Wiltshire
Wintanceaster	Winchester, Hampshire

PART ONE
The King

ONE

It began with three ships.

Now there were four.

The three ships had come to the Northumbrian coast when I was a child, and within days my elder brother was dead and within weeks my father had followed him to the grave, my uncle had stolen my land and I had become an exile. Now, so many years later, I was on the same beach watching four ships come to the coast.

They came from the north, and anything that comes from the north is bad news. The north brings frost and ice, Norsemen and Scots. It brings enemies, and I had enemies enough already because I had come to Northumbria to recapture Bebbanburg. I had come to kill my cousin who had usurped my place. I had come to take my home back.

Bebbanburg lay to the south. I could not see the ramparts from where our horses stood because the dunes were too high, but I could see smoke from the fortress's hearths being snatched westward by the wild wind. The smoke was being blown inland, melding with the low grey clouds that scudded towards Northumbria's dark hills.

It was a sharp wind. The sand flats that stretched towards

Lindisfarena were riotous with breaking waves that seethed white and fast towards the shore. Further out the waves were foam-capped, their spume flying, turbulent. It was also bitterly cold. Summer might have just come to Britain, but winter still wielded a keen-edged knife on the Northumbrian coast and I was glad of my bearskin cloak.

'A bad day for sailors,' Berg called to me. He was one of my younger men, a Norse who revelled in his skill as a swordsman. He had grown his long hair even longer in the last year until it flared out like a great horsetail beneath the rim of his helmet. I had once seen a Saxon seize a man's long hair and drag him backwards from his saddle, then spear him while he was still flailing on the turf.

'You should cut your hair,' I told him.

'In battle I tie it up!' he called back, then nodded seawards. 'They will be wrecked! They're too close to shore!'

The four ships were following the shore but struggling to stay at sea. The wind wanted to drive them ashore, to strand them on the flats, to tip them there and break them apart, but the oarsmen were hauling on their looms as the steersmen tried to force the bows away from the breakers. Seas shattered on their bows and spewed white along their decks. The beam wind was too strong to carry yards or sail-cloth aloft and so their heavy sails were stowed on deck.

'Who are they?' my son asked, spurring his horse alongside mine. The wind lifted his cloak and whipped his horse's mane and tail.

'How would I know?' I asked.

'You've not seen them before?'

'Never,' I said. I knew most of the ships that prowled the Northumbrian coast, but these four were strangers to me. They were not trading vessels, but had the high prows and low freeboard of fighting ships. There were beast-heads on their prows, marking them as pagans. The ships were large.

Each, I reckoned, held forty or fifty men who now rowed for their lives in spiteful seas and bitter wind. The tide was rising, which meant the current was running strongly northwards and the ships were battling their way south, their dragon-crested prows bursting into spray as the cross-seas smashed into their hulls. I watched the nearest ship rear to a wave and half vanish behind the cold seas that shattered about her cutwater. Did they know there was a shallow channel that curled behind Lindisfarena and offered shelter? That channel was easily visible at low tide, but now, in a flooding sea that was being wind-churned to frenzy, the passage was hidden by scudding foam and seething waves, and the four ships, oblivious of the safety the channel offered, rowed past its entrance to struggle on towards the next anchorage that would give them safety.

They were heading for Bebbanburg.

I turned my horse southwards and led my sixty men along the beach. The wind was stinging sand against my face.

I did not know who they were, but I knew where the four ships were going. They were heading for Bebbanburg, and life, I thought, had suddenly become more difficult.

It took us only moments to reach the Bebbanburg channel. The breaking waves pounded the beach and seethed into the harbour mouth, filling the narrow entrance with a swirling grey foam. That entrance was not wide, as a child I had often swum across it, though never when an ebbing tide ran strong. One of my earliest memories was of watching a boy drown as the tide swept him from the harbour channel. His name had been Eglaf, and he must have been six or seven years old when he died. He was the son of a priest, the only son. Strange how names and faces from the distant past come to mind. He had been a small, slight boy, dark-haired and funny, and I had liked him. My elder brother had dared him to swim the channel, and I remember my brother laughing as Eglaf vanished in the welter of dark sea and whipping white caps. I had been crying, and my brother had slapped me around the head. 'He was weak,' my brother said.

How we despise weakness! Only women and priests are allowed to be weak. Poets too, perhaps. Poor Eglaf had died because he wanted to appear as fearless as the rest of us, and in the end he had merely proved he was just as stupid. 'Eglaf,' I said his name aloud as we cantered down the sand-blown beach.

'What?' my son shouted.

'Eglaf,' I said again, not bothering to explain, but I think that so long as we remember names, so long those people live. I am not sure how they live; whether they are spirits drifting like clouds or whether they live in an afterworld. Eglaf could not have gone to Valhalla because he did not die in battle, but of course he was a Christian too, so he must have gone to their heaven, which made me feel even more sorry for him. Christians tell me they spend the rest of time singing praises to their nailed god. The rest of time! Eternity! What kind of swollen-headed god wants to hear himself being praised for ever? Which thought put me in mind of Barwulf, a West Saxon thegn who had paid four harpists to chant songs of his battle-deeds, which were next to none. Barwulf had been a fat, selfish, greedy pig of a man; just the sort who would want to hear himself being praised for ever. I imagined the Christian god as a fat, scowling thegn brooding in his mead hall and listening to lackeys telling him how great he was.

'They're turning!' my son called, breaking my thoughts, and I looked to my left and saw the first ship turning towards the channel. It was a straightforward entrance, though an inexperienced shipmaster could be fooled by the strong tidal

6

currents close inshore, but this man was experienced enough to anticipate the danger and he drove his long hull straight and true. 'Count the men on board,' I ordered Berg.

We reined the horses on the channel's northern bank where the sand was heaped with dark bladderwrack, sea shells, and bleached scraps of wood. 'Who are they?' Rorik asked me. He was a boy, my new servant.

'They're probably Norse,' I said, 'like you.' I had killed Rorik's father and wounded Rorik in a messy battle that had driven the pagans from Mercia. I had felt remorse at injuring a child, he had been only nine when I struck him with my sword, Wasp-Sting, and my guilt had driven me to adopt the boy, just as Ragnar the Elder had adopted me so long ago. Rorik's left arm had healed, though it would never be as strong as his right, but he could hold a shield and he seemed happy. I liked him.

'They're Norse!' he echoed happily.

'I think so,' I said. I was not certain, but there was something about the ships that suggested they were Norse rather than Danish. The great beasts on the prow were more flamboyant, and the short masts were raked further aft than on most Danish ships. 'Don't go too deep!' I called to Berg, who had spurred his horse up to its fetlocks in the swirling shallows.

The tide surged through the channel, the waves flicked white by the wind, but I was staring at the further shore that lay just fifty or sixty yards away. There was a small strip of sand on that far shore that would soon be covered by the flooding tide, then dark rocks that climbed to a high wall. It was a stone wall, which, like so much else in Bebbanburg, had been built since my father's time, and in the centre of that wall was the Sea Gate. Years before, terrified that I would attack him, my uncle had sealed both the Low Gate and the High Gate, which together formed the main entrance to the fortress, and he had built the Sea Gate, which could only be approached by ship or by a path along the beach that led beneath the seaward ramparts. In time his terror had subsided, and, because supplying Bebbanburg through the Sea Gate was both inconvenient and time-consuming, he had reopened the two southern gates, but the Sea Gate still existed. Behind it was a steep path climbing to a higher gate that pierced the wooden palisade surrounding the whole long summit of the rock on which Bebbanburg was built.

Men were gathering on the fighting platform of the high palisade. They waved, not to us, but to the arriving ships, and I thought I heard a cheer from those high ramparts, but perhaps that was my imagination.

I did not imagine the spear. A man hurled it from the palisade, and I watched it fly dark against the dark clouds. For a heartbeat it seemed to hang in the air, and then, like a stooping falcon, it plummeted to thump hard into the shallow water just four or five paces short of Berg's horse. 'Get it,' I told Rorik.

I could hear jeers from the ramparts now. The spear might have fallen short, but it had been a mighty throw all the same. Two more spears fell, both splashing uselessly into the channel's centre. Then Rorik brought me the first spear. 'Hold the blade low,' I said.

'Low?'

'Close to the sand.'

I dismounted, hauled up the heavy mail coat, pulled open the laces, and took aim. 'Hold it still,' I ordered Rorik, and then, when I was sure the men in the bows of the leading ship were watching, I pissed on the blade. My son chuckled, and Rorik laughed. 'Now give it to me,' I ordered the boy, and took the ash-haft from him. I waited. The leading ship was racing into the channel now, the breaking waves seething along her hull as the oarsmen dragged on their blades.

Her high prow, a dragon with open mouth and glaring eyes, reared above the white water. I drew my arm back, waited. It would be a difficult throw, made even more difficult by the force of the wind and by the weight of the bearskin cloak that tried to drag my arm down, but I had no time to unclasp the heavy fur. 'This,' I shouted at the ship, 'is Odin's curse!'

Then I hurled the spear.

Twenty paces.

And the piss-soaked blade struck true, just as I had aimed it. It struck the dragon's eye, and the shaft quivered there as the ship slid past us, tide-driven, going into the calm inner waters of the wide shallow harbour that lay sheltered from the storm by the great rock on which the fortress stood.

My fortress. Bebbanburg.

Bebbanburg.

From the day it was stolen from me I had dreamed of recapturing Bebbanburg. My uncle had been the thief, and now his son, who dared call himself Uhtred, held the great fort. Men said it could not be taken except by treachery or by starvation. It was massive, it was built on the great rock that was almost an island, it could only be approached on land by a single narrow track, and it was mine.

I had once come so close to recapturing the fort. I had taken my men through the Low Gate, but the High Gate had been closed just in time, and so my cousin still ruled in the great fort beside the turbulent sea. His wolf's head banner flew there, and his men jeered from the ramparts as we rode away, and as the four ships coursed through the channel to find safe anchorage in the shallow harbour.

'A hundred and fifty men,' Berg told me, then added, 'I think.'

'And some women and children,' my son said.

'Which means they've come to stay,' I said, 'whoever they are.'

We skirted the harbour's northern edge where the beach was hazy from the fires on which my cousin's tenants smoked herrings or made salt by boiling sea-water. Those tenants now cowered in their small houses that edged the harbour's inland shore. They were frightened of us, and of the newly arrived ships, which were dropping anchor stones amidst the smaller fishing craft that rode out the vicious wind in Bebbanburg's safe water. A dog barked in one of the turf-roofed cottages and was immediately silenced. I spurred my horse between two of the houses and up onto the slope beyond. Goats fled our approach, and the goatherd, a small girl perhaps five or six years old, whimpered and hid her head in her hands. I turned at the low crest to see the crews of the four ships were wading ashore with heavy bundles on their shoulders. 'We could slaughter them as they come ashore,' my son suggested.

'We can't now,' I said, and pointed to the Low Gate, which barred the narrow isthmus leading to the fort. Horsemen were appearing there, emerging from the skull-decorated arch and galloping towards the harbour.

Berg chuckled and pointed to the nearest ship. 'Your spear is still there, lord!'

'That was a lucky throw,' my son said.

'It was not luck,' Berg said reprovingly, 'Odin guided the weapon.' He was a pious young man.

The horsemen were directing the newly arrived sea-warriors towards the hovels of the village rather than towards the great stronghold on its high rock. The crews of the ships dumped their bundles on the shore and added sheaves of spears, piles of shields, and heaps of axes and swords. Women carried small children ashore. The wind brought snatches of voices and of laughter. The newcomers had plainly come to stay, and, as if to show that they now possessed the land, a man planted a flag on the foreshore, grinding its staff into the shingle. It was a grey flag, snapping in the cold wind. 'Can you see what's on it?' I asked.

'A dragon's head,' Berg answered.

'Who flies a dragon's head?' my son asked.

I shrugged. 'No one I know.'

'I would like to see a dragon,' Berg said wistfully.

'It might be the last thing you ever see,' my son remarked.

I do not know if there are dragons. I have never seen one. My father told me they lived in the high hills and fed on cattle and sheep, but Beocca, who had been one of my father's mass priests and my childhood tutor, was certain that all the dragons are sleeping deep in the earth. 'They are Satan's creatures,' he had told me, 'and they hide deep underground waiting for the last days. And when the horn of heaven sounds to announce Christ's return they will burst from the ground like demons! They will fight! Their wings will shadow the sun, their breath will scorch the earth, and their fire will consume the righteous!'

'So we all die?'

'No, no, no! We fight them!'

'How do you fight a dragon?' I had asked him.

'With prayer, boy, with prayer.'

'So we do all die,' I had said, and he had hit me around the head.

Now four ships had brought the dragon's spawn to Bebbanburg. My cousin knew he was under attack. He had been safe for years, protected by his impregnable fortress and by Northumbria's kings. Those kings had been my enemies. To attack Bebbanburg I would have had to fight through Northumbria and defeat the armies of Danes and Norsemen who would gather to protect their land, but now the king in Eoferwic was my son-in-law, my daughter was his queen, the pagans of Northumbria were my friends, and

I could ride unmolested from the Mercian frontier to the walls of Bebbanburg. And for a whole month I had been using that new freedom to ride my cousin's pastures, to harry his steadings, to kill his sworn men, to steal his cattle, and to flaunt myself in sight of his walls. My cousin had not ridden to confront me, preferring to stay safe behind his formidable ramparts, but now he was adding to his forces. The men who carried their shields and weapons ashore must have been hired to defend Bebbanburg. I had heard rumours that my cousin was prepared to pay gold for such men, and we had been watching for their arrival. Now they were here.

'We outnumber them,' my son said. I had close to two hundred men camped in the hills to the west, so yes, if it came to a fight, we would outnumber the newcomers, but not if my cousin added his garrison troops to their ranks. He now commanded over four hundred spears, and life had indeed become more difficult.

'We're going down to meet them,' I said.

'Down?' Berg asked, surprised. There were only sixty of us that day, fewer than half the enemy's number.

'We should know who they are,' I said, 'before we kill them. That's just being polite.' I pointed towards a wind-bent tree. 'Rorik!' I called to my servant, 'cut a branch off that hornbeam and hold it like a banner.' I raised my voice so all my men could hear, 'turn your shields upside down!'

I waited till Rorik was brandishing a ragged branch as a symbol of truce, and until my men had clumsily turned their shields so that their symbols of the wolf's head were upside down, and then I walked Tintreg, my dark stallion, down the slope. We did not go fast. I wanted the newcomers to feel sure that we came in peace.

Those newcomers came to meet us. A dozen men escorted by a score of my cousin's horsemen straggled onto the patch of pastureland where the villagers' goats grazed on thistles.

The horsemen were led by Waldhere, who commanded Bebbanburg's household troops and whom I had met just two weeks before. He had come to my encampment in the western hills with a handful of troops, a branch of truce, and an impudent demand that we left my cousin's land before we were killed. I had scorned the offer and belittled Waldhere, but I knew him to be a dangerous and experienced warrior, blooded many times in fights against marauding Scots. Like me he wore a bearskin cloak and had a heavy sword hanging at his left side. His flat face was framed by an iron helmet that was crested by an eagle's claw. His short beard was grey, his grey eyes grim, and his mouth a wide slash that looked as if it had never smiled. The symbol painted on his shield was the same as mine, the grey wolf's head. That was the badge of Bebbanburg and I had never abandoned it. Waldhere held up a gloved hand to halt the men who followed him and spurred his horse a few paces closer to me. 'You've come to surrender?' he demanded.

'I forget your name,' I said.

'Most people spew shit from their arse,' he retorted, 'you manage it with your mouth.'

'Your mother gave birth through her arse,' I said, 'and you still reek of her shit.'

The insults were routine. One cannot meet an enemy without reviling him. We insult each other, then we fight, though I doubted we would need to draw swords today. Still, we had to pretend. 'Two minutes,' Waldhere threatened, 'then we attack you.'

'But I come in peace,' I indicated the branch.

'I will count to two hundred,' Waldhere said.

'But you only have ten fingers,' my son put in, making my men laugh.

'Two hundred,' Waldhere snarled, 'and then I'll ram your branch of truce up your arsehole.'

'And who are you,' I directed that question to a man who had walked up the slope to join Waldhere. I assumed he was the leader of the newcomers. He was a tall, pale man with a shock of yellow hair that swept back from a high forehead and fell down his back. He was dressed richly with a golden collar about his neck and golden arm rings. The buckle of his belt was gold, and the crosspiece of his sword's hilt shone with more gold. I guessed he was about thirty years old. He was broad-shouldered, with a long face, very pale eyes, and ink-marks of dragon heads on his cheeks. 'Tell me your name,' I demanded.

'Don't answer!' Waldhere snarled. He spoke English, even though my question had been in Danish.

'Berg,' I said, still looking at the newcomer, 'if that shit-mouthed bastard interrupts me one more time I will assume he has broken the truce and you may kill him.'

'Yes, lord.'

Waldhere scowled, but did not speak. He was outnumbered, but every moment we lingered on the pasture brought more of the newcomers, and they came with shields and weapons. It would not be long before they outnumbered us.

'So who are you?' I asked again.

'I am named Einar Egilson,' he answered proudly, 'men call me Einar the White.'

'You are Norse?'

'I am.'

'And I am Uhtred of Bebbanburg,' I told him, 'and men call me by many names. The one I am most proud of is Uhtredærwe. It means Uhtred the Wicked.'

'I have heard men tell of you,' he said.

'You have heard of me,' I said, 'but I have not heard of you! Is that why you have come? Do you suppose your name will become famous if you kill me?'

'It will,' he said.

14

'And if I kill you, Einar Egilson, will it add to my renown?'
I shook my head as an answer to my own question. 'Who
will mourn you? Who will remember you?' I spat towards
Waldhere. 'These men have paid you gold to kill me. You
know why?'

'Tell me,' Einar said.

'Because since I was a little child they have tried to kill
me and they have failed. Always failed. Do you know why
they failed?'

'Tell me,' he said again.

'Because they are cursed,' I said. 'Because they worship
the nailed god of the Christians and he will not protect them.
They despise our gods.' I could see a hammer carved from
white bone at Einar's throat. 'But years ago, Einar Egilson,
I put the curse of Odin on them, I called Thor's anger on
them. And you would take their soiled gold?'

'Gold is gold,' Einar said.

'And I threw the same curse at your ship,' I said.

He nodded, touched the white hammer, but said nothing.

'I will either kill you,' I told Einar, 'or you will come to
join us. I will not offer you gold to join me, I will offer you
something better. Your life. Fight for that man,' I spat towards
Waldhere, 'and you will die. Fight for me and you will live.'

Einar said nothing, but just stared at me solemnly. I was
not certain that Waldhere understood the conversation, but
he hardly needed to understand it. He knew our words were
hostile to his master. 'Enough!' he snarled.

'All of Northumbria hates these men,' I ignored Waldhere
and still spoke to Einar, 'and you would die with them? And
if you choose to die with them we shall take the gold that
is gold that will not be your gold. It will be my gold.' I looked
at Waldhere. 'Have you finished counting?'

He did not answer. He had hoped more men would join
him, enough men to overwhelm us, but our numbers were

15

about equal, and he had no wish to start a fight he was not sure of winning. 'Say your prayers,' I told him,' because your death is near.' I bit my finger and flicked it at him. He made the sign of the cross, while Einar just looked worried. 'If you have the courage,' I told Waldhere, 'I'll wait for you tomorrow at Ætgefrin.' I flicked the finger again, the sign of a curse being cast, and then we rode westwards.

When a man cannot fight he should curse. The gods like to feel needed.

We rode westwards in the dusk. The sky was dark with cloud and the ground sodden from days of rain. We did not hurry. Waldhere would not follow us, and I doubted my cousin would accept the offer of battle at Ætgefrin. He would fight, I thought, now that he had Einar's hardened warriors to add to his own, but he would fight on ground of his choosing, not of mine.

We followed a valley that climbed slowly to the higher hills. This was sheep country, rich country, but the pastures were empty. The few steadings that we passed were dark with no smoke coming from their roof-holes. We had ravaged this land. I had brought a small army north, and for a month we had savaged my cousin's tenants. We had driven off their flocks, stolen their cattle, burned their storehouses, and torched the fishing craft in the small harbours north and south of the fortress. We had killed no folk except those who wore my cousin's badge and the few who had offered resistance, and we had taken no slaves. We had been merciful because these people would one day be my people, so instead we had sent them to seek food from Bebbanburg where my cousin would have to feed them even as we took away the food that his land provided.

'Einar the White?' my son asked.

'Never heard of him,' I said dismissively.

'I have heard of Einar,' Berg put in. 'He is a Norseman who followed Grimdahl when he rowed into the rivers of the white land.' The white land was the vast expanse that lay somewhere beyond the home of the Danes and the Norse, a land of long winters, of white trees, white plains, and dark skies. Giants were said to live there, and folk who had fur instead of clothes, and claws that could rip a man open from the bellybutton to the spine.

'The white land,' my son said, 'is that why he's called the White?'

'It is because he bleeds his enemies white,' Berg said.

I scoffed at that, but still touched the hammer at my neck. 'Is he good?' my son asked.

'He's a Norseman,' Berg said proudly, 'so of course he is a great fighter!' He paused. 'But I have also heard him called something else.'

'Something else?'

'Einar the Unfortunate.'

'Why unfortunate?' I asked.

Berg shrugged. 'His ships go aground, his wives die.' He touched the hammer hanging at his neck so that the misfortunes he described would not touch him. 'But he is known to win battles too!'

Unfortunate or not, I thought, Einar's one hundred and fifty hardened Norse warriors were a formidable addition to Bebbanburg's strength, so formidable that my cousin was evidently refusing to let them into his fortress for fear that they would turn on him and become the new owners of Bebbanburg. He was quartering them in the village instead, and I did not doubt that he would soon give them horses and send them to harry my forces. Einar's men were not there to defend Bebbanburg's walls, but to drive my men far away from those ramparts. 'They'll come soon,' I said.

'They'll come?'

17

'Waldhere and Einar,' I said. 'I doubt they'll come tomorrow, but they'll come soon.' My cousin would want to end this quickly. He wanted me dead. The gold at Einar's neck and around his wrists was evidence of the money my cousin had paid to bring warriors to kill me, and the longer they stayed the more gold they would cost him. If not tomorrow, I thought, then within the week.

'There, lord!' Berg called, pointing northwards.

A horseman was on the northern hill.

The man was motionless. He carried a spear, its blade slanting downwards. He watched us for a moment, then turned and rode beyond the distant crest. 'That's the third today,' my son said.

'Two yesterday, lord,' Rorik said.

'We should kill one or two of them,' Berg said vengefully.

'Why?' I asked. 'I want my cousin to know where we are. I want him to come to our spears.' The horsemen were scouts and I assumed they had been sent by my cousin to watch us. They were good at their business. For days now they had formed a wide loose cordon around us, a cordon that was invisible for much of the time, but I knew it was always there. I caught a last glimpse of another horseman just as the sun sank behind the western hills. The dying sun reflected blood-red off his spear-point, then he was gone into the shadows as he rode towards Bebbanburg.

'Twenty-six head of cattle today,' Finan told me, 'and four horses.' While I had been taunting my cousin by taking men close to his fort, Finan had been hunting for plunder south of Ætgefrin. He had sent the captured cattle on a drove road that would take them eventually to Dunholm. 'Erlig and four men took them,' he told me, 'and there were scouts down south, just a couple.'

'We saw them north and east,' I said, 'and they're good,' I added grudgingly.

18

'And now he has a hundred and fifty new warriors?' Finan asked dubiously.

I nodded. 'Norsemen, all of them hired spears under a man called Einar the White.'

'Another one to kill then,' Finan said. He was an Irishman and my oldest friend, my second-in-command and my companion of uncounted shield walls. He had grey hair now, and a deeply lined face, but so, I guessed, did I. I was getting old, and I wanted to die peacefully in the fortress that was mine by right.

I had reckoned it would take me a year to capture Bebbanburg. First, through the summer, autumn, and winter, I would destroy the fortress's food supply by killing or capturing the cattle and sheep that lived on the wide lands and green hills. I would break the granaries, burn the haystacks, and send ships to destroy my cousin's fishing boats. I would drive his frightened tenants to seek shelter behind his high walls so that he would have many mouths and little food. By spring they would be starving, and starving men are weak, and by the time they were eating rats we would attack.

Or so I hoped.

We make plans, but the gods and the three Norns at the foot of Yggdrasil decide our fate. My plan was to weaken, starve, and eventually kill my cousin and his men, but wyrd bið ful ãræd.

I should have known.

Fate is inexorable. I had hoped to tempt my cousin into the valley east of Ætgefrin where we could make the two streams run red with their blood. There was little shelter at Ætgefrin. It was a hilltop fort, one built by the ancient people who lived in Britain before even the Romans came. The old fort's earthen walls had long decayed, but the shallow remnant

19

of the ditch still ringed the high summit. There was no settlement there, no buildings, no trees, just the great hump of the high hill under the incessant wind. It was an uncomfortable place to camp. There was no firewood, and the nearest water was a half-mile away, but it did have a view. No one could approach unseen, and if my cousin did dare send men then we would see them approaching and we would have the high ground.

He did not come. Instead, three days after I had confronted Waldhere, we saw a single rider approach from the south. He was a small man riding a small horse, and he was wearing a black robe that flapped in the wind, which still blew strong and cold from the distant sea. The man gazed up at us, then kicked his diminutive beast towards the steep slope. 'It's a priest,' Finan said sourly, 'which means they want to talk instead of fight.'

'You think my cousin sent him?' I asked.

'Who else?'

'Then why's he coming from the south?'

'He's a priest. He couldn't find his own arse if you turned him around and kicked it for him.'

I looked for any sight of a scout watching us, but saw none. We had seen none for two days. That absence of scouts persuaded me that my cousin was brewing mischief, and so we had ridden to Bebbanburg that day and gazed at the fortress where we saw the mischief for ourselves. Einar's men were making a new palisade across the isthmus of sand that led to Bebbanburg's rock. That, it seemed, was the Norsemen's defence, a new outer wall. My cousin did not trust them inside his stronghold, so they were making a new refuge that would have to be overcome before we could assault first the Low Gate and then the High. 'The bastard's gone to ground,' Finan had growled at me, 'he's not going to fight us in the country. He wants us to die on his walls.'

'His three walls now,' I said. We would have to cross the new palisade, then the formidable ramparts of the Low Gate, and there would still be the big wall pierced by the High Gate.

But that new wall was not the worst news. The two new ships in Bebbanburg's harbour were what made my heart sink. One was a fighting ship, smaller than the four we had watched arrive but, like them, flying Einar's banner of the dragon's head, and alongside her was a fat-bellied trading ship. Men were carrying barrels ashore, wading through the shallow water to dump the supplies on the beach just outside the Low Gate.

'Einar's bringing him food,' I said bleakly. Finan said nothing. He knew what I was feeling; despair. My cousin now had more men, and a fleet to bring his garrison food. 'I can't starve them now,' I said, 'not while those bastards are there.'

Now, late in the afternoon and under a glowering sky, a priest came to Ætgefrin, and I assumed he had been sent by my cousin with a gloating message. He was close enough now for me to see that he had long black hair that hung greasily either side of a pale, anxious face that stared up at our earthen wall. He waved, probably wanting a return wave that would reassure him that he would be welcome, but none of my men responded. We just watched as his weary gelding finished the climb and carried him over the turf rampart. The priest staggered slightly when he dismounted. He looked around him and shuddered at what he saw. My men. Men in mail and leather, hard men, men with swords. None spoke to him, we all just waited for him to explain his arrival. He finally caught sight of me, saw the gold at my throat and on my forearms, and he walked to me and dropped to his knees. 'You're Lord Uhtred?'

'I'm Lord Uhtred.'

'My name is Eadig, Father Eadig. I've been looking for you, lord.'

'I told Waldhere where he could find me,' I said harshly. Eadig looked up at me, puzzled. 'Waldhere, lord?'

'You're from Bebbanburg?'

'Bebbanburg?' He shook his head. 'No, lord, we come from Eoferwic.'

'Eoferwic!' I could not hide my surprise. 'And "we"? How many of you are there?' I looked southwards but saw no more riders.

'Five of us left Eoferwic, lord, but we were attacked.'

'And you alone lived?' Finan said accusingly.

'The others drew the attackers away, lord.' Father Eadig spoke to me rather than to Finan, 'they wanted me to reach you. They knew it was important.'

'Who sent you?' I demanded.

'King Sigtryggr, lord.'

I felt a cold pulse shiver around my heart. For a moment I dared not speak, frightened of what this young priest would say. 'Sigtryggr,' I finally said, and wondered what crisis would provoke my son-in-law to send a messenger. I feared for my daughter. 'Is Stiorra ill?' I asked urgently. 'The children?'

'No, lord, the queen and her children are well.'

'Then . . .'

'The king requests your return, lord,' Eadig blurted out, and took a rolled parchment from inside his robe. He held it out to me.

I took the crushed parchment, but did not unroll it. 'Why?'

'The Saxons have attacked, lord. Northumbria is at war.' He was still on his knees, gazing up at me. 'The king wants your troops, lord. And he wants you.'

I cursed. So Bebbanburg must wait. We would ride south.

TWO

We rode next morning. I led one hundred and ninety-four men, together with a score of boys who were servants, and we rode south through rain and wind and beneath clouds as dark as Father Eadig's robe. 'Why did my son-in-law send a priest?' I asked him. Sigtryggr, like me, worshipped the old gods, the real gods of Asgard.

'We do his clerical work, lord.'

'We?'

'We priests, lord. There are six of us who serve King Sigtryggr by writing his laws and charters. Most . . .' he hesitated, 'it's because we can read and write.'

'And most pagans can't?' I asked.

'Yes, lord.' He blushed. He knew that those of us who worshipped the old gods disliked being called pagans, which is why he had hesitated.

'You can call me a pagan,' I said, 'I'm proud of it.'

'Yes, lord,' he said uneasily.

'And this pagan can read and write,' I told him. I had the skills because I had been raised as a Christian, and the Christians value writing, which is, I suppose, a useful thing. King Alfred had established schools throughout Wessex where boys were molested by monks when they were not being forced to learn their letters. Sigtryggr, curious about how the Saxons ruled in southern Britain, had once asked me whether he should do the same, but I had told him to teach boys how to wield a sword, hold a shield, guide a plough, ride a horse, and butcher a carcass. 'And you don't need schools for that,' I had told him.

'And he sent me, lord,' Father Eadig went on, 'because he knew you would have questions.'

'Which you can answer?'

'As best I can, lord.'

Sigtryggr's message on the parchment merely said that West Saxon forces had invaded southern Northumbria and that he needed my forces in Eoferwic as soon as I could reach that city. The message had been signed with a scrawl that might have belonged to my son-in-law, but also bore his seal of the axe. The Christians claim that the one great advantage of reading and writing is that we can be sure a message is real, but they fake documents all the time. There is a monastery in Wiltunscir that has the skill to produce charters that look as if they are two or three hundred years old. They scrape old parchments, but leave just enough of the original writing visible so that the new words, written over the old in weak ink, are hard to read, and they carve copies of seals, and the faked charters all claim that some ancient king granted the church valuable lands or the income from customs' dues. Then the abbots and bishops who paid the monks for the forged documents take them to the royal court to have some family thrown out of its homestead so that the Christians can get richer. So I suppose reading and writing really are useful skills.

'West Saxon forces,' I asked Father Eadig, 'not Mercians?'

'West Saxons, lord. They have an army at Hornecastre, lord.'

'Hornecastre? Where's that?'

'East of Lindcolne, lord, on the River Beina.'

'And that's Sigtryggr's land?'

'Oh yes, lord. The frontier's not far away, but the land is Northumbrian.'

I had not heard of Hornecastre, which suggested it was not an important town. The important towns were those built on the Roman roads, or those which had been fortified into burhs, but Hornecastre? The only explanation I could think of was that the town made a convenient place to assemble forces for an attack on Lindcolne. I said as much to Father Eadig, who nodded eager agreement. 'Yes, lord. And if the king isn't in Eoferwic then he requests that you join him in Lindcolne.'

That made sense. If the West Saxons wanted to capture Eoferwic, Sigtryggr's capital city, then they would advance north up the Roman road and would need to storm the high walls of Lindcolne before they could approach Eoferwic. But what did not make sense was why there was war at all.

It made no sense because there was a treaty of peace between the Saxons and the Danes. Sigtryggr, my son-in-law and King of Eoferwic and of Northumbria, had made the treaty with Æthelflaed of Mercia, and he had surrendered land and burhs as the price for that peace. Some men despised him for that, but Northumbria was a weak kingdom, and the Saxon realms of Mercia and Wessex were strong. Sigtryggr needed time, men, and money if he was to withstand the Saxon onslaught he knew was coming.

It was coming because King Alfred's dream was turning into reality. I am old enough to remember a time when the Danes ruled almost all of what is now England. They captured Northumbria, took East Anglia, and occupied all of Mercia. Guthrum the Dane had then invaded Wessex, driving Alfred and a handful of men into the marshes of Sumorsæte, but

Alfred had won the unlikely victory at Ethandun, and ever since the Saxons had inexorably worked their way northwards. The old kingdom of Mercia was in Saxon hands now, and Edward of Wessex, Alfred's son and the brother of Æthelflaed of Mercia, had reconquered East Anglia. Alfred's dream, his passion, had been to unite all the lands where the Saxon tongue was spoken, and of those lands only Northumbria was left. There might be a peace treaty between Northumbria and Mercia, but we all knew the Saxon onslaught would come.

Rorik, the Norse boy whose father I had killed, had been listening as I talked to Father Eadig. 'Lord,' he asked nervously, 'whose side are we on?'

I laughed. I was born a Saxon, but raised by Danes, my daughter had married a Norseman, my dearest friend was Irish, my woman was a Saxon, the mother of my children had been Danish, my gods were pagan, and my oath was sworn to Æthelflaed, a Christian. Whose side was I on?

'All you need to know, boy,' Finan growled, 'is that Lord Uhtred's side is the one that wins.'

The rain was slashing down now, turning the drove path we followed into thick mud. The rain fell so hard I had to raise my voice to Eadig. 'You say the Mercians haven't invaded?'

'Not as far as we know, lord.'

'Just West Saxons?'

'Seems so, lord.'

And that was strange. Before Sigtryggr captured the throne in Eoferwic I had tried to persuade Æthelflaed to attack Northumbria. She had refused, saying she would not start a war unless her brother's troops were fighting alongside her men. And Edward of Wessex, her brother, had been adamant that she refuse. He insisted Northumbria could only be conquered by the combined armies of Wessex and Mercia, yet now he had marched alone? I knew there was a faction in the West Saxon court that insisted Wessex could conquer Northumbria without Mercian help, but Edward had always been more cautious. He wanted his sister's army alongside his own. I pressed Eadig, but he was sure there had been no Mercian attack. 'At least not when I left Eoferwic, lord.'

'It's just rumours,' Finan said scornfully. 'Who knows what's happening? We'll get there and find it's nothing but a god-damned cattle raid.'

'Scouts,' Rorik said. I thought he meant that a handful of West Saxon scouts had been mistaken for an invasion, but instead he was pointing behind us, and I turned to see two of the horsemen watching us from a ridge. They were hard to see through the drenching rain, but they were unmistakable. The same small, fast horses, the same long spears. We had seen no scouts for a couple of days, but they were back now and following us.

I spat. 'Now my cousin knows we're leaving.'

'He'll be happy,' Finan said.

'They look like the men who ambushed us,' Father Eadig said, staring at the distant scouts and making the sign of the cross. 'There were six of them on fast horses and carrying spears.' Sigtryggr had sent the priest with an armed escort who had sacrificed their lives so that Eadig alone could escape.

'They're my cousin's men,' I told Father Eadig, 'and if we catch any of them I'll let you kill them.'

'I couldn't do that!'

I frowned at him. 'You don't want revenge?'

'I am a priest, lord, I can't kill!'

'I'll teach you how, if you like,' I said. I doubt I shall ever understand Christianity. 'Thou shalt not kill!' their priests teach, then encourage warriors to give battle against the heathen, or even against other Christians if there is a

27

half-chance of gaining land, slaves, or silver. Father Beocca had taught me the nailed god's ten commandments, but I had long learned that the chief commandment of the Christians was 'Thou shalt make my priests wealthy'.

For two more days the scouts followed us southwards until, in a wet evening, we reached the wall. The wall! There are many wonders in Britain; the ancient people left mysterious rings of stone, while the Romans built temples, palaces, and great halls, yet of all those wonders it is the wall that amazes me the most.

The Romans, of course, had made it. They had made a wall across Britain, clear across Northumbria, a wall that stretched from the River Tinan on Northumbria's eastern coast to the Cumbrian coast on the Irish Sea. It ended close to Cair Ligualid, though much of the wall's stone there had been pillaged to make steadings, yet still most of the wall existed. And not just a wall, but a massive stone rampart, wide enough for men to walk two abreast on its top, and in front of the wall was a ditch and an earthen bank and behind it was another ditch, while every few miles was a fort like the one we called Weallbyrig. A string of forts! I had never counted them, though once I had ridden the wall from sea to sea, and what amazing forts! There were towers from which sentries could gaze into the northern hills, cisterns to store water, there were barracks, stables, storerooms, all made of stone! I remembered my father frowning at the wall as it twisted its way into a valley and up the further hill, and he had shaken his head in wonder. 'How many slaves did they need to build this?'

'Hundreds,' my elder brother had said, and six months later he was dead, and my father had given me his name, and I became the heir to Bebbanburg.

The wall marked the southern boundary of Bebbanburg's lands, and my father had always left a score of warriors in

Weallbyrig to collect tolls from travellers using the main road that linked Scotland to Lundene. Those men were long gone, of course, driven out when the Danes conquered Northumbria during the invasion that had cost my father his life and left me an orphan with a noble name and no land. No land because my uncle had stolen it. 'You are lord of nothing,' King Alfred had once snarled at me, 'lord of nothing and lord of nowhere. Uhtred the godless, Uhtred the landless, and Uhtred the hopeless.'

He had been right, of course, but now I was Uhtred of Dunholm. I had taken that fort when we defeated Ragnall and killed Brida, and it was a great fort, almost as formidable as Bebbanburg. And Weallbyrig marked the northern limit of Dunholm's lands, just as it marked the southern edge of Bebbanburg's domain. If the fort had another name, I did not know it, we called it Weallbyrig, which just means the fort of the wall, and it had been built where the great wall crossed a low hill. The years and the rain had made the ditches shallow, but the wall itself was still strong. The buildings had lost their roofs, but we had cleared the debris from three of them and brought rafters from the woods near Dunholm to make new roofs, which we layered with turf, and then we constructed a new shelter on top of the look-out tower so sentries were protected from wind and rain as they stared northwards.

Always northwards. I thought about that often. I do not know how many years it is since the Romans left Britain. Father Beocca, my childhood tutor, had told me it was over five hundred years, and perhaps he was right, but even back then, however long ago it was, the sentries gazed north. Always north towards the Scots, who must have been as much trouble then as they are now. I remember my father cursing them, and his priests praying that the nailed god would humble them, and that always puzzled me because the Scots were Christians too. When I was just eight years old my father had allowed me to ride with his warriors on a punitive cattle raid into Scotland, and I remember a small town in a wide valley where the women and children had crowded into a church. 'You don't touch them!' my father had commanded, 'they have sanctuary!'

'They're the enemy,' I protested, 'don't we want slaves?'

'They're Christians,' my father explained curtly, and so we had taken their long-haired cattle, burned most of their houses, and ridden home with ladles, spits, and cooking pots, indeed with anything that our smithy could melt down, but we had not entered the church. 'Because they're Christians,' my father had explained again, 'don't you understand, you stupid boy?'

I did not understand, and then, of course, the Danes had come, and they tore the churches apart to steal the silver from the altars. I remember Ragnar laughing one day. 'It is so kind of the Christians! They put their wealth in one building and mark it with a great cross! It makes life so easy.'

So I learned that the Scots were Christians, but they were also the enemy, just as they had been the enemy when thousands of Roman slaves had dragged stones across Northumbria's hills to make the wall. In my childhood I was a Christian too, I knew no better, and I remember asking Father Beocca how other Christians could be our enemies.

'They are indeed Christians,' Father Beocca had explained to me, 'but they are savages too!' He had taken me to the monastery on Lindisfarena and he had begged the abbot, who was to be slaughtered by the Danes within half a year, to show me one of the monastery's six books. It was a huge book with crackling pages, and Beocca turned them reverently, tracing the lines of crabbed handwriting with a dirty fingernail. 'Ah!' he had said. 'Here it is!' He turned the book so I could see the writing, though because it was in Latin it meant nothing at all to me. 'This is a book,' Beocca told me, 'written by Saint Gildas. It's a very rare book. Saint Gildas was a Briton, and his book tells of our coming! The coming of the Saxons! He did not like us,' he had chuckled when he said that, 'for of course we were not Christians then. But I want you to see this because Saint Gildas came from Northumbria, and he knew the Scots well!' He turned the book and bent over the page. 'Here it is! Listen! "As soon as the Romans returned home,"' he translated as his finger scratched along the lines, '"there eagerly emerged the foul hordes of Scots like dark swarms of worms who wriggle out of cracks in the rocks. They had a greed for bloodshed, and were more ready to cover their villainous faces with hair than cover their private parts with clothes."' Beocca had made the sign of the cross after he closed the book. 'Nothing changes! They are thieves and robbers!'

'Naked thieves and robbers?' I had asked. The passage about private parts had interested me.

'No, no, no. They're Christians now. They cover their shameful parts now, God be praised.'

'So they're Christians,' I said, 'but don't we raid their land too?'

'Of course we do!' Beocca had said. 'Because they must be punished.'

'For what?'

'For raiding our land, of course.'

'But we raid their land,' I insisted, 'so aren't we thieves and robbers too?' I rather liked the idea that we were just as wild and lawless as the hated Scots.

'You will understand when you are grown up,' Beocca had said, as he always did when he did not know the answer. And now that I was grown up I still did not understand Beocca's argument that our war against the Scots was right-eous punishment. King Alfred, who was nobody's fool, often said that the war that raged across Britain was a crusade of Christianity against the pagans, but whenever that war crossed into Welsh or Scottish territory it suddenly became something else. Then it became Christian against Christian, and it was just as savage, just as bloody, and we were told by the priests that we did the nailed god's will, while the priests in Scotland said exactly the same thing to their warriors when they attacked us. The truth, of course, was that it was a war about land. There were four tribes in one island, the Welsh, the Scots, the Saxons, and the Northmen, and all four of us wanted the same land. The priests preached incessantly that we had to fight for the land because it had been given to us as a reward by the nailed god, but when we Saxons had first captured the land we had all been pagans. So presumably Thor or Odin gave us the land.

'Isn't that true?' I asked Father Eadig that night. We were sheltering in one of Weallbyrig's fine stone buildings, protected from the relentless wind and rain by Roman walls, and warmed by a great fire in the hearth.

Eadig gave me a nervous smile. 'It's true, lord, that God sent us to this land, but it wasn't the old gods, it was the one true God. He sent us.'

'The Saxons? He sent the Saxons?'

'Yes, lord.'

'But we weren't Christians then,' I pointed out. My men, who had heard it all before, grinned.

'We weren't Christians then,' Eadig agreed, 'but the Welsh who had this land before us were Christians. Except they were bad Christians, so God sent the Saxons as a punishment.'

'What had they done?' I asked. 'The Welsh, I mean. How were they bad?'

'I don't know, lord, but God wouldn't have sent us unless they deserved it.'

32

'So they were bad,' I said, 'and God preferred to have bad pagans in Britain instead of bad Christians? That's like killing a cow because it has a lame hoof and replacing it with a cow that has the staggers!'

'Oh, but God converted us to the true faith as a reward for punishing the Welsh!' he said brightly. 'We're a good cow now!'

'So why did God send the Danes?' I asked him. 'Was he punishing us for being bad Christians?'

'That is a possibility, lord,' he said uncomfortably, as if he was not quite sure of his answer.

'So where does it end?' I asked.

'End, lord?'

'Some Danes are converting,' I said, 'so who does your god send to punish them when they become bad Christians? The Franks?'

'There's a fire,' my son interrupted us. He had drawn aside a leather curtain and was staring north.

'In this rain?' Finan asked.

I went to stand beside my son, and, sure enough, somewhere in the far northern hills, a great blaze made a glow in the sky. Fires mean trouble, but I could not imagine any raiding party being loose in this night of rain and wind. 'It's probably a steading that caught fire,' I suggested.

'And it's a long way away,' Finan said.

'God's punishing someone,' I said, 'but which god?'

Father Eadig made the sign of the cross. We watched the distant blaze for a short while, but no more fires showed, then the rain damped the far flames and the sky darkened again.

We changed the sentries in the high tower, then slept.

And in the morning the enemy came.

'You, Lord Uhtred,' my enemy commanded, 'will go south.'

He had come with the morning rain and the first I knew

of his arrival was when the sentries in the look-out tower clanged the iron bar that served as our alarm bell. It was an hour or so after dawn, though the only hint of the sun was a ghostly paleness in the eastern clouds. 'There are people out there,' one of the sentries told me, pointing north, 'on foot.'

I leaned on the tower's parapet and stared into the patchy mist and rain as Finan climbed the ladder behind me. 'What is it?' he asked.

'Maybe shepherds?' I suggested. I could see nothing. The rain was less violent now, just a steady drenching.

'They were running towards us, lord,' the sentry said.

'Running?'

'Stumbling anyway.'

I stared, but saw nothing.

'There were horsemen too,' Godric, who was the second sentry, said. He was young and not too clever. Until a year before he had been my servant and he was liable to see enemies in any shadow.

'I didn't see horsemen, lord,' the first sentry, a reliable man called Cenwulf, said.

Our horses were being saddled ready for the day's journey. I wondered if it was worth taking scouts north to discover if there really were men out there and who they were and what they wanted. 'How many men did you see?' I asked.

'Three,' Cenwulf said.

'Five,' Godric said at the same time, 'and two horsemen.'

I gazed north and saw nothing except the rain falling on bracken. Drifts of ragged mist hid some of the further swells in the land. 'Probably shepherds,' I said.

'There were horsemen, lord,' Godric said uncertainly, 'I saw them.'

No shepherd would ride a horse. I gazed into the rain

34

and mist. Godric's eyes were younger than Cenwulf's, but his imagination was also a lot more fanciful.

'Who in Christ's name would be out there at this time of morning?' Finan grumbled.

'No one,' I said, straightening up, 'Godric's imagining things again.'

'I'm not, lord!' he said earnestly.

'Dairymaids,' I said, 'he thinks of nothing else.'

'No, lord!' he blushed.

'How old are you now?' I asked him. 'Fourteen? Fifteen? That's all I ever thought about at your age. Tits.'

'You haven't changed much,' Finan muttered.

'I did see them, lord,' Godric protested.

'You were dreaming of tits again,' I said, then stopped. Because there were men on the rain-soaked hills.

Four men appeared from a fold in the ground. They were running towards us, running desperately, and a moment later I saw why, because six horsemen came out of the mist, galloping to cut the fugitives off. 'Open the gate!' I shouted to the men at the tower's foot. 'Get out there! Bring those men here!'

I scrambled down the ladder, arriving just as Rorik brought Tintreg. I had to wait as the girth was tightened, then I hauled myself into the saddle and followed a dozen mounted men out onto the hillside. Finan was not far behind me. 'Lord!' Rorik was shouting at me as he ran from the fort. 'Lord!' He was holding my heavy sword belt with the scabbarded Serpent-Breath.

I turned, leaned from the saddle and just drew the sword, leaving belt and scabbard in Rorik's hands. 'Go back to the fort, boy.'

'But . . .'

'Go back!'

The dozen men who had been already mounted ready to

leave the fort were well ahead of me, all riding to cut off the horsemen who pursued the four men. Those horsemen, seeing they were outnumbered, sheered away and just then a fifth fugitive appeared. He must have been hiding in the bracken beyond the skyline and now ran into view, leaping down the slope. The horsemen saw him and turned again, this time towards the fifth man, who, hearing their hooves, twisted away, but the leading rider slowed, calmly levelled a spear, then thrust its blade into the fugitive's spine. For a heartbeat the man arched his back, staying on his feet, then the second rider overtook him, back-swung an axe and I saw the bright sudden mist of blood. The man collapsed instantly, but his death had distracted and delayed his pursuers and so saved his four companions, who were now guarded by my men.

'Why didn't that stupid fool stay hidden?' I asked, nodding to where the six horsemen had surrounded the fallen man.

'That's why,' Finan answered, and pointed towards the northern skyline where a crowd of horsemen was appearing from the mist. 'God save us,' he said, making the sign of the cross, 'but it's a god-damned army.'

Behind me the sentries on the tower were clanging the iron bar to bring the rest of my men to the fort's ramparts. A gust of rain blew heavy and sudden, lifting the cloaks of the horsemen who lined the skyline. There were dozens of them. 'No banner,' I said.

'Your cousin?'

I shook my head. In the grey and rain-smeared light it was hard to see the distant men, but I doubted my cousin would have had the courage to bring his garrison this far south through a dark night. 'Einar, perhaps?' I asked, but in that case who had they been chasing? I spurred Tintreg towards my men, who guarded the four fugitives.

'They're Norsemen, lord!' Gerbruht shouted as I approached.

The four were soaked through, shaking with cold, and terrified. They were all young, fair-haired, and had inked faces. When they saw my drawn sword they dropped to their knees. 'Lord, please!' one of them said.

I looked north and saw that the army of horsemen had not moved. They just watched us. 'Three hundred men?' I guessed.

'Three hundred and forty,' Finan said.

'My name,' I said to the men who knelt in the wet heather, 'is Uhtred of Bebbanburg.' I saw the fear on their faces and let them feel it for a few heartbeats. 'And who are you?'

They muttered their names. They were Einar's men, sent to scout for us. They had ridden for much of the previous afternoon, and, not finding our trail, had camped in a shepherd's hut in the western hills, but just before dawn the horsemen to the north had disturbed their sleep and they had run, abandoning their own horses in their panic. 'So who are they?' I nodded at the horsemen to the north.

'We thought they were your men, lord!'

'You don't know who's chasing you?' I asked.

'Enemies, lord,' one of them said miserably and unhelpfully.

'So tell me what happened.'

The five men had been sent by Einar to look for us, but three of the mysterious mounted scouts had discovered them in the wolf-light just before the sun rose behind the thick eastern clouds. The shepherd's shelter had been in a hollow and they had managed to drag one of the surprised scouts from his saddle and drive off the remaining two. They had killed the one man, but, while they did that, the surviving two scouts had driven off their horses.

'So you killed the man,' I asked them, 'but did you ask him who he was?'

'No, lord,' the oldest of the four survivors confessed.

'We didn't understand his language. And he struggled, lord. He drew a knife.'

'Who did you think he was?'

The man hesitated, then muttered that he thought their victim was my follower.

'So you just killed him?'

The man shrugged, 'Well, yes, lord!' They had then hurried south, only to discover they were being pursued by a whole army of horsemen.

'You killed a man,' I said, 'because you thought he served me. So why shouldn't I kill you?'

'He was shouting, lord. We needed to silence him.'

That was reason enough and I supposed I would have done the same. 'So what do I do with you?' I asked. 'Give you to those men?' I nodded at the waiting horsemen. 'Or just kill you?' They had no answer to that, but nor did I expect one.

'Be kindest just to kill the bastards,' Finan said.

'Lord, please!' one of them whispered.

I ignored him because a half-dozen horsemen had left the far hilltop and were now riding towards us. They came slowly as if to assure us they meant no harm. 'Take those four bastards back to the fort,' I ordered Gerbruht, 'and don't kill them.'

'No, lord?' the big Frisian sounded disappointed.

'Not yet,' I said.

My son had come from the fort and he and Finan rode with me to meet the six men. 'Who are they?' my son asked.

'It's not my cousin,' I said. If my cousin had pursued us he would be flaunting his banner of the wolf's head, 'and it's not Einar.'

'So who?' my son asked.

A moment later I knew who it was. As the six horsemen drew closer I recognised the man who led them. He was mounted on a fine, tall, black stallion, and wore a long blue cloak that was spread across the horse's rump. He had a golden cross hanging from his neck. He rode straight-backed, his head high. He knew who I was, we had met, and he smiled when he saw me staring at him. 'It's trouble,' I told my companions, 'it's damned trouble.'

And so it was.

The man in the blue cloak was still smiling as he curbed his horse a few paces away. 'A drawn sword, Lord Uhtred?' he chided me. 'Is that how you greet an old friend?'

'I'm a poor man,' I said, 'I can't afford a scabbard,' I pushed Serpent-Breath into my left boot, sliding her carefully till the blade was safely lodged beside my calf and the hilt was up in the air.

'An elegant solution,' he said, mocking me. He himself was elegant. His dark blue cloak was astonishingly clean, his mail polished, his boots scoured of mud, and his beard close-trimmed like his raven-dark hair that was ringed with a golden circlet. His bridle was decorated with gold, a gold chain circled his neck, and the pommel of his sword was bright gold. He was Causantín mac Áeda, King of Alba, known to me as Constantin, and beside him, on a slightly smaller stallion, was his son, Cellach mac Causantín. Four men waited behind the father and son, two warriors and two priests, and all four glowered at me, presumably because I had not addressed Constantin as 'lord King'.

'Lord Prince,' I spoke to Cellach, 'it's good to see you again.'

Cellach glanced at his father as if seeking permission to answer.

'You can talk to him!' King Constantin said, 'but speak slowly and simply. He's a Saxon so he doesn't understand long words.'

'Lord Uhtred,' Cellach said politely, 'it's good to see you again too.' Years before, when he was just a boy, Cellach had been a hostage in my household. I had liked him then and I still liked him, though I supposed one day I would have to kill him. He was about twenty now, just as handsome as his father, with the same dark hair and very bright blue eyes, but not surprisingly he lacked his father's calm confidence.

'Are you well, boy?' I asked and his eyes widened slightly when I called him 'boy', but he managed a nod in reply. 'So, lord King,' I looked back to Constantin, 'what brings you to my land?'

'Your land?' Constantin was amused by that. 'This is Scotland!'

'You must speak slowly and simply, lord,' I told him, 'because I don't understand nonsense words.'

Constantin laughed at that. 'I wish I didn't like you, Lord Uhtred,' he said, 'life would be so much simpler if I detested you.'

'Most Christians do,' I said, looking at his dour priests.

'I could learn to detest you,' Constantin said, 'but only if you choose to be my enemy.'

'Why would I do that?' I asked.

'Why indeed!' The bastard smiled, and he seemed to have all his teeth, and I wondered how he had managed to keep them. Witchcraft? 'But you won't be my enemy, Lord Uhtred.'

'I won't?'

'Of course not! I've come to make peace.'

I believed that. I also believed that eagles laid golden eggs, fairies danced in our shoes at midnight, and that the moon was carved from good Sumorsæte cheese. 'Maybe,' I said, 'peace would be better discussed by a hearth with some pots of ale?'

40

'You see?' Constantin turned to his scowling priests, 'I assured you Lord Uhtred would be hospitable!'

I allowed Constantin and his five companions to enter the fort, but insisted the rest of his men waited a half-mile away where they were watched by my warriors who lined Weallbyrig's northern rampart. Constantin, feigning innocence, had asked that all his men be allowed through the gate, and I had just smiled at him for answer and he had the grace to smile back. The Scottish army could wait in the rain. There would be no fighting, not so long as Constantin was my guest, but still they were Scots, and no one but a fool would invite over three hundred Scottish warriors into a fort. A man might as well open a sheepfold to a pack of wolves.

'Peace?' I said to Constantin after the ale had been served, bread broken, and a flitch of cold bacon carved into slices.

'It is my Christian duty to make peace,' Constantin said piously. If King Alfred had said the same thing I would have known he was in earnest, but Constantin managed to mock the words subtly. He knew I did not believe him, any more than he believed himself.

I had ordered tables and benches fetched into the large chamber, but the Scottish king did not sit. Instead he wandered around the room, which was lit by five windows. It was still gloomy outside. Constantin seemed fascinated by the room. He traced a finger up the small remaining patches of plaster, then felt the almost imperceptible gap between the stone jambs and lintel of the door. 'The Romans built well,' he said almost wistfully.

'Better than us,' I said.

'They were a great people,' he said. I nodded. 'Their legions marched across the world,' he went on, 'but they were repelled from Scotland.'

'From or by?' I asked.

He smiled. 'They tried! They failed! And so they built these forts and this wall to keep us from ravaging their province.' He stroked a hand along a row of narrow bricks. 'I would like to visit Rome.'

'I'm told it's in ruins,' I said, 'and haunted by wolves, beggars, and thieves. You'd think yourself at home, lord King.'

The two Scottish priests evidently spoke the English tongue because each of them muttered a reproof at me, while Cellach, the king's son, looked as if he was about to protest, but Constantin was quite unmoved by my insult. 'But what ruins!' he said, gesturing his son to silence. 'What marvellous ruins! Their ruins are greater than our greatest halls!' He turned towards me with his irritating smile. 'This morning,' he said, 'my men cleared Einar the White from Bebbanburg.'

I said nothing, indeed I was incapable of speech. My first thought was that Einar could no longer supply the fortress with food and that the vast problem of his ships was solved, but then I plunged into renewed despair as I understood that Constantin had not attacked Einar on my behalf. One problem was solved, but only because a much greater obstacle now stood between me and Bebbanburg.

Constantin must have sensed my gloom because he laughed. 'Cleared him out,' he said, 'scoured him from Bebbanburg, sent him scurrying away! Or perhaps the wretched man is dead? I'll know soon enough. Einar had fewer than two hundred men and I sent over four hundred.'

'He also had the ramparts of Bebbanburg,' I pointed out.

'Of course he didn't,' Constantin said scornfully, 'your cousin wouldn't let a pack of Norsemen through his gates! He knows they'd never leave. If he had let Einar's men into the fortress he'd have invited a knife in his back. No, Einar's men were quartered in the village, and the palisade they were building outside the fort was unfinished. They'll be gone by now.'

'Thank you,' I said sarcastically.

'For doing your work?' he asked, smiling, then came to the table and at last sat down and helped himself to some ale and food. 'Indeed I did do your work,' he went on. 'You can't besiege Bebbanburg till Einar is defeated, and now he is! He was hired to keep you away from the fortress and to supply your cousin with food. Now, I hope, he's dead, or at least running for his miserable life.'

'So thank you,' I said again.

'But his men have been replaced by my men,' Constantin said in an even tone. 'My men are occupying the steadings now, just as they are occupying the village at Bebbanburg. As of this morning, Lord Uhtred, my men have taken all of Bebbanburg's land.'

I looked into his very blue eyes. 'I thought you'd come to make peace.'

'I have!'

'With seven, eight hundred warriors?'

'Oh, more,' he said airily, 'many more! And you have how many? Two hundred men here? And another thirty-five in Dunholm?'

'Thirty-seven,' I said, just to annoy him.

'And led by a woman!'

'Eadith is fiercer than most men,' I said. Eadith was my wife and I had left her in charge of the small garrison that guarded Dunholm. I had also left Sihtric there in case she forgot which end of a sword did the damage.

'I think you'll find she's not fiercer than my men,' Constantin said, smiling. 'Peace would be a very good idea for you.'

'I have a son-in-law,' I pointed out.

'Ah, the formidable Sigtryggr, who can put five, six hundred men into the field? Maybe a thousand if the southern jarls support him, which I doubt! And Sigtryggr

43

must keep men on that southern frontier to keep the jarls on his side. If indeed they are on his side. Who knows?'

I said nothing. Constantin was right, of course. Sigtryggr might be king in Eoferwic and call himself King of Northumbria, but many of the most powerful Danes on the Mercian frontier had yet to swear him loyalty. They claimed he had surrendered too much land to make peace with Æthelflaed, though I suspected they were willing to surrender themselves rather than fight in a losing war to preserve Sigtryggr's kingdom.

'And it's not just the jarls,' Constantin went on, rubbing salt into the wound. 'I hear the West Saxons are making rude noises there.'

'Sigtryggr's at peace with the Saxons,' I said.

Constantin smiled. That smile was beginning to infuriate me. 'One result of being a Christian, Lord Uhtred, is that I feel a sympathy, even a fondness, for my fellow Christian kings. We are the Lord's anointed, His humble servants, whose duty it is to spread the gospel of Jesus Christ across all lands. King Edward of Wessex would love to be remembered as the man who brought the pagan kingdom of Northumbria under the shelter of Christian Wessex! And your son-in-law's peace treaty is with Mercia, not with Wessex. And many West Saxons say the treaty should never have been concluded! They say it's time Northumbria was brought into the Christian community. Did you not know that?'

'Some West Saxons want war,' I conceded, 'but not King Edward. Not yet.'

'Your friend Ealdorman Æthelhelm seeks to persuade him otherwise.'

'Æthelhelm,' I said vengefully, 'is a stinking turd.'

'But he's a Christian stinking turd,' Constantin said, 'so it's my religious duty, surely, to encourage him?'

44

'Then you're a stinking turd too,' I said, and the two Scottish warriors who accompanied Constantin heard my tone and stirred. Neither seemed to speak English, they had their own barbarous tongue, and one growled incomprehensibly.

Constantin raised a hand to calm the two men. 'Am I right?' he asked me.

I nodded reluctantly. Ealdorman Æthelhelm, my genial enemy, was the most powerful noble in Wessex, and also King Edward's father-in-law. And it was no secret that he wanted a quick invasion of Northumbria. He wanted to be remembered as the man who forged Englaland, and whose grandson became the first King of all Englaland. 'But Æthelhelm,' I said, 'does not lead the West Saxon army. King Edward does, and King Edward is younger, which means he can afford to wait.'

'Perhaps,' Constantin said, 'perhaps.' He sounded amused, as if I was being naive. He leaned across the table to pour more ale into my cup. 'Let us talk of something else,' he said, 'let us talk of the Romans.'

'The Romans?' I asked, surprised.

'The Romans,' he said warmly, 'and what a great people they were! They brought the blessings of Christianity to Britain and we should love them for that. And they had philosophers, scholars, historians, and theologians, and we would do well to learn from them. The wisdom of the ancients, Lord Uhtred, should be a light to guide our present! Don't you agree?' He waited for me to answer, but I said nothing. 'And those wise Romans,' Constantin went on, 'decided that the frontier between Scotland and the Saxon lands should be this wall.' He was looking into my eyes as he spoke and I could tell he was amused even though his face was solemn.

'I hear there's a Roman wall further north.'

'A ditch,' he said dismissively, 'and it failed. This wall,' he waved towards the ramparts that were visible through one of the windows, 'succeeded. I have thought about the matter, I have prayed about it, and it makes sense that this wall should be the dividing line between our peoples. Everything to the north will be Scotland, Alba, and everything to the south can belong to the Saxons, Englaland. There'll be no more argument about where the frontier lies, every man will be able to see the border clearly marked across our island by this great stone wall! And though it won't stop our people from cattle-raiding, it will make such raids more difficult! So you see? I am a peacemaker!' He smiled radiantly at me. 'I have proposed all this to King Edward.'

'Edward doesn't rule in Northumbria.'

'He will.'

'And Bebbanburg is mine,' I said.

'It was never yours,' Constantin said harshly. 'It belonged to your father, and now it belongs to your cousin.' He suddenly snapped his fingers as if he had remembered something. 'Did you poison his son?'

'Of course not!'

He smiled. 'It was well done if you did.'

'I did not,' I said angrily. We had captured my cousin's son, a mere boy, and I had let Osferth, one of my trusted men, look after both him and his mother, who had been taken captive with her son. Mother and son had both died of a plague the year before, but inevitably men said that I had poisoned them. 'He died of the sweating fever,' I said, 'and so did thousands of others in Wessex.'

'Of course I believe you,' Constantin said carelessly, 'but your cousin is now in need of a wife!'

I shrugged. 'Some poor woman will marry him.'

'I have a daughter,' Constantin said musingly, 'perhaps I should offer the girl?'

'She'll be a cheaper price than you'll pay trying to cross his ramparts.'

'You think I fear Bebbanburg's walls?'

'You should,' I said.

'You planned to cross those ramparts,' Constantin said, and there was no amusement in his manner any more, 'and do you believe I am less willing and less able than you?'

'So your peace,' I said bitterly, 'is conquest.'

'Yes,' he said bluntly, 'it is. But we are merely moving the frontier back to where the Romans so wisely placed it.' He paused, enjoying my discomfiture. 'Bebbanburg, Lord Uhtred,' he went on, 'and all its lands are mine.'

'Not while I live.'

'Is there a fly buzzing in here?' he asked. 'I heard something. Or was it you speaking?'

I looked into his eyes. 'You see the priest over there?' I jerked my head towards Father Eadig.

Constantin was puzzled, but nodded. 'I'm surprised, pleased, that you have a priest for company.'

'A priest who spoiled your plans, lord King,' I said.

'My plans?'

'Your men killed his escort, but Father Eadig got away. If he hadn't reached me I'd still be at Ætgefrin.'

'Wherever that is,' Constantin said lightly.

'The hill your scouts have been watching this past week and more,' I said, realising at last who the mysterious and skilful watchers had been. Constantin gave a very slight nod, acknowledging that his men had indeed been haunting us. 'And you'd have attacked me there,' I went on, 'why else would you be here instead of at Bebbanburg? You wanted to destroy me, but now you find me behind stone walls and killing me will be much more difficult.' That was all true. If Constantin had caught me in open country his forces would have chopped my men into pieces, but he would pay a high price if he tried to assault Weallbyrig's ramparts.

He seemed amused by the truth I had spoken. 'And why, Lord Uhtred, would I want to kill you?'

'Because he's the one enemy you fear,' Finan answered for me.

I saw the momentary grimace on Constantin's face. Then he stood, and there were no more smiles. 'This fort,' he said harshly, 'is now my property. All the land to the north is my kingdom. I give you till sundown today to leave my fort and my frontier, which means that you, Lord Uhtred, will go south.'

Constantin had come to my land with an army. My cousin had been reinforced by Einar the White's ships. I had fewer than two hundred men, so what choice did I have?

I touched Thor's hammer and made a silent vow. I would take Bebbanburg despite my cousin, despite Einar, and despite Constantin. It would take longer, it would be hard, but I would do it.

Then I went south.

PART TWO
The Trap

THREE

We arrived at Eoferwic, or Jorvik as the Danes and Norse call it, on the next Sunday, and were greeted by the ringing of church bells. Brida, who had been my lover before she became my enemy, had tried to eradicate Christianity in Eoferwic. She had murdered the old archbishop, slaughtered many of his priests, and burned the churches, but Sigtryggr, the new ruler in the city, did not care what god any man or woman worshipped so long as they paid their taxes and kept the peace, and so the new Christian shrines had sprung up like mushrooms after rain. There was also a new archbishop, Hrothweard, a West Saxon who was reputed to be a decent enough man. We arrived around midday under a bright sun, the first sun we had seen since we had ridden from Ætgefrin. We rode to the palace, close by the rebuilt cathedral, but there I was told that Sigtryggr had gone to Lindcolne with his forces. 'But the queen is here?' I asked the elderly doorkeeper as I dismounted.

'She rode with her husband, lord.'

I grunted disapprovingly, though my daughter's taste for danger did not surprise me, indeed it would have astonished me if she had not ridden south with Sigtryggr. 'And the children?'

'Gone to Lindcolne too, lord.'

I flinched from the aches in my bones. 'So who's in charge here?'

'Boldar Gunnarson, lord.'

I knew Boldar as a reliable, experienced warrior. I also thought of him as old, though in truth he might have been a year or two younger than I was and, like me, he had been scarred by war. He had been left with a limp thanks to a Saxon spear that had torn up his right calf, and he had lost an eye to a Mercian arrow, and those wounds had taught him caution. 'There's no news of the war,' he told me, 'but of course it could be another week before we hear anything.'

'Is there really war?' I asked him.

'There are Saxons on our territory, lord,' he said carefully, 'and I don't suppose they've come here to dance with us.' He had been left with a scanty garrison to defend Eoferwic, and if there really was a West Saxon army rampaging in southern Northumbria then he had best hope it never reached the city's Roman ramparts, just as he had best pray to the gods that Constantin did not decide to cross the wall and march south. 'Will you be staying here, lord?' he asked, doubtless hoping my men would stiffen his diminished garrison.

'We'll leave in the morning,' I told him. I would have gone sooner, but our horses needed rest and I needed news. Boldar had no real idea what happened to the south, so Finan suggested we talked to the new archbishop. 'Monks are always writing to each other,' he said, 'monks and priests. They know more about what's going on than most kings! And they say Archbishop Hrothweard's a good man.'

'I don't trust him.'

'You've never met him!'

'He's a Christian,' I said, 'and so are the West Saxons. So who would he rather have on the throne here? A Christian or Sigtryggr? No, you go and talk to him. Wave your crucifix at him and try not to fart.'

My son and I walked east, leaving the city through one of the massive gates and following a lane to the river bank where a row of buildings edged a long wharf used by trading ships that came from every port of the North Sea. Here a man could buy a ship or timber, cordage or pitch, sailcloth or slaves. There were three taverns, the largest of which was the Duck, which sold ale, food, and whores, and it was there that we sat at a table just outside the door. 'Nice to see the sun again,' Olla, the tavern's owner, greeted me.

'Be nicer still to see some ale,' I said.

Olla grinned, 'And it's good to see you, lord. Just ale? I've a pretty little thing just arrived from Frisia?'

'Just ale.'

'She won't know what she's missing,' he said, then went to fetch the ale while we leaned against the tavern's outside wall. The sun was warm, its reflections sparkling on the river where swans paddled slowly upstream. A big trading ship was tied up nearby and three naked slaves were cleaning her. 'She's for sale,' Olla said when he brought the ale.

'Looks heavy.'

'She's a pig of a boat. You wanting to buy, lord?'

'Not her, maybe something leaner?'

'Prices have gone up,' Olla said, 'better to wait till there's snow on the ground.' He sat on a stool at the table's end. 'You want food? The wife's made a nice fish stew and the bread's fresh baked.'

'I'm hungry,' my son said.

'For fish or Frisians?' I asked.

'Both, but fish first.'

Olla rapped the table and waited until a pretty young girl came from the tavern. 'Three bowls of the stew, darling,' he said, 'and two of the new loaves. And a jug of ale, some

53

butter, and wipe your nose.' He waited till she had darted back indoors. 'You got any lively young warriors that need a wife, lord?' he asked.

'Plenty,' I said, 'including this lump,' I gestured at my son.

'She's my daughter,' he said, nodding at the door where the girl had vanished, 'and a handful. I found her trying to sell her younger brother to Haruld yesterday.' Haruld was the slave-dealer three buildings upriver.

'I hope she got a good price,' I said.

'Oh, she'd have driven a hard bargain, that one. Fleas don't grow old on her. Hanna!' he shouted, 'Hanna!'

'Father?' The girl peered around the door.

'How old are you?'

'Twelve, father.'

'See?' he looked at me, 'ready for marriage.' He reached down and scratched a sleeping dog between the ears. 'And you, lord?'

'I'm already married.'

Olla grinned. 'Been a while since you drank my ale. So what brings you here?'

'I was hoping you'd tell me.'

He nodded. 'Hornecastre.'

'Hornecastre,' I confirmed. 'I don't know the place.'

'Nothing much there,' he said, 'except an old fort.'

'Roman?' I guessed.

'What else? The West Saxons rule up to the Gewasc now,' he sounded gloomy, 'and for some reason they've sent men further north to Hornecastre. They planted themselves in the old fort and as far as I know they're still there.'

'How many?'

'Enough. Maybe three hundred? Four?' That sounded like a formidable war-band, but even four hundred men would have a hard time assaulting Lindcolne's stone walls.

'I was told we were at war,' I said bitterly. 'Four hundred

men sitting in a fort might be a nuisance, but it's hardly the end of Northumbria.'

'I doubt they're there to pick daisies,' Olla said. 'They're West Saxons and they're on our land. King Sigtryggr can't just leave them there.'

'True.' I poured myself more ale. 'Do you know who leads them?'

'Brunulf.'

'Never heard of him.'

'He's a West Saxon,' Olla said. He got his news from folk who drank in his tavern, many of them sailors whose ships traded up and down the coast, but he knew of Brunulf because of a Danish family who had been ejected from their steading just north of the old fort and who had sheltered in the Duck for a night on their way north to lodge with relatives. 'He didn't kill any of them, lord.'

'Brunulf didn't?'

'They said he was courteous! But the whole village had to leave. Of course they lost their livestock.'

'And their homes.'

'And their homes, lord, but not one of them was so much as scratched! Not a child taken as a slave, not a woman raped, nothing.'

'Gentle invaders,' I said.

'So your son-in-law,' Olla went on, 'took over four hundred men south, but I hear he wants to be gentle too. He'd rather talk the bastards out of Hornecastre than start a war.'

'So he's become sensible?'

'Your daughter is, lord. She's the one who insists we don't prod the wasps' nest.'

'And here's your daughter,' I said, as Hanna brought a tray laden with bowls and jugs.

'Put it there, darling,' Olla said, tapping the table top.

'So how much did Haruld offer you for your brother?' I asked her.

'Three shillings, lord.' She was bright-eyed, brown-haired, with an infectiously cheeky grin.

'Why did you want to sell him?'

'Because he's a turd, lord.'

I laughed. 'You should have taken the money then. Three shillings is a good price for a turd.'

'Father wouldn't let me.' She pouted, then pretended to have a bright idea. 'Maybe my brother could serve you, lord?' She made a ghastly grimace. 'Then he'd die in a battle?'

'Go away, you horrible thing,' her father said.

'Hanna!' I called her back. 'Your father says you're ready to be married.'

'Another year, maybe,' Olla put in quickly.

'You want to marry this one?' I asked, pointing to my son.

'No, lord!'

'Why not?'

'He looks like you, lord,' she said, grinned, and vanished.

I laughed, but my son looked offended. 'I do not look like you,' he said.

'You do,' Olla said.

'God help me then.'

And god help Northumbria, I thought. Brunulf? I knew nothing of him, but assumed he was competent enough to be given command of several hundred men, but why had he been sent to Hornecastre? Was King Edward trying to provoke a war? His sister Æthelflaed might have made peace with Sigtryggr, but Wessex had not signed the treaty, and the eagerness of some West Saxons to invade Northumbria was no secret. But sending a few hundred men a small distance into Northumbria, ejecting the nearby Danes without slaughter, and then settling into an old fort did not sound like a savage invasion. Brunulf and his men, I decided, were in Hornecastre as a provocation, designed to make us attack them and so start a war we would lose. 'Sigtryggr wants me to join him,' I told Olla.

'If he can't talk them out of the fort then he's hoping you'll scare them out,' he said flatteringly.

I tasted the fish stew and discovered I was ravenous. 'So why is the price of ships going up?' I asked.

'You won't believe this, lord. It's the archbishop.'

'Hrothweard?'

Olla shrugged. 'He says it's time the monks went back to Lindisfarena.'

I stared at him. 'He says what?'

'He wants to rebuild the monastery!' Olla said.

There had been no monks on Lindisfarena for half a life-time, not since marauding Danes had killed the last of them. In my father's time it had been the most important Christian shrine in all Britain, surpassing even Contwaraburg, attracting hordes of pilgrims who came to pray beside Saint Cuthbert's grave. My father had profited because the monastery was just north of the fortress, on its own island, and the pilgrims spent silver buying candles, food, lodging, and whores in Bebbanburg's village. I had no doubt that the Christians wanted to rebuild the place, but right now it was in Scottish hands. Olla jerked his head eastwards along the bank. 'See that pile of timber? It's all good seasoned oak from Sumorsæte. That's what the archbishop wants to use. That and some stone, so he needs a dozen ships to carry it all.'

'King Constantin might not approve,' I said grimly.

'What's it got to do with him?' Olla asked.

'You hadn't heard? The damned Scots have invaded Bebbanburg's land.'

'Sweet Christ! Truly, lord?'

'Truly. That bastard Constantin claims Lindisfarena is part

of Scotland now. He'll want his own monks there, not Hrothweard's Saxons.'

Olla grimaced. 'The archbishop won't like that! The damned Scots in Lindisfarena!'

I had a sudden thought and frowned as I considered it. 'You know who owns most of the island?' I asked Olla.

'Your family, lord,' he said, which was a tactful answer.

'The church owns the monastery ruins,' I said, 'but the rest of the island belongs to Bebbanburg. Do you think the archbishop asked my cousin's permission to build there? He doesn't need it, but life would be easier if my cousin agreed.'

Olla hesitated. He knew how I felt about my cousin. 'I think the suggestion came from your cousin, lord.'

Which was exactly what I had suddenly suspected. 'That weasel shit,' I said. From the moment that Sigtryggr became King of Northumbria my cousin must have known that I would attack him, and he had doubtless made the suggestion to Hrothweard so that the church would support him. He would turn the defence of Bebbanburg into a Christian crusade. Constantin had at least ended that hope, I thought.

'But before that,' Olla went on, 'the mad bishop tried to build a church there. Or he wanted to.'

I laughed. Any mention of the mad bishop always amused me. 'He did?'

'So Archbishop Hrothweard wants to stop that nonsense. Of course you never know what to believe about that crazy bastard, but it was no secret that the fool wanted to build a new monastery on the island.'

The mad bishop might have been mad, but he was no bishop. He was a Danish jarl named Dagfinnr who had declared himself the Bishop of Gyruum and given himself a new name, Ieremias. He and his men occupied the old fort at Gyruum, just south of Bebbanburg's land on the southern bank of the River Tinan. Gyruum was part of Dunholm's holdings, which made Ieremias my tenant, and the only time I had met him was when he had dutifully come to the larger fortress to pay me rent. He had arrived with a dozen men, who he called his disciples, all of them mounted on stallions except for Ieremias himself, who straddled an ass. He wore a long grubby robe, had greasy white hair hanging to his waist, and a sly look of amusement on his thin, clever face. He had laid fifteen silver shillings on the grass, then hitched up his robe. 'Behold,' he announced grandly, then pissed on the coins. 'In the name of the Father, the Son, and the other one,' he said as he pissed, then grinned at me. 'Your rent, lord, a little damp, but blessed by God Himself. See how they sparkle now? A miracle, yes?'

'Wash them,' I told him.

'And your feet too, lord?'

So the crazy Ieremias wanted to build on Lindisfarena? 'Did he ask my cousin's permission?' I asked Olla.

'I wouldn't know, lord. I haven't seen Ieremias or his horrible ship for months.'

The horrible ship was called *Guds Moder*, a dark, untidy war vessel that Ieremias used to patrol the coast just beyond Gyruum. I shrugged. 'Ieremias is no threat,' I decided, 'if he farts northwards then Constantin will crush him.'

'Perhaps,' Olla sounded dubious.

I stared at the river as it slid past the busy wharves, then watched a cat stalk along the rail of a moored ship before leaping down to hunt rats in the bilge. Olla was telling my son about the horse races that had to be postponed because Sigtryggr had led most of Eoferwic's garrison south, but I was not listening, I was thinking. Plainly the permission to build the new monastery must have been given weeks ago, before even Constantin had led his invasion. How else would the archbishop have his piles of wood and masonry ready to be shipped?

'When did Brunulf occupy Hornecastre?' I asked,

interrupting Olla's enthusiastic account of a gelding he reckoned was the fastest horse in Northumbria.

'Let me think,' he frowned, pausing a few heartbeats, 'must be the last new moon? Yes, it was.'

'And the moon's almost full,' I said.

'So . . .' my son began, then went silent.

'So the Scots invaded a few days ago!' I said angrily. 'Suppose Sigtryggr hadn't been distracted by the West Saxons, what would he have done when he heard about Constantin?'

'Marched north,' my son said.

'But he can't, because the West Saxons are pissing all over his land to the south. They're allied!'

'The Scots and the West Saxons?' my son sounded incredulous.

'They made a secret treaty weeks ago! The Scots get Bebbanburg, and the West Saxon church gets Lindisfarena,' I said, and I was sure I was right. 'They get a new monastery, relics, pilgrims, silver. The Scots get land, and the church gets rich.'

I was sure I was right, though in fact I was wrong. Not that it mattered in the end.

Olla and my son were silent until my son shrugged. 'So what do we do?'

'We start killing,' I said vengefully.

And next day we rode south.

'No killing,' my daughter said firmly.

I growled.

Sigtryggr was no longer in Lindcolne. He had left most of his army to defend the walls and had ridden with fifty men to Ledecestre, a burh he had ceded to Mercia, to plead with Æthelflaed. He wanted her to influence her brother, the King of Wessex, to withdraw his troops from Hornecastre.

'The West Saxons want us to start a war,' my daughter

said. She had been left in command of Lindcolne, leading a garrison of almost four hundred men. She could have confronted Brunulf with that army, but she insisted on leaving the West Saxons undisturbed. 'You probably outnumber the bastards in Hornecastre,' I pointed out.

'I probably don't,' she said patiently, 'and there are hundreds more West Saxons waiting across the border, just looking for an excuse to invade us.'

And that was true. The Saxons in southern Britain wanted more than an excuse, they wanted everything. In my lifetime I had seen almost all of what is now called Englaland in Danish hands. The long ships had rowed up the rivers, piercing the land, and the warriors had conquered Northumbria, Mercia, and East Anglia. Their armies had overrun Wessex, and it had seemed inevitable that the country would be called Daneland, but fate had decreed otherwise and the West Saxons and Mercians had fought their way northwards, fought bitterly and suffered mightily, so that now only Sigtryggr's Northumbria stood in their way. When Northumbria fell, and eventually it would, then all the folk who spoke the English tongue would live in one kingdom. Englaland.

The irony, of course, was that I had fought on the side of the Saxons all the way from the south coast to the edge of Northumbria, but now, thanks to my daughter's marriage, I was their enemy. Such is fate! And fate now decreed that I was being told what to do by my daughter!

'Whatever you do, father,' she said strictly, 'don't stir them up! We haven't confronted them, talked to them, or threatened them! We don't want to provoke them!'

I looked across at her brother, who was playing with his nephew and niece. We were in a great Roman house built at the very summit of Lindcolne's hill, and from the eastern edge of its wide garden we could see for miles across a sunlit

61

country. Brunulf and his men were out there somewhere. My son, I thought, would like nothing better than to fight them. He was blunt, cheerful, and headstrong, while my daughter, so dark compared to her brother's fair complexion, was subtle and secretive. She was clever too, like her mother, but that did not make her right.

'You're frightened of the West Saxons,' I said.

'I respect their strength.'

'They're bluffing,' I said, and hoped I was right.

'Bluffing?'

'This isn't an invasion,' I said angrily, 'it's just a distraction! They wanted your armies in the south while Constantin attacks Bebbanburg. Brunulf isn't going to attack you here! He doesn't have enough men. He's just here to keep you looking south while Constantin besieges Bebbanburg. They're in league, don't you see?' I slapped the garden's stone parapet. 'I shouldn't be here.'

Stiorra knew I meant that I should be at Bebbanburg and touched my arm as if to soothe me. 'You think you can fight your cousin and the Scots?'

'I have to.'

'You can't, father, not without our army to help.'

'All my life,' I said bitterly, 'I have dreamed of Bebbanburg. Dreamed of taking it back. Dreamed of dying there. And what have I done instead? Helped the Saxons conquer the land, helped the Christians! And how do they repay me? By allying themselves with my enemy.' I turned on her, my voice savage. 'You're wrong!'

'Wrong?'

'The West Saxons won't invade if we attack Brunulf. They're not ready. They will be one day, but not yet.' I had no idea if what I said was true, I was just trying to persuade myself it was the truth. 'They need to be hurt, punished, killed. They need to be frightened.'

'No, father,' she was pleading now. 'Wait to see what Sigtryggr agrees with the Mercians? Please?'

'We're not at war with the Mercians,' I said.

She turned and gazed across the cloud-dappled hills. 'You know,' she said, quietly now, 'that some West Saxons say we should never have made the peace. Half their Witan say Æthelflaed betrayed the Saxons because she loves you, the other half say the peace must be kept until they're so strong that we'll never resist them.'

'So?'

'So the men who want war are just waiting for a cause. They want us to attack. They want to force King Edward's hand, and even your Æthelflaed won't be able to resist the call to fight. We need time, father. Please. Leave them alone. They'll go away. Go to Ledecestre. Help Sigtryggr there. Æthelflaed will listen to you.'

I thought about what she had said and decided she was probably right. The West Saxons, fresh from their triumph over East Anglia, were spoiling for a war, and it was a war I did not want. I wanted to drive the Scots from Bebbanburg's land and to do that I needed Northumbria's army, and Sigtryggr would only help me attack northwards if he was certain that he had peace with the southern Saxons. He had gone to Ledecestre to plead with Æthelflaed, hoping her influence with her brother would secure that peace, but despite my daughter's urgent pleading my instinct said that the road to Bebbanburg lay through Hornecastre, not through Ledecestre. And I have always trusted instinct. It might defy reason and sense, but instinct is the prickle at the back of the neck that tells you danger is close. So I trust instinct.

So next day, despite all my daughter had said, I rode to Hornecastre.

*   *   *

Hornecastre was a bleak place, though the Romans had valued it enough to build a stone-walled fort just south of the River Beina. They had built no roads, so I assumed the fort had been made to guard against ships coming upriver, and those ships would have belonged to our ancestors, the first Saxons to cross the sea and take a new land. And it was good land, at least to the north where low hills provided rich pasture. Two Danish families and their slaves had settled in nearby steadings, though both had been told to leave as soon as the West Saxons occupied the ancient fort. 'Why weren't the Danes living in the fort?' I asked Egil. He was a sober, middle-aged man with long plaited moustaches who had grown up not far from Hornecastre, though now he served in Lindcolne's garrison as commander of the night watchmen. When the West Saxons had first occupied Hornecastre's fort he had been sent with a small force to watch them, which he had done from a safe distance, until Sigtryggr's caution had caused him to be summoned back again to Lindcolne. I had insisted that he return to Hornecastre with me. 'If we assault the fort,' I had told him, 'it will help to have a man who knows it. I don't. You do.'

'A man called Torstein lived there,' Egil said, 'but he left.'

'Why?'

'It floods, lord. Torstein's two sons were drowned in a flood, lord, and he reckoned the Saxons had put a curse on the place. So he left. There's a stream this side of the fort, a big one, and the river beyond? And the walls on that far side have fallen in places. Not on this side, lord,' we were watching from the north, 'but on the southern and eastern sides.'

'It looks formidable enough from here,' I said. I was staring at the fort, seeing its stone ramparts rearing gaunt above an expanse of rushes. Two banners hung on poles above the northern wall and a sullen wind occasionally lifted one to reveal the dragon of Wessex. The second banner must have been made from heavier cloth because the wind did not stir it. 'What does the left-hand banner show?' I asked Egil.

'We could never make it out, lord.'

I grunted, suspecting that Egil had never tried to get close enough to see that second banner. Smoke from cooking fires drifted up from the ramparts and from the fields to the south where, evidently, a part of Brunulf's force was camped. 'How many men are there?' I asked.

'Two hundred? Three?' Egil sounded vague.

'All warriors?'

'They have some magicians with them, lord.' He meant priests.

We were a long way off from the fort, though doubtless the men on its walls had seen us watching from the low hilltop. Most of my men were hidden in the shallow valley behind. 'Is there anything there besides the fort?'

'A few houses,' Egil said dismissively.

'And the Saxons haven't tried to come further north?'

'Not since the first week they were here, lord. Now they're just sitting there.' He scratched his beard, trying to pinch a louse. 'Mind you,' he went on, 'they could have been roaming around, but we wouldn't know. We were ordered to stay away from them, not to upset them.'

'That was probably wise,' I said, reflecting that I was about to do the very opposite.

'So what do they want?' Egil asked in an annoyed tone.

'They want us to attack them,' I said, but if Egil was right and the West Saxons could put two or three hundred men behind the stone walls, then we would need at least four hundred men to storm the ramparts, and for what? To possess the ruins of an old fort that no longer guarded anything of value? Brunulf, the West Saxon commander, would know that too, so why did he stay? 'How did they get here?' I asked. 'By boat?'

'They rode, lord.'

'And they're miles from the nearest West Saxon forces,' I said, speaking more to myself than to Egil.

'The nearest are at Steanford, lord.'

'Which is how far?'

'A half day's ride, lord,' he said vaguely, 'maybe?'

I was riding Tintreg that day and I spurred him down the long slope, pushed through a hedge, across a ditch, and up the low rise beyond. I took Finan and a dozen men with me, leaving the rest hidden. If the West Saxons had a mind to chase us away then we would have no choice but to flee northwards, but they seemed content to watch from their walls as we drew closer. One of their priests joined the warriors on the ramparts and I saw him lift a cross and hold it in our direction. 'He's cursing us,' I said, amused.

Eadric, a Saxon scout, touched the cross hanging about his neck, but said nothing. I was staring at a stretch of grassland just to the north of the fort. 'Look at the pasture on this side of the stream,' I said, 'what do you see there?'

Eadric had eyes as good as Finan's and he now stood in his stirrups, shaded his face with a hand and stared. 'Graves?' he sounded puzzled.

'They're digging something,' Finan said. There seemed to be several mounds of freshly-turned earth.

'You want me to look, lord?' Eadric asked.

'We all will,' I said.

We rode slowly towards the fort, leaving our shields behind as a sign we did not want battle, and for a time it seemed the West Saxons were content just to watch as we explored the pasture on our side of the river where I could see the mysterious heaps of earth. As we rode closer I saw that the mounds had not been excavated from graves, but from trenches. 'Are they building a new fort?' I asked, puzzled.

'They're building something,' Finan said.

'Lord,' Eadric said warningly, but I had already seen the dozen horsemen leave the fort and ride to where a ford crossed the stream.

We numbered fourteen men, and Brunulf, if he was trying to avoid trouble, would bring the same number, and so he did, but when the horsemen were in the centre of the stream where the placid water almost reached up to their horses' bellies, they all stopped. They bunched there, ignoring us, and it seemed to me that they argued, and then, unexpectedly, two men turned and rode back to the fort. We were at the pasture's edge by then, the grass lush from the recent rain, and as I spurred Tintreg forward I saw it was no fort they were making, nor graves, but a church. The trench had been dug in the form of a cross. It was meant to be the building's foundation and it would eventually be half filled with stone to support the wall pillars. 'It's big!' I said, impressed.

'Big as the church in Wintanceaster!' Finan said, equally impressed.

The dozen remaining emissaries from the fort were now spurring from the river. Eight were warriors like us, the rest were churchmen, two priests in black robes, and a pair of monks in brown. The warriors wore no helmets, carried no shields, and, apart from their sheathed swords, no weapons. Their leader, on an impressive grey stallion that stepped high through the long grass, wore a dark robe edged with fur above a leather breastplate over which hung a silver cross. He was a young man with a grave face, a short beard, and a high forehead beneath a woollen cap. He reined in his restless horse, then looked at me in silence as if expecting me to speak first. I did not.

'I am Brunulf Torkelson of Wessex,' he finally said. 'And who are you?'

'You're Torkel Brunulfson's son?' I asked.

He looked surprised at the question, then pleased. He nodded. 'I am, lord.'

'Your father fought beside me at Ethandun,' I said, 'and fought well! He slew Danes that day. Does he still live?'

'He does.'

'Give him my warm greeting.'

He hesitated and I sensed he wanted to thank me, but there was a pretence that had to be spoken first. 'And whose greeting is that?' he asked.

I half smiled, looking along the line of his men. 'You know who I am, Brunulf,' I said. 'You called me "lord", so don't pretend you don't know me.' I pointed at the oldest of his warriors, a grizzled man with a scar across his forehead. 'You fought beside me at Fearnhamme. Am I right?'

The man grinned, 'I did, lord.'

'You served Steapa, yes?'

'Yes, lord.'

'So tell Brunulf who I am.'

'He's . . .'

'I do know who he is,' Brunulf interrupted, then gave me a slight nod of his head. 'It is an honour to meet you, lord.' Those words, spoken courteously, caused the eldest of the two priests to spit on the grass. Brunulf ignored the insult. 'And may I ask what brings Uhtred of Bebbanburg to this poor place?'

'I was about to ask what brought you here,' I retorted.

'You have no business here,' it was the spitting priest who spoke. He was a strongly built man, broad-chested, older than Brunulf by perhaps ten or fifteen years, with a fierce face, short-cropped black hair, and an undeniable air of authority. His black robe was made of finely woven wool, and the cross on his chest was of gold. The second priest was a much smaller man, younger, and plainly very nervous of our presence.

I looked at the older priest. 'And who are you?' I demanded.

'A man doing God's business.'

'You know my name,' I said mildly, 'but do you know what they call me?'

'Satan's earsling,' he snarled.

'Perhaps they do,' I said, 'but they also call me the priest-killer, but it's been many years since I last slit the belly of an arrogant priest. I need the practice.' I smiled at him.

Brunulf held up a hand to check whatever retort was about to be made. 'Father Herefrith fears you are trespassing, Lord Uhtred.' Brunulf, plainly, was not looking for a fight. His tone was courteous.

'How can a man trespass on his own king's land?' I asked.

'This land,' Brunulf said, 'belongs to Edward of Wessex.'

I laughed at that. It was a brazen statement, as outrageous as Constantin's claim that all the land north of the wall belonged to the Scots. 'This land,' I said, 'is a half-day's ride north of the frontier.'

'There is proof of our claim,' Father Herefrith said. His voice was a deep, hostile growl, and his gaze even more unfriendly. I guessed he had been a warrior once, he had scars on one cheek, and his dark eyes betrayed no fear, only challenge. He was big, but it was all muscle, the kind of muscle a man develops from years of practising sword-skill. I noticed that he stood his horse apart from the rest of Brunulf's followers, even from his fellow priest, as if he despised their company.

'Proof,' I said scornfully.

'Proof!' he spat back. 'Though we need prove nothing to you. You're shit from the devil's arse and you trespass on King Edward's land.'

'Father Herefrith,' Brunulf seemed disturbed by the older priest's belligerence, 'is a chaplain to King Edward.'

'Father Herefrith,' I said, keeping my voice mild, 'was born from a sow's arsehole.'

Herefrith just stared at me. I had been told once that there is a tribe of men far beyond the seas who can kill with a look, and it seemed as if the big priest was trying to emulate them. I looked away from him before it became a contest, and saw that the second banner, the one that had not stretched in the small wind, had now been taken down from the fort's ramparts. I wondered if a war party was assembling to follow that banner to our destruction. 'Your royal chaplain, born of a sow,' I spoke to Brunulf, though I was still watching the fort, 'says he has proof. What proof?'

'Father Stepan?' Brunulf passed my question to the nervous younger priest.

'In the year of our lord 875,' the second priest answered in a high, unsteady voice, 'King Ælla of Northumbria ceded this land in perpetuity to King Oswald of East Anglia. King Edward is now the ruler of East Anglia and thus is the true and rightful inheritor of the gift.'

I looked at Brunulf and had the impression that here was an honest man, certainly a man who did not look convinced by the priest's statement. 'In the year of Thor 875,' I said, 'Ælla was under siege from a rival, and Oswald wasn't even the King of East Anglia, he was a puppet for Ubba.'

'Nevertheless—' the older priest insisted, but stopped when I interrupted him.

'Ubba the Horrible,' I said, staring into his eyes, 'who I killed beside the sea.'

'Nevertheless,' he spoke loudly as if challenging me to interrupt him again, 'the grant was made, the charter written, the seals impressed, and the land so given.' He looked to Father Stepan, 'is that not so?'

'It is so,' Father Stepan squeaked.

Herefrith glared at me, trying to kill with his eyes. 'You are trespassing on King Edward's land, earsling.'

Brunulf flinched at the insult. I did not care. 'You can produce this so-called charter?' I asked.

For a moment no one answered, then Brunulf looked at the younger priest. 'Father Stepan?'

'Why prove anything to this sinner?' Herefrith demanded angrily. He spurred his horse forward a pace. 'He is a priest-killer, hated by God, married to his Saxon whore, spewing the devil's filth.'

I sensed my men stirring behind me and raised a hand to calm them. I ignored Father Herefrith and looked at the younger priest instead. 'Charters are easy to forge,' I said, 'so entertain me and tell me why the land was given.'

Father Stepan glanced at Father Herefrith as if looking for permission to speak, but the older priest ignored him.

'Tell me!' I insisted.

'In the year of our lord 632,' Father Stepan said nervously, 'Saint Erpenwald of the Wuffingas came to this river. It was in flood and could not be crossed, but he prayed to the Lord, struck the river with his staff, and the waters parted.'

'It was a miracle,' Brunulf explained a little shamefacedly.

'Strange,' I said, 'that I never heard that tale before. I grew up in Northumbria, and you'd think a northern lad like me would have heard a marvellous story like that. I know about the puffins that sang psalms, and the holy toddler who cured his mother's lameness by spitting on her left tit, but a man who didn't need a bridge to cross a river? I never heard that tale!'

'Six months ago,' Father Stepan continued, as if I had not spoken, 'Saint Erpenwald's staff was discovered on the river bed.'

'Still there after two hundred years!'

'Much longer!' one of the monks put in, and received a glare from Father Herefrith.

'And it hadn't floated away?' I asked, pretending to be amazed.

'King Edward wishes to make this a place of pilgrimage,' Father Stepan said, again ignoring my mockery.

'So he sends warriors,' I said menacingly.

'When the church is built,' Brunulf said earnestly, 'the troops will withdraw. They are here only to protect the holy fathers and to help construct the shrine.'

'True,' Father Stepan added eagerly.

They were telling lies. I reckoned their reason to be here was not to build some church, but to distract Sigtryggr while Constantin stole the northern part of Northumbria, and perhaps to provoke a second war by goading Sigtryggr into an assault on the fort. But why, if that is what they wanted, had they been so unprovocative? True, Father Herefrith had been hostile, but I suspected he was a bitter and angry priest who did not know how to be courteous. Brunulf and the rest of his company had been meek, trying to placate me. If they wanted to provoke a war they would have defied me and they had not, so I decided to push them. 'You claim this field is King Edward's land,' I said, 'but to reach it you must have travelled over King Sigtryggr's land.'

'We did, of course,' Brunulf agreed hesitantly.

'Then you owe him customs' dues,' I said. 'I assume you brought tools?' I nodded at the cross-shaped trenches. 'Spades? Mattocks? Even timber to build your magic shrine perhaps?'

For a heartbeat there was no answer. Brunulf, I saw, glanced at Father Herefrith, who gave an almost imperceptible nod. 'That's not unreasonable,' Brunulf said nervously. For a man planning a war, or trying to provoke one, it was an astonishing concession.

'We will think on the matter,' Father Herefrith said harshly, 'and give you our answer in two days.'

My immediate impulse was to argue, to demand we meet the next day, but there was something strange about Herefrith's sudden change of attitude. Till this moment he had been hostile and obstructive, and now, though still hostile, he was cooperating with Brunulf. It was Herefrith who had given the signal that Brunulf should pretend to agree about paying customs' dues, and Herefrith who had insisted on waiting for two days, and so I resisted my urge to argue. 'We will meet you here in two days,' I agreed instead, 'and make sure you bring gold to that meeting.'

'Not here,' Father Herefrith said sharply.

'No?' I responded mildly.

'The stench of your presence fouls God's holy land,' he snarled, then pointed northwards. 'You see the woodland on the skyline? Just beyond it there's a stone, a pagan stone.' He spat the last three words. 'We shall meet you by the stone at mid morning on Wednesday. You can bring twelve men. No more.'

Again I had to resist the urge to anger him. Instead I nodded agreement. 'Twelve of us,' I said, 'at mid morning, in two days' time, at the stone. And make sure you bring your fake charter and plenty of gold.'

'I'll bring you an answer, pagan,' Herefrith said, then turned and spurred away.

'We shall meet in two days, lord,' Brunulf said, plainly embarrassed by the priest's anger.

I just nodded and watched as they all rode back to the fort.

Finan watched too. 'That sour priest will never pay,' he said, 'he wouldn't pay for a morsel of bread if his own poor mother was starving.'

'He will pay,' I said.

But not in gold. The payment, I knew, would be in blood. In two days' time.

FOUR

The stone where Father Herefrith had insisted we meet was a rough pillar, twice the height of a man, standing gaunt above a gentle and fertile valley an hour's easy ride from the fort. It was one of the strange stones that the old people had placed all across Britain. Some stones stood in rings, some made passages, some looked like tables made for giants, and many, like the one on the valley's southern crest, were lonely markers. We had ridden north from the fort, following a cattle path, and when I reached the stone I touched the hammer hanging at my neck and wondered what god had wanted the stone put beside the path, and why. Finan made the sign of the cross. Egil, who had grown up in the River Beina's valley, said that his father had always called the pillar Thor's Stone, 'but the Saxons call it Satan's Stone, lord.'

'I prefer Thor's Stone,' I said.

'There were Saxons living here?' my son asked.

'When my father arrived, yes, lord.'

'What happened to them?'

'Some died, some fled, and some stayed as slaves.'

The Saxons had now had their revenge because, just north of the crest on which the stone stood and beside a ford of the Beina, was a burned-out steading. The fire had been recent, and Egil confirmed that it had been one of the few places that Brunulf's men had destroyed. 'They forced everyone to leave,' he said.

'None was killed?'

He shook his head. 'The folk were told they had to go before sundown, but that was all. They even said the man who led the Saxons was apologetic.'

'Strange way to start a war,' my son remarked, 'being apologetic.'

'They want us to draw the first blood,' I said.

My son kicked a half-burned beam. 'Then why burn this place?'

'To persuade us to attack them? To provoke revenge?' I could think of no better explanation, but why then had Brunulf been so meek when he met me?

Brunulf's men had burned the hall, barn, and cattle byres. Judging by the size of the blackened remnants the steading had been prosperous, and the folk who lived there must have thought it a safe place because they had built no palisade. The ruins lay just yards from the river, where the ford had been trampled by the hooves of countless cattle, while upstream of the steading an elaborate fish trap had been made clear across the river. The trap had silted up, becoming a crude dam, which, in turn, had flooded the pastures to form a shallow lake. A few cottages remained unharmed, enough to offer us crowded shelter, while lengths of charred timber made good fires on which we roasted mutton ribs. I posted sentries in the woodland to our south, and more in a stand of willows on the ford's further bank.

My son was apprehensive. More than once he left the fire and walked to the steading's southern edge to stare at the gaunt stone on the skyline. He was imagining men there, shapes in the darkness, the glint of fire reflected from sword-blades. 'Don't fret,' I told him after moonrise, 'they won't be coming.'

'They want us to think that,' my son said, 'but how do we know what they're thinking?'

'They're thinking that we're fools,' I told him.

'And maybe they're right,' he muttered as he reluctantly sat and joined us. He looked back into the southern darkness where a glow on the clouds showed where Brunulf's men had their fires in the fort and in the fields beyond. 'There are three hundred of them.'

'More than that!' I said.

'Suppose they decide to attack?'

'Our sentries will let us know. That's why we have sentries.'

'If they come on horseback,' he said, 'we won't have much time.'

'So what would you do?' I asked.

'Move,' he said, 'go north a couple of miles.' The flames showed the concern on his face. My son was no coward, but even the bravest man must have known what danger we faced by lighting fires to show our position so close to an enemy who outnumbered us by at least two to one.

I looked at Finan. 'Should we move?'

He half smiled. 'You're running a risk, sure enough.'

'So why am I doing that?'

Men leaned forward to listen. Redbad, a Frisian who was sworn to my son, had been playing a soft tune on his pan pipes, but he paused, his face anxious, watching me. Finan grinned, the firelight reflecting bright from his eyes. 'Why are you doing it?' he asked. 'Because you know what the enemy will do, that's why.'

I nodded. 'And what will they do?'

Finan frowned as he thought about my question. 'The godforsaken bastards are laying a trap, is that right?'

I nodded again. 'The godforsaken bastards think they're being clever, and their godforsaken trap will catch us two days from now. Why two days? Because they need tomorrow to get it ready. Maybe I'm wrong, maybe they'll close the trap tonight, but I don't think they will. That's the risk. But we need to persuade them that we suspect nothing. That we're lambs waiting for the slaughterer's knife, and that's why we're staying here. So that we look like innocent little lambs.'

'Baaaaa,' one of my men said, and then, of course, they all had to bleat until the steading sounded like Dunholm on market day, and they all found it funny.

My son, who did not join in the laughter, waited for the noise to stop. 'A trap?' he asked.

'Work it out,' I said, then went to bed to work it out for myself.

I could have been wrong. As I lay in a flea-infested hovel listening to men singing and other men snoring I decided I was wrong about the reason for the West Saxon presence at Hornecastre. They were not there to draw men away from Constantin's invasion, because Edward was not such a fool as to exchange a slice of Northumbria for a new monastery on Lindisfarena. He hoped to be king of all the Saxon lands one day, and he would never yield Bebbanburg's rich hills and pastures to the Scots. And why grant Bebbanburg, one of the great fortresses of Britain, to an enemy? So I decided it was more likely an unfortunate coincidence. Constantin had marched south while the West Saxons marched north, and there was probably no connection between the two. Probably. Not that it mattered. What mattered was Brunulf's presence in the old fort beside the river.

I thought about Brunulf and Father Herefrith. Which one had been in command?

I thought about men turning back rather than riding to meet us.

I wondered about a banner disappearing from the fort's wall.

And strangest of all, I marvelled at the cordial tone of the confrontation. Usually, when enemies meet before fighting, it offers an opportunity for insult. That exchange of insults is almost a ritual, but Brunulf had been humble, courteous, and respectful. If the purpose of his presence on Northumbrian soil was to provoke an attack that would give Wessex a reason to break the truce, then why had he not been hostile? Father Herefrith, it was true, had been belligerent, but he was the only one who had tried to goad me to fury. It was almost as if the others had wanted to avoid a fight, but if so, why invade at all?

They had lied, of course. There was no ancient charter giving the land to East Anglia, and Saint Erpenwald's staff, if the wretched man ever had one, must have vanished years ago, and they surely had no intention of paying gold as customs' dues, but none of those lies was a challenge. The challenge was their presence; their mild, unthreatening presence. And yet Wessex wanted a fight? Why else be here?

And then I understood.

Suddenly.

In the middle of that night, watching through the hovel's door at the glow of fire touching the southern clouds, I understood. The idea had been there all day, half formed, nagging at me, but suddenly it took shape. I knew why they were here.

And I was fairly sure I knew when the fight would start; in two days.

So I knew why, and I thought I knew when, but where? That question kept me awake. I was wrapped in an otter-skin cloak, lying by the door of one of the cottages and

78

listening to the low murmur of voices around the dying fires. The charred posts, beams, and rafters of the destroyed hall had provided us with convenient firewood, and that thought made me wonder whether Brunulf really had brought logs to build a church. If indeed, he had any real intention of building anything, but that was his ostensible reason for being here, and he had gone to the trouble of digging a church's foundations, so either he had brought logs with him or he planned to cut down trees for timber. I had not seen much mature woodland in these gentle hills, but there had been the stand of old growth oak and chestnut that had barred our path as we had ridden northwards from Hornecastre. I had been impressed by the fine trees, wondering why they had not been felled to make more pasture or to sell as timber.

After leaving Brunulf we had ridden north along the rough cattle path that led through the belt of woodland that lay like a barrier across the path on a slight, almost imperceptible ridge. That ridge stood about halfway between the ruined steading and the old fort. So Brunulf must ride through the trees if he was to meet us at the stone, and that thought brought me fully awake and alert. Of course! It was so simple! I gave up trying to sleep. I did not need to dress or pull on boots because we were all sleeping, or trying to sleep, fully clothed in case the West Saxons did attempt a surprise assault on the steading. I doubted it would come because I reckoned they had other plans, but I had ordered it because it did no harm to keep my men alert. I buckled Serpent-Breath around my waist, and walked into the night, taking the path southwards. Finan must have seen me leave because he ran to catch up. 'Can't sleep?'

'They're going to attack Wednesday morning,' I said.

'You know that?'

'Not for certain. But I'll wager Tintreg against that spavined nag you call a horse that I'm right. Brunulf will come to talk with us sometime in mid morning, and that's when they'll attack. On Woden's day,' I smiled in the night, 'and that's a good omen.'

We had left the steading behind and were walking up a long and very gentle slope of pastureland. I could hear the sound of the river off to my right. The moon was clouded, but just enough light came through the thinner patches to show us the path and to reveal the woodland as a great dark barrier between us and the fort. 'The fight they want will be there,' I said, nodding at the trees.

'In the wood?'

'On the far side, I think. I can't be sure, but I think so.'

Finan walked in silence for a few paces. 'But if they want a fight beyond the trees, why tell us to wait on this side?'

'Because they want us to, of course,' I said mysteriously. 'A bigger question is how many men they'll bring.'

'Every man they have!' Finan said.

'No, they won't.'

'You sound very sure,' he said dubiously.

'Have I ever been wrong?'

'Sweet Christ, you want the whole list?'

I laughed. 'You met Archbishop Hrothweard. What's he like?'

'Oh, he's a nice fellow,' he spoke warmly.

'Really?'

'Couldn't have been nicer. He reminded me of Father Pyrlig, except he isn't fat.'

That was a recommendation. Pyrlig was a Welsh priest, and a man with whom it was good to drink or stand beside in the shield wall. I would have trusted my life to Pyrlig, indeed he had saved it more than once. 'What did you talk about?'

'The poor fellow was upset about Constantin. He asked about him.'

'Upset?'

'It'll be hard to rebuild Lindisfarena without Constantin's permission.'

'Constantin might give permission,' I said. 'He's a Christian. Of sorts.'

'Aye, that's what I said.'

'Did he ask about Bebbanburg?'

'He asked if I thought Constantin would capture it.'

'And you said?'

'Not in my lifetime. Unless he starves them out.'

'Which he will,' I said, 'by spring.' We walked in silence for a while. 'It's strange,' I broke the silence, 'that Brunulf is building a church and Hrothweard is rebuilding a monastery. Coincidence?'

'People build all the time.'

'True,' I allowed, 'but it's still strange.'

'You think they're really building a church here?' he asked.

I shook my head. 'But they have to have a reason for being here, and that's as good a reason as any. What they really want is a war.'

'Which you're going to give them?'

'Am I?'

'If you fight,' Finan said suspiciously, 'then yes.'

'I'll tell you what I plan,' I said. 'On Wednesday we rid ourselves of these bastards, then we go south and smack King Edward to stop any similar nonsense, and after that we capture Bebbanburg.'

'That simple?'

'Yes,' I said, 'that simple.'

Finan laughed, then saw my face in the moonlight. 'Christ,' he said, 'you're going to fight Constantin and your cousin? How in hell do we do that?'

'I don't know,' I said, 'but I'm going back to Bebbanburg this year. And I'm going to capture it.' I gripped my hammer and saw Finan put a finger on the cross he wore. I had no idea how I would capture the fortress, I just knew my enemies believed they had scared me away from my father's lands, and I would let them believe that until my swords turned that land red.

We had reached the gaunt stone that stood tall beside the path. I touched it, wondering if it still possessed some dark power. 'He was very specific,' I said.

'The priest?'

'About meeting us here. Why not meet us by the woodland?' I asked. 'Or closer to the fort?'

'You tell me.'

'He wants us to be here,' I said, still touching the great stone pillar, 'so that we can't see what happens on the other side of the trees.'

Finan still looked puzzled, but I gave him no time to ask questions. Instead I walked on south towards the trees and whistled through my fingers. I heard a brief answering whistle, then Eadric appeared at the woodland's edge. He was probably the best of my scouts, an older man with a poacher's uncanny ability to move silently through tangled woods. He carried a horn, which he would blow if the West Saxons came from the fort, but he said all had been quiet since sundown. 'They haven't even sent out scouts, lord,' he said, evidently disgusted by the enemy's lack of precautions.

'If I'm right . . .' I began.

'. . . which he always is,' Finan put in.

'There'll be men leaving the fort tomorrow. I want you to watch for them.'

Eadric scratched his beard, then grimaced. 'What if they leave from the far side?'

'They will,' I said confidently. 'Can you find a place to watch the southern walls?'

82

He hesitated. The land around the fort was mostly flat with few coppices or other hiding places. 'There's bound to be a ditch,' he finally allowed.

'I need to know how many men leave,' I said, 'and which direction they take. You'll have to bring the news back after dark tomorrow.'

'I'll have to find a place tonight then,' he said cautiously, meaning that he would be seen if he tried to find a hiding place in the daylight, 'and if they find me tomorrow . . .' he left the sentence unfinished.

'Say you're a deserter, show them your cross, and tell them you're tired of serving a pagan bastard.'

'Well, that's true enough,' he said, making Finan laugh.

The three of us followed the track through the wood till I could see the fort's ramparts outlined by the glow of the fires burning in its courtyard. The cattle path led gently downhill for over a mile, running straight as a Roman road across the pastureland. Two mornings from now Brunulf would follow that path, bringing eleven men and, doubtless, an apologetic refusal to pay any gold to Sigtryggr. 'If Brunulf has any sense,' I said, 'and I suspect he does, he'll send scouts to make sure we're not ambushing the path in the wood.' The woodland was the key. It was a massive tract of old trees, of fallen trunks, of tangling ivy, and thorny undergrowth. I wondered why it was not being tended, why no foresters had thinned out the brush or pollarded the trees, and why no charcoal was being made here, or great oaks turned into valuable timber. Probably, I thought, because there was a dispute about ownership, and, until a law court gave a judgement, no one could claim rights over the wood. 'And if we do set an ambush here,' I went on, 'and Brunulf sends scouts first, he'll find it.'

'So no ambush,' Finan said.

'It's the only place,' I said, 'so it has to be here.'

'Sweet Jesus,' Finan swore in frustration.

Eadric grunted. 'If you asked me to scout it, lord, I wouldn't search the whole wood. It's too big. I'd just search maybe a bowshot either side of the path?'

'And if I was Brunulf,' Finan added, 'I wouldn't fear an ambush here at all.'

'No?' I asked. 'Why not?'

'Because it's in full view of the fort! When he's riding to the place where he knows we're meeting him? If we wanted to kill him why wouldn't we wait till he reaches the stone? Why kill him in view of the fort?'

'You're probably right,' I said, and that thought gave me a little comfort even as it mystified Finan even further. 'But tomorrow he'll probably send scouts here,' I was talking to Eadric now, 'just to look at the land before Woden's day, so tell your men to get out of here before dawn.'

I sounded certain, but of course the doubts harried me. On Woden's day would Brunulf search the wood before riding through it? Eadric was right, it was a large wood, but a horseman could gallop along the edges quickly enough, even if searching the thick undergrowth would take time. But I could see nowhere else that would serve as well for an ambush. 'And why,' Finan asked me again, 'do you want to ambush him here at all? You'll just attract three hundred angry Saxons from the fort! If you wait till he's at the stone,' he jerked his head back towards the steading, 'we can slaughter the lot of them and no one in the fort will know a thing. They won't see it!'

'That's true,' I said, 'that's very true.'

'So why?' he asked.

I grinned at him. 'I'm thinking like my enemy. You should always plan your battles from the enemy's point of view.'

'But . . .'

I hushed him. 'Not so loud. You might wake three hundred

angry Saxons.' There was no chance of waking men so far away, but I was enjoying mystifying Finan. 'Let's go this way,' I said, and led my companions westwards, walking on the open ground beside the tree line. By daylight we would have been seen from the fort's walls, but I doubted our dark clothing would show against the black loom of the dense wood. The ground sloped towards the river, and it was a deceptive slope, steeper than it appeared. If one of Brunulf's scouts rode this way he would soon lose sight of the track and would surely conclude that no one planning an ambush against men on the road would wait in this lower wood, simply because they could not see their prey. That gave me some hope. 'We won't need more than fifty men,' I said, 'all of them mounted. We'll conceal them in these lower trees and have some scouts higher up the slope to tell us when Brunulf is almost at the wood.'

'But . . .' Finan began again.

'Fifty should be enough,' I interrupted him, 'but that really depends on how many men leave the fort tomorrow.'

'Fifty men!' Finan protested. 'And the West Saxons have over three hundred.' He jerked his head southwards. 'Three hundred! And only a mile away.'

'Poor innocent bastards,' I said, 'and they have no idea what's about to happen to them!' I turned back towards the track. 'Let's try and sleep.'

Instead I lay awake, worrying I might be wrong.

Because if I was, Northumbria was doomed.

I grew angry the next day.

The Lady Æthelflaed, ruler of Mercia, had made peace with Sigtryggr, and Sigtryggr had yielded valuable land and formidable burhs to secure that peace. That surrender of land had offended some of the powerful Danish jarls in southern Northumbria, and those men were now refusing to serve him, though whether that meant they would refuse to fight when the invasion came was something we did not yet know. What I did know was that West Saxon envoys had witnessed the treaty, they had travelled to Ledecestre's church to see the oaths taken, and they had brought written approval from King Edward for the peace his sister had negotiated.

No one was fooled, of course. Sigtryggr might have purchased peace, but only for a while. The West Saxons had conquered East Anglia, making that once proud country part of Wessex, while Æthelflaed had restored the frontier of Mercia to where it had been before the Danes came to ravage Britain. Yet the years of war had left the armies of Wessex, Mercia, and Northumbria blood-battered, and so the peace treaty had been largely welcomed because it gave all three countries a chance to train new young warriors, to repair walls, to forge spear-blades, and to bind the willow shields with iron. And it gave Mercia and Wessex the time to create new and bigger armies that would eventually surge north-wards and so unite the Saxon people into one new land called Englaland.

Now Wessex wanted to break the peace, and that made me angry.

Or rather, a faction in the West Saxon court wanted the peace broken. I knew because my people in Wintanceaster kept me informed. Two priests, a tavern-keeper, one of the household warriors, King Edward's wine steward, and a dozen other folk sent messages that were carried north by merchants. Some of the messages were written, others were whispered quietly and retold to me weeks later, but in the last year all confirmed that Æthelhelm, Edward's chief advisor and father-in-law, was pushing for a swift invasion of Northumbria. Frithestan, the Bishop of Wintanceaster and a fierce supporter of Æthelhelm, had preached a vituperous

Christmas sermon complaining that the north still lay under pagan power, and demanding to know why Wessex's Christian warriors were not doing the nailed god's will by destroying Sigtryggr and every other Dane or Norse south of the Scottish border. Edward's wife, Ælflæd, had rewarded the bishop's Christmas sermon by giving him an elaborately embroidered stole, a maniple hemmed with garnets, and two tail-feathers from the cockerel that had crowed three times when someone said something that the nailed god did not like. Edward gave the bishop nothing, which confirmed rumours that Edward and his wife disagreed, not only about the desirability of invading Northumbria, but just about everything else. Edward was no coward, he had led his armies well in East Anglia, but he wanted time to impose his authority on the lands he had conquered; there were bishops to appoint, churches to build, land to be given to his followers, and walls to be strengthened around his newly captured towns. 'In time,' he had promised his council, 'in time we will take the north. But not yet.'

Except Æthelhelm did not want to wait.

I could not blame him for that. Before my son-in-law became king in Eoferwic, I had urged the same thing on Æthelflaed, telling her time after time that the northern Danes were disorganised, vulnerable, and ripe for conquest. But she, like Edward, wanted more time, and she wanted the security of larger armies, and so we had been patient. Now I was the vulnerable one. Constantin was stealing much of the north, and Æthelhelm, the most powerful ealdorman in Wessex, wanted an excuse to invade the south. In one way he was right; Northumbria was ripe for conquest, but Æthelhelm wanted a victory over Sigtryggr for one reason only; to make certain that his grandson would be king of a united Englaland.

Edward, King of Wessex and Æthelhelm's son-in-law, had

secretly married a Centish girl long before he became king. They had a son, Æthelstan, whose mother had died at birth. Edward then married Æthelhelm's daughter, Ælflæd the feather-giver, and had more children, one of whom, Ælfweard, was widely regarded as the ætheling, the crown prince, of Wessex. Except, in my view, he was not. Æthelstan was older, he was a legitimate son despite the rumours of bastardy, and he was a stalwart, brave, and impressive young man. Edward's sister Æthelflaed, like me, supported Æthelstan's claim to be the heir, but we were opposed by the richest, most influential ealdorman in Wessex. And I had no doubt that Brunulf and his men were in Northumbria to provoke the war that Æthelhelm wanted. Which meant that the peace party in Wessex would be proved wrong and Æthelhelm right, and he would gain the renown of being the man who united the Saxons into one nation, and that renown would make him unassailable. His grandson would be the next king, and Æthelstan, like Northumbria, would be doomed.

So I had to stop Brunulf and defeat Æthelhelm.

With fifty men.

Hidden in a wood.

At dawn.

We were among the lower trees long before the first light leaked in the east. Birds flapped among the leaves in panic when we arrived and I feared the West Saxon scouts would realise we had caused the disturbance, but if Brunulf had scouts in the wood they raised no alarm. He had sent horsemen to explore the trees before nightfall, a task they had done in a desultory way, and, because I had withdrawn my scouts, they found nothing, but I worried he might have left sentries to watch the woods all night. It seemed he had not, and, as far as I could tell, only the panicked birds and the beasts of the dark were aware of our arrival. We dismounted, forced our way through the thick undergrowth, and, once we were close to the southern edge of the trees, we waited as the wood settled.

I knew it would be a long wait because Brunulf would not leave the fort till full daylight, but I had not wanted to reach the wood after the dawn in case the sight of birds fleeing the trees alerted the West Saxons. Finan, still puzzled as to what I planned, had given up pressing me and now sat with his back against the moss-covered trunk of a fallen oak and stroked a stone down a sword already as sharp as the shears wielded by the three fates. My son played dice with two of his men, and I took Berg aside. 'I need to talk,' I told him.

'I've done something bad?' he asked anxiously.

'No! I have a job for you.'

I led him to a place where we would not be overheard. I liked Berg Skallagrimmrson and trusted him totally. He was a young Norseman, strong, loyal, and skilled. I had saved his life, which gave him reason to be grateful to me, but his loyalty went far beyond gratitude. He was proud to be one of my men, so proud that he had tried to ink my wolf's head badge on his cheek, and was always offended when folk asked him why he was wearing pig heads on his face and that had given me pause before speaking to him, but he was thorough, dependable, and, despite his slow manner, clever. 'When we've finished today,' I told him, 'I'll have to go south.'

'South, lord?'

'If it all goes well, yes. But if it goes badly?' I shrugged and touched my hammer. Ever since we had left the steading I had been watching and listening for omens, but nothing had suggested the will of the gods yet. Except this was Woden's day, and that was surely a good sign.

'We will fight, yes?' He looked anxious, as if he feared he might not have a chance to use his sword.

'We will,' I said, hoping that was true, 'but I'm only expecting around thirty enemies.'

'Only thirty?' Berg sounded disappointed.

'Maybe a few more,' I said. Eadric had returned the previous evening bringing the news I had expected. A party of horsemen, Eadric reckoned there were twenty-five to thirty of them, had left the fort and ridden south. Eadric had been concealed in a ditch not far from the West Saxons, so had been unable to follow the horsemen and thus discover whether they turned east or west once they were out of sight of the ramparts. My guess was east, but only daylight would reveal that truth. 'But those thirty,' I went on, 'will fight like bastards.'

'Is good,' Berg said happily.

'And I want prisoners!'

'Yes, lord,' he said dutifully.

'Prisoners,' I repeated. 'I don't want you happily slaughtering every man you see.'

'I will not, I promise,' he touched the hammer hanging about his neck.

'And when it's over,' I said, 'I will go south and you will go north, and I will give you gold. A lot of gold!'

He said nothing, but just stared at me with wide, solemn eyes.

'I'll send eight men with you,' I said, 'all Norse or Danes, and you are to find your way back to Eoferwic.'

'Eoferwic,' he repeated the name uncertainly.

'Jorvik!' I used the Norse name, and he brightened. 'And in Jorvik,' I went on, 'you will buy three ships.'

'Ships!' He sounded surprised.

'You know, big wooden things that float.'

'I know what a ship is, lord,' he assured me earnestly.

'Good! Then you buy three of them, each for a crew of about thirty to forty men.'

'Fighting ships, lord?' he asked. 'Or trading vessels?'

'Fighting ships,' I said, 'and I need them soon. Maybe in two weeks? I don't know. Maybe longer. And when you are in Eoferwic,' I went on, 'you're not to go into the city. Buy your food at the Duck tavern. You remember where that is?'

He nodded, 'I remember, lord. It is just outside the city, yes? But we're not to go into Eoferwic?'

'You might be recognised. Wait at the Duck. You'll have plenty of work to do, patching up the ships you bought, but if you go into the city someone will recognise you and will know you serve me.' Plenty of folk in that city had seen my men passing through, and someone could easily remember the tall, good-looking and long-haired Norseman with the smudged wolf-heads on his cheeks, indeed I hoped they would remember him.

Berg was a splendid young man, but a young man who had no guile. None. He could no more tell a convincing lie than jump over the moon, and if he did lie he blushed, shuffled his feet, and looked pained. His honesty was blazingly apparent, as plain as the pigs on his face; he was, in a word, trustworthy. If I told Berg to keep his mission secret then he would, but he would still be recognised, and that was what I wanted. 'Can you keep a secret?' I asked him.

'Yes, lord!' He touched the hammer at his neck. 'On my honour!'

I lowered my voice, forcing him to lean closer. 'We can't capture Bebbanburg,' I said.

'No, lord?' he sounded disappointed.

'The Scots are there,' I said, 'and though I'm willing to fight battles, I can't fight a whole nation. And the Scots are vicious bastards.'

'I have heard that,' he said.

I lowered my voice even more. 'So we are going to Frisia.'

'Frisia!' he sounded surprised.

'Shhh!' I hushed him, though no one could have over-heard us.

'The Saxons will invade Northumbria,' I told him, 'and the Scots will hold the north, and there's nowhere left for us to live. So we must cross the sea. We'll find new land. We'll make a new home in Frisia, but no one must know!'

He touched the hammer again. 'I will say nothing, lord! I promise.'

'The only people you can tell,' I said, 'are the men who sell you the ships because they have to know we need ships sound enough to cross the sea. And you can tell Olla who owns the Duck, but no one else!'

'No one, lord, I swear it!'

By telling those few people I was certain the rumour would reach all of Eoferwic and half of Northumbria before the sun went down, and within a week or so my cousin would hear the story that I was abandoning Britain and sailing to Frisia.

My cousin might be under siege, but he would somehow be smuggling messengers in and out of the fortress. There was a sallyport on the seaward ramparts, a small hole in the wooden wall that led to the cliff-top. It was no use as a way of attacking Bebbanburg because it was impossible to approach the hole unseen; to reach it a man must walk along the bare beach and clamber up a precipitous slope immediately beneath the high ramparts. A man might reach it unseen at night-time, but my father had always insisted that at night the sallyport was firmly blocked from the inside, and my cousin, I was sure, would do the same. I suspected he had managed to get men away through the sallyport, perhaps picked up from the beach beneath by a fishing vessel in the fog, and I did not doubt that the news that I had purchased ships would eventually reach him. He might not believe the Frisian story, but Berg did, and Berg was so transparently honest that his tale would be utterly convincing. At worst the news would cause my cousin to doubt what I intended.

'Remember,' I said, 'only tell the men who sell you the ships, and you can tell Olla.' Olla, I knew, would not be able to resist spreading the rumour. 'You can trust Olla.'

'Olla,' Berg repeated the name.

'And his tavern has everything you need,' I said, 'decent ale, good food, and pretty whores.'

'Whores, lord?'

'Girls who . . .'

'Yes, lord, I also know what a whore is,' he said, sounding disapproving.

'And Olla has a daughter,' I told him, 'looking for a husband.'

He brightened at that. 'She is pretty, lord?'

'Her name is Hanna,' I said, 'and she is as gentle as a dove, soft as butter, obedient like a dog and pretty as the dawn.' At least the last claim was true. I looked eastwards and saw that the sky was touched with the first faint light of day. 'Now,' I went on, 'most important. Olla knows you're my man, but no one else must know, no one! If anyone asks, say you've come from southern Northumbria, that you're leaving your land before the Saxons invade. You're going home across the sea. You are leaving Britain, running away.'

He frowned, 'I do understand, lord, but . . .' he paused, plainly unhappy at the thought of running from enemies. He was a brave young man.

'You'll like it in Frisia!' I said earnestly.

Before I could say any more Rorik, my servant, came running through the trees, dodging thorns, 'Lord, lord!'

'Quietly!' I told him. 'Quietly!'

'Lord!' he crouched beside me, 'Cenwulf sent me. There are horsemen coming from the fort!'

'How many?'

'Three, lord.'

Scouts, I thought. Rorik had been posted with Cenwulf and two other sentries further up the slope in a place from where they could see the fort to the south. 'We'll talk later,' I told Berg, then returned to where my fifty men waited, and cautioned them to silence.

The three scouts followed the path into the wood, but they made no effort to explore east or west. They seemed to linger a long time. Cenwulf, who was watching them, told me they went to the wood's northern edge from where they could see a dozen of my men with their riderless horses clustered about the distant stone, and that sight seemed to reassure them because they turned and rode back south. They went slowly, evidently satisfied that no danger lurked among the trees. By now the sun was well up, dazzling in the east and touching a few wispy clouds with bright edges of glowing gold. It promised to be a fine day, at least for us. If I was right. If.

I sent Rorik back to join the hidden sentries, and then nothing happened. A deer wandered onto the pasture from the upper wood to sniff the air, then she heard something that turned her back into the trees. I was tempted to join the sentries to see the fort myself, but resisted the urge. My watching the ramparts would not make anything happen any sooner, and the less movement we made, the better. The gold at the cloud edges faded to a vaporous white. I was sweating beneath my war gear. I wore a leather jerkin under a mail coat, and woollen trews tucked into boots that were made heavy by iron strips sewn into the leather. My forearms were ringed with silver and gold, the marks of a warlord. I wore a gold chain at my neck with a common bone hammer suspended from a link. Serpent-Breath was belted at my waist, while my shield, helmet, and spear were lodged against a tree.

'Maybe he's not coming,' Finan grumbled at mid morning.

'Brunulf will come.'

'He's not going to pay us anything, so why should he?'

'Because if he doesn't come,' I said, 'there can't be a war.'

Finan looked at me as though I was moon-touched mad. He was about to speak when Rorik appeared again, breathless. 'Lord . . .' he began.

'They've left the fort?' I interrupted him.

'Yes, lord.'

'Told you,' I said to Finan, then to Rorik. 'How many?'

'Twelve, lord.'

'Are they carrying a banner?'

'Yes, lord, with a worm on it.'

He meant the dragon banner of Wessex, which is what I had expected. I patted Rorik on the head, told him to stay with me, then called for my men to ready themselves. Like them I pulled on my helmet with its greasy, stinking leather liner. It was my finest helmet, the one with a silver wolf crouching on its crest. I dragged it down over my ears, then closed the cheek-pieces and let Rorik fasten the laces over my chin. He gave me a dark cloak that he tied at my neck, handed me my gloves, then held my horse while I used a fallen log as a mounting block. I settled into Tintreg's saddle, then took the heavy iron-bound shield from Rorik. I pushed my left arm through the loop and gripped the handle. 'Spear,' I said, 'and Rorik?'

'Lord?'

'Stay at the back. Stay out of trouble.'

'Yes, lord,' he said too quickly.

'I mean it, you horrible boy. You're my standard-bearer, not a warrior. Not yet.'

I had dressed in war finery. Most days I did not trouble with a cloak, I left the arm rings behind, and wore a plain helmet, but in the next few minutes I would be deciding the fate of three nations, and that surely deserved some show. I gave Tintreg a friendly slap on the neck and nodded to Finan, who, like me, was glittering with silver and gold. I glanced behind and saw my fifty men were all mounted. 'Quietly now,' I told them, 'walk out slow! There's no need for haste!'

We walked the horses out of the wood onto the pasture-land. Two hares raced away towards the river. We were still on the lower ground, invisible to both the fort and to Brunulf, who was leading his unsuspecting men north along the cattle path that led to the stone beyond the woodland. I was relying on Cenwulf, an experienced and older man, to give me a signal. 'We just wait now,' I called, 'we just wait.'

'Why don't you wait till they're out of sight of the fort?' Finan asked sourly.

'Because I'm not the man who picked this place for a fight,' I said, mystifying him still further, and then I raised my voice so that all my men could hear the explanation. 'When we move,' I said, confident that my voice would not carry beyond the grassy bowl that hid us, 'you'll see a dozen horsemen riding under the banner of Wessex. Our job is to protect them! Those twelve must live. They're going to be attacked by between twenty-five and thirty men! I want those men taken prisoner! Kill some if you must, but I must have some prisoners! Especially their leaders! Look for the richest mail and helmets and make sure you capture those bastards!'

'Oh, sweet Jesus,' Finan said, 'now I understand.'

'I want prisoners!' I stressed.

Rorik climbed into his saddle and hoisted the flag of the wolf's head, and just then Cenwulf appeared at the wood's margin and waved both arms above his head. I touched the hammer hanging from the gold chain. 'Let's go!' I called. 'Let's go!'

Tintreg must have been bored by waiting, because one touch of the spurs sent him leaping ahead. I clung to him, then all of us were climbing the short slope and our spear-points were lowered as we neared the crest. 'When did you realise?' Finan shouted at me.

'Two nights ago!'

'You could have told me!'

'I thought it was obvious!'

'You tricksy bastard!' he said admiringly.

Then we were over the crest and I saw that the gods were with me.

Nearest us, on the path not a quarter-mile away, was Brunulf with his horsemen. They had stopped, astonished because other horsemen had appeared to their east. The far riders were carrying shields and had drawn swords. I saw Brunulf turn back southwards. He was accompanied by two black-robed priests, and one panicked, spurring towards the trees, and Brunulf shouted at him to turn back. I saw him point towards the fort, but it was already too late.

Too late because the far horsemen were galloping to cut off their retreat. I could see about thirty of them, and when they had left the fort the previous day they had doubtless ridden under the banner of the West Saxon dragon, but now they rode beneath the flag of the red axe. The flag was far off, but it was huge, its red axe clearly visible, and I had no doubt that the same badge was painted on the riders' shields.

It was Sigtryggr's badge, but these were not Sigtryggr's men. They were West Saxons who were pretending to be Danes, West Saxons under orders to slaughter their fellow West Saxons and so provoke a war. Brunulf and his delega-tion were to die, watched by their comrades in the fort, who would send word back to Æthelhelm and to Edward that the treacherous Northumbrians had agreed to a truce and then attacked and killed the envoys. It was a clever scheme, doubtless devised by Æthelhelm himself. He wanted to provoke a war, but he had learned that Sigtryggr was capable of restraint, that Sigtryggr, indeed, would do almost anything to avoid a confrontation, so if Sigtryggr would not attack Edward's men, then Æthelhelm's warriors would wear the badge of the red axe and do the killing themselves.

Except we were there, and I was in a vengeful mood.

My cousin was still in Bebbanburg.

Æthelhelm was trying to destroy my daughter and her husband.

Constantin had humiliated me by driving me from my ancestral land.

I had not seen Eadith, my wife, in a month.

So someone had to suffer.

FIVE

Neither Brunulf nor any of his men saw us at first. They could not take their eyes from the horsemen coming from their east, horsemen carrying Northumbrian shields and bright-bladed swords, horsemen intent on killing. Brunulf's first instinct had been to turn back towards the fort, but half the approaching riders swerved southwards to cut off that retreat. Then one of his men looked west and saw us coming. He shouted a warning, Brunulf turned, and I was close enough to see the look of panic on his face. He had thought he was riding to a talk of peace, and instead death was closing on him from two sides. He wore mail, but no helmet. Nor did he carry a shield. The two priests with him had no protection at all. Brunulf half drew his sword, then hesitated, perhaps hoping that if he offered no resistance he would be given a chance to surrender.

'We're on your side!' I shouted at him. He seemed either too dazed or too scared to understand. 'Brunulf!' I bellowed his name. 'We're on your side!'

Berg and my son had spurred to join me, one on either side, and I knew they had agreed to protect me. I lurched Tintreg to my right, driving Berg's horse away. 'Don't crowd me!' I snarled.

'Take care, lord!' he called. 'You're . . .' He was probably about to say 'old', but wisely thought better of it.

The men carrying Sigtryggr's banner had seen us now and they slowed, uncertain. Half a dozen turned towards Brunulf's party, and I heard one shout that they should attack, and another man yelled that they should retreat, and that confusion was their doom.

We crossed the track south of Brunulf and his men. 'We're on your side!' I shouted at him again, and I saw him nod. Then we were past him. We carried spears and were galloping, while the enemy, fewer in number, were armed with swords and were uncertain what they should do. Some seemed frozen in indecision while others managed to turn their horses and spur away eastwards, but one man, plainly lost in terror and confusion, urged his horse towards us, and all I needed to do was level the spear and lean into the blow. There was anger in me and I nudged Tintreg to the right and thrust the spear's thick ash shaft forward with the weight of horse and man behind the blade that glanced off the rim of his shield, pierced his mail, broke through leather, skin, and muscle, and ripped into his belly. I let go of the shaft and just grabbed his helmet and pulled him out of the saddle, blood welling around the spearhead. His left foot was trapped in the stirrup and he was dragged, screaming, leaving a smear of blood on the morning turf.

'I'm not that old,' I called to Berg, then pulled Serpent-Breath from her scabbard.

'Prisoners!' Finan shouted, and I suspected he was shouting at me because I had so blatantly ignored my own insistence that we take men captive.

I cut at a man who managed to bring up his shield in time to block the blow. I saw that the red axe was bright, newly painted over an old badge that had been half scraped from the shield's willow-boards. The man lunged at me and missed, his blade wasted on my saddle's cantle. His bearded face, framed by a close-fitting helmet, was a grimace of desperate savagery that suddenly changed to horror, eyes widening, as Berg's spear thrust into his back. The blow was so savage that I saw the spearhead push the mail outwards at the man's chest. He opened his mouth, I had a glimpse of missing teeth, and then bright blood bubbled and spilled from his lips.

'Sorry, lord, not a prisoner,' Berg said, drawing his sword. 'I do better.'

'Lord!' Finan shouted and I saw him point his sword east. A half-dozen men were galloping away.

'Those are the ones I want,' I called to Berg. The six men were well mounted, one had a fine helmet plumed in black horsehair, another rode a horse whose trappings were of gold, but what really betrayed them as the leaders was the presence of the standard-bearer, who glanced behind, saw our pursuit, and desperately hurled away the huge flag with its cumbersome staff and false badge.

Behind me men were throwing down shields and raising their arms to show they no longer wanted to fight. Brunulf's followers seemed safe, huddled around their banner, while my son was herding prisoners, shouting at them to dismount and yield their swords. So we did have prisoners, but not the ones I wanted, and I touched the spurs to Tintreg's flanks. It was a horse race now, and the six men had a fair start on us, but three of my men were mounted on the smaller, lighter stallions we used for scouting, stallions that were much faster than big beasts like Tintreg, and two of those riders still had spears. They raced alongside the fugitives, then one of them, Swithun, swerved in fast and thrust with his spear, not at a rider, but at the legs of the leading horse. There was a brief howl of pain, then a tumble of flailing legs, the horse rolling, falling, screaming pathetically now,

101

and the thrown rider was pinned beneath the stallion's body as it slid along the grass, then a second horse ploughed into the thrashing beast and also went down, the other riders were desperately yanking reins to avoid the chaos, and my men closed on them. The man with the black horsehair plume leaped his horse over one of the fallen beasts and looked to be getting away, but Berg reached out and seized the plume, pulled, and the rider was jerked backwards in the saddle and almost fell. Berg seized the man's arm, pulled again, and this time he did topple. The helmet, loosened by Berg's first tug, came off and rolled away as the man sprawled on the turf. He still had his sword, and he stood, snarling, and slashed the long blade at Berg's horse, but the young Norseman was out of reach so the man turned to face the next rider.

Me.

And I understood why, two days before, the two men had left Brunulf's envoys and returned to the fort rather than come to meet us. They must have recognised me and known I would recognise them, and not just recognise them, but smell the rancid reek of treachery, because facing me, ready to gut Tintreg with his heavy blade, was Brice.

I had a warrior called Brice once, a mean little bastard, who had finally died beneath a Danish blade when we captured Ceaster. Maybe the name made men mean, because the Brice who faced me was just such another malevolent creature. He was red-haired and grey-bearded, a warrior who had fought a score of battles for his master, Æthelhelm, and a man whom Æthelhelm chose whenever there was filthy work needed. It was Brice who had been sent to capture Æthelstan in Cirrenceastre, and Æthelstan would doubtless have died if we had not thwarted the attempt. Now Brice had been trusted to start a war, and he had been thwarted again. He roared in anger as he lunged his sword at Tintreg's belly. I had turned the stallion, deliberately taking my sword arm away from Brice and he saw the opening and lunged, hoping to disembowel the stallion, but I parried the hard stroke with my left stirrup, the blade piercing the leather to strike against one of the iron strips in my boot. It still hurt, but not half as much as the iron rim of my shield that I slammed down onto Brice's skull. The blow felled him instantly. I hoped I had not killed the bastard because that was a pleasure which must wait.

'Want me to kill him?' Kettil, one of my Danes, must have seen Brice stir.

'No! He's a prisoner. Kill that instead,' I pointed to the horse that had been brought down by Swithun's spear and was now struggling with a broken leg. Kettil dismounted, exchanged his sword for Folcbald's axe, and did the necessary. All six fugitives had been subdued, all six were now prisoners.

Folcbald, one of my enormous Frisian warriors, was holding a tall prisoner by the scruff of his neck, or rather by the man's mail coat, half hoisting him off the turf that was suddenly splashed by the blood of the horse Kettil killed. 'This one says he's a priest,' Folcbald told me cheerfully. He dropped the man and I saw it was Father Herefrith who was wearing a mail coat over his priestly robe. He glared at me, but said nothing.

I smiled and dismounted. I gave Tintreg's reins to Rorik, who had rescued the vast flag of the red axe. I sheathed Serpent-Breath and dropped my shield onto the turf, 'So,' I spoke to Father Herefrith, 'you're one of King Edward's chaplains?'

He still said nothing.

'Or are you Ealdorman Æthelhelm's pet sorcerer?' I asked. 'That fool there,' I pointed to Brice, who was still prone on the grass, 'is Æthelhelm's man. He's stupid too, a brute. Good for killing and wounding, very talented at hitting people and skewering them, but he has the brains of a slug. Lord Æthelhelm always sends a clever person along to tell Brice who to hit and who not to hit. That's why he sent you.'

Father Herefrith just gave me his flat stare, the one that tried to kill by sheer force.

I smiled again. 'And Lord Æthelhelm told you to provoke a war. He needs to hear that King Sigtryggr's men attacked you. That's why you insulted me two days ago. You wanted me to hit you. One blow of mine would have been enough! Then you could have ridden home and bleated to Lord Æthelhelm that I had broken a truce by striking you. That I attacked you! Isn't that what you wanted?'

His face betrayed nothing. He stayed silent. Flies settled on the dead horse's head.

'That failed,' I went on, 'so you were forced to pretend to be King Sigtryggr's men. You always did intend to do that, of course, which is why you brought the shields painted with the red axe, but perhaps you hoped the deception wouldn't be necessary? But it was, and now that has failed too.' I raised my right hand and touched a gloved finger to the scar on his cheek. He flinched. 'You didn't get that scar by preaching a sermon,' I said, 'did one of your choirboys fight back?'

He stepped back to avoid my gloved hand. He still said nothing. He had an empty scabbard hanging at his waist, which told me he had broken the church's rules by carrying a sword. 'Are you a priest?' I asked him. 'Or just pretending to be one?'

'I am a priest,' he growled.

'But not always. You were a warrior once.'

'And still am!' he spat at me.

'One of Æthelhelm's men?' I asked, genuinely interested in his answer.

'I served Lord Æthelhelm,' he said, 'until God convinced me I would achieve more as a servant of the church.'

'Your god did tell you a pack of lies, didn't he!' I pointed to a sword, a fine weapon lying in the grass. 'You were a warrior,' I said, 'so I'll give you that sword and you can fight me.' He did not respond to that, did not even blink. 'Isn't that what your god wants?' I asked. 'My death? I'm shit from the devil's arse, the devil's earsling, isn't that what you called me? Oh, and priest-killer! I'm proud of that one.' He just stared at me with loathing as I stepped a pace closer. 'And you said that I was married to a Saxon whore, and for that, priest, I'm going to give you what you want, I'm going to give you provocation. This is for my Saxon wife.' And then I hit him on the cheek I had touched, and he more than flinched. He fell sideways, blood showing on his face. 'Only the provocation comes too late for you,' I said. 'Aren't you going to fight back? It's the only war you'll get!'

He stood and moved towards me, but I hit him again, this time in the mouth, and hard enough to hurt my knuckles, and I felt the crunch of teeth breaking. He went down a second time and I kicked him in the jaw. 'That's for Eadith,' I told him.

Finan had been watching from horseback and now made a pretend noise as if the kick had hurt him and not Father Herewith. 'That wasn't nice of you,' he said, then grimaced a second time as the priest spat out a tooth and a mouthful of blood. 'He might have had to preach a sermon this Sunday.'

'I never thought of that.'

'And we have company,' Finan said, nodding southwards.

A stream of horsemen was coming from the fort. Brunulf, I saw, was riding to intercept them, and so I left Father Herewith under Folcbald's care, hauled myself back into Tintreg's saddle, and went to meet them.

There was a moment's confusion as eager young men from the fort looked for enemies to attack, but Brunulf shouted

105

at them to sheathe their weapons, then turned his horse towards me. He looked anxious, confused, and appalled. I checked Tintreg, waited for Brunulf to join me, then looked up at the sky. 'I'm glad the rain held off,' I said, as he came close.

'Lord Uhtred,' he began, then seemed not to know what to say.

'I never minded rain when I was young,' I went on, 'but as I get older? You're too young to know.' I said the last few words to Father Stepan, the young priest who had been accompanying Brunulf when suddenly a peaceful stretch of pastureland was turned into a charnel house. 'I suppose,' I was still talking to Stepan, 'that you were on your way to tell me that you refused to pay customs' dues to King Sigtryggr?'

Father Stepan looked at Brice, who had staggered to his feet. Blood had run from his scalp to paint his gaunt cheeks and grey beard red. Skull wounds always bleed profusely. Stepan crossed himself, then managed to nod to me. 'We were, lord.'

'I never expected you to pay,' I said. I looked back to Brunulf. 'You owe me thanks.'

'I know, lord,' he said, 'I know.' He looked pale. He was just beginning to understand how close he had come to death that day. He looked past me, and I twisted in the saddle to see that Father Herefrith was being marched towards us. The priest's mouth was a mess of blood.

'Whose man are you?' I demanded of Brunulf.

'King Edward's,' he said, still staring at Father Herefrith.

'And Edward sent you?'

'He—' he began, and then seemed not to know what to say.

'Look at me!' I snarled, startling him. 'Did King Edward send you?'

'Yes, lord.'

'He sent you to start a war?'

'He said we were to do whatever Ealdorman Æthelhelm commanded us.'

'He told you that himself?'

Brunulf shook his head. 'The order was brought from Wintanceaster.'

'By Father Herefrith?' I guessed.

'Yes, lord.'

'Was the order written?'

He nodded.

'You have it still?'

'Father Herefrith . . .' he began.

'Destroyed it?' I suggested.

Brunulf looked to Father Stepan for help, but found none. 'I don't know, lord. He showed it to me, and then . . .' he shrugged.

'And then he destroyed it,' I said. 'And yesterday Herefrith, Brice, and their men left to go south. What did they tell you?'

'That they were riding to bring reinforcements, lord.'

'But they said you could trust me to keep the truce? To meet you at the stone?'

'Yes, lord, but they said once you heard we wouldn't retreat, you'd besiege the fort, so they went south to bring reinforcements.'

There were now at least two hundred of Brunulf's men on the pasture, most of them mounted and all of them puzzled. They had gathered behind Brunulf, and some were staring at the fallen shields with the red axes, while others recognised my wolf's head badge. We were the enemy, and I could hear the West Saxons murmuring. I silenced them. 'You were sent here,' I shouted, 'to be killed! Someone wanted an excuse to start a war, and you were that excuse!

These men were to betray you,' I pointed at Brice and Father Herefrith. 'Is he a priest?' I asked Father Stepan.

'Yes, lord!'

'They were sent to kill your commander! To kill him and as many other West Saxons as they could! Then I would have been blamed! But . . .' I paused and looked at the anxious faces and realised that many of them must have fought under my command at some time. 'But,' I went on, 'there is a peace treaty between Northumbria and Mercia, and your King Edward does not wish to break that truce. You have done nothing wrong! You were led here and you were lied to. Some of you have fought for me in the past, and you know I do not lie to you!' That was not true, we always lie to men before battle, telling them that victory is certain even when we fear defeat, but by telling them I could be trusted I was telling Brunulf's men what they wanted to hear, and there were murmurs of agreement. One man even shouted that he would willingly fight for me again. 'So now,' I went on, 'you will go back south. You will not be attacked. You will take your weapons, and you will go in peace! And you will go today!' I looked at Brunulf, who nodded agreement.

I took Brunulf aside. 'Tell your men to go south to the Gewasc,' I told him, 'and to stay there for three days. You know where it is?'

'I do, lord.'

I had thought about taking their horses to slow their journey, but they outnumbered us by more than three to one, and if any had decided to resist I would lose the subsequent argument. 'You're coming with me,' I told Brunulf. I saw he was about to protest. 'You owe me your life,' I told him harshly, 'so you can give me three or four days of that life as thanks. You and Father Stepan both.'

He half smiled in rueful acknowledgement. 'As you say, lord,' he agreed.

'You have a second-in-command?'

'Headda,' he nodded towards an older man.

'He's to keep those men prisoner,' I pointed towards the survivors of Brice's troops, 'and go to the Gewasc. Tell him you'll join him in a week or so.'

'Why the Gewasc?'

'Because it's far from Ledecestre,' I said, 'and I don't want Lord Æthelhelm to know what happened here. Not until I tell him.'

'You think Lord Æthelhelm is at Ledecestre?' He sounded nervous.

'The last I heard,' I said, 'was that King Sigtryggr was meeting the Lady Æthelflaed at Ledecestre. Æthelhelm won't be far away. He wants to make certain their negotiations fail.'

So we would ride to Ledecestre.

And afterwards I would go home.

To Bebbanburg.

Headda led Brunulf's chastened men southwards and we rode east to Lindcolne where I snatched a few moments with my daughter. 'You can go back to Eoferwic,' I told her, 'because there won't be a war. Not this year.'

'No? What did you do?'

'Killed some West Saxons,' I said, and then before she could tear me limb from limb, explained what had happened. 'So they won't invade this year,' I finished.

'Next year?' Stiorra asked.

'Probably,' I said bleakly. We stood on the high Roman-built terrace and watched storm clouds move north across the countryside. Great grey swathes of rain showed in the far distance. 'I must go,' I told her, 'I have to reach Æthelhelm before he does more damage.'

'What will you do if there's war?' she asked, meaning

how would I resolve my love for her with my oath to Æthelflaed.

'Fight,' I said shortly, 'and hope to live long enough to settle in Frisia.'

'Frisia!'

'Bebbanburg's lost,' I said. I did not know if she believed me, but it would do no harm for Stiorra to spread that rumour too.

We rode south on the great Roman road that led to Ledecestre, but a few miles down that road a merchant travelling north told me that the great lords of the Saxon lands were all met at Godmundcestre instead. The merchant was a Dane, a gloomy man called Arvid who traded in iron ore. 'There's going to be war, lord,' he told me.

'When is there not?'

'The Saxons have an army at Huntandun. Their king is there!'

'Edward!'

'Is that his name? His sister too.'

'And King Sigtryggr?'

Arvid sneered. 'What can he do? He has not enough men. All he can do is fall to his knees and ask for mercy.'

'He's a fighter,' I said.

'A fighter!' Arvid was scornful. 'He made peace with the woman. Now he has to make peace with her brother. And Jarl Thurferth has already made peace! He gave up Huntandun and took the cross.' Jarl Thurferth was one of the Danish lords who had refused to swear loyalty to Sigtryggr. He owned vast tracts of farmland on what was now the border between Danish and Saxon territories, and if the West Saxon armies marched north then Thurferth's estates would be among the first to fall, and if Arvid was right then Thurferth had preserved that property by yielding his burh at Huntandun, by being baptised and by swearing allegiance

110

to Edward. Thurferth had never been a great warrior, but nevertheless his surrender to Edward surely meant that other Danish jarls in southern Northumbria would follow his lead and so expose Sigtryggr to attack. All that preserved Sigtryggr was his fragile peace treaty with Æthelflaed, a treaty that Ealdorman Æthelhelm was determined to shatter.

So we hurried on south, no longer on our way to Ledecestre, but following the wider Roman road that eventually led to Lundene. The burh at Huntandun guarded a crossing of the Use, and it had always been a bastion protecting Northumbria's southern frontier. Now it was gone, surrendered to Edward's forces. I touched the hammer at my neck and wondered why the old gods surrendered so cravenly to the nailed god? Did they not care? The Saxons and their intolerant religion crept ever nearer to Eoferwic and to capturing Northumbria, and one day, I thought, the old religion would vanish and the nailed god's priests would pull down the pagan shrines. In my lifetime I have seen the Saxons beaten back to a husk, clinging for existence in a stinking bog, and then fighting back until now the great dream of a single country called Englaland was temptingly close. So Sigtryggr's truce would eventually end and Wessex would attack, and then what? Eoferwic could not be held. The walls were stout and well-maintained, but if a besieging army was willing to accept the casualties then they could attack in a half-dozen places, and they would eventually cross the ramparts and carry their swords into a terrified city. The Christians would rejoice, while those of us who loved the more ancient gods would be driven away.

If we wanted to survive the Christian onslaught, then the price for their victory had to be too high. That was why I wanted Bebbanburg, because the cost of capturing that fortress was exorbitant. Constantin would not have succeeded yet. His best hope was still to starve my cousin out, but that might take months. If he tried an assault then his Scottish warriors had only one narrow approach, and they would die on that path. Their bodies would pile beneath the ramparts, the ditch would stink of their blood, ravens would feast on their guts, widows would weep in Constantin's hills, and the white bones of Alba's warriors would be left as a warning to the next attacker.

And Frisia? I wondered, as we hurried southwards, how far the nailed god had captured that land. I had heard that some folk still worshipped Thor and Odin across the sea, and there were times when I was genuinely tempted to go there and establish my own realm, to be a sea-lord beside the grey sea. But to lose Bebbanburg? To abandon a dream? Never.

Before we left Lindcolne I had sent Berg and his companions north towards Eoferwic. I gave the young Norseman a purse of gold and told him again all that I wanted. I made the men scrape the wolf's heads from their shields so that no one would think they were my followers. 'But my cheeks!' Berg had said, worried. 'I wear your badge on my face, lord!'

'I don't think it matters,' I said, not wanting to tease him that the inked patches looked more like drunken pigs than savage wolves. 'We'll run that risk.'

'If you say so, lord,' he had said, still worried.

'Let your hair hang over your face,' I suggested.

'Good idea! But . . .' He had suddenly looked aghast.

'But?'

'The girl? Olla's daughter? She might think it strange? My hair?'

Not nearly as strange as pigs on his cheeks, I thought, but again I spared him. 'Girls don't worry about things like that,' I assured him, 'just so long as you don't smell too bad. They're oddly fussy about that. Now go,' I had said, 'just go! Buy me three ships and wait in Eoferwic till you hear from me.'

He rode north, and we were riding south taking Brunulf, Father Herefrith, and Brice with us. Brice and the priest had their hands tied and wore ropes about their necks, the ropes' bitter ends held by my men. Brice just glowered for most of the journey, but Father Herefrith, realising how many of my men were Christians, promised that the fury of the nailed god would be unleashed on them if they did not release him. 'Your children will be born dead!' he shouted on the first day of our journey. 'And your wives will rot like spoiled meat! Almighty God will curse you. Your skin will be purulent with boils, your bowels will leak watery filth, your cocks will shrivel!'

He went on shouting such threats until I dropped back to ride beside him. He ignored me, just glaring at the road ahead. Gerbruht, a good Christian, was holding the rope that led to the priest's neck. 'He has a mouth, lord,' Gerbruht said.

'I envy him,' I said.

'Envy him, lord?'

'Most of us have to lower our trews to shit.'

Gerbruht laughed. Herefrith just looked even angrier.

'How many teeth do you have left?' I asked him, and, as I expected, he did not answer. 'Gerbruht? You have pincers?'

'Of course, lord,' he patted a saddlebag. Many of my men carried pincers in case a horse half cast a shoe.

'Needle?' I asked him. 'Thread?'

'Not me, lord,' Gerbruht said, 'but Godric always has a needle and thread. So does Kettil.'

'Good!' I looked at Herefrith. 'If you don't keep your filthy mouth shut,' I told him, 'I'll borrow Gerbruht's pincers and pull out every tooth you have left. Then I'll sew your mouth shut.' I smiled at him. He shouted no more threats.

Father Stepan looked distressed, I assumed at my harshness, but then, when he was out of earshot of the scowling

113

Father Herefrith, he surprised me. 'Saint Apollonia had her mouth sewn shut, lord,' he said.

'You're saying I'm making the bastard a saint?'

'I don't know if the story is true,' he went on, 'some say she just lost all her teeth. But if you have toothache, lord, you should pray to her.'

'I'll remember that.'

'But she did not preach like Father Herefrith, and no, I do not think he is a saint.' He crossed himself. 'Our God is not cruel, lord.'

'He seems so to me,' I said bleakly.

'Some of his preachers are cruel. It is not the same thing.'

I had no taste for a theological discussion. 'Tell me, father,' I said, 'is Herefrith really a chaplain to King Edward?'

'No, lord, he is chaplain to Queen Ælflæd, but,' the young priest shrugged, 'it is perhaps the same thing?'

I snorted at that. The West Saxons had never honoured the king's wife by calling her queen, I do not know why, but evidently Æthelhelm's daughter had taken the title, no doubt at her father's urging. 'It's not the same thing,' I said, 'if the rumour about Edward and Ælflæd is true.'

'Rumour, lord?'

'That they're on bad terms. That they don't speak to each other.'

'I wouldn't know, lord,' he said, reddening. He meant he did not want to gossip. 'But all marriages have their tribulations, is that not so, lord?'

'They have their pleasures too,' I said.

'Praise God.'

I smiled at his warm tone. 'So you're married?'

'I was, lord, but only for a few weeks. She died of the sweat. But she was a sweet woman.'

We halted a day's march north of Huntandun, where I summoned two of my Saxon men, Eadric and Cenwulf, and sent them ahead equipped with shields we had taken from Brice's men. They were not the shields they had used to ambush Brunulf, but two that had been left in the fort, and each showed a leaping stag. The standard that had been removed from the rampart on the day I first went to Hornecastre had shown the same badge, Æthelhelm's badge. Brice had recognised me that day, which is why he and a companion had turned back from the meeting and taken down the flag. He might be dumb as an ox, but he had the sense to know I would have smelled trouble if I had seen Æthelhelm's emblem. 'Find the biggest tavern in Huntandun,' I told Eadric, 'and drink there.' I gave him coins.

He grinned. 'Just drink, lord?'

'If you have trouble entering the town,' I said, 'say you're Æthelhelm's men.'

'And if they question us?'

I gave him my own gold chain, though I took the hammer from it first. 'Tell them to mind their own damned business.' The chain would mark him as a man of authority, far outranking any guards on Huntandun's gates.

'And once we're there we just drink, lord?' Eadric asked again.

'Not quite,' I said, then told him what I wanted, and Eadric, who was nobody's fool, laughed.

And next day we followed him south.

We never reached Huntandun, nor needed to. Some few miles north of the town we saw a mass of horses grazing in pastureland to the east of the road and, beyond them, the dirty white roofs of tents above which gaudy standards flapped in a fitful wind. The dragon of Wessex flew there, as did Æthelflaed's weird goose flag, and Æthelhelm's banner of the leaping stag. There were flags showing saints, and flags flaunting crosses, and flags showing both saints and

115

crosses, and hidden among them was Sigtryggr's banner of the red axe. This was where the lords were meeting, not in the newly surrendered Huntandun, but in tents erected around a solid-looking farmstead. A harried-looking steward saw us approach and waved us towards a pasture. 'Who are you?' he called.

'Sigtryggr's men,' I answered. We were not flying my banner, but carrying the red axe flag that Brice and Herefrith had used in their attempt to deceive Brunulf.

The steward spat. 'We weren't expecting any more Danes,' he said in apparent disgust.

'You never expect us,' I said, 'that's why we usually beat the shit out of you.'

He blinked at me and I gave him a smile. He took a pace back and pointed to a nearby pasture. 'Leave your horses there,' he sounded nervous now, 'and no one is to carry weapons, no one.'

'Not even Saxons?' I asked.

'Only the guards of the royal household,' he said, 'no one else.'

I left most of my men guarding our horses, along with our discarded swords, spears, axes, and seaxes, then led Finan, Brunulf, my son, and our two captives towards the farmstead. Smoke rose thick from cooking fires that burned between the tents. A whole ox was being spit-roasted on one fire, the spit's handle turned by two half-naked slaves while small boys fed the roaring blaze with newly split logs. A huge man, the size of Gerbruht, rolled a barrel towards a nearby tent. 'Ale,' he shouted, 'make way for ale!' He saw the barrel was rolling straight towards me and tried to stop it. 'Whoa!' he shouted. 'Sorry, lord, sorry!'

I skipped safely aside, then saw Eadric and Cenwulf waiting close to the farmstead's huge barn. Eadric grinned, evidently relieved to see me, and held out my gold chain as

I approached. 'They've strapped King Sigtryggr to a sawhorse, lord,' he said, 'and now they're chopping his bits off, bit by bit.'

'That bad, eh?' I hung the chain around my neck again. 'So it worked?'

He grinned. 'It worked well, lord. Maybe too well?'

'Too well?'

'They want to march north tomorrow. They just can't decide who gets the pleasure of killing you, and how.'

I laughed. 'They're going to be disappointed then.'

I had sent Eadric and Cenwulf to spread a rumour in Huntandun that Æthelhelm's treachery had worked. They had told a tale of my betrayal, how I had attacked Brunulf and his followers, how I had ignored a flag of truce and slaughtered priests and warriors. The rumour had evidently done its work, though doubtless Æthelhelm was wondering where it came from and why he had heard nothing from any of the men he had sent north to start a war. He would still be content. He was getting what he wanted.

For the moment.

The meeting was being held in the vast barn, an impressive building larger than most mead halls. 'Who owns the barn?' I asked a guard standing at one of the big doors. He wore the badge of Wessex, carried a spear, and was evidently one of Edward's household troops.

'Jarl Thurferth,' he said, after glancing at us to make sure none of us carried weapons, 'and now we own him.' The guard made no attempt to stop us. I had spoken to him in his own language, and, though my cloak was a poor and threadbare thing, beneath it he could see I wore a golden chain of nobility. Besides, I was older and grey-haired, and so he just assumed both my rank and my right to be present, though he did frown slightly when he saw Brice and Herefrith with their hands tied.

'Thieves,' I explained curtly, 'who deserve royal justice.' I looked at Gerbruht. 'If either of the bastards speak,' I told him, 'you can bite their balls off.'

He bared his dirty teeth. 'A pleasure, lord.'

We slid into the back of the barn. As I entered I pulled the hood of the shabby cloak over my head to shadow my face. There were at least a hundred and fifty men inside the barn, which, after the day's sunlight, seemed dim, the only light coming through the two great doorways. We stood behind the crowd looking towards a crude platform that had been constructed at the barn's further end. Four banners were hung on the high wall behind the platform, the dragon of Wessex, Æthelflaed's goose, a white banner with a red cross, and, much smaller than the others, Sigtryggr's flag with its red axe. Beneath them six chairs were set on the platform, each draped with a cloth to add dignity. Sigtryggr sat in the chair furthest left, his one eye downcast and his face suffused with gloom. Another Northman, I assumed he was a Northman because he wore his hair long and had inked patterns on his cheeks, sat furthest to the right, and that had to be Jarl Thurferth who had supinely surrendered his lands to the West Saxons. He was fidgeting. King Edward of Wessex was in one of the three chairs that had been elevated above the others by a short stack of planks. He had a thin face and, to my surprise, I saw his hair was going grey at the temples. To his left and on a slightly lower chair was his sister, Æthelflaed, and her appearance shocked me. Her once beautiful face was drawn, her skin pale as parchment, and her lips were clamped together as if she tried to subdue pain. She, like Sigtryggr, had her eyes lowered. The third raised chair, on Edward's right hand, was occupied by a sullen-looking boy who had a moon face, indignant eyes, and wore a golden circlet about his unkempt brown hair. He could not have been more than thirteen or fourteen, and he sprawled in his seat, looking disdainfully at the crowd beneath him. I had never seen the lad before, but assumed he was Ælfweard, Edward's son, and Ealdorman Æthelhelm's grandson.

Æthelhelm sat next to the boy. Big, bluff, genial Æthelhelm, though right now he wore a stern expression. He was gripping an arm of his chair and leaning slightly forward as he listened to a speech that was being delivered by Bishop Wulfheard. No, it was a sermon, not a speech, and the bishop's words were being applauded by a row of priests and a handful of mailed warriors who stood in the deep shadows behind the six thrones. Of the throne's occupants only Æthelhelm was applauding. He rapped a hand on the chair's arm and occasionally nodded, though always with a look of regret as though he was saddened by what he was hearing.

In truth he could not have been happier. 'Every kingdom divided shall be brought to ruin!' the bishop yelped. 'Those are the words of Christ! And who here doubts that the lands north of here are Saxon lands! Purchased by Saxon blood!'

'He's been talking the best part of an hour, I should think, maybe longer,' Eadric grumbled to me.

'He's just begun then,' I said. A man standing in front of us tried to hush me, but I growled at him and he quickly turned away.

I looked back to Wulfheard, who was an old enemy of mine. He was Bishop of Hereford, but spent his time wherever the King of Wessex might be in residence, because, though Wulfheard might preach about heavenly powers, the only power he craved was earthly. He wanted money, land, and influence, and he largely succeeded because his ambition was well-served by a mind that was subtle, clever, and ruthless. He was impressive to look at; tall, stern, with a hook of a nose and deep-set dark eyes beneath thick brows that had turned grey with age. He was formidable, but his weakness was a fondness for whores. I could not blame him for that, I like whores myself, but Wulfheard, unlike me, pretended to be a man of impeccable rectitude.

The bishop had paused to drink ale or wine, and the six occupants of the chairs all stirred as if stretching tired limbs. Edward leaned over to whisper something to his sister, who nodded wearily, while her nephew Ælfweard, the sullen-looking boy, yawned. 'I do not doubt,' the bishop startled the boy by beginning again, 'that the Lady Æthelflaed made her peace with King Sigtryggr with nothing but Christian motives, with charitable motives, and in the fervent hope that the light of Christ would illuminate his dark pagan soul and bring him to a knowledge of our Saviour's grace!'

'True,' Æthelhelm said, 'so true.'

'Slimy bastard,' I growled.

'But how could she know,' the bishop asked, 'how could any of us know, of the treachery which lurks in Lord Uhtred's soul? Of the hatred he nurtures for us, the children of God!' The bishop paused, and it seemed he gave a great sob. 'Brunulf,' he shouted, 'that great warrior for Christ, dead!' The priests behind him wailed, and Æthelhelm shook his head. 'Father Herefrith!' the bishop shouted even louder, 'that martyred man of God, dead!'

The guards might have thought we were disarmed, but I had kept a knife and I slid it through Herefrith's clothes to prick his arse. 'One word,' I whispered, 'one word and you're dead.' He shivered.

'Our good men,' the bishop still spoke with a sob, 'were killed by a pagan! Slaughtered by a savage! And it is time!' He raised his voice. 'It is past time, that we scourged this pagan savage from our land!'

'Amen,' Æthelhelm said, nodding, 'amen.'

'Praise God,' one of the priests called.

'Hearken!' the bishop shouted. 'Hearken to the words of the prophet Ezekiel!'

'Must we?' Finan muttered.

'"And I will make them one nation!"' the bishop thundered, '"And one king shall be king to them! And they shall be no more two nations!" You hear that? God has promised to make us one nation, not two, with one king, not two!' He turned his fierce gaze onto Sigtryggr. 'You, lord King,' he snarled, and managed to infuse the last two words with utter scorn, 'will leave us today. Tomorrow this truce expires, and tomorrow King Edward's forces will march north! An army of God will march! An army of faith! An army of truth! An army dedicated to revenge the deaths of Brunulf and Father Herefrith! An army led by the risen Christ and by our king and by Lord Æthelhelm!' King Edward frowned slightly, offended, I suspected, by the suggestion that Æthelhelm was his equal in leading the West Saxon army, but he did not contradict the bishop. 'And with that mighty force,' Wulfheard went on, 'will march the men of Mercia! Warriors led by Prince Æthelstan!'

It was my turn to frown. Æthelstan had been given command of Mercia's army? I approved of that, but I knew Æthelhelm wanted nothing more than to kill Æthelstan and so ease his grandson's path to the throne, and now Æthelstan was being sent into Northumbria with a man who wanted him dead? I wondered why Æthelstan was not seated on a throne like his half-brother, Ælfweard, then I saw him among the warriors standing with the priests behind the six chairs. And that was significant, I thought. Æthelstan was the elder son, yet he was not given the same honours as the sullen, plump Ælfweard. 'It will be a united Saxon army,' Wulfheard exulted, 'the army of Englaland, an army of Christ!' the bishop's voice grew louder. 'An army to avenge our martyred dead and to bring everlasting glory to our church! An army to make one Saxon nation under one Saxon king!'

'Ready?' I asked Finan.

He just grinned.

'The pagan Uhtred has brought the wrath of God upon himself,' the bishop was almost screaming now, spittle spraying from his mouth as his hands stretched towards the barn's rafters. 'The peace is over, broken by Uhtred's cruel deception, by his insatiable hunger for blood, by his betrayal of all that we treasure, by his vicious attack upon our honour, upon our piety, upon our devotion to God, and upon our yearning for peace! It is not our doing! It is his, and we must give him the war he so fervently desires!'

Men cheered. Sigtryggr and Æthelflaed looked distraught, Edward was frowning, while Æthelhelm was shaking his head as if overcome by misery at getting exactly what he wanted.

The bishop waited until the crowd was silent. 'And what does God desire of us?' he bellowed. 'What does he want of you?'

'He wants you to stop spewing filth, you whoremonger,' I shouted, breaking the silence that followed his two questions.

Then I pushed my way through the crowd.

SIX

I had peeled back the hood and thrown the shabby cloak from my shoulders before I forced a path through the crowd with Finan following close behind me. There were gasps as I was recognised, then murmurs, and finally angry protests. Not all the crowd was irate. Some men grinned, anticipating entertainment, and a handful called a greeting to me. Bishop Wulfheard stared in shock, opened his mouth to speak, found he had nothing to say, and so looked desperately at King Edward in the hope that the king would exercise his authority, but Edward seemed similarly astonished to see me, and said nothing. Æthelflaed was wide-eyed and almost smiling. The protests grew as men bellowed that I should be ejected from the barn, and one young man decided to be a hero and stepped into my path. He wore a dark red cloak that was clasped at his throat by a silver badge of the leaping stag. All Æthelhelm's household warriors wore the dark red cloaks, and a group of them muscled their way through the crowd to reinforce the young man, who held out a hand to stop me. 'You—' he began.

He never finished whatever he wanted to say because I just hit him. I did not mean to hit him so hard, but the anger was in me, and he folded over my fist, suddenly breathless, and I pushed him away so that he staggered and fell onto the dirty straw. Then, just before we reached the makeshift platform, one of Edward's guards confronted us with a levelled spear, but Finan came past me and stood in front of the blade. 'Try it, lad,' he said quietly, 'please, please, just try it.'

'Stand back!' Edward found his voice, and the guard backed away.

'Take him away!' Æthelhelm shouted. He was talking to his household warriors, and meant them to drag me away, but two of Edward's guards, who alone were permitted to carry weapons in the king's presence, mistook him and pulled away the red-cloaked young man instead. The voices of Edward and Æthelhelm had silenced the barn, though murmuring began again as I clambered awkwardly onto the dais. Finan stayed below the dais, facing the crowd and daring any man to interfere with me. Sigtryggr, like every other person in the barn, stared at me in surprise. I winked at him, then went onto one knee before Æthelflaed. She looked so ill, so pale, so thin.

'My lady,' I said. She had reached out a hand, a thin hand, and I kissed it, and when I looked up after the kiss I saw tears in her eyes, but she was smiling. 'Uhtred,' she said my name softly, nothing else.

'Your oath-man still, my lady,' I said, and turned to her brother to whom I bowed my head respectfully. 'Lord King,' I said.

Edward, who wore the emerald crown of his father, lifted a hand to silence the crowd. 'I am surprised to see you, Lord Uhtred,' he said stiffly.

'I bring you news, lord King,' I said.

'News is always welcome. Good news especially.'

'I think you'll discover that this is very good news, lord King,' I said as I stood up.

'Let us hear it,' the king commanded. The crowd was utterly silent now. Some men who had fled Wulfheard's tedious sermon had flocked back to the barn's open doors and were jostling to get inside.

'I'm not a man of words, lord King,' I said as I walked slowly towards Wulfheard. 'I'm not like Bishop Wulfheard. The whores at the Wheatsheaf in Wintanceaster tell me he doesn't stop talking even when he's humping them.'

'You foul—' Wulfheard began.

'Though they say,' I interrupted him fiercely, 'that he's so quick with them that it's never a long sermon. More like a gabbled blessing. In the name of the Father, the Son, and the ho, ho, ho, oh!'

A few men laughed, but stopped when they saw the anger on Edward's face. He had not been particularly religious as a youngster, but now that he was at the age when men begin to contemplate their deaths he lived in fear of the nailed god. But Æthelflaed, who was older and deeply pious, did laugh, though her laughter turned into a cough. Edward was about to protest my words, but I forestalled him. 'So,' I was talking to the whole assembly now, my back to an outraged Wulfheard, 'Brunulf is dead?'

'You killed him, you bastard,' a man, braver than the rest, called.

I looked at him. 'If you think I'm a bastard then you step up here now, the king will give us swords, and you can prove it.' I waited, but he did not move, and so I just nodded to my son.

Who stepped aside so Brunulf could walk through the crowd. He had to elbow his way through the press of men, but gradually, as some recognised him, a passage was made for him. 'So,' I said again, 'Brunulf is dead? Did anyone here see him die? Did anyone here see his corpse?' No one answered, though there were gasps and whispers as men realised who

125

was approaching the platform. He reached it, and I stretched down a hand to help him up onto the planks. 'Lord King,' I turned to Edward, 'may I present your man Brunulf?'

No one spoke. Edward looked at Æthelhelm, who had suddenly found the rafters of the barn's roof intensely interesting, then back to Brunulf, who had knelt to him.

'Does he smell dead to you, lord King?' I asked.

Edward's face twitched in what might have been a smile. 'He does not.'

I turned on the crowd. 'He's not a corpse! It seems I didn't kill him! Brunulf, are you dead?'

'No, lord.'

The barn was so silent you could have heard a flea cough. 'Were you attacked in Northumbria?' I asked Brunulf.

'I was, lord.'

Edward gestured for Brunulf to stand, and I beckoned him closer to me. 'Who attacked you?' I demanded.

He paused for a heartbeat, then, 'Men carrying King Sigtryggr's badge.'

'That badge?' I asked, pointing to Sigtryggr's banner with its red axe that hung high above the platform.

'Yes, lord.'

There were growls from the hall, but they were silenced by those men who wanted to hear Brunulf's words. Sigtryggr frowned when he heard that the men who had attacked Brunulf had carried his badge, but he made no protest. Æthelhelm cleared his throat, shifted uncomfortably in his chair, then went back to staring at the rafters. 'And you successfully fought these men off?' I asked.

'You did, lord.'

'And how many of your men died?'

'None, lord.'

'None?' I asked louder.

'Not one, lord.'

'Not one of your West Saxons died?'

'None, lord.'

'Were any injured?'

He shook his head. 'None, lord.'

'And of the men carrying the badge of the red axe. How many of those died?'

'Fourteen, lord.'

'And the rest you captured?'

'You captured them, lord.'

Æthelhelm was now staring at me, apparently unable to speak or even move.

'And were they King Sigtryggr's men?' I asked.

'No, lord.'

'Then whose men were they?'

Brunulf paused again, this time to look directly at Æthelhelm. 'They were Lord Æthelhelm's men.'

'Louder!' I insisted.

'They were Lord Æthelhelm's men!'

And then there was uproar. Some men, many of them wearing the dark red cloak and the silver stag badge of Æthelhelm's household, were bellowing that Brunulf lied, but others were shouting for silence or demanding that Brunulf be allowed to tell more of his tale. I let the commotion continue as I walked to Æthelhelm's chair and leaned close to him. His grandson, Prince Ælfweard, strained to hear what I said, but I spoke too softly. 'I have Brice here,' I told Æthelhelm, 'and I have Father Herefrith. They're both scared shitless of me, so they won't lie to save your miserable hide. Do you understand me, lord?'

He gave an almost imperceptible nod, but said nothing. The men in the hall were clamouring to know more, but I ignored them. 'So, lord,' I went on, still whispering, 'you'll say they disobeyed you, and then you'll agree with everything I propose. Everything. Do we have an agreement, lord?'

'You bastard,' he muttered.

'Do we have an agreement?' I insisted, and, after a slight pause, he gave a small nod. I patted his cheek.

And then we did agree. We agreed that Brice had exceeded his orders, that he had tried to provoke a war on his own initiative, and that the decision to attack Brunulf had been taken by him and by Father Herefrith alone, in contradiction of Ealdorman Æthelhelm's strict orders. All Æthelhelm had wanted, he declared, was to build a church to the glory of Saint Erpenwald of the Wuffingas, and he had never, not for a moment, thought that pious act might provoke violence. And it was agreed that Brice would be handed over to Edward's men to receive the king's justice, while Father Herefrith would be disciplined by the church.

We agreed that the truce already in place between Æthelflaed and Sigtryggr would be extended until All Saints' Day the following year. I wanted three years, but Edward insisted on the shorter period and I had no sway over him as I did over Æthelhelm, and so I accepted the condition. All Saints' Day came late in the campaigning season, too close to winter for comfort, and I reckoned it gave Sigtryggr almost two years of peace.

And lastly I insisted on taking hostages to ensure the good behaviour of Northumbria's enemies. That was not popular. Some men shouted that if Wessex or Mercia were to yield hostages, then Northumbria should do the same, but Æthelhelm, prompted by a glance from me, supported the proposal. 'Northumbria,' he said grudgingly, 'did not break the truce. It was our men who did that.' You could almost see the pain on his face as he spoke. 'The transgressor,' he said, flinching, 'must pay the price.'

'And who,' King Edward demanded of me, 'are to be your hostages?'

'I only want one, lord King,' I said, 'just one. I want the

heir to your throne,' I paused and saw the fear on Æthelhelm's face. He thought I meant his grandson, Ælfweard, who also looked horrified, but then I slid the hook out of their frightened guts, 'I want Prince Æthelstan.'

Who I loved like a son.

And for over a year he would be mine.

And so would Sigtryggr's army.

Brice died that same day.

I had never liked him. He was a dull, brutal, unthinking man, or he was until the afternoon of his death when he was brought with tied hands to the space in front of Edward's tent, and at that moment he impressed me.

He made no attempt to blame Æthelhelm even though he was being executed for obeying Æthelhelm's commands. He could have called out the truth, but he had sworn his oath to the ealdorman, and he kept that oath to the end.

He knelt in front of a priest and made his confession, he received absolution and was given the last rites. He did not protest, neither did he weep. He stood when the priest was finished and turned towards the king's tent, and only then did he flinch.

He had expected a guard from the king's household troops to kill him, a man experienced in war who would do the job swiftly, and indeed a great hulking brute of a man had been waiting for him at the place of execution. The brute's name was Waormund, and Waormund was a giant of a man who could kill an ox with one blow of a sword. He was a man to put at the centre of a shield wall to terrify an enemy, but while Brice was being shriven, Waormund's place had been taken by Ælfweard, the king's son, and, seeing the youngster, Brice shuddered.

He went to his knees again. 'Lord Prince,' he said, 'I beg you to let me die with my hands free.'

'You'll die as I choose,' Ælfweard said. He had a high voice, not quite broken, 'and I choose to leave your hands tied.'

'Free his hands,' I called. I was one of two hundred or more men who were watching the execution, and most of them supported me by murmuring agreement.

'You will be silent,' Ælfweard commanded me.

I walked to him. He was plump, like his mother, with a petulant face. He had curling brown hair, ruddy cheeks, blue eyes, and an expression of disdain. He carried a sword that looked too big for him, and he twitched the blade as I came close, but one look into my eyes persuaded him to leave the weapon low. He wanted to be defiant, but I could see the fear in his slightly protuberant eyes. 'Waormund,' he commanded, 'tell the Lord Uhtred to mind his business.'

Waormund lumbered towards me. He really was a giant, a whole head taller than me, with a flat, grim face slashed from his right eyebrow to his lower left jaw by a scar. He had a bristling brown beard, eyes dead as stone, and a thin-lipped mouth that seemed set in a permanent grimace. 'Let Prince Ælfweard do his duty,' he growled at me.

'When the prisoner's hands are freed,' I said.

'Make him go away!' Ælfweard whined.

'You heard . . .' Waormund began.

'You don't serve me,' I interrupted him, 'but I am a lord and you are not, and you owe me respect and obedience, and if you fail to give me either then I shall fillet you. I've killed bigger fools than you,' I doubted that was true, but it did no harm for Waormund to hear it, 'but none more stupid. Now both of you will wait while I free Brice's hands.'

'You can't—' Waormund began, and I slapped him. I slapped him hard across the face, and he was so astonished that he just stood there like a stunned heifer.

'Don't tell me what I can or cannot do, ceorl,' I snapped

at him. 'I told you to wait, so you will wait.' I walked away from him, going to Brice, and I gave Finan a tiny nod as I went. Then I stepped behind Brice, drew the knife I was not supposed to be carrying, and cut through the hide rope that had bound him. I looked past him and saw the scarlet curtain hanging in the entrance of the king's tent move slightly.

'Thank you, lord,' Brice said. He massaged his freed wrists. 'A man should die with his hands free.'

'So he can pray?'

'Because I don't deserve to die like a common thief, lord. I'm a warrior.'

'Yes,' I said, 'you are.' I was facing him now, my back to Waormund and to Prince Ælfweard, while Finan had stepped behind Brice. 'And you're a warrior who kept his oath,' I added.

Brice glanced around the circle of men who watched us. 'He didn't come to see this.' He meant Æthelhelm.

'He's ashamed of himself,' I said.

'But he made sure I'd die this way, lord, and not by being hanged. And he'll look after my wife and children.'

'I'll make sure he does.'

'But he lets the boy kill me,' Brice said in disgust, 'and that boy will butcher me. He likes hurting people.'

'You did too.'

He nodded. 'I've repented my sins, lord.' He looked past me, gazing up into the cloudless sky, and for a heartbeat there was a hint of tears in his eyes. 'You think there's a heaven, lord?'

'I think there's a mead hall called Valhalla where brave warriors go after death. A mead hall filled with friends and feasts.'

Brice nodded. 'But to get there, lord, a man must die with a weapon in his hand.'

'Is that why you wanted your hands untied?'

He did not answer, but just looked at me, and I saw the confusion in him. He had been raised a Christian, at least I assumed he had, but the stories of the old gods were still whispered about the night-time fires, and the fear of the corpse-ripper who feeds on the dead in Niflheim was not forgotten, despite all that the priests preached. I still carried the knife and now I reversed it and held the hilt towards Brice. 'It's not a sword,' I said, 'but it is a weapon. Hold it tight.' I kept my fingers closed firmly around Brice's knuckles so that he could not release the blade nor, for that matter, lunge it at my belly.

He did not try. 'Thank you, lord,' he said.

And Finan struck. He had hidden a seax under his tunic, and, while I spoke to Brice, he slid the weapon free and, as soon as he saw that Brice had good hold of the knife, he slashed the short blade across the nape of Brice's neck. Brice died instantly, with no time even to know he was dying, and the knife was still in his grasp as he fell. I kept my grip on his hand as his body collapsed, and only when I was certain that he was dead did I prise his fingers from the hilt.

'You . . .' Ælfweard began to protest in a shrill voice, but went silent as Finan whirled the seax's blooded blade in a series of air-whistling cuts and slashes too fast for the eye to follow.

So Brice died, and, stupid as he was, he will have his place on the benches in Valhalla's hall. We shall meet again.

I walked away, but a touch on my elbow turned me back fast. I thought for a heartbeat that Waormund or Ælfweard was attacking me, but it was a servant who bowed low and told me I was summoned to the king's tent. 'Now, if it please you, lord.'

It did not matter whether I was pleased or displeased, a king's summons could hardly be ignored and so I followed the servant past the guards and pushed through the scarlet curtain. It was cool inside the tent, smelling of crushed grass. There were tables, chairs, chests, and a large bed on which a dark-haired girl with large eyes sat watching us. The king dismissed the servant, but ignored the girl, instead going to a table littered with broken loaves, a block of cheese, documents, a book, quills, horn cups, and two silver jugs. The crown of Wessex with its emeralds lay discarded in the muddle. Edward poured himself a beaker of wine and looked at me questioningly. 'Please, lord,' I said.

He poured another beaker and brought it to me himself, then sat, nodding to a second, smaller chair. 'So Brice was a pagan?'

'A pagan and a Christian, I suspect.'

'And he did not deserve to die.' It was not a question, but a statement.

'No, lord.'

'But it was a necessary death,' he said. I did not respond. Edward sipped his wine and brushed a scrap of dirt from his blue robe. 'I didn't know,' he went on, 'that my son had been given the job of killing him. I am glad you intervened.'

'Brice deserved a quick end,' I said.

'He did,' he agreed, 'yes, he did.' I had not seen Edward for some years, and thought he looked old now, though he was much younger than me. He was, I suppose, in his early forties then, but his hair had gone grey at the temples, his short beard was grey, and his face was lined. I could see his father in that face. I remembered Edward as a young and uncertain prince, since when I had heard rumours of too much wine and too many women, though the gods know the same rumours could be spread of any lord, but I had also heard that he cared deeply about his country, was pious, and I knew he had proved a notable warrior in his conquest of East Anglia. It had been difficult for him, if not impossible, to live up to his father's reputation, but as Alfred's death receded in time so Edward had grown in authority and achievement. 'You do know,' he said suddenly, 'that we shall attack Northumbria?'

'Of course, lord.'

'The truce will be kept. In truth it's convenient for me. We need time to impose law on the lands we've taken.' He meant the next year would be spent rewarding his followers with estates, and making sure they had trained warriors who could march north under the dragon banner of Wessex. He frowned as a priest came into the tent clutching an armful of documents. 'Not now, not now,' the king said irritably, waving the man off. 'Later. Who has your oath, Lord Uhtred?'

'Your sister.'

He seemed surprised by that. 'Still?'

'Indeed, lord.'

He frowned. 'Yet you would fight for Sigtryggr?'

'Your sister hasn't demanded otherwise, lord.'

'And if she did?'

I tried to avoid the question. 'You have nothing to fear from me, lord King. I'm an old man with aching joints.'

Edward offered me a grim smile. 'My father tried to control you and said it couldn't be done. He also advised me never to underestimate you. He said you look stupid but act clever.'

'I thought it was the other way around, lord.'

He smiled dutifully at that, then returned to the question I had tried to avoid. 'So what happens if my sister demands your service?'

'Lord,' I said, 'all I want is to retake Bebbanburg.' I knew that would not satisfy him, so added, 'but that is probably impossible now that Constantin is there, so I am planning to retire to Frisia.'

He frowned. 'I asked,' he said precisely, and in a voice that was just like his father's, 'what you would do if my sister demanded your oath-service.'

'I would never draw my sword against your sister, lord, never.'

It was not the full answer he wanted, but he did not press me any further. 'You know what is happening at Bebbanburg?'

'I know Constantin is besieging the fortress,' I said, 'but nothing more.'

'He's trying to starve your cousin,' Edward said. 'He's left over four hundred men there under a leader called Domnall, and Domnall is a very capable commander.'

I did not ask how he knew. Edward would have inherited his father's vast number of spies and informants, and no king in Britain was better supplied with news, much of it sent by churchmen who were incessantly writing letters, and I did not doubt that Edward had plenty of informants in both Scotland and Northumbria. 'There's a sea gate,' I said, 'and the fortress can be supplied by ship.'

'No longer,' Edward said confidently. 'The coast is guarded by a Norseman and his ships. A man originally hired by your cousin.'

'Einar the White?'

He nodded. 'Constantin has purchased his loyalty.'

That surprised me. 'Constantin told me he'd attack Einar.'

'Why fight when you can buy? Einar's ships patrol the coast now.' Edward sighed. 'Constantin is no fool, though I'm not sure how useful Einar will be. He calls himself Einar the White, but he's also known as Einar the Unfortunate.' He gave a mirthless smile. 'What did you like to tell me years ago? That fate is inexorable?'

'Wyrd bið ful āræd,' I said.

'Maybe Einar's fate is to be unfortunate? You must hope so.'

'Why unfortunate, lord?' I asked.

'I'm told he's wrecked three ships.'

'Then maybe he's fortunate to be alive?'

135

'Maybe,' he smiled thinly, 'but I am told the nickname is deserved.' I hoped he was right. I touched the hammer hanging around my neck and said a silent prayer that Einar proved to be the unlucky one. Edward saw the gesture and frowned.

'But with or without Einar's ships,' I said, 'Bebbanburg is almost impossible to capture. That's why I'm thinking of Frisia.'

'Frisia!' Edward said contemptuously, his disbelief plain, and I feared my cousin's reaction might be the same. 'Bebbanburg,' he went on, 'is surely difficult to assault, but it can be starved, and your cousin has over two hundred men inside Bebbanburg, well over two hundred. They need a lot of food! He could have held the fortress with half that number, but he's a cautious man and he's going to starve sooner rather than later. And one of his granaries burned. Did you know that?'

'I didn't, lord.' I felt a surge of pleasure at my cousin's ill-fortune, then a pang of fear as I thought how such a fire would help Constantin.

'Your cousin evicted the useless mouths from the fortress,' Edward went on, 'but he's kept too many fighting men inside. They will starve, and a starved garrison will prove easy to conquer.' I touched the hammer again, risking his displeasure. 'But it does not suit me,' Edward sounded bitter suddenly, 'for Constantin to rule Bebbanburg's land. He had the impudence to demand all the land north of the wall! He sent an envoy, a bishop, to propose a new frontier! But Bebbanburg is Saxon land. It always has been! And it should be, and it will be, a part of Englaland. You might be old, feeble, and have aching joints, Lord Uhtred, but you will drive Constantin out of your ancestral land!'

I shrugged. 'I want Bebbanburg more than you, lord King, but I also know the fortress. If I had a thousand men?'

I shrugged again. 'I hold Dunholm, and Dunholm is almost as formidable as Bebbanburg. I had thought to dream of Bebbanburg and die in Dunholm, but when your army invades Northumbria, lord, Frisia will be a safer place for me.' I said that loudly, not for Edward's benefit, but for the wide-eyed girl who listened from the bed. The king might not believe my story of Frisia, but let the girl spread the rumour that I was not going to Bebbanburg.

'If you do not take Bebbanburg,' Edward said savagely, 'then I will, and my man will rule there instead of you. Is that what you want?'

'Better you than the Scots, lord.'

He grunted, then stood to show we were finished, and so I stood too. 'You asked to take Æthelstan as your hostage,' he said as we walked towards the tent's doorway, 'why?'

'Because he's like a son to me,' I said, 'and because I would preserve his life.'

Edward well knew what I implied, he knew who threatened Æthelstan. He nodded. 'Good,' he said softly. 'My sister has protected him these many years. Now you will do it for a year.'

'You could preserve his life yourself, lord,' I said.

He paused and lowered his voice. 'Ealdorman Æthelhelm is my most powerful lord. He leads too many men, and has too many followers who owe him their lands and their fortunes. To oppose him openly is to risk civil war.'

'But he'll start just such a war,' I said, 'to keep Æthelstan from succeeding.'

'Then that will be Æthelstan's problem,' the king said bleakly, 'so teach him well, Lord Uhtred, teach him well, because my sister can no longer protect him.'

'She can't?'

'My sister,' he said, 'is dying.'

And my heart seemed to stop.

And just then an indignant Ælfweard pushed aside the scarlet curtain. 'That man Uhtred, father . . .' he began, then stopped abruptly. He had evidently not known I was in the tent.

'That man Uhtred what?' Edward asked.

Ælfweard offered his father a perfunctory bow. 'I was told to kill the prisoner. He interfered.'

'So?' Edward demanded.

'He should be punished,' Ælfweard protested.

'Then punish him,' Edward said, and turned away.

Ælfweard frowned, looked from me to his father, then back to me. If he had possessed any sense he would have stepped aside, but his pride was hurt. 'Do you not bow to royalty, Lord Uhtred?' he demanded in his high voice.

'I bow to those I respect,' I said.

'You call me "lord",' he insisted.

'No, boy, I don't.'

He was shocked. He mouthed the word 'boy', but said nothing, just stared indignantly at me. I took a pace forward, forcing him back. 'I called your father "boy",' I said, 'until the day he accompanied me across the walls of Beamfleot. We killed Danes that day, spear-Danes, sword-Danes, fierce warriors. We fought, boy, and we made a great slaughter, and on that day your father deserved to be called lord and deserved all the respect I still give him. But you're still reeking of your mother's tit, boy, and until you prove to me that you're a man then you stay a boy. Now get out of my way, boy.'

He did. And his father said nothing. And I left.

'He's not a bad boy,' Æthelflaed told me.

'He's pampered, rude, insufferable.'

'People say that about you.'

I growled at that, making her smile. 'And you?' I asked her, 'your brother says you're ill.'

She hesitated. I could see she wanted to deny the fact, but then she relented and sighed. 'I'm dying,' she said.

'No!' I protested, but I could see the truth in her eyes. Her beauty was overlaid by age and pain, her skin looked somehow fragile, as if it had thinned, her eyes were darker, yet she still could smile and still had grace. I had found her in her tent, behind her flag, which showed a white goose holding a cross in its beak and a sword in a webbed foot. I had mocked that badge often enough. The goose was the symbol of Saint Werburgh, a Mercian nun who had miraculously evicted a flock of geese from a wheatfield, though why that counted as a miracle was beyond my understanding, any child of ten could do the same thing, but I knew Werburgh was precious to Æthelflaed, and she was precious to me. I pulled a chair beside hers and sat, taking one of her thin hands in mine. 'I know a healer . . .' I began.

'I have had healers,' she said tiredly, 'so many healers. But Ælfthryth sent me a clever man, and he's helped.' Ælfthryth was her younger sister who had married the ruler of Flanders. 'Father Casper makes a potion that takes away much of the pain, but he had to go back to Flanders because Ælfthryth is sick too.' She sighed and made the sign of the cross. 'Some days I feel better.'

'What are you suffering from?'

'Pain, here,' she touched a breast, 'deep inside. Father Casper taught the sisters how to make his potion, and that helps. Prayer helps too.'

'Then pray more,' I said. Two nuns, presumably the sisters who nursed Æthelflaed, sat in the shadows at the back of the tent. Both watched me suspiciously, though neither could hear a word we spoke.

'I pray day and night,' Æthelflaed said with a wan smile, 'and I pray for you too!'

'Thank you.'

'You'll need prayer,' she said, 'with Æthelhelm as your enemy.'

'I just pulled his teeth,' I said. 'You were there.'

'He'll want revenge.'

I shrugged. 'So what will he do? Attack me in Dunholm? I wish him luck with that.'

She patted my hand. 'Don't be arrogant.'

'Yes, my lady,' I said, smiling, 'so why doesn't your brother just smack Æthelhelm down?'

'Because it would mean war,' she said bleakly. 'Æthelhelm is popular! He's generous! There isn't a bishop or abbot in Wessex who doesn't take his money, he's friends with half the nobles. He gives feasts! And he doesn't want the throne for himself.'

'Just for his grandson, that piece of puke.'

'It's all he cares about,' Æthelflaed said, 'that Ælfweard becomes king, and my brother knows that the West Saxon Witan will vote that way. They've been bought.'

'And Æthelstan?' I asked, though I knew the answer.

'You did well to demand him as a hostage. He'll be safer with you than he is here.'

'Which is why I asked for him,' I said, then frowned. 'Would Æthelhelm really dare to kill him?'

'He'd dare to arrange his death, but no one would know. Do you ever read the scriptures?'

'Every day,' I said enthusiastically, 'not a moment passes that I don't have a quick read of Ieremias or dip into Ezekiel.'

She smiled, amused. 'What a barbarian you are! Have a priest tell you the story of Urias.'

'Urias?'

'Just remember the name,' she said, 'Urias Hetthius.'

'Talking of priests,' I said, 'who is Hrothweard?'

'The Archbishop of Eoferwic,' she said, 'as you well know.'

'A West Saxon,' I said.

'He is, and he's a good man!'

'Did the good man take Æthelhelm's gold?' I asked.

'Oh no, he's a good, pious man,' she said briskly, then hesitated and frowned. 'He was an abbot,' she went on more tentatively, 'and I remember his house receiving a generous grant of land. Twenty hides in Wiltunscir. It was a long way from his abbey.'

'He got land instead of gold?'

She still frowned. 'Men give land to the church all the time.'

'And Æthelhelm is Ealdorman of . . .'

'Wiltunscir,' she finished the sentence for me, then sighed. 'Æthelhelm is buying lords in Mercia now, showering them with gold. He wants the Mercian Witan to appoint Ælfweard as my successor.'

'No!' I was shocked by the suggestion. That sullen, callow boy to be King of Mercia!

'He proposed a marriage between Ælfweard and Ælfwynn,' she said. Ælfwynn was her daughter. She was a frivolous girl, pretty and irresponsible. I liked her, probably more than her mother did, which is why Æthelflaed's next words surprised me. 'I said no,' she went on, 'because I think Ælfwynn should succeed me.'

'You think what?' I blurted out.

'She's a princess of Mercia,' Æthelflaed said firmly, 'and if I can rule Mercia, why can't she? Why must a man always be the next ruler?'

'I adore Ælfwynn,' I said, 'but she doesn't have your good sense.'

'Then she can marry Cynlæf Haraldson,' Æthelflaed said, 'and he'll advise her. He's a strong young man.'

I said nothing. Cynlæf Haraldson was a young, handsome West Saxon warrior, but of no great birth, which meant he did not bring Ælfwynn the power of a big noble house, and he was of no great achievement either, which meant he did not have the reputation to attract men to follow him. I thought him shallow, but there was no point in saying so to Æthelflaed, who had always been charmed by his looks, manners, and courtesy.

'Cynlæf will protect her,' Æthelflaed said, 'and so will you.'

'You know I'm fond of her,' I said, and that was an evasion. What she wanted to hear was that I would support Ælfwynn as I had supported her, that Ælfwynn would have my oath. I was saved from having to say more by Rorik, my servant, who slapped a hand on the tent flap and came nervously out of the sunlight.

'Lord?' he said, then remembered to bow to Æthelflaed.

'What is it?'

'King Sigtryggr is leaving, lord. You wanted me to tell you.'

'I'm riding north with him,' I told Æthelflaed.

'Then go,' she said.

I stood and bowed to her. 'I will protect Ælfwynn,' I said, and that would have to satisfy her. Saying that much did not commit my oath to Ælfwynn, and Æthelflaed knew it, but she smiled anyway and held out her hand.

'Thank you,' she said.

I bent and kissed her hand, then held onto it. 'The best fate,' I said, 'is for you to get well. Become healthy! You're the best ruler Mercia has ever had, so be well and go on ruling.'

'I shall do my best.'

Then I shocked the two nuns by bending further and kissing Æthelflaed on the mouth. She did not resist. We had been lovers, I still loved her, and I love her to this day. I sensed a slight sob as we kissed.

'I shall come again,' I promised her, 'after I've taken Bebbanburg.'

'Not Frisia?' she asked mischievously. So the rumour was spreading.

I lowered my voice. 'I'm going to Bebbanburg next. Tell no one.'

'Dear Lord Uhtred,' she said softly, 'everyone knows you're going to Bebbanburg. Perhaps I'll visit you there?'

'You must, my lady, you must. You will be treated like the queen you are.' I kissed her hand again. 'Till we meet in the north, my lady,' I said, then reluctantly released her fingers and followed Rorik out of the tent.

I never saw her again.

My men and Sigtryggr's men rode together, going north. The sun shone, it was warm, and the summer air was filled with the sound of hooves and the jingle of harnesses. 'I hate Saxons,' Sigtryggr said.

I did not answer. To my right was a field thick with growing wheat, a reminder of how rich this land was. Dust drifted from our passing.

'You've bought me at least a year,' Sigtryggr said, 'thank you.'

I saw a falcon high in the warm air, hovering, its wings motionless except for a slight quiver as it stared intensely at the ground where some creature was doomed. I watched it, hoping to see the bird stoop, but it just stayed there, effortlessly riding the high wind. An omen? Maybe an omen of peace, except I did not want peace. I was carrying my sword towards Bebbanburg.

'They smell different,' Sigtryggr said vengefully. 'They reek of the Saxon stink! Rotted turnips! That's what they smell like, rotted turnips! Smug, self-satisfied turnips!'

I twisted in my saddle and looked at Æthelstan, who was riding next to my son a few paces behind us and who, thankfully, was out of earshot of Sigtryggr's spleen. 'Prince Æthelstan,' I called, 'do Danes and Norsemen smell?'

'The Danes stink of curdled cheese, lord,' he called back cheerfully, 'while the Norse reek of bad fish.'

Sigtryggr snorted. 'I hope the Saxons do break the truce, Prince Æthelstan,' he said loudly, 'then I will have the pleasure of killing you.' He knew I would never allow it, but he enjoyed making the threat.

He looked older. I remembered the gleeful young battle-warrior who had leaped up the ramparts of Ceaster as he tried to kill me. A lord of war. I had taken one of his eyes and he had taken my daughter, and now we were friends, but a few months of kingship had put lines on his face and taken the joy from his soul.

'And that bastard Thurferth!' he spat. 'He's no better! He calls himself a Dane and lifts his arse for the Christians? I'd nail the treacherous bastard to a cross.' His anger was justified. The Danish lords who ruled Northumbria's southern burhs had the power to give Sigtryggr a formidable army, but their fear was proving stronger than their loyalty. I suspected most would follow Thurferth and give their allegiance to both the West Saxons and to the nailed god. 'They'll even march with the Saxons,' Sigtryggr said bitterly.

'Probably.'

'And what do I do then?' It was not a real question, more a cry of despair.

'You come to live in Bebbanburg,' I said mildly.

We rode in silence for a half-mile as the road dropped to a shallow ford where the horses paused to drink. I rode ahead a few paces and checked Tintreg in the road's dusty centre, just listening to the day's silence.

Sigtryggr followed me. 'I can't fight the Scots and the Saxons,' he said. He sounded grudging, not wanting me to think him a coward, 'not at the same time.'

'The Saxons will keep the truce,' I assured him, and I was sure I was right.

'Next year,' he said, 'or maybe the year after, the armies of Mercia and Wessex will come north. I can hold them. I have just enough men. At the very least I can make them wish they'd never heard of Northumbria. And with your men? We can darken the earth with their filthy blood.'

'I won't fight against Æthelflaed,' I told him, 'she has my oath.'

'Then you can kill the bastard West Saxons,' he said vengefully, 'and I'll kill the Mercians, but I can't fight if I don't have enough men.'

'True.'

'And to throw Constantin back to his hovels? I can do it, but at what price?'

'A high price,' I said, 'the Scots fight like angry polecats.'

'So . . .' he began.

'I know,' I interrupted him. 'You can't throw away the best part of your army fighting the Scots, at least not till you've beaten back the Saxons.'

'You understand?'

'Of course I understand,' I said. And he was right. Sigtryggr commanded a small army. If he led it north to evict the Scots from Bebbanburg's land he would be inviting a war with Constantin, who would welcome a chance to weaken Northumbria's army. Sigtryggr might well win the first battles, driving Domnall's four hundred men northwards, but after that the howling devils of Niflheim would emerge from the Scottish hills, and the battles would become grimmer. Sigtryggr, even if he won, would lose the men he needed to stave off the Saxon assault.

He gazed north to where the day's heat shimmered above low hills and thick woods. 'So you'll wait to attack Bebbanburg?' he asked. 'You'll wait till we've driven off the Saxons?'

'I can't wait.'

Sigtryggr looked pained. 'Without those bastard Thurferth's troops,' he said, 'and the rest of those slimy toads in the south, I can't assemble more than eight hundred men. I can't lose a hundred to Constantin.'

'I'll want a hundred and fifty from you,' I said, 'maybe two hundred, and if I'm right, not one of those men will be scratched. I can't wait because by next spring Constantin will have starved the bastard out and he'll be sitting inside Bebbanburg, so I'm going there now, and I'm going to capture it,' I touched the hammer, 'and I need your help.'

'But—' he said.

And I interrupted him again.

By telling him how we would conquer the unconquerable, and how his men would suffer no casualties in the conquest.

Or so I hoped. I gripped the hammer. Wyrd bið ful āræd.

PART THREE
The Mad Bishop

SEVEN

'We're going to Frisia,' I told Eadith.

She just stared at me in astonishment.

I had ridden north to Eoferwic where I spent one night, feasting with Sigtryggr, my daughter and, of all people, the new Archbishop Hrothweard. He was indeed a decent man, or seemed so to me. He flinched when I told him what had happened in Hornecastre. 'It seems God was on your side, Lord Uhtred,' he said gently, 'you snatched peace from the jaws of war.'

'Which god?' I asked him.

He laughed, then asked me what I thought would happen at Bebbanburg and I gave him the same answer that Finan had given him, that Constantin would find an assault too costly, but that he hardly needed to expend troops on the fortress walls when hunger would do the job for him. Hrothweard shook his head sadly. 'So Saint Cuthbert's monastery, if it is rebuilt, will host Scottish monks.'

'And that worries you?' I asked him.

He thought about his answer. 'It shouldn't,' he finally said. 'They will be godly men, I am sure.'

'But you will lose the money that pilgrims bring,' I said.

He liked that retort, and his long face lit up with delight as he pointed a goose-leg at me. 'You like to think the worst of us, Lord Uhtred!'

'But it's true, isn't it?'

He shook his head. 'Lindisfarena is a holy place. An island of prayer. I would like to appoint its new abbot if God wills it, only to be certain that he is worthy of the island and will not bring God's church into disrepute. And a worthy man, Lord Uhtred, would not be a greedy man, whatever you might think.'

'I think Bishop Ieremias has dreams of being the next abbot,' I said mischievously.

Hrothweard laughed. 'Poor man! What do men call him? The mad bishop?' He chuckled. 'There are those who urge me to excommunicate him, but what good would that do? He is sorely mistaken, I'm sure, but unlike some I can think of,' he looked at me with humour in his eyes, 'he worships the one god. He is, I think, harmless. In grievous error, of course, but harmless.'

I liked the man. Like Father Pyrlig, he wore his faith lightly, but his piety, kindness, and honesty were obvious. 'I shall pray for you,' he said, on parting, 'whether you like it or not.'

I made no attempt to see Berg on that brief visit, though my daughter told me he had purchased three ships and was now repairing them on the wharves close to the Duck tavern. Now, back in Dunholm, I told Eadith of those ships, and of my plans to cross the sea to Frisia. It was night-time, and we talked in the house I had built above the main gate. In daylight the house gave us a fine view southwards, but now all that could be seen were the glow of fires from the small town below the fortress and the sparks of uncountable stars spread across the heavens. The house had been an extravagance. It had meant building a gatehouse tunnel to support it, and two chambers flanking the tunnel, one to house our servants and the other for the gate's guards. A set of stairs led from our servants' quarters into our private rooms, and I was inordinately proud of those stairs. They were rare! Of course every Roman town that had kept its walls had steps leading to the ramparts, but I had rarely seen stairs in the buildings we made. Many halls had an upper floor, but those platforms, which we usually used for sleeping, were reached by ladders, and sometimes by a ramp, but I had always admired how the Romans had made stairs inside their houses, and so I had ordered some built, though admittedly the Dunholm stair was made from wood and not from finely-cut stone. Building our house above the entrance tunnel meant thrusting a new rampart out over the approach road, and, because there were sentries on that rampart's high platform, I kept my voice low, though not quite low enough to prevent our conversation from being overheard.

'Frisia!' Eadith exclaimed.

'There are islands,' I said, 'off the Frisian coast. We'll take one, build a fortress and make it home.' I could see a mixture of disbelief and disappointment on her face. 'Frisia is Christian,' I said, reassuring her, because she was a Christian and, despite all my persuasion, had never reverted to the worship of my older gods, 'well, it's mostly Christian,' I went on, 'and you won't find it a strange place. Their language is so close to ours that you can understand everything!'

'But,' she began, and gestured around our chamber that was lit by small rushlights that glowed on the woven wall hangings, on the big woollen rug and the heap of furs that was our bed.

'I've made too many enemies,' I said bleakly. 'Æthelflaed is dying, so she can't protect me, the West Saxons have never loved me, and Æthelhelm hates me, my cousin sits in Bebbanburg like a great toad, and Constantin would like nothing more than to squash me like a louse.'

'Sigtryggr . . .' she began.

'Is doomed,' I said firmly. 'The Saxons will attack next year or the year after, and he might hold them off for a couple of months, but after that? They'll keep coming, and Constantin will see his opportunity and start taking more land in the north of Northumbria.'

'But Sigtryggr's looking to you for help!' she protested.

'And that's what I'm giving him,' I said. 'We're making a new land in Frisia. He'll be welcome!'

'Sigtryggr knows about this?'

'Of course he does,' I said. I heard a scraping noise beneath the window that looked onto the approach road. It was probably the sound of a spear-butt dragging on the gate's fighting platform and it suggested someone was listening to our conversation.

Eadith again looked about the room with its comforts. 'I've grown fond of Dunholm,' she said plaintively.

'I'm giving it to Sihtric. He knows Dunholm. He was born here, he grew up here, and his father was the lord here.' Sihtric was the bastard son of Jarl Kjartan the Cruel, a man who had been my dreadful enemy as a child. Sihtric had none of his father's viciousness, but he was just as capable a warrior, and, starting as my servant, he had become one of my most trusted war-leaders. 'A few men can stay with him,' I said, 'mostly the older men, and he can recruit and train new men. They'll all be Christians, of course. Once the Saxons rule here, there'll be no room for pagans.'

'What about Bebbanburg?' Eadith asked.

'A year ago,' I said bleakly, 'I thought I had a chance of taking it. Now? My cousin holds it, and Constantin wants it. I might defeat my cousin, but I can't defeat the Scots as

152

well. I'm old, my love, I can't fight for ever.' I paused and half turned towards the ramparts. 'But don't tell anyone, not yet.'

And next day, of course, everyone in Dunholm knew of my plans.

We were going to Frisia.

I trusted Eadith. Some men thought that stupid of me because she had once been my enemy, but now she was my friend as well as my wife, and how can there be love without trust? So, later that night, when I was certain we could not be overheard, I told her the truth. The earlier conversation had been solely for the benefit of whoever might have been listening on the rampart outside our chamber, and I knew the conversation would eventually reach my cousin.

His first reaction, I'm sure, would be disbelief, but the story would be persistent and the evidence for its truth overwhelming. It would not make him drop his guard, but it would sow doubt, and doubt would be enough. And if I was wrong, and Eadith could not be trusted, then I had just removed that doubt. He would know I was coming.

Eadith did not betray me, but I never discovered all those who did.

I found a few, and hanged them from the nearest tree, but only after I had fed them misleading information they could pass on to my enemies. Still, I am certain there were many others I never discovered. I looked, of course. I looked for men who suddenly had more gold or silver than they should, or whose wives flaunted fine linen dresses with elegant embroidery, or men who would not meet my eyes, or who stood too close as I talked with Finan or with my son. I watched for men who paid too much attention to Eadith, or whose servants made efforts to be over-friendly with Rorik, my own servant.

But I never discovered all who betrayed me, nor did my enemies ever discover all who betrayed them.

I spent good money on my own spies, just as my enemies spent gold to spy on me. I had all those men who served Edward in Wintanceaster, and I had a wine-steward, a clerk, and a blacksmith who were in Æthelhelm's employment. I had no one in my cousin's service. I had tried to find a man or woman who could tell me what happened inside Bebbanburg, but my efforts were never successful, though I did hear a great deal of my cousin's doings from folk scattered up and down the east coast, and even from across the sea in Frisia. The same harbour taverns brought me news from Scotland because, again, I had no spies in Constantin's court.

My cousin, I was sure, had someone watching me. Perhaps it was one of my own men? Or a priest in Eoferwic? Or a merchant in Dunholm? I did not know who, but I knew such men existed. And he had folk listening to rumours as I did. Christians had the strange habit of confessing their worst behaviour to their sorcerers, and many of those priests sold what they learned, and my cousin took care to donate money to churches and churchmen. I doubted that Cuthbert, my blind priest, took my cousin's money. Cuthbert was loyal, and took a relish in passing me scraps he heard from such confessions. 'Would you believe it, lord? Swithun and Vidarr's wife! I'm told she's ugly.'

'Not truly ugly, but spiteful.'

'Poor boy, he must be desperate.'

Not every man or woman who sent me news was a spy. Priests, monks, and nuns constantly exchanged letters, and many were happy to share what they had learned from some faraway abbey, and merchants were always keen to pass on gossip, though inevitably much of that information was wrong, and almost always it was long out of date by the time it made its way to Northumbria.

But now, in the days following the meetings at Hornecastre, I also had Æthelstan's spies on my side. They did not know that. They probably thought they were keeping the young prince supplied with news while he suffered the ordeal of being my hostage, but Æthelstan promised to pass on much of what they told him. He was a Christian, of course, and was accompanied by three priests as well as six servants, four of whom were plainly warriors just pretending to be servants. 'Do you trust them?' I asked him as we hunted for deer in the hills north of Dunholm. It was a week since I had arrived back from Eoferwic, and, to bolster the rumour that I was leaving for Frisia, I had ordered my servants to start packing our goods.

'I trust them with my life,' Æthelstan said. 'They're all Mercian warriors, given to me by the Lady Æthelflaed.'

'And the priests?'

'I don't trust Swithred, but the other two?' He shrugged. 'They're young and full of noble ideals. I asked them to be my priests, they weren't imposed on me.'

I smiled at that. Æthelstan was about twenty-two or twenty-three in that year, no older than the two young priests. 'And Father Swithred was imposed on you?' I asked.

'By my father. Maybe he just sends news to him?'

'And any letters he sends,' I said, 'will be read by the king's clerks, who might be in Æthelhelm's pay.'

'So I assume,' he said.

Swithred was an older man, maybe forty or even fifty, with a scalp as bald as an egg, sharp dark eyes, and a perpetual frown. He resented being among pagans and let the resentment show. 'Have you noticed,' I had asked him as we journeyed north, 'that at least half my men are Christians?'

'No Christian can serve a heathen lord,' he had answered gruffly, then reluctantly added, 'lord.'

'You mean by serving me they cease to be Christians?'

'I mean that they place themselves in dire need of redemption.'

'They have their own church in Dunholm,' I had told him, 'and a priest. Would you provide the same for pagans in Wessex or Mercia?'

'Of course not!' he had said. He had been riding a tall grey horse, a fine beast, and he rode it well. 'Might I ask,' he had said, then seemed to think better of his question.

'Ask,' I had said.

'What arrangements will be made for Prince Æthelstan's comfort?'

He meant what arrangements would be made for his own comfort, but I pretended to believe that his concern was solely for the prince. 'He's a hostage,' I had told him, 'so we'll probably keep him in a cattle byre or maybe in a pig shed, fasten his ankles with chains and feed him slops and water.'

Æthelstan, who had been listening, laughed. 'Don't believe him, father.'

'And if even one West Saxon crosses the frontier,' I had continued, 'I'll cut his throat. And yours too!'

'This is not amusing, lord,' Father Swithred had said sternly.

'He will be treated as the prince that he is,' I had assured him, 'with honour, with comfort, and with respect.'

And so he was. Æthelstan feasted with us, hunted with us, and worshipped in the small church inside Dunholm's walls. He had become more pious as he grew into manhood. He still had his fierce joy in life, a hunger for activity, and an appetite for laughter, but now, much like his grandfather Alfred, he prayed every day. He read Christian texts, guided by the two young priests he had brought with him to Dunholm. 'What changed you?'

I asked as we waited on the edge of some woodland. We were armed with hunting bows. I was never a good archer, but Æthelstan had already killed two fine beasts with an arrow apiece.

'You changed me,' he said.

'Me!'

'You persuaded me I could be king, and if I'm to be king, lord, then I must have God's blessing.'

I raised the bow and notched an arrow as leaves sounded loud in the wood, but no beast appeared and the noise subsided. 'What's wrong with having Thor and Woden on your side?'

He smiled at that. 'I'm a Christian, lord. And I try to be a good one.' I made a grumbling noise, but said nothing. 'God won't reward me,' he said, 'if I do evil.'

'The gods have looked after me,' I said truculently.

'By sending you to Frisia?'

'Nothing wrong with Frisia.'

'It isn't Bebbanburg.'

'When you become king,' I said, watching the trees as I spoke, 'you'll discover that some ambitions can be fulfilled and some cannot. The important thing is to recognise which is which.'

'So you won't go north to Bebbanburg?' he asked.

'I told you, I'm going to Frisia.'

'And when you reach,' he paused, then stressed the next word, 'Frisia, will there be fighting?'

'There's always fighting, lord Prince.'

'And this fighting in,' again the slight pause, 'Frisia will be fierce?'

'Fighting always is.'

'Then you will allow me to fight alongside you?'

'No!' I spoke more vehemently than I had intended. 'The fight will be none of your concern. The enemies I fight will

157

not be your enemies. And you're my hostage, so I have a duty to keep you alive.'

He was gazing at the tree line, waiting for prey, his bow half drawn, though the arrow was still pointing to the ground. 'I owe you a lot, lord,' he said. 'You have protected me, I know that, and one way to repay you is to help you in your battles.'

'And if you die in battle,' I said brutally, 'then I've just done Æthelhelm a favour.'

He nodded, accepting that truth. 'The Lord Æthelhelm,' he said, 'wanted me to command the troops he sent to Hornecastre. He asked my father to appoint me, but father sent Brunulf instead.'

'Urias Hetthius,' I said.

He laughed at that. 'You were well educated!'

'By Lady Æthelflaed.'

'My clever aunt,' he said approvingly, then took his hand off the bow's cord to make the sign of the cross, doubtless saying a silent prayer for her recovery at the same time. 'Yes, Æthelhelm thought he could arrange my death in battle.'

Urias Hetthius was a soldier who served King David, who, in turn, was a hero to Christians. I had asked Father Cuthbert, my blind priest and good friend, who Urias was, and he had chuckled. 'Uriah! That's how we pronounce his name, lord. Uriah the Hittite. He was an unlucky man!'

'Unlucky?'

'He was married to a beautiful woman,' Cuthbert had told me wistfully, 'one of those girls you look at and you can't look away!'

'I've known a few,' I had said.

'And you married them, lord,' Cuthbert had said with a grin. 'Well David wanted to bounce on the bed with Uriah's wife, so he sent a message to Uriah's commander and told him to put the poor man in the front rank of the shield wall.'

'And he died?'

'Oh he did, lord! Poor bastard was cut to pieces!'

'And David . . .' I had begun.

'Bounced the pretty wife, lord, probably from dawn to dusk and back to dawn again. Lucky man!'

And Æthelhelm had wished that fate on Æthelstan. He had wanted him isolated deep in Northumbria in the hope that we would slaughter him. 'So if you think I'm going to risk your life in battle,' I told Æthelstan, 'you're dreaming. You'll stay well away from any fighting.'

'In Frisia,' Æthelstan said pointedly.

'In Frisia,' I repeated.

'So when do you leave?' he asked.

But that I could not answer. I was waiting for news. I wanted my spies or Æthelstan's informants to tell me what my enemies planned. Some folk wondered why I did not march straight to Bebbanburg, or, if they believed the rumours, sail directly to Frisia. Instead I lingered at Dunholm; hunting, practising sword-craft, and feasting. 'What are you waiting for?' Eadith asked me one day.

The two of us were riding in the hills west of Dunholm, hawks on our wrists, trailed by a dozen men who guarded me whenever I left the fortress. None of those men were in earshot. 'I can take fewer than two hundred warriors to Bebbanburg,' I told her, 'and my cousin has at least that many behind his ramparts.'

'But you're Uhtred,' she said loyally.

I smiled at that. 'And Uhtred knows the ramparts of Bebbanburg,' I said, 'and I don't want to die under those walls.'

'So what will change?'

'My cousin is getting hungry. One of his granaries burned.

So he'll be negotiating for someone to help him, someone to bring him food. But the coast is guarded by Einar's ships, so whoever takes the food north will need a fleet because they'll have to fight their way to the Sea Gate.' For a time I had suspected Hrothweard, but my daughter assured me that the archbishop was neither collecting food nor recruiting shipmasters, and my own meeting with the man had convinced me that she spoke the truth.

'And when that fleet sails,' Eadith began, then paused as she saw what I intended. 'Oh!' she said, 'I see! Your cousin will be expecting ships!'

'He will.'

'And one ship looks much like another!' She was a clever woman, as clever as she was beautiful.

'But I can't put to sea,' I said, 'until I know where that fleet is and who commands it and when it will sail.'

It was a time of waiting for news. I knew much of what happened on Bebbanburg's land because I sent scouts to watch Constantin's men, and they reported that Domnall, Constantin's commander, was still content to starve the fortress into submission. Scottish troops had garrisoned two of the forts on the Roman wall. Both garrisons were small because Constantin had other worries; there were aggressive Norsemen in the far north of his country and the ever troublesome kingdom of Strath Clota to the west. Both needed troops to contain them, so his men on the wall were simply there to enforce his claim to Bebbanburg's land and, of course, to warn him if we brought an army north. He would be alarmed when he heard that the truce between the Saxons and Sigtryggr had been renewed for over a year, and my fear was that he would order an assault on Bebbanburg's ramparts to forestall any attempt by Sigtryggr and myself to drive him away, but his spies would be reassuring him that Sigtryggr was strengthening the walls of Lindcolne and Eoferwic, readying himself for the inevitable attack that would come when the truce ended. There would be no hint of any preparations to attack Constantin's men, and common sense would convince him that Sigtryggr would not want to lose men in a war against Scotland when he was about to face a larger war against the southern Saxons. Constantin was willing to wait, knowing that the fortress would eventually starve. And perhaps Constantin even believed my tale of going to Frisia. He had to be contemplating an assault on Bebbanburg's walls, but he knew how slaughterous that attack would be, and the news he received from the south suggested he did not need to sacrifice scores of his men to gain a prize that would eventually be given to him by hunger.

So all of us in Britain were waiting for news. It was a time of rumours, of whispered tales that were designed to mislead and that sometimes were true. A merchant selling fine leather promised me that the town reeve of Mældunesburh, Æthelhelm's home town in Wiltunscir, had told him the ealdorman planned to invade Northumbria with or without King Edward's help. A priest in far-off Contwaraburg wrote that Edward was making an alliance with Constantin whereby both men would invade Northumbria and divide the land between them. 'I swear this,' the priest wrote, 'on the holy blood of Christ Himself, and assure you that the battles will begin on the Feast Day of Saint Gunthiern.' Saint Gunthiern's feast was already past when the letter reached Archbishop Hrothweard in Eoferwic, but still one of his clerks copied the words and gave them to my daughter, who, in turn, sent them to me.

In the end the news I wanted came from Merewalh who commanded Æthelflaed's household warriors. Merewalh was an old friend and a loyal supporter of Æthelflaed, who, he wrote, had commanded him to tell me that supplies were being sent to the East Anglian port of Dumnoc where a fleet was being assembled. 'She has this on the authority of Father Cuthwulf, who is mass priest to Lord Æthelhelm, and she prays you will not reveal his name, and Father Cuthwulf moreover tells her that if God wills it then the Lord Æthelhelm's fleet will put to sea after the feast of Saint Eanswida.'

And that made sense. Saint Eanswida's feast day was at the end of the harvest, a time when food was plentiful, and, if a man wanted to supply a besieged fortress with the food that would enable it to hold out for another year, then the late summer was the time to act. And of all the men in Britain who hated me, who wanted revenge on me, Æthelhelm was the most dangerous. I had always thought him the likeliest man to help my cousin, but I could not be sure until Merewalh's letter arrived.

And so, leaving Sihtric and eighteen men to hold Dunholm, I moved the rest of my followers with all their wives, children, servants, and slaves to Eoferwic. We were going to Frisia, I told them, and then I took three men and went to Dumnoc instead.

I chose three Saxon Christians as my companions because I suspected that Dumnoc, an East Anglian town that was newly conquered by the West Saxons, might be in a vengeful mood against both Northmen and pagans. I took Cerdic, one of my older men who was slow of wit but loyal to a fault. Oswi was much younger, and had served me since he was a boy. Now he was a lithe and eager fighter. The third was Swithun, a West Saxon who looked angelic, had a quick smile and a ready laugh, but also had the sly instincts and nimble fingers of a thief.

The four of us took passage on a West Saxon ship that

had berthed in Eoferwic with a cargo of Frankish glassware and was now returning to Lundene with her belly full of Northumbrian hides and silver bars. The shipmaster, Renwald, was glad of the gold we paid him and for our long knives, though he doubted I would be of much use in a fight. 'But you other three look useful,' he said.

Swithun grinned at him. 'Grandpa can fight,' he said, 'I know he don't look much, but he's a scoundrel in a scrap. Aren't you, grandpa!' he shouted at me, 'you're a right old bastard in a bundle!'

Since I had received the news about Dumnoc I had stopped shaving. I no longer bothered to comb my hair. I wore the oldest, dirtiest clothes I could find, and, on arriving in Eoferwic, I had practised walking with a stoop. Finan and my son had both told me I was a fool, that I had no need to go to Dumnoc, and that either of them would gladly go in my place, but my life's ambition depended upon what I would find in the East Anglian port, and I trusted no one but myself to travel there and discover what mischief was brewing.

'Mind you,' Renwald went on, 'if we're attacked by anything larger than a fishing boat, then your knives won't make much difference.' None of us carried swords or seaxes, only knives, because I did not want to announce to the men in Dumnoc that we were warriors.

'Are there pirates?' I mumbled.

'What did he say?'

'Speak up, grandpa!' Swithun shouted.

'Are there pirates?' I half shouted back, making sure I dribbled into the white stubble on my chin.

'He wants to know if there are pirates,' Swithun told Renwald.

'There are always pirates,' Renwald said, 'but they're mostly small craft these days. I haven't seen any Danish longships since King Edward captured the rest of East Anglia. God be praised.'

'God be praised,' I echoed piously, and made the sign of the cross. For this journey and for this cause, I was pretending to be a Christian, and even wore a crucifix instead of a hammer. I was also pretending that Swithun was my grandson, a pretence he had taken up with indecent enthusiasm.

Renwald, naturally, wanted to know where we had come from and why we were travelling, and Swithun spun a story about being driven from our land north of the wall. 'It was the Scots,' he said, spitting over the side of the ship.

'I heard those scavenging bastards had come south,' Renwald said. 'So you were Bebbanburg's tenants?'

'Grandpa rented from the old Lord Uhtred,' Swithun said, meaning my father. 'He's been on that land a lifetime, but his wife's father had land in East Anglia, so we're hoping it's still there.'

Renwald doubted that any Saxon had held onto East Anglian land in the last years of Danish rule. 'But you never know!' he said, 'a few did.'

'I want to be buried there,' I mumbled.

'What did he say?'

'He wants to be buried with his family,' Swithun explained, then added, 'silly old fool.'

'I understand that!' Renwald insisted. 'Better to rise with your family on the day of judgement than with strangers.'

'Amen,' I growled.

The story satisfied Renwald. Not that he was suspicious, merely curious. We were journeying down the Use, letting the current carry us with just the occasional touch of an oar to keep the boat on course. She was named *Rensnægl*, 'Because she's slow as a snail,' Renwald explained cheerfully. 'She's not quick, but she's sturdy.' He had a crew of six men,

164

a large crew for a trading ship, but he often carried valuable cargo and he reckoned the extra hands were a worthwhile precaution against the small boats that preyed on passing vessels. He leaned on the steering-oar to take *Rensnægl* into the river's centre where the current was strongest. 'And there'll be rich pickings soon,' he said balefully.

'Rich pickings?' Cerdic asked.

'Folk are leaving.' He glanced up at the sky, judging the wind. 'The days of the pagan in Britain are numbered,' he said.

'God be praised,' I muttered.

'Even Uhtred of Bebbanburg!' Renwald sounded surprised. 'No one thought he'd leave, but he's got ships in Eoferwic and he's brought his families there.'

'I heard he bought the ships to go to Bebbanburg,' Swithun offered.

'No man takes his families to war,' Renwald said scornfully. 'No, he's off and away! Going to Frisia, I hear.' He pointed ahead. 'That's where we join the Humbre,' he said, 'be a quick voyage down to the sea now!'

It was my abandonment of Dunholm and the decision to move the women and children, much of the livestock, and all our goods that had given substance to the rumour that we were going to Frisia. My men had arrived in Eoferwic with fifteen ox-drawn wagons loaded with beds and spits, cauldrons and rakes, scythes and grindstones, indeed with anything we could carry. Renwald was right, of course, when he said that no man went to war with ships filled with women and children, let alone with all their household goods, and I was certain my cousin would soon hear that I had left the safety of Dunholm with everything I possessed. He needed to hear more though, he needed to hear we had enough ships to carry all the people, animals, and belongings we would take to Frisia.

So, before leaving Eoferwic, I had given my son more of my diminishing stock of gold coins, and told him to buy or hire as many large trading ships as he needed. 'Put wooden stalls in the ships,' I had told him, 'enough for two hundred horses, and do the work at Grimesbi.'

'Grimesbi!' My son was surprised.

Grimesbi was a fishing port at the mouth of the Humbre, downriver from Eoferwic. It was a gaunt, windswept place, far less comfortable than Eoferwic, but also much closer to the sea. I still did not know how I was to recapture Bebbanburg, but the only thing I could be certain of was that my cousin was negotiating for a fleet to sail to his relief, and, if Merewalh's message was true, then that fleet was assembling at Dumnoc. I now needed to know when it would sail and how many ships would make the passage. The priest who had betrayed Æthelhelm had said the fleet would not put to sea till after Saint Eanswida's day, and that was still some weeks away, so I had time to explore the East Anglian port and plan how I would replace Æthelhelm's ships with my own. And those ships, my ships, would be at Grimesbi, close to the sea, ready to sail to make my cousin's nightmares real.

I did not doubt that my cousin would hear of our new ships and of the presence of our families, and by now, I suspected, he was beginning to believe the Frisian story. He must have reckoned that even I would not fight a war against both Bebbanburg and Constantin, that I had abandoned my dream. He would still want to know where I was and might be puzzled when I did not travel to Grimesbi with the rest of my men, but Sigtryggr and my daughter had announced that I was ill and lying in a sickbed in their palace.

When rumours fly, when false tales are being told, be the storyteller.

I was going to Dumnoc.

*   *   *

I had been to Dumnoc before, long ago, and had been trapped in its largest tavern, the Goose, and the only way to escape had been to start a fire that had caused panic in the town and had scattered the enemies who had surrounded the building. The fire had spread, eventually consuming most of the town. All that had been left was a few houses at the town's edge and the tall, rickety platform from which folk had kept a look-out for enemy ships creeping through the treacherous sandbanks at the river's mouth. I had expected Renwald to be cautious as we approached those notorious shoals, but he did not hesitate, aiming *Rensnægl* between the outermost withies that marked the channel. 'They've taken away the false marks,' he said.

'False marks?' Cerdic asked.

'For years they had withies which were meant to mislead you. Now they mark the real channel. Row, boys!' His men were hauling hard on the oars to bring *Rensnægl* safe through the outer shallows and to escape the freshening weather. The wind was gusting high to send white-crested waves scudding across the shoals. Clouds darkened the western sky, hiding the sun and promising foul weather. 'My father,' Renwald went on, 'saw a fifty-oared dragon boat high and dry on that bank,' he jerked his head south to where the white caps fretted across a bulge of hidden sand. 'Poor bastards had gone aground at high tide. Spring tide at that. They followed the false marks and were rowing as if the devil himself was up their arse. Bastards spent a fortnight trying to get that thing to float again, but it never did. They either drowned or starved, and the townsfolk just watched them die. Nine or ten of them managed to swim ashore, and the reeve let the womenfolk kill them.' He leaned on the steering-oar and *Rensnægl* veered up the main channel. 'Of course that was the old days, before the Danes took the place.'

'Now it's Saxon again,' I said.

'What did he say?' Renwald asked.

'Speak up, grandpa!' Swithun bellowed. 'You're muttering!'

'Now it's Saxon again!' I shouted.

'And pray God it stays that way,' Renwald said.

The oarsmen pulled hard. The tide was ebbing and the sharp south-west wind buffeted *Rensnægl*'s bow. The small waves were spiteful and I did not envy men who were further out to sea in this rising wind. It would be a cold rough night. Renwald must have thought the same because he cocked an eye at the high scudding clouds that streamed from the darker clouds in the west. 'Reckon I might lay up for a day or two,' he said, 'and let this weather pass. But it's not a bad place to be stranded.'

The town looked much the same as it had before I burned it. It was still dominated by a church with a tower crowned by a cross. Guthrum had been King of East Anglia back then, and, though he was Danish, he had converted to Christianity. Smoke drifted from a score of fires on the muddy beach, either smoking tall racks of herrings or boiling wide, shallow salt pans. The nearest houses were built on sturdy wooden pillars, and green slime on the thick trunks showed that the highest tides almost reached the lower floors. The river's bank was hidden by a long wharf and two piers, which in turn were crowded with ships. 'Looks like Lundene!' Renwald said in astonishment.

'All sheltering from the weather?' I suggested.

'Most of them were here two months ago,' he said, ' they brought supplies for King Edward's army, but I'd have thought they'd have long ago returned to Wessex. Ah!' This last exclamation was because he had seen an empty gap on the long wharf that stretched along the river's southern bank. He pushed the loom of the steering-oar, and the *Rensnægl* turned slowly towards the space, but just then a man shouted from one of the two piers.

168

'Not there!' he shouted. 'Not there! Sheer off, damn you! Sheer off!'

In the end we tied outboard of a Frisian trader moored along the western pier, and the man who had chased us away from the inviting space on the wharf clambered aboard to demand a berthing fee. Gulls screamed overhead, soaring and wheeling in the stiffening wind. 'That gap's for the king's ship,' the man explained, counting the silver that Renwald had given him.

'The king is coming?' Renwald asked.

'We're ordered to leave that wharf free in case he does come. He hasn't yet, but he might. An angel might come and wipe my wife's bum too, but that hasn't happened yet either. Now, you've paid your wharfage, so let's work out the customs' dues, shall we? What's your cargo?'

I left Renwald haggling and led my three men ashore. The Goose was still the largest building on the harbour front, and it looked much the same as it did before I had burned the old tavern, but the new one had been built to the same design, and its timbers had been bleached by sun and salt to the same silvery sheen. The tavern's sign, which showed an indignant goose, swung and creaked in the wind. We pushed through the door into a crowded room, but found two benches with a barrel for a table by a window that had its shutters open to the wharf. It was still two hours till sundown, but the tavern was noisy with half-drunken men. 'Who are they?' Cerdic asked.

'Lord Æthelhelm's men,' I said. I had recognised a couple, while others in the room wore the distinctive dark red cloak of Æthelhelm's household warriors. They would have recognised me too, except I had taken care to pull the scruffy hood over my head, to straggle hair across my face, and to walk with a stoop and a limp. I also sat in the shadow of a window shutter. I had closed and latched the shutters when we first sat down, but men bellowed at us to open them again. The room was smoky from a hearth, and the breeze through the window helped sweep the smoke away.

'Why are they all here?' Cerdic asked.

'They finished the conquest of East Anglia,' I said, 'and they're waiting for the ships to take them home.' That, I suspected, was not true, but it was doubtless the story being spread in the small town, and it satisfied Cerdic.

'You have money?' a truculent voice demanded.

Swithun tipped some silver onto the barrel table. 'You have ale?' he asked the man who had confronted us. I kept my head lowered.

'Ale, food, and whores, boys. What's your pleasure?'

The whores worked in the attic that was reached by a ladder in the room's centre. A table of rowdy men was just beneath the ladder, and every time a girl climbed or descended they banged the table top and roared appreciation. 'Listen,' I hissed to my three men, 'these bastards will be looking for a fight. Don't let them provoke you.'

'And if they ask who we are?' Oswi was nervous.

'We're servants to the Archbishop of Eoferwic,' I said, 'and we're travelling to Lundene to buy silk.' I had decided the tale I had told Renwald would not work ashore. Men would ask who my wife's family were, and I had no convincing answer. It was better to pose as strangers, and Oswi was right to be nervous. The men in the Goose had the confidence of warriors who knew each other, who loved to show off to each other, and who despised strangers. They were also either drunk or well on the way to being drunk. Fights would start soon enough, but I reckoned men might be cautious before challenging servants of the church.

A huge cheer greeted a man descending the ladder. He was a big man, broad shouldered, with fair hair cropped short. He jumped from the ladder onto the nearest table and bowed to the company, first in one direction, then to the other. 'His name,' I said, 'is Hrothard.'

'You know him, lord?' Cerdic seemed impressed.

'Don't call me lord,' I snarled. 'Yes, I know him. He's one of Æthelhelm's dogs.' I had been surprised that Hrothard was not with Brice at Hornecastre. I knew him because he had been Brice's second-in-command when they attempted to kill the young Æthelstan in Cirrenceastre, an attempt I had thwarted. Hrothard was very like Brice; a brutal fighter who did his lord's bidding without pity or remorse.

Hrothard now grinned at his comrades. 'I wore out two of the beauties, boys! But there's a ripe little Danish plum just waiting for you!' Another cheer filled the room.

'When things calm down,' I said to Swithun, then paused as a harried girl brought pots and a jug of ale to the table. I waited till she was gone, threading her way through benches and groping hands. 'When it's quieter,' I told him, 'you'll go up the ladder.'

He grinned, but said nothing.

'Find out what the girls know. Be clever about it. Don't let them think you're interested, just let them talk.'

That was why we were here, to learn what was brewing in this remote harbour town on the eastern edge of Britain. I doubted any of the tavern's whores would know much, but every little scrap of information was useful. I had already learned much just by coming here. The town was filled with warriors who should have returned home by now. The marker withies in the treacherous entrance had been aligned with the real channel rather than left to tempt enemy boats onto a wrecking shoal, and that meant that the new rulers of this town were expecting more ships and did not want to lose them. And the real ruler of this town, I had no doubt, was Æthelhelm, and Æthelhelm wanted his revenge on me.

And I knew just what that revenge would be.

171

I just did not know exactly how he would do it.

'Jesus,' Cerdic said, 'look at that!' He was gazing through the window, and whatever he had seen had also attracted the attention of other men, who pushed through the door to gaze at the river.

Where a ship had appeared.

I had never seen a ship like her. She was white! Her timbers had been bleached pale by the sun, or more likely had been given a soaking with limewash. The white faded to sour dark green at the waterline, suggesting the limewash had been scoured by the rough seas. She was long and handsome, a Danish vessel I thought, by the look of her, but she was plainly in Saxon hands for her high prow was topped with a cross that glinted silver. Her sail was furled on the yard, but even that looked as if it was made from white sailcloth. A banner had wrapped itself around a shroud so that it flapped impotently, but just as her steersman turned her towards the empty space on the wharf the flag freed itself and streamed proudly out to the east. The banner showed a white stag leaping against a black background.

'Lord Æthelhelm,' Swithun murmured.

'Silence now!' Hrothard had gone to the door, seen the ship, and now bellowed at the half-drunken men who had crowded out of the tavern to welcome the white ship. 'Show respect!'

I was standing on the bench to see above the heads of the men who had gone to the wharf to watch the ship's arrival. Some, a few, wore hats that they pulled off as the vessel slowed. She was, I thought, beautiful. She left hardly a ripple as she ghosted into the sheltered water between the piers. Her lines were perfect, the timbers curved by craftsmen so that she seemed to rest on the water rather than plough through it. The oars gave a last pull and then were thrust out of the oar-holes in the ship's side and brought inboard as the steersman expertly brought her into the waiting gap. Lines were thrown, men hauled, and she nestled gently into the wharf. 'The *Ælfswon,*' a man said admiringly.

The bright swan, a good name, I thought. The rowers slumped on the benches. They must have pulled hard to bring the bright swan through the rising wind and against the spiteful waves heaping at the harbour mouth. Behind them, at the stern of the ship, I saw a group of helmeted warriors, their mail covered by dark red cloaks. They leaped onto the wharf and other men threw them their shields. There were six of them. Was Æthelhelm here?

Two wharf slaves put a wooden walkway across the narrow gap between the ship and the pier. There was a pile of crates and barrels amidships that half hid the people waiting to come ashore, but then two priests appeared, crossed the planks, and after them came a group of women, all of them hooded. The women and the priests stood on the wharf, waiting.

A tall man, his helmet crested with black horsehair and wearing a black cloak, strode over the walkway. It was not Æthelhelm. This man was taller. I saw a glint of gold at his neck as he turned to wait for the last passenger to alight. It was a girl. She was dressed in white and was bare-headed so that her long fair hair streamed in the rising wind. She was slender, tall, and evidently nervous because, as she reached the walkway's centre, she seemed to lose her balance. For a heartbeat I thought she would fall into the water, but then the tall man in the horsehair helmet reached out, took her arm, and guided her to safety.

The men outside the tavern began to applaud by clapping their hands and stamping their feet. The girl seemed surprised by the noise and turned towards us, and the clear sight of her face made the breath catch in my throat. She was young, blue-eyed, pale, unscarred, wide-mouthed, beautiful, and utterly miserable. I guessed she was thirteen or fourteen, and she was plainly still unmarried or else she would have bound her hair. Two of the women wrapped a fur-trimmed cloak about her thin frame, and one of them pulled the cloak's hood over the girl's long hair. The tall man then took her elbow and led her away from the wharf, the women and priests following, all of them protected by the six spear-carrying warriors. The girl hurried by the tavern with her head bowed.

'Who in Christ's name is she?' Swithun asked.

'Ælswyth, of course,' one of the men outside the window had overheard the question.

The tall man in the black-tailed helmet walked beside Ælswyth, towering over her by at least a head. He glanced towards us and I instinctively shrank back into the shadows. He did not see me, but I recognised him.

'And who's Ælswyth?' Swithun asked, still gazing at the hooded figure. He, like every man on the waterfront, was transfixed by her.

'Where are you from?' the man demanded.

'Northumbria.'

'That's Lord Æthelhelm's youngest daughter. And you northern rats had better get used to her.'

'I could get used to that,' Swithun said reverently.

'Because she's going to live in your stinking country, poor lass.'

And the man escorting Ælswyth was Waldhere, my cousin's war-leader.

And my cousin lacked a wife.

Æthelhelm had planned his exquisite revenge. He was going to Bebbanburg.

EIGHT

We slept on a pile of filthy straw in an empty stall of the Goose's stables, sharing the stinking space with six other men. A sliver of hacksilver bought the four of us a breakfast of rock-hard bread, sour cheese, and watery ale. The noise of thunder made me look at the sky, but though the wind still blew hard and the clouds were grey and low, there was no rain and no sign of a storm. Then I realised the thunder was the sound of empty barrels being rolled along the street beyond the tavern yard. I went to the gate and saw men pushing half a dozen vast tuns inland. Another man led a string of pack mules laden with panniers heaped with salt.

I called Swithun to me and gave him silver. 'Spend the day here,' I told him, meaning the Goose. 'Don't get in a fight. Don't get drunk. Don't boast. And keep your ears open.'

'Yes, lo—' he managed to stop before saying lord. He took great delight in calling me grandpa when any stranger was in earshot, but when we were alone he found it almost impossible not to say 'lord'. We were alone now, but there was a score of men in the yard, some splashing water on their faces from a wooden horse trough, others using a latrine along the eastern wall. The latrine was just a deep ditch, topped with a wooden bench, and supposedly flushed by a stream. It stank.

'Just let the girls talk, and listen to them!'

'I will, lo— and,' he hesitated, then looked down at the silver shillings. He seemed surprised by my generosity. 'Is it all right if I?' he hesitated again.

'They're not going to talk to you unless you pay them,' I said, 'and you're not paying them for words, are you?'

'No, lor—'

'Then do your duty.' I doubted any of the girls would be awake yet, but Swithun headed eagerly into the tavern's great room.

Oswi looked aggrieved. 'I could have done—'

'This afternoon,' I interrupted him, 'it will be your turn this afternoon. Swithun will be worn out by then. Now let's get out of this stench.'

I was curious to discover where the barrels were going, but it took hardly a moment to find the answer because, before we had gone thirty paces from the back gate of the tavern yard, the squealing began. A gang of men was butchering pigs in a wide street that led east into the countryside. Two men wielded axes, the rest had knives and saws. The animals screamed, knowing their fate, the axes swung, and jets of blood spattered on house walls and puddled in the street's ruts. Dogs yapped at the edge of the slaughter, ravens lodged on the roofs, and women used jugs, bowls, and pails as they tried to collect the fresh blood to mix with oats. The butchers were crudely cutting away shoulders, bellies, loins, and hams that were tossed to men packing the great barrels with layers of meat and salt. The trotters were packed as well, along with the kidneys, but much of the animals was being tossed aside. Heads, guts, hearts, and lungs were being discarded, and the dogs fought over the offal, and women snatched up scraps as yet more screaming beasts were driven forward and had their skulls split open by the blunt blades. The waste of heads and hearts was proof that these men were in a hurry.

'It ain't right,' Cerdic muttered.

'Wasting the heads like that?' I asked.

'Pigs are clever, lord . . .' he flinched, 'sorry. My father kept pigs. He always said they were clever. Pigs know! You have to surprise a pig when you kill him. It's only fair.'

'They're only pigs!' Oswi said scornfully.

'It ain't right. They know what's happening.'

I let them argue. I was remembering that Father Cuthwulf, who spied for Æthelflaed, had said that the fleet would put to sea after the feast of Saint Eanswida, and we were still weeks away from that day. But just as I spread tales to mislead my enemies, so might Æthelhelm. If this frantic butchery meant anything it surely meant that the fleet would sail much sooner than Saint Eanswida's day. Maybe within the next few days? Maybe even today! Why else would Ælswyth be here? Her father would not expect the girl to wait for weeks in this bleak East Anglian town, nor would he want his troops idle for so long. 'We're going to the harbour,' I told Oswi and Cerdic.

I had found a rough stick in the tavern's piles of firewood and I leaned on it as I limped past the Goose. I kept my back bent. It made for slow progress, of course, but I hoped that no one seeing a shabby old man limping broken-backed would suspect it was Uhtred the Warlord. I let Cerdic support one elbow as we crossed the uneven gap between land and wharf. The stick thumped on the planks, and when Cerdic released me I staggered slightly. The wind was stronger here, still whistling in the moored ships' rigging and whipping the river into hustling white caps.

The one long wharf ran along the river's bank, and the two

piers jutted from it, the rickety structures so crowded with ships that most were moored side by side, sometimes three ships were lashed together, the outer two depending on the inside craft to hold them safe to the pier or wharf. The *Ælfswon* lay halfway down the long wharf, manned by a dozen men who I suspected had slept aboard. There was no more room in the town. Every tavern was crowded, and if Æthelhelm, or whoever commanded these troops, did not move them soon there would be trouble. Idle men make mischief, especially idle men supplied with ale, whores, and weapons.

Most of the ships, I reckoned, were trading craft. They had wider bellies and lower prows than the fighting ships. A few looked abandoned. One ship was half full of water, her timbers blackened by neglect. She had no sail bent on her yard, while one severed shroud lifted in the brisk wind, but she still had another ship moored outboard of her. Other ships were laden with barrels and crates, the cargo carefully stowed amidships, and all those ships had three or four men aboard. I counted fourteen such trading boats that looked ready for sea. Then there were the fighting ships, which were leaner, longer, and more menacing. Most, like the *Ælfswon*, had a cross on their prow. There were eight of them, including the *Ælfswon*, and all eight had men aboard, and most had clean waterlines. I stopped beside one and peered down into the scummy water and saw how the ship had recently been beached so that the weed could be scraped from her hull. A clean hull adds speed to a ship, and speed wins battles at sea. 'What are you looking at, cripple?' a man demanded.

'God bless you,' I called, 'God bless you.'

'Piss off and die,' the man growled, then made the sign of the cross. A cripple meant bad luck. No sailor would willingly go to sea with a cripple aboard, and even a cripple close to a ship might bring a malevolent spirit.

I obeyed the first of his commands by limping further up the pier. I had counted sixteen pairs of benches on the ship, which meant thirty-two oarsmen. The *Ælfswon* and the two ships moored fore and aft of her were even bigger. Say fifty men aboard each and that meant Æthelhelm's eight fighting ships could carry four hundred warriors, with still more on the cargo vessels. He had an army.

And I had no doubt where that army was going. To Bebbanburg. My cousin was a widower, so Æthelhelm would provide him with a bride. My cousin was being starved into surrender, so Æthelhelm would take him food. My cousin had men enough to defend Bebbanburg's ramparts, but not enough to retake his lands, and so Æthelhelm would bring him warriors.

And what did Æthelhelm receive in return? He became master of northern Northumbria, and celebrated as the man who drove the Scots from Saxon land. He would have a secure fortress from which to launch an invasion of Sigtryggr's kingdom from the north, an attack that would split my son-in-law's forces when Edward invaded from the south. And he would take a fortress so formidable that he could openly defy Edward of Wessex. He could insist that Æthelstan be disinherited, or else all northern England would become the enemies of Wessex. And, sweetest of all perhaps, Æthelhelm would gain his revenge on me.

'Good morrow,' a friendly voice shouted, and I saw Renwald taking a piss off the pier's edge, 'still nasty weather!' He and his crew had plainly slept aboard the *Rensnægl* that lay outboard of the Frisian trading ship. They had rigged a sailcloth awning across the *Rensnægl*'s stern to give them shelter from the wind.

'You'll lay up for a couple of days?' I asked.

'You're limping!' he said, frowning.

'Just an ache in the hip.'

He looked up at the low clouds. 'We'll lay up till this passes. There'll be some rain and wind, and then we'll leave. Did you find your family?'

'I'm not sure they're here any longer.'

'I pray they are,' he said generously.

'If I have to go back north,' I asked, 'will you take us? I'll pay you.'

He chuckled at that. 'I'm for Lundene! But you'll find plenty of ships going north!' He looked up at the clouds again. 'This will probably clear today, so we'll leave tomorrow. Give the weather time to settle, eh? Then sail on tomorrow's ebb.'

'I'll pay you well,' I said. I was beginning to fear I needed to return to the Humbre sooner than I had expected, and I had learned to trust Renwald.

He did not respond to my offer because he was gazing fixedly seawards. 'Good God almighty,' he said, and I turned to see a ship coming into the river. 'Poor bastard must have had a rough night of it,' Renwald added, making the sign of the cross.

The approaching ship looked dark under the dark sky. She was a fighting ship, long and low, with her sail brailed tight to her yard and banks of oars pulling her upstream. She looked ragged, with torn scraps of sailcloth and broken rigging flying loose in the wind. Her prow reared high and was capped by a cross from which streamed a long black pennant. She turned towards the piers, the small waves fretting white at her bows and her tired oarsmen fighting against wind, current, and tide.

Her steersman pointed the dark ship towards the *Ælfswon*, and I waited for the *Ælfswon*'s crew to shout at her to veer off, but to my surprise they were waiting with mooring lines. The lines were thrown, the oars shipped, and the newcomer was hauled in to settle beside the longer, white-hulled vessel.

'He is privileged,' Renwald said enviously, then shook his head. 'I'm sorry, I'm going to Lundene! But you'll find a ship going north.'

'I hope so,' I responded, then walked back down the pier to see who or what the dark ship had brought.

'May God bless you all!' a shrill voice called loud enough to be heard above the wind's howling and the crying of the gulls, 'in the name of the Father, and of the Son, and of the other one, my blessing on you!'

Ieremias had come to Dumnoc.

Ieremias, the mad bishop who was no bishop at all and who might not even have been mad, was my tenant, paying rent to the lord of Dunholm. This was the man who had brought me fifteen silver shillings and then pissed on them. His real name was Dagfinnr Gundarson, but Jarl Dagfinnr the Dane had turned himself into Bishop Ieremias of Gyruum, and today, as his dirty-looking ship was berthed alongside the pristine *Ælfswon*, he appeared in the bright robes of a bishop and carrying a crozier; a bishop's staff that was nothing more than a shepherd's crook, though Ieremias's crozier had a hook of silver. 'God bring you health!' he shouted, his long white hair lifting to the wind, 'and God bring you healthy sons and fertile women! God bring you good crops and plump fruit! May God multiply your flocks and increase your herds!' He lifted his arms to the dull heavens, 'I pray this, God! I pray that Thou bless these people and by Thy great mercy piss mightily upon all their enemies!'

It began to rain.

I was surprised the rain had held off for so long, but suddenly it began, hard spitting at first, but growing quickly into a vicious downpour. Ieremias cackled, then he must have seen me. He could not recognise me, of course, I wore the hood of my cloak over my head and he was looking through drenching rain from the wharf to where we stood on a pier, but he saw a bent-backed cripple, and immediately pointed his crozier towards me. 'Heal him, God! Shower Thy mercy upon that broken man!' His voice pierced through the sound of the rainstorm. 'Straighten him, Lord! Lift Your curse from him! I ask this in the name of the Father, the Son, and of the other one!'

'*Guds Moder*,' I muttered.

'Lord?' Cerdic asked.

'That's the name of his ship,' I said, 'God's mother, and don't call me lord.'

'Sorry, lord.'

I had been told that the *Guds Moder* was a shambles, a half-wrecked ship with gaping seams and frayed rigging that would sink if it so much as struck a ripple, but she would never have survived this weather if she had not been in good repair. Ieremias just wanted her to look dirty and uncared for. Loose lines blew ragged from the mast, but I could see that beneath that raggedness was a taut and seaworthy ship, a fighting ship. Ieremias had turned away from me and now crossed over the *Ælfswon*'s deck followed by four of his men, all in mail and wearing helmets. He kept praying or preaching as he crossed the wharf, though I could no longer hear him. We followed.

The rain was malevolent, streaming off the town's thatched roofs and flooding the alleys. Ieremias did not care. He preached as he walked. Two of Æthelhelm's warriors had met him, and now led him past the Goose, where he insisted on stopping to shout through the open door. 'Whores and wine-guzzlers,' he bellowed, 'the scriptures forbid both! Repent you miserable sons of Beelzebub! You bibbers of ale and tuppers of tarts! Repent!' Men stared in astonishment from the Goose's door at the gaunt, rain-drenched bishop in his embroidered vestments who harangued them. 'Who hath woe?' he demanded. 'Who hath babbling? They that

182

guzzle wine! That is the word of God, you bastard bibbling babblers! Thine eyes shall behold strange women! The scriptures say that! Believe me! I have beheld strange women, but by the grace of God I am redeemed! I am sanctified! I am saved from strange women!'

'Bastard's mad,' Cerdic said.

I was not so sure. Somehow the mad bastard had outlived Brida's rule in Northumbria. She had hated Christians with a malevolence, but Ieremias had survived her slaughterous campaign against his god. He possessed a fort at Gyruum, but he had never needed it. Perhaps, I thought, Brida had recognised someone as moon-touched as herself, or else she had smelt that Ieremias's religion was a joke.

One of Æthelhelm's guards plucked at Ieremias's elbow, plainly wanting to persuade the ranting prophet out of the rain and into a fire-warmed hall, and Ieremias let himself be led on. We followed, passing the street where the pig blood was being washed from walls by rain, then to the edge of the town where a substantial hall had been built on a slight rise of ground. It was a fine hall, steep roofed and thickly thatched, and big enough, I estimated, to feast two hundred men. Beside it were stables, storehouses, and a barn, the buildings surrounding a courtyard where two spearmen wearing Æthelhelm's dark red cloaks were guarding the hall's door. Ieremias was led inside. I doubted we could follow, nor did I want to risk an attempt to enter the hall in case I was recognised, but a group of beggars was huddled beneath a thatched shelter at one end of the barn, and I joined them there. I sent Oswi back to the Goose, but kept Cerdic with me.

We waited. We sat hunched, crammed with legless, blind, gibbering beggars. One of the women, her face a mess of weeping ulcers, crawled towards the hall door and was kicked back by one of the guards. 'You were told to wait over there,' the spearman snarled, 'and be grateful his lordship allows it!'

His lordship? Was Æthelhelm here? If so, I thought, then coming to Dumnoc had been a terrible mistake, not because I feared he would recognise me, but if he was in the town then surely his fleet was ready to sail and I had no chance of joining my ships and men before he arrived at Bebbanburg. I sat shivering, worrying, and waiting.

It was past midday when the rain finally ended. The wind still gusted, but it had lost much of its spite. Two hounds came from the hall, wandered around in the mud and puddles for a while, then lifted their legs against a post. A girl brought the two guards at the hall door pots of ale, then stood chatting and laughing with them. I could just see over the rain-darkened thatch of the town to where a fishing boat was heading for sea, her sail bellying taut in the chill wind. A watery sun glinted on the far waves. The weather was improving, and that meant Æthelhelm's fleet could go to sea.

'Onto your knees, you earslings,' a guard suddenly shouted at us. 'If you've got knees, that is. If you haven't, just grovel best you can! And make a line!'

A large group was coming from the hall. There were helmeted guards in their red cloaks, two priests, and then I saw Æthelhelm, bluff and genial, his arm around his daughter, who tried to lift the hem of her pale dress out of the mud. She still looked miserable, though her misery could not mask her delicate beauty. She was pale, her face flawless, and her slender frame making her appear fragile despite her height. Waldhere, my cousin's warrior, was on her other side. His broad shoulders were draped by a black cloak beneath which he wore mail. He had no helmet. Behind him was Æthelhelm's brute, Hrothard, grinning at something the ealdorman had just said, and last of all came Ieremias,

184

resplendent in his damp bishop's robes. I took a handful of mud and smeared it on my face, then made sure the hood was covering my eyes.

'Charity is our duty,' I heard Æthelhelm say as he approached us, 'if we want God's favour then in turn we must favour his most unfortunate children. When you are mistress of the north, my dear, you must be charitable.'

'I will, father,' Ælswyth answered dully.

I dared not look up. I could see Æthelhelm's soft leather boots that were trimmed with silver and smeared with mud, and I could see his daughter's tapestry slippers, their fine embroidery clogged with dirt. 'God bless you,' Æthelhelm said and dropped a silver shilling into my neighbour's hand. I held out both my hands and kept my head bowed. 'What ails you?' Æthelhelm asked. He was standing directly in front of me.

I said nothing.

'Answer his lordship,' Hrothard growled.

'He's . . . he's . . . he's,' Cerdic stuttered next to me.

'He's what?' Hrothard demanded.

'An id . . . id . . . idiot, lord.'

A shilling dropped into my hands, then another into Cerdic's hand. 'And you?' Æthelhelm asked him. 'What ails you?'

'An id . . . idiot too.'

'God bless both you idiots,' Æthelhelm said, and walked on.

'Touch this!' Ieremias was coming behind the father and daughter, and he dangled a grubby strip of grey cloth in front of our eyes. 'This was a gift to me from Lord Æthelhelm and it has power, my children, great power! Touch it! This is the very girdle the mother of Christ was wearing when her son was crucified! Look! You can see his blessed blood upon it! Touch it, my children, and be healed!' He was right in front of me. 'Touch it, you half-brained fool!' He nudged me with a boot. 'Touch the cloth of Gud's moder and your wits will return like birds to their nest! Touch it and be healed! This cloth rested on the blessed womb that held our Lord!'

I raised the hand holding the shilling and brushed the strip of cloth with my knuckles, and as I did so, Ieremias leaned down and yanked my ragged-bearded chin to force my head up. He stooped over me and stared into my eyes. 'You will be healed, you fool,' he said passionately, 'the devils that possess you will flee from my touch! Believe and be healed,' and as he spoke I saw a sudden puzzlement cross his gaunt features. He had wide mad brown eyes, scarred cheeks, a hawk nose, and wild white hair. He frowned.

'Thank you, lord,' I muttered and dropped my head.

There was a pause that seemed to last for ever, then he stepped on. 'Touch it,' Ieremias commanded Cerdic, and I felt relief wash through me. I had only met Ieremias once, and on that first occasion I had been dressed in a warlord's finery, but somehow he had seen something familiar in the muddy mad beggar whose face he had tilted towards his own.

'Now go! Limp away, crawl, wriggle off, just go!' a guard shouted at us as the notables went back to the hall.

'Don't hurry,' I whispered to Cerdic. I used my stick, I bent my back and I walked slowly down the gentle slope towards the nearest houses, and I had never felt so vulnerable in all my life. I was remembering the night I went to Cippanhamm because Alfred had disguised himself as a harpist to spy on Guthrum's Danes who had captured the town. That had been a night of heart-stopping fear, of sheer terror, and I felt the same now as I limped back through Dumnoc to the Goose. Swithun was drinking at a table, and, seeing us at the door, he joined us to tell me that Oswi was in the loft. 'He went up that ladder like a squirrel chasing nuts.'

'Then get him down the ladder now,' I said, 'because we're leaving.'

'Now?'

'Get him! I don't care what he's doing, just pull him off the poor girl and get him down here.'

My haste was not just because I feared I had been recognised, but also because everything I had seen in Dumnoc suggested that Æthelhelm's fleet was about to set sail. My son and Finan should have moved our people and ships to Grimesbi by now, and I needed to get back to that port fast, and that meant finding a ship going north. I used Æthelhelm's shilling to buy a pot of ale that Cerdic and I shared as we waited for Swithun, but as soon as he and Oswi joined us I hurried them out of the tavern and led them towards the westernmost pier where Renwald's ship was moored. I could see men readying their boats for sea. The storm had passed, the wind had settled into a brisk south-westerly, the white caps were smaller, and there were even patches of sunlight on the far green countryside.

'Lord!' Swithun sounded scared.

I turned and saw Æthelhelm's red-cloaked household warriors coming down the street from the hall. Hrothard led them, and he was pointing at buildings, sending men into shops, into taverns, and even into the big church. Three men ran to the door of the Goose and stood there, barring it.

'In here,' I said desperately. There was a row of huts on the wharf, and I forced open one of the doors to find a space crammed with coiled lines, bolts of sailcloth, heaps of folded nets, a barrel of caulking pitch, and sacks of the sea-coal used to melt the pitch. 'We have to hide,' I said, 'and fast!'

We tore the chandler's supplies apart, making a den at

187

the very back of the hut and then piling nets and sailcloth to conceal the hole we had made. The last thing I did before crawling over the messy heap and taking cover was to kick over the barrel of pitch so that the thick liquid broke through its crust and slowly seeped across the floor just inside the door. I had tried to bar or wedge the door, but found nothing to use, so just wrestled another barrel to block the entrance. Then we crouched in our hiding place, pulled a bolt of sail-cloth over our heads, and were almost suffocated by the smell of pitch and coal.

The wall of the hut was flimsy, with great chinks between the weathered planks. I could see through one such gap and watched as men spread along the wharf to search the ships. Two of them stood very close. 'They'll never find him,' one said.

'He's not here!' the other said scornfully. 'That silly bastard Dane is just dreaming. He's mad anyway. He's no more a bishop than I am.'

'He's a sorcerer. People are scared of him.'

'I'm not.'

'You are!'

Hrothard shouted at the two, demanding to know if they had searched the huts. 'We'd better look,' one said wearily.

A moment later I heard the door thump open. One of the men cursed. 'I'm not going in there.'

'He's not here!' the other man shouted. 'He's miles away, you stupid bastard,' he added in a low voice.

'Sweet Jesus,' Swithun breathed in my ear.

I could see men with leashed hounds that were sniffing uselessly at doorways and alleys. The dogs sniffed at the huts too, but the stink of the pitch was overwhelming, and the dogs passed on. We crouched, scarce daring to breathe, but as the afternoon wore on the excitement died and the search was evidently abandoned. More cargo was brought to the wharves and loaded onto ships, and then there was another commotion as Ieremias left and Lord Æthelhelm walked down to the harbour to bid him farewell. I did not hear any of their conversation, but I crawled up onto the mess of nets and used my knife to lever a gap between two planks and saw *Guds Moder* being rowed downriver towards the sea. The sun was setting, it was about high tide, and small waves were slapping against the underside of the wharf's planking. I went back to our hiding place and peered through another chink to see Lord Æthelhelm and six of his guards walking back into town. 'They're not leaving today,' I said.

'Tomorrow then?' Swithun asked.

'Probably,' I said, and knew I was too late. Even if fate was with me and I found a ship that would leave for the north at dawn I would never make Grimesbi in time. Æthelhelm's fleet would sail past the mouth of the Humbre and make landfall at Bebbanburg long before I could rouse my men, man the ships, and set sail in pursuit.

I felt the gloom of failure, and instinctively reached for my hammer and found myself clutching a cross instead. I cursed fate and needed a miracle.

I did not know what to do and so did nothing.

We stayed in the hut. The hue and cry had long died away. I doubt Æthelhelm truly believed I was in Dumnoc, but Ieremias's suspicion had forced him to make the search which had found nothing, though doubtless it had allowed his men to plunder the houses they had searched. Swithun, meanwhile, told me about his talkative whore. 'She said there are almost four hundred warriors in the town, lord.'

'How did she know?'

'One of them told her,' he said, as if the answer was obvious, which I suppose it was.

'What else?'

'Their horses were driven back to Wiltunscir, lord.'

That was useful to know, and made sense too. If Æthelhelm had wanted to take all his horses to Bebbanburg he would need at least another six or seven ships, and the time to make stalls in the ships' bellies. And he had no need of horses at Bebbanburg. It was enough to land his troops, lead them through the Sea Gate, and then flaunt his presence by flying his leaping stag banner from the fortress walls. Constantin was already reluctant to lose men by assaulting the ramparts, and the knowledge that food and new warriors had reinforced my cousin's garrison would surely persuade him to abandon the siege.

And I could do nothing to stop Æthelhelm.

I remember my father growling advice. My brother had still been alive and we were having a rare meal when just the three of us were at the hall's high table. My father had never much liked me, but then there were very few folk he did like, and he had directed the advice towards my brother, ignoring me. 'You'll have to make choices,' he had said, 'and from time to time you'll make the wrong choices. We all do.' He had frowned into the gloom of the night-time hall where a harpist was picking at his strings. 'Stop tinkling,' he had shouted.

The harpist had stopped playing. A hound had whined under the table and was lucky to avoid a kicking.

'But it's better to make the wrong choice,' my father had continued, 'than to make no choice at all.'

'Yes, father,' my brother had replied dutifully. He had made a choice a few weeks later, and it would have been better if he had made none because he had lost his head and I had become the heir to Bebbanburg. Now I remembered my father's advice and wondered what choices I had. None, as far as I could see. I suspected Æthelhelm's fleet would sail the next day, and after that I would have to go

190

back to Grimesbi and wait for the news that my cousin had found a new bride and had become stronger than ever.

So I needed a miracle.

Swithun, Oswi, and Cerdic slept. Whenever one of them snored I would kick them awake, though no guards were nearby. I put a bolt of sailcloth over the sticky pitch and opened the hut door to gaze into the darkness. Why had Ieremias left? He was plainly allied with Æthelhelm, so why not sail to Bebbanburg with him? The question nagged me, but I could find no answer.

I sat in the hut's doorway and listened to the wind's noise, the rattle of rigging, the slap of water on hulls, and the creak of boats moving to the wind. Small rushlights showed on a couple of ships. I could not stay in the hut. When dawn came I knew the harbour would become busy. Men would be boarding boats and more cargo would be loaded. We needed to leave, but despair made me indecisive. I finally thought of Renwald. He would doubtless leave Dumnoc on the tide and sail for Lundene, but perhaps gold could persuade him to go north to the Humbre instead. Then I would head home for Dunholm, my pretence to have abandoned it over, and my dreams of Bebbanburg ended.

Two men walked up the wharf. I sat very still, but neither looked in my direction. One of them farted and they both laughed. I could hear birdsong, so knew the dawn must be close, and a few moments later I saw the first faint swordblade's edge of grey light in the eastern sky. I had to move. If I stayed in the hut we would be discovered. The first men had already come to the wharf and more would soon follow.

But something else came first.

The miracle.

The miracle came at daybreak.

It came from the cold grey sea.

191

Five ships, their menacing shapes dark against the dawn.

They came on the flooding tide, their oar banks rising and falling like wings, their sails dark-furled at the tops of their masts.

They came with dragon-heads, beast-prows, and the first glimpse of dawn's glory glinted from helmets, spearheads and axes.

They came fast and they came with flames. Fire and ships do not go well together, I fear fire at sea more than I fear the storm-filled anger of Ran the sea-goddess, but these ships dared to carry lighted torches that flared bright and left wavering trails of smoke above their wakes.

The fifth ship, last in line, was not carrying a beast-head, instead her high prow was topped by a cross, and for a moment I thought she must be the *Guds Moder*, Ieremias's ship, but then I saw that this craft was longer and heavier, and that her mast was more raked. Even as I watched her I saw the flames burst in her bows as men lit flaming torches.

'Wake up!' I bellowed at my men. 'And come! Hurry!'

I had moments, only moments. Maybe I did not have enough time, but I had no choice now but to escape, and so I led my three men along the wharf and up the western-most pier. The few men already on the wharf ignored us, staring instead at the approaching fleet, while the sentry on the gaunt look-out tower must have been asleep, but he was awake now, and he had seen the five ships and began clanging a bell. It was too late. The whole purpose of the look-out was to see ships when they were still at sea, not when they were just yards away from delivering fire, havoc, and death to Dumnoc.

I jumped onto the empty ship, crossed its deck and leaped onto *Rensnægl*. 'Wake up!' I bellowed at Renwald who was already awake, but confused. He and his crew had been sleeping at the *Rensnægl's* stern, under a sailcloth awning.

He just stared at the four of us. 'You have to get under way!' I snarled at him.

'Sweet Christ!' he said, staring past me to the pier's far end where one of the five ships had rammed a moored vessel, splintering her planks. The first flaming torches were thrown. Two of the attacking ships were rowing into the centre of the harbour, into the wide space between the two piers, and each slammed into the moored boats at the landward end where the piers joined the wharf, and I saw mailed men armed with spears and shields clambering ashore to make two shield walls, each barring access to a pier. Dogs were howling in the town, the church bell began to toll, and still the sentry on the look-out tower rang his alarm. 'What in God's name?' Renwald asked.

'He's called Einar the White,' I told him, 'and he's come to burn Æthelhelm's fleet.'

'Einar?' Renwald seemed dazed.

'He's a Norseman,' I said, 'in the pay of King Constantin of Scotland.' I could not be sure of that, but Edward of Wessex had told me that Einar had changed sides, seduced by Scottish gold, and I could not think who else might have come to Dumnoc to destroy the fleet gathered to relieve Bebbanburg. 'Now cast off!' I ordered Renwald.

He turned to stare at the Norsemen who had made a shield wall across the pier. There might have been thirty men in that wall, more than enough to defend its narrow width. The light was growing, making the world grey and black.

'Give me your sword!' I called to Renwald.

'We can't fight them!' he said, appalled.

I wanted the sword to cut his mooring lines. Einar's men were already doing that for us. A group was running along the pier, severing or casting off the mooring lines of smaller boats. They wanted to cause chaos. They would burn or break the larger ships destined to relieve Bebbanburg, but they would also scatter Dumnoc's trading and fishing fleets. When they saw men aboard a moored boat or saw cargo heaped in a belly they were boarding to look for plunder, and I wanted to cut *Rensnægl* free before they saw us. 'I don't want to fight them,' I snarled and ran back to the stern where I knew Renwald kept his weapons. I ducked under the awning, pushed two of his crewmen aside, and snatched up a long-sword. I ripped it out of its leather scabbard.

'Lord!' Swithun shouted.

I turned to see that two Norsemen had already spied that the *Rensnægl* was crewed, and they could see too that she had cargo in her belly. They must have smelt plunder because they jumped onto the next ship and were about to leap onto ours.

'No!' Renwald tried to bar my way. I pushed him hard so that he tripped and fell into the cargo, then I turned as a mailed warrior jumped onto our deck. He carried no shield, just a naked sword, and his bearded face was framed by a helmet with cheek-pieces so that all I could see of him were his eyes, eager and wide. He thought us easy prey. He saw the sword in my hand, but reckoned I was some elderly Saxon sailor, no match for a Norse warrior, and he simply lunged his blade at me, thinking to pierce my belly and then rip the sword aside to spill my guts on the *Rensnægl*'s deck.

It was simple to parry the lunge. Renwald's sword was old, rusty, and probably blunt, but she was heavy too, and my parry threw his lunge wide to my left, and before he could recover the blade I punched him in the face with the sword's pommel. It struck the edge of his helmet, but with enough force to stagger him backwards. He was still trying to bring his sword back to face me when I plunged Renwald's blade deep into his guts. The sword was blunt, but still the point pierced his mail, ripped through the leather jerkin beneath, and gouged into his bladder. He gave a strangled cry and threw himself at me, his free hand flailing to claw my face and pry out my eyes, but I snatched his beard with my free hand and pulled him hard towards me, using his lunge against him, and I stepped aside, kept pulling, and he stumbled past me, his momentum pulling the sword from his belly, and then his legs struck the *Rensnægl*'s upper strake and he went overboard. There was a splash, a yelp, then he was gone, dragged down by his mail.

The second man had been content to watch his companion slaughter a crew of miserable Saxons, but the death of his companion had been so swift that he had been given no chance to help. Now he wanted revenge, but he did not think to attack Swithun, Oswi, or Cerdic, who stood unarmed at the bows of *Rensnægl*, instead he leaped, snarling, onto the pile of cargo and faced me. He saw a shabby, grey-haired man with an ancient rusty sword, and he must have thought I had merely been lucky to survive the first attack, and he leaped again, this time aiming to sever my head with a sweeping cut of his sword. He was young, angry, fair-haired, and had ravens inked onto his cheeks. He was also a fool, a hot-headed young fool. There were ten of us aboard the *Rensnægl*, and he had watched me kill his companion with the skill of a trained warrior, but he only saw a crew of Saxons, while he was a Norse warrior, a wolf from the north, and he would teach us how Norsemen treated impudent Saxons. He swung his sword as he leaped at me. The sword cut was massive, wild, a killing blow that should have sliced through my neck, but it was also as obvious as the first man's opening lunge. I saw it coming from the corner of my eye as I turned towards him, and I felt the battle-joy surge, the knowledge that the enemy has made a mistake, and the certainty that another brave man was about to join the benches I had crowded in Valhalla's mead hall.

Time seemed to slow as the sword flashed towards me. I saw the youngster grimace with the effort of putting all his strength into that blade, and then I just ducked.

I ducked straight down, the sword whipped above my head, and I stood again with my rusty blade pointing skywards, and the Norseman, still coming forward, impaled himself on Renwald's old sword. The point slid into his chin, through his mouth, up behind his nose, into his brain, and then jarred against the top of his skull. He seemed frozen suddenly, head-pierced, and his hand suddenly lost its force and his sword clattered onto the *Rensnægl*'s deck. I let go of my blade, pushed him away from me, and snatched up his good weapon. I slashed at the stern mooring line, cutting it with three blows, then tossed the sharp blade to Cerdic. 'Cut the bow line!' I shouted. 'Then the spring! Quick!'

Cerdic picked up the sword and used his huge strength to cut the two lines with two strokes, thus freeing *Rensnægl*, and the tide immediately drifted us away from the pier. A third Norseman had seen what had happened, he could see one of his comrades lying on our cargo, his body in spasms and the sword still jammed in his skull. The man jumped onto the boat we had been lashed against and he shouted angrily at us, but the flooding tide was running strong and we were already out of his reach.

We were also in danger of running aground. Swithun had seen that the dying Norseman was wearing a fine scabbard plated with silver, and was now trying to unbuckle the belt. 'Leave it!' I snarled. 'Get an oar! Cerdic, an oar! Hurry!'

Cerdic, usually so slow, was quick to seize an oar and used it to thrust the *Rensnægl* off the glistening mudbank that loomed to our left. I dragged the rusty sword free of the dying man's head and used it to cut at the lines holding the awning that was suspended above the ship's stern and which obstructed the helmsman's platform. 'Get a steering-oar!'

I called to Renwald. 'And put your men at the oars! And get the sail up!'

I put the rusty sword onto the dying man's hand. He was making choking noises, his eyes flicking left and right, but he seemed incapable of moving his arms or legs. I retrieved the good sword from the *Rensnægl*'s bows, checked that the poor youngster still had the old sword lying on his palm, then put him out of his misery. Blood welled and spilled across the cargo of hides, and just then a flare of light erupted to my right. One of Æthelhelm's ships had caught fire and the flames leaped up the tarred shrouds and spread along the yard. Renwald's crew, who had seemed too stunned to move when the Norsemen attacked us, now scrambled to push oars through the holes in the *Rensnægl*'s side-strakes. 'Row!' Renwald shouted. He may have been confused by the dawn's panic and slaughter, but he was seaman enough to grasp the danger of running aground. I dropped the sword and unhanked the halliard that was secured to the mast base, then dropped the yard until it was just above the deck where Oswi, standing on the dead man's belly, used a knife to cut the lashings that were holding the furled sail tight. The dark brown canvas dropped and I hauled the yard back up as one of Renwald's crewmen seized the steerboard sheet and pulled it taut. Another man tightened the bæcbord sheet, and I felt the boat steady herself. The wind was behind us, coming from the south-west, but the tide was running strongly against us, and we needed both oars and sail to make headway. Renwald had managed to slide the steering-oar into place and pulled its loom so that the *Rensnægl* slowly turned and slowly gathered way and slowly drew away from the gleaming mud towards the river's centre.

And in Dumnoc's harbour there was slaughter.

NINE

The *Rensnægl* lived up to her name by creeping with painful slowness across the river, her bluff bows slapping irritably against the incoming tide. That flood tide would end soon and there would be slack water, and then the river's current would help carry us to sea, but till then it was hard work to make even small progress. On shore there was killing, while on the two piers ships were burning. Some of those ships had been cut loose and were drifting upstream. The sun was above the horizon now and I could see men forming a shield wall in the open space in front of the Goose. They would soon charge the smaller Norse walls barring the piers, but it was already too late to save most of the ships. Only the few tethered to the wharf built along the river bank had been spared, among them Æthelhelm's own craft, the *Ælfswon*. I could see men crowded aboard her, some holding long oars ready to fend off any burning ship that threatened to drift onto the white ship's flank.

'We'd do better by sailing upstream,' Renwald called to me, 'we'd be well away from those bastards then.'

He meant that by riding the tide inland to the shallower river reach we would be safe from any pursuit by the raiding vessels, all of which had to draw twice as much water as the *Rensnægl*. He was right, of course, but I shook my head. 'We're going to sea,' I told him, 'and then you're taking us north to Grimesbi.'

'We're sailing to Lundene,' Renwald said.

I picked up the young Norseman's good sword and pointed the blade's reddened tip towards Renwald. 'You will take us,' I said slowly and clearly, 'to Grimesbi.'

He stared at me. Till now he had thought me a decrepit old man who had sailed to East Anglia to find a family grave, but I was stooped no longer. I stood straight, I spoke harshly instead of mumbling, and he had just watched me kill two men in the time it would have taken him to gut a herring. 'Who are you?' he asked.

'My name,' I told him, 'is Uhtred of Bebbanburg.'

For a moment he seemed unable to speak, then he looked at his crewmen, who had checked their rowing and were gazing open-mouthed at me. 'Lads,' Renwald said, then needed to clear his throat before he could speak again, 'we're going to Grimesbi. Now row!'

'You'll be paid,' I promised him, 'and generously. You can keep this sword for a start.' I cleaned the blade's tongue on the cargo of hides, then pushed the sword under the low steering platform.

The *Rensnægl* had managed to cross the river to the northern bank where the tidal current was weaker, but still the heavy ship made pitiful progress despite her six oars and the big sail. We were inching our way towards the sea, while on the other bank Einar the White was demonstrating why he was also called the Unfortunate.

It must have seemed a good idea to put men ashore to bar the way onto the two piers while the rest of his force destroyed Æthelhelm's fleet, but those two outnumbered shield walls were under savage attack from enraged West

Saxons, who had poured out of the town's alleys and streets to make their own shield walls. The Norsemen, I thought, had to be tired. They had arrived at dawn, and must be wearied by a night of rowing against the wind. The eastern shield wall seemed to be holding, but I watched as the other gave way and its surviving men fled across moored boats to regain the safety of the nearest of Einar's ships. But that ship was not safe at all. The tide was pinning it against the pier, and furious Saxons followed the fugitives and leaped onto the trapped ship's bows. I could see blades rising and falling, see men leaping overboard into the shallows, see men dying. That ship was lost.

But so was much of Æthelhelm's fleet. At the end of the piers the smoke was thickening to darken the dawn sky as ships caught fire. Some of the smaller trading craft had been manned by Norsemen and were being sailed out of the turmoil, following us downriver, while behind them at least three of Æthelhelm's warships were ablaze. His own vessel, the *Ælfswon*, appeared to have survived, as had two other big West Saxon war craft that shared the long wharf, but much of the rest of his fleet was burning, sinking, or captured. The crew of Einar's largest ship, the dark-hulled boat with the cross at its prow, was still hurling flaming torches into Æthelhelm's smaller boats, but she began to pull away as the surviving shield wall retreated. Another of Einar's ships went close to that eastern pier, and I saw Norsemen leaping aboard her, then she backed her oars to carry them safely away from Saxon vengeance. The big ship, the one with the cross, was the last to leave the burning chaos, and as she came from a roiling bank of smoke I saw a flag unfurled at her masthead. For a moment the flag seemed reluctant to fly, then the wind caught the fabric and it streamed out to show a red hand holding a cross. 'Whose badge is that?' I asked.

'She's a Scottish ship,' Renwald answered, 'and that's Domnall's flag.'

'Constantin's man?'

'And a happy man too,' Renwald said, looking back at the chaos of broken ships and burning hulls.

Five ships had come to Dumnoc in the dawn, but only four left, though they were accompanied by a dozen captured cargo vessels. Einar, if he lived, must have assumed that the *Rensnægl* was one of those captured vessels because, as the larger warships overtook us at the river's mouth, not one made an attempt to stop us. Instead a man waved from the steersman's platform of Domnall's dark ship, and we waved back, and then the *Rensnægl*'s bows met the larger seas of the open water and we shipped the oars and let the big sail carry us north along the coast.

'She's called the *Trianaid*,' Renwald said, nodding at the Scottish ship.

'*Trianaid*?' I asked.

'Means the trinity,' he said. 'I usually see her in the Forth, I've never seen her this far south before.'

'I thought Constantin's ships were all fighting Norsemen up in the islands?'

'Most are, but he keeps the *Trianaid* closer to home.'

'He keeps her at Bebbanburg now,' I said bitterly.

'He does, lord, so he does.'

The only consolation was knowing that the *Trianaid*, like Einar's fleet, would be having an uncomfortable time at Bebbanburg. They could not use the fort's own harbour, which could only be reached by the narrow channel that ran directly beneath the northern ramparts and past the heavily defended Sea Gate. Any ship using that channel would be assailed by spears and rocks, which meant that Einar's ships must shelter in the shallow anchorage between Lindisfarena and the mainland. It was a difficult and cramped refuge, and in a gale it was downright dangerous. When I was a child a Scottish trader had taken refuge there, and during the night the storm worsened and we woke to discover that the ship had been driven ashore, and I remember my father's delight when he realised that the vessel and its cargo were now his property. He had let me ride with the warriors who galloped over the sands at low tide to surround the stranded ship. The five crewmen had promptly surrendered, of course, but my older brother had ordered them killed anyway. 'They're Scots!' he told me. 'Vermin! And you know what you do with vermin.'

'They're Christians,' I had protested. In those days, when I was about seven or eight years old, I was still trying to be a good little Christian and so avoid Father Beocca's feeble beatings.

'They're Scots, you fool,' my brother had said. 'You get rid of the bastards! Do you want to kill one of them?'

'No!'

'You're a pathetic weakling,' he had said scornfully, then had drawn his sword to rid the world of vermin.

In the end the stranded ship proved to hold nothing more valuable than sheepskins, one of which became my bed cover for the next two years. I was remembering that tale as Renwald gave the steering-oar to one of his crew, then pulled the young Norseman's sword from beneath the stern platform. He turned the hilt, admiring the silver wire twisted around the crosspiece. 'It's a valuable weapon, lord,' he said.

'Probably Frankish,' I said, 'and you'll find it more useful than that piece of rusty iron you call a sword.'

He smiled. 'I can keep it?'

'Keep it, sell it, do what you like with it. But keep the blade greased. It's a pity to let a good sword turn to rust.'

He pushed it back into the narrow space. 'So you're going to Bebbanburg, lord?'

I shook my head. 'We're going to Frisia.'

'Which is why you went to Dumnoc first?' he asked shrewdly.

'I had business in Dumnoc,' I said harshly, 'and now we're leaving for Frisia.'

'Yes, lord,' he said, plainly disbelieving me.

We ran before the wind, though in truth the *Rensnægl* never ran. She lumbered heavily as Einar's fleet steadily drew ahead of us. I watched his ships sail through a sparkling sea lit by a sun shining between ragged clouds that scattered to the north and east. I instinctively tried to touch my hammer as a way of thanking Thor for the miracle, and my fingers found the cross, and I wondered if that symbol had brought me good fortune. That was one of Christianity's strongest arguments, that fate smiled on Christians. A Christian king, their sorcerers argued, won more battles, received higher rents, and spawned more sons than a pagan ruler. I hoped that was not true, but I took care in that moment to mutter a prayer of thanks to the Christian god who had arranged for fate to smile on me in the last few hours. 'Æthelhelm won't be sailing today,' I said.

'He'll need more than a day or two to recover from that morning surprise,' Renwald agreed. 'He lost some good ships.'

'He won't be happy,' I said happily. My miracle had come. Einar had given me what I so desperately needed, time. Æthelhelm had planned to take food and reinforcements to Bebbanburg, but most of the food and many of his ships were now destroyed.

Then fate smiled on me again.

Just north of Dumnoc the River Wavenhe empties to the sea. A few fishing families lived in driftwood hovels built at the river's mouth, which was marked by a wide stretch of fretting waves, a hint to a sailor that the anchorage beyond, though inviting, was dangerous to approach. Inland, bright under the sun, was a great lake, and beyond that, I knew, was a tangle of lakes, rivers, creeks, mudbanks, reeds, and marshland that was home to birds, eels, fish, frogs, and mud-covered folk. I had never sailed into the Wavenhe, though I had heard of shipmasters who had risked the entrance shoals and lived, but now, as Einar's fleet drew level with the river's mouth, a ship came from the anchorage.

I had heard that Ieremias, the mad bishop, was a brilliant seaman, and so he must have been because he had left Dumnoc late in the afternoon and had surely entered the Wavenhe in the encroaching darkness, and now the *Guds Moder* came from the river, sailing through the shoals with a confident assurance. Her sail, bellying away from us, was decorated with a cross. She came fast, sliding into the open sea with her tattered rigging flying ragged to the wind. I could just see Ieremias's white hair lifting to that same wind. He was the helmsman.

I had wondered why Ieremias had left Dumnoc early instead of waiting for Æthelhelm's fleet to sail, and now I had the answer. I had assumed he was allied to Æthelhelm, a natural supposition after I had seen the warm greeting that Æthelhelm had given him. I had also heard Ieremias boast of Æthelhelm's gift, the stained girdle that had supposedly belonged to Christ's mother and was most probably a strip of dirty cloth torn from a kitchen slave's tunic. And an alliance between Æthelhelm and Ieremias made sense. Ieremias might be mad, but he still possessed an anchorage and a fort at the mouth of the River Tinan, and so long as Constantin claimed Bebbanburg's land, then so long did Ieremias own the northernmost fort of Northumbria. He also had ships and men, and best of all he knew the Northumbrian coast as well as any man alive. I doubted the West Saxon shipmasters knew where the shoals and rocks lurked, but Ieremias did, and if Æthelhelm planned a voyage to the fortress he would do well to have Ieremias as his guide. I had not questioned my assumption that he was Æthelhelm's ally until now, when I saw his dark-hulled ship come from the River Wavenhe to join Einar's fleet. I saw him wave to the *Trianaid*, then the *Guds Moder* turned north to sail in company with Æthelhelm's enemies.

'He scouted Dumnoc for them,' I said.

'I thought he was Lord Æthelhelm's ally,' Renwald was as surprised as I was.

'So did I,' I admitted. And now, it seemed, Ieremias was allied with the Scots. I gazed at his ship and reflected that it did not really matter whose ally he was, he was certainly my enemy.

The Scots were my enemies.

The West Saxons were my enemies.

Bebbanburg's garrison was my enemy.

Ieremias was my enemy.

Einar the White was my enemy.

So fate had better be my friend.

We sailed on northwards.

Grimesbi was smaller than Dumnoc, but had the same weatherbeaten houses, the same homely smells of salt, wood fires, and fish, and the same sea-hardened folk struggling to haul a living from the long cold waves. There were wharves, piers, and a shallow anchorage, while beyond the town's ditch lay a bleak marsh. Grimesbi, though, was Northumbrian, which, in that year, meant that the reeve was a Dane; a hard-faced, strong-fisted man called Erik, who treated me with a wary civility. 'So you're leaving, lord?' he asked me.

'For Frisia,' I said.

'That's what I heard,' he said, then paused to pick something out of his broad nose. He flicked whatever he discovered onto the tavern floor. 'I'm supposed to levy a charge on everything you take out of the port,' he went on. 'Horses, household goods, trade goods, everything except your victuals and your people.'

'And you pay that levy to King Sigtryggr?'

'I do,' he said cautiously, because he knew that I knew that he only paid a part of what he owed to the king and that, probably, a criminally small part. 'I pay that and the wharfage fees to Jorvik.'

'Of course you do,' I said, and laid a gold coin on the table. 'I think Sigtryggr would forgive me if I didn't pay, don't you?'

His eyes widened. The last time I had laid up in Grimesbi the wharf fee had been a penny a day, and the coin on the table would pay for a fleet to stay a whole year. 'I reckon he would forgive you, lord,' Erik said. The coin vanished.

I laid a silver coin where the gold had been. 'I'm taking three of my ships to sea,' I told him, 'and I'll be gone for a fortnight, maybe longer. But I'm not taking my women and children with me. They'll stay here.'

'Women bring ill luck at sea, lord,' he said, eyeing the coin and waiting to discover what it was meant to buy.

'The women need to be protected,' I said. 'I could leave warriors here, but I need all my men. We're sailing for Frisia to take land.' He nodded to show that he believed me, which maybe he did or maybe he didn't. 'I don't need women and children aboard,' I went on, 'not if I'm fighting some Frisian lord for a patch of defensible land.'

'Of course not, lord.'

'But the women must be safe,' I insisted.

'I have a dozen good men to keep order,' he said.

'So when I return,' I said, 'or when I send for the families, they'll all be safe and unmolested?'

'I swear it, lord.'

'Sigtryggr is sending men to guard them,' I said. I had

sent a message to Sigtryggr, and I was sure he would send some warriors, 'but those men won't arrive for a day or two.'

He reached for the coin, but I placed a hand over it. 'If my women are molested,' I said, 'I will come back here.'

'I swear their safety, lord,' he said. I moved my hand, and the second coin vanished. We each spat on a palm and shook on the agreement.

My son had brought six ships to Grimesbi, which was now crowded by my people. The women, children, and heavy cargo had travelled downriver on the ships, while my men had ridden their horses from Eoferwic. Every tavern was full, and some families were living aboard the three warships that were tied to the town's longest wharf. Nearby, on a pier, were three big trading ships that my son had purchased. 'There's not enough room for two hundred horses,' he told me gloomily, 'we'll be lucky to ship sixty. But they were the only ships for sale.'

'They'll do,' I said.

Berg was now equipping the three ships to carry horses. 'Lots of folk have asked why, lord,' he told me, 'and I tell them what you told me to say. That I don't know. But they all seem to know we're going to Frisia.'

'That's good,' I said, 'that's very good. And you don't need to keep that a secret any longer.' Berg was building stalls in the ships' bellies, a necessary precaution to keep frightened horses still while they were at sea, and, because Berg was in charge, the work was being done well and I did not have the heart to tell him that the ships would probably never be needed. They were just a part of the deception, an attempt to persuade folk that I really had abandoned any thought of recapturing Bebbanburg and instead planned to take my people and their livestock to a new land. Doubtless, I thought morosely, I could eventually sell the three ships, but almost certainly for less than I had paid for them. A dozen men were working in the nearest boat, their hammers and saws loud as they rigged the stout stalls. 'But stop the work now,' I told Berg, 'and take the beast-heads off the three warships.'

'Take them off, lord?' He sounded shocked. Two of the war boats had fine dragon-heads, newly carved, while the third and largest ship had a magnificent wolf's head. Berg had made them to please me, and now I was demanding that he lift them off the prows.

'Take them off,' I said, 'and put Christian crosses in their place.'

'Crosses!' Now he really was shocked.

'Big ones,' I said. 'And the folk living on those three boats? They have to leave today. They can camp in the trading ships instead. We're setting sail at dawn tomorrow.'

'Tomorrow,' he echoed me excitedly.

'And one last thing,' I said, 'the horses are here?'

'Stabled all through the town, lord.'

'You have a grey, don't you?'

'Hræzla! He's a good horse!'

'Dock his tail,' I said, 'and bring me the hair.'

He stared at me as if I was mad. 'You want Hræzla's tail?'

'Do that first,' I said, 'then make the crosses. My son will provision the boats.' My son already had men bringing supplies to the wharf. I had told him he needed to buy two weeks' supply of food and ale; enough to feed one hundred and sixty-nine men.

Because that was the number I was taking northwards. One hundred and sixty-nine warriors to fight against my cousin, against the forces of Æthelhelm, and against the King of Scotland. They were good men, almost all of them battle-hardened with just a smattering of young ones who had yet to stand in a shield wall and learn the terror of fighting an enemy who is close enough for you to smell the ale on his breath.

I had paid Renwald handsomely. I had few coins left, so I had given him one of my arm rings, a fine piece of silver carved with runes. 'I took that one,' I said, 'in a fight just north of Lundene. That's the name of the man I killed,' I pointed to the runes, 'Hagga. He shouldn't have died. Not that day, anyway.'

'He shouldn't?'

'They were just scouting. Six of them and eight of us. We were hawking. Hagga chose to fight.' I remembered Hagga. He had been a young man, well mounted, with a fine helmet that was too big for him. The helmet had cheek-pieces and was decorated with a snarling face etched onto its crown. I suppose he had thought we would be easy prey because none of us was in mail and two of our hunting party were women, and he had screamed insults, challenged us, and we had given him the fight he wanted, though it was soon over. I had hit the helmet hard with Serpent-Breath and, because it was too big for him, it had turned and half blinded him. He had screamed pathetically as he died.

I had looked over at the *Rensnægl*, moored against one of Grimesbi's piers. 'Buy yourself a faster ship,' I told Renwald.

He had shaken his head. 'She serves me well, lord. She's like me, slow but sure.'

'Dependable,' I said. 'And when this is all over,' I went on, 'you can depend on me as a friend.'

'In Frisia, lord?' he asked, smiling.

'In Frisia,' I said, returning the smile.

'You'll go with my prayers, lord.'

'For that,' I said warmly, 'and for all you did, thank you.'

At sunset I walked with Finan, following a path that led beside a drainage ditch outside the town. I had told him much of what had happened in Dumnoc, but he was eager to know more, though first I asked him about Æthelstan and was assured that the young prince was safe in Sigtryggr's hall. 'He wanted to come with us,' Finan said.

'Of course he did.'

'But I told him it was impossible. Christ, can you imagine the trouble if he died while he was a hostage? God save us!'

'He knows he can't come,' I said.

'He still wanted to.'

'And get himself killed? Then I'd be blamed for that and the truce would be over and we'd all be up to our necks in shit.'

'You mean we're not?'

'Maybe up to our armpits,' I allowed.

'That bad, eh?' We walked in silence for a few paces. 'So?' he asked, 'Lord Æthelhelm was in Dumnoc?'

'Giving away silver,' I said, and then told Finan more of the tale, and ended by describing how I planned to capture Bebbanburg.

He listened, saying nothing till I had finished, and then, 'King Edward told you there were four hundred Scots at Bebbanburg?'

'Led by a man called Domnall.'

'He's said to be a beast in a fight.'

'So are you.'

He smiled at that. 'So four hundred Scots?'

'That's what Edward said. But that might include the garrisons Constantin left on the wall forts, so I reckon he has at least two hundred and fifty men at Bebbanburg.'

'And how many men does your cousin have?'

'I'm not sure, but he can muster at least three hundred. Edward reckoned he had two hundred in the fort.'

'And Einar?'

'He lost a ship and men at Dumnoc, but he still has four crews left.'

'Say another hundred and twenty?'

'At least that,' I said.

'And Æthelhelm will take how many?'

'If he even goes now,' I said, 'he'll take as many as he can. Three hundred? Maybe more.'

'Ieremias?'

'Fifty, maybe sixty. But he won't be at Bebbanburg.'

'He won't?' Finan sounded dubious. He frowned, then picked up a stone and skimmed it across a green-scummed pond. 'How do you know Ieremias isn't on his way to Bebbanburg with Einar right now?'

'I don't.'

'So you're just guessing.'

'Ieremias is betraying everyone,' I said, 'so he won't want to appear as if he's chosen sides. If he sails to Bebbanburg he has to either anchor with Einar's ships, in which case my cousin knows he's been betrayed, or he puts into Bebbanburg harbour, in which case Constantin learns the same. Ieremias wants to be on the winning side, so he's on everyone's side. He might be mad, but he's not stupid. I tell you, he'll have gone to Gyruum to wait things out.'

He nodded, accepting the argument. 'But still,' he said, 'if we get inside we'll probably be fighting three hundred men?'

'Nearer two hundred.'

'And fighting uphill?'

'Part of the time.'

'And we could have another four or five hundred outside, trying to stab us in the back?'

'Yes.'

'Not to mention the bastard Scots, who won't be happy.'

'They never are.'

'Well, that's true,' he said. He skimmed another stone and watched it sink through the pond's dark scum. 'And Sigtryggr won't help you?'

'He'll help me,' I said, 'but he won't join an assault on the ramparts. He needs all his men for when the truce ends.'

Finan walked a few paces to where a dead tree stood gaunt and black at the pond's margin. No other trees grew nearby, and this one had been dead so long that the trunk was split open, fungus grew thick in the gaping rift, and the only branches left were a pair of thick and drooping stumps. Dozens of cloth scraps were nailed or tied to those forlorn branches. 'A prayer tree,' Finan said. 'Did a saint live here?'

'A god lived here.'

He looked at me, amused. 'A god? You're telling me a god chose to live in this godforsaken place?'

'Odin built a hall here.'

'Sweet Jesus, but you have strange gods. Or maybe your fellow Odin just likes swamps?' He drew a knife from his belt. 'You think the gods listen to prayers?'

'I wouldn't if I were a god. Can you imagine it? All those moaning women, whining children, and miserable men?'

'You're a rare warrior,' he said, 'but let's be grateful you're not a god.' He cut a strip from his jerkin, then found a crack in one of the branches and wedged the cloth into place. I saw him close his eyes and mutter a prayer, though whether he prayed to Odin or to the Christian god I did not ask. 'The thing is, lord,' he said, staring at the strip of cloth, 'I can't think of a better way to capture the place.'

'Nor can I, short of raising a thousand men. And I can't afford that. I'm running out of money.'

He laughed. 'Aye, you've been pissing it away like Bishop Wulfheard in a brothel.' He reached up and touched the ragged cloth. 'So let's do it, lord. Let's just do it.'

I found Eadith in Grimesbi's small church. The town might have been Danish and most of its inhabitants pagans, but it depended on ships and sailors for its prosperity, and no harbour town became rich by turning away trade. Christian seamen could see the cross atop the church's roof from a mile away and know they would be welcome. Besides, as I have never tired of telling my Christian followers, we pagans rarely persecute Christians. We believe there are many gods, so we accept another man's religion as his own affair, while Christians, who perversely insist that there is only one god, think it their duty to kill, maim, enslave, or revile anyone who disagrees. They tell me this is for our own good.

Eadith had not gone to the church to pray, but rather to use its floor, which, unencumbered by any furniture, was a wide empty space on which she had spread a bolt of linen. The cloth was light blue. 'I'm sorry about the colour,' Eadith told me. She was on her hands and knees, crawling across the material with two other women. 'It must have been dyed with woad,' she said, 'I asked for a darker colour, but he only had dark cloth in wool.'

'Wool would be too heavy,' I said.

'But this linen was expensive,' she looked worried.

'And the white won't show well against it,' Ethne, Finan's wife, said.

'Then use black.'

'We have no black cloth!' Eadith said.

'He does,' I said, looking at the priest who stood frowning by his altar.

'He does?' Eadith asked.

'He's wearing it,' I said. 'Cut his robe up!'

'Lord! No!' The priest backed into a corner. He was a small man, bald, with a pinched face, and anxious eyes.

'Paint it on,' Finan suggested. 'Use pitch.' He nodded at the priest. 'That miserable robe won't make two stags, and you need one on each side. There'll be plenty of pitch down at the harbour.'

'Good idea!' the priest said hurriedly. 'Use pitch!'

'It won't dry in time,' Ethne said, 'one side might, but we have to turn it over to paint the second side.'

'Charcoal?' the priest suggested nervously.

'Pitch,' I said, 'on one side only. Then sew it to the *Hanna*'s sail.' The *Hanna* was one of the three ships Berg had purchased. She had been called the *Saint Cuthbert*, but Berg, hating the Christian name, had changed it to *Hanna*. 'Hanna?' I had asked him.

'Yes, lord,' he had blushed.

'Olla's daughter?'

'Yes, lord.'

'The girl who wanted to sell her brother into slavery?'

'That one, lord, yes.'

I had stared at him, deepening his blush. 'You do know,' I had asked him, 'that it's unlucky to change a ship's name?'

'I know, lord. But if a virgin pisses in the bilge? Then it is all right, yes? My father always said you find a virgin and you ask her to pee in . . .' his voice had faded away and he had gestured at the renamed *Hanna*, 'and then it is good, yes? The gods will not mind.'

'You found a virgin in Eoferwic?' I asked, astounded.

He had blushed again. 'I did, lord, yes.'

'Hanna?'

He had gazed at me with pathetic, puppy eyes, afraid that I disapproved. 'She is so lovely, lord,' he had blurted out, 'and perhaps, when this is finished . . .' He was too nervous to finish the question.

'When this is finished,' I said, 'and we've won, then you can go back to Eoferwic.'

'And if we don't win?' he had asked anxiously.

'If we don't win, Berg,' I had said, 'then we'll all be dead.'

'Ah!' he had beamed at me. 'Then we must win, lord, yes?'

And to win we needed the tail hairs from Berg's horse, a bolt of pale blue linen, some pitch, and the favour of the gods. 'It has to be enough,' I said to Eadith that night. I had found it hard to sleep, and so walked down to the harbour and watched a crescent moon shudder its reflection on the estuary beyond the anchorage, while, on the wharf, my three warships shivered to the night wind. The *Hanna*, the *Eadith* and the *Stiorra*. Berg had named the ships for women, choosing two for me and one for himself. I suppose, if I had chosen the names, I would have picked Gisela, the mother of my children, and Æthelflaed, who had received my oath, which I had never broken, but Berg's choices were good too. I smiled at the memory of Berg's nervousness and at the thought of a twelve- or thirteen-year-old girl reducing a warrior like him to quivers. What was he, I wondered, eighteen, nineteen? He had stood in the shield wall, he had faced swordsmen and spear-warriors, he had killed and known the battle-joy, but a pretty face and a tangle of brown hair had him shaking like a fifteen-year-old in his first fight.

'What are you thinking?' Eadith asked as she came to join me. She slipped her arm through mine and leaned her head on my shoulder.

'Of the power of women,' I said.

She squeezed my arm, but said nothing.

I was looking for omens and finding none. No birds flew, even the dogs in the town were silent. I knew my sleepless-ness came from the anticipation of battle, from the fear that I had miscalculated. 'Is it past midnight? I asked Eadith.

'I don't know. I don't think so. Maybe?'

'I should sleep.'

'You leave at dawn?'

'Before, if I can.'

'And how long is the voyage?'

I smiled. 'If I get wind? Two days. Without it? Three.'

'So in two or three days,' she began, then her voice faltered.

'We fight the first battle,' I finished the sentence for her.

215

'Dear God,' she said, and I think it was a prayer. 'And the second?'

'Maybe two days later?'

'You'll win,' she said. 'You're Uhtred, you always win.'

'We must win,' I said. Neither of us spoke for a while, but just listened to the creak of boats and the sigh of the wind and the small slap of the waves. 'If I don't come back,' I began, and she tried to hush me. 'If I don't come back,' I insisted, 'then take our people to Eoferwic. Sigtryggr will look after you.'

'Won't he have marched north?'

'He should have left by now, but if I don't survive then he'll be back in Eoferwic very soon.'

'You'll survive,' she said very firmly. 'I gave the emerald ring to the church and said a prayer.'

'You did what?' I asked, astonished.

'I gave the emerald to the church,' she said. She had possessed a rich emerald set in a gold ring that had been given to her by Æthelred who had been my enemy and her lover. She never wore it, and I knew she kept it, not out of any sentimentality, but because its value offered her some security in a dangerous world.

'Thank you,' I said.

'I did not tell the priest why,' she said, 'but I asked him to pray for us.'

'He'll build himself a new house instead,' I said, amused.

'So long as he prays he can build himself a mead hall.' She shivered as she gazed at the moon's long reflection. 'The flag is finished, and the horsehair.'

'Thank you.'

'You'll come back!' she said fiercely.

I thought how I had always wanted to die at Bebbanburg. But not yet, not yet. 'More likely I'll send for you,' I said. 'Look for the ships in two, maybe three weeks from now.'

216

'I won't stop praying.'

I turned and drew her away from the harbour. I needed sleep. To bed, and tomorrow we would sail towards battle.

The estuary was calm in the summer's dawn. The water was the colours of silver and slate, and they moved slowly, as if the sea-goddess was breathing in her sleep. On the wharf it was all confusion as men tossed shields, mail coats and weapons onto the three ships that were already heavy with supplies. There were barrels of ale, barrels of salted herrings, barrels of twice-baked bread, barrels of salt pork, and dozens of empty barrels. There were heaps of sacks stuffed with straw and all lashed down in the ships' shallow bellies. All three ships had crosses on their prows; gaunt, high crosses made of newly split wood. My son commanded the *Stiorra*, Finan was master of the *Hanna*, and I would board the *Eadith*. 'Say your goodbyes,' I shouted along the wharf. 'The day's wasting!' The sun was almost above the horizon, touching the silver and slate with shivers of gold.

Finan was no seaman, so I had given him Berg who, like all Norsemen, knew how to steer a ship and weather a storm. I had rather Finan had been on the *Eadith* with me, we had been together ever since we met, but in these next days we would fight in three groups, and it was better that he stayed with his men throughout. 'I hope it stays calm,' he said.

'I want a fierce southern wind,' I answered, 'so say your prayers.'

He touched the cross hanging at his breast. 'Jesus,' he said, 'we've been dreaming of this moment for years.'

I impulsively embraced him. 'Thank you for staying,' I said.

'Staying?'

'You could have returned to Ireland.'

He grinned. 'And not see the story's end? Sweet Jesus, of course I stayed.'

'It's not the end of the story,' I said, 'I gave Æthelflaed a promise to look after her daughter.'

'God, you're a fool!' he laughed.

'And Æthelstan is unfinished business.'

'So life won't be dull after this,' he said, 'I was getting worried.'

'Go,' I told him, 'we're leaving.'

Now I held Eadith in my arms. She was crying softly. Other men were saying similar farewells to their women or to their children.

I stroked Eadith's red hair. 'I'll send for you,' I promised her.

Then it was time to board and the mooring lines were cast off and men thrust with oars to push the ships away from the wharf. There was a clatter as the oars were threaded through holes in the hull, or, on my ship, dropped between the tholes. I pointed to the men on the three forward bæcbord benches and shouted at them to give a couple of strokes to swing the *Eadith*'s bows towards the open water. I saw Renwald watching from the *Rensnægl*, and waved to him and he waved back. Eadith called a farewell, her voice almost lost among the cries of the gulls, and the ship named for her rocked slightly as the hull turned. I touched the hammer at my breast and prayed to the gods that they would be good to us, then I took hold of the steering-oar. 'Together now!' I called and all the oar-blades swung forward and waited poised above the harbour's calm water. 'Row!'

And so our three ships headed into the estuary, their high bows breaking the still waters. We rowed with long strokes, not hurrying, just driving the hulls down the channel between the withies, then curving east towards the rising sun. There were no other ships in sight.

We passed the Raven's Beak, that long treacherous spit of sand that guards the Humbre's mouth, and there we turned north, and a whisper of south-western wind gave me hope that we could soon raise a sail. Men tired by rowing do not fight as well as unwearied men.

We were three ships in a summer's dawn, and we were going to war.

TEN

The voyage took longer than I had anticipated and much longer than I hoped. We had left Grimesbi in a calm, but by midday the whisper of south-west wind had veered to the north-west, and risen to half a gale. That was a bad omen. Then, some time that afternoon, we rowed through a patch of white-topped waves littered with oars and shattered timbers. They were the remnants of a broken ship, and as plain a warning as any I have ever received from the gods. Had the crosses on our bows angered Ran, the sea-goddess? I had no beast to sacrifice, so while Gerbruht steered the *Eadith* I opened a vein in my right arm, my sword arm, and dripped blood into the sea and told Ran that the crosses were only on the ships' prows so that I could win a victory that would bring the gods pleasure.

I thought her anger had not been assuaged because we had difficulty finding shelter that night. We rowed close to the land, near enough to hear the seethe of angry waves assaulting the shore, and as the light faded I feared we must head east into open water and weather the heavy seas through the darkness, but in the very last light Ran showed us a creek, and our three boats nosed carefully into a wind-fretted anchorage. There were no lights ashore, no fires, no smell of woodsmoke, just endless reeds and mudflats. At low tide during that restless night the *Eadith*'s keel bumped on sand or mud. The air was cold, brought by the malevolent north wind, which also gave us rain.

The second day was almost as bad, except in the afternoon the wind backed as suddenly as it had veered the day before. It still blew hard, churning the seas, but at least it blew in a direction that helped us and we could raise the sails and run before the new wind. The three prows shattered the waves, and my men, resting from their oars, had to bail the ships constantly. By evening we were sailing in a more westerly direction, following Northumbria's coast, but all day we had stood well offshore so that anyone glimpsing our sails through the squalls would think we were heading for Scotland or even further north towards the lands of the Norsemen. We saw few ships, just some fishing craft working close to land.

I had hoped to reach my destination on the third day, but the weather had slowed us, and on that third evening, by which time I had thought to have fought our first skirmish, we found shelter in the mouth of the River Wiire. On the river's northern bank stood a fine stone building that had been an abbey church before the Danes came, and I could remember the day that Ragnar's fierce warriors had slaughtered the monks, ransacked the treasury, and burned the monastery. The church, being stone, resisted the fire, though the roof had fallen in to leave scorched walls and the stump of a bell tower. As we rowed into the river's mouth I saw that a new roof had been made for the church, and that smoke was coming from the hole at its ridge. More smoke blew in the gusting wind from the straggle of small houses that crouched around the old church, while eight small fishing craft were either moored in the river or else had been hauled onto the shingle where still more smoke rose from the fires that dried herrings on the foreshore. Two small children whose job was to keep the gulls away from the herring racks fled when we arrived, but were beaten back to their work by a man who then stood and stared at us. Other folk watched from the small settlement. The crosses on our prows would persuade them we were neither Danes nor Norse, but even so they must have been nervous. I waved to them, but none responded.

Then, just before the sun disappeared behind the western hills, a small boat pushed off from the beach. Two men rowed, and a third sat at the stern. The *Eadith* was closest to the shore and so the boat headed for us. I had ordered all my pagans to hide their hammers, and told those who had inked faces to pretend to be sleeping beneath the benches. I wore a cross, but feared I would be recognised, and so I crouched in the cramped space beneath the helmsman's platform at the stern, and pulled a cloak's hood over my head while Swithun, who had proved himself a clever young man during the visit to Dumnoc, waited to receive the visitors. I had given Swithun my gold chain to wear, and a fine woollen cloak trimmed with otter fur.

'The peace of God be upon this ship,' the boat's passenger hailed us. He was dressed as a priest, though I doubted he had been ordained by the church. 'I'm coming aboard!' he called as his small craft came alongside, and then, without any invitation, he clambered over the *Eadith*'s side. 'And who in Christ's name are you?' he demanded.

The River Wiire marked the southernmost boundary of Ieremias's land, and any priest here was liable to have been appointed by the mad bishop, who claimed his authority came directly from the nailed god rather than from Contwaraburg or Rome. This priest was a short man with a mass of brown curls, a beard in which a heron could have nested, and a wide grin which showed he had three teeth left. He did not wait for anyone to answer his question, but went on to demand payment. 'If you're staying through till dawn you must pay the fee! Sorry about that. It isn't our rules, but God's law.'

The priest spoke in Danish, and Swithun, who could struggle by in that language, pretended he did not understand. 'You want something?' he asked in English, speaking very slowly and a little too loudly.

'Money! Coin! Silver!' The priest used a grubby finger to mime counting coins into his palm.

'How much?' Swithun asked, still speaking very slowly.

'You haven't told me who you are!' the priest protested, and I muttered a translation from the shadows.

'Does the fee depend on the answer?' Swithun demanded, and again I offered a translation.

The priest grinned. 'Of course it does! If you're some piss poor East Anglian hailing from a fly-ridden river bog with a cargo of dog turds and goose shit, then it's cheaper than if you're a god-damned West Saxon who's carrying Frankish mail and Neustrian wine! Are you West Saxon?'

'He is,' I provided the answer, 'and you are?'

'Father Yngvild, and your lord owes me a shilling a ship. Three shillings for a night's shelter,' he smirked, knowing it was an absurd demand.

'Three pennies,' Swithun, who was following the conversation well enough, offered.

I translated, and Yngvild frowned at me. 'Who is that?' he asked Swithun. He could not see me because I was in shadow and well cloaked.

'My harpist,' Swithun said, letting me translate, 'and he's ugly so he must stay out of sight.'

'Three pennies is not enough,' Yngvild said, evidently satisfied with Swithun's explanation, 'make it six.'

'Three,' Swithun insisted.

'Five.'

'Three!'

'Done.' Yngvild grinned again because he had bargained in English and evidently believed he had tricked us in some way. 'Now who are you?' he demanded.

Swithun straightened and looked stern. 'I am Prince Æthelstan,' he announced grandly, 'son of Edward of Wessex, Ætheling of the West Saxons, and sent here by my father and by his sister, Æthelflaed, Lady of Mercia.'

Yngvild stared at him with an expression of pure awe. He opened his mouth to speak, but just stammered helplessly. I had told Swithun to tell the lie confidently, and he had, and now he stood tall and commanding, gazing the shorter priest in the eye. 'You are . . .' Yngvild at last managed to say something.

'You call me lord!' Swithun snapped.

'You call him lord,' I growled menacingly.

Yngvild glanced about the ship, but saw nothing except tired warriors wearing crosses. In truth no prince of Wessex would have sailed this far north without counsellors, priests, and a fearsome guard of household warriors, but Yngvild of the Wiire had no experience of princes, and I had long learned that the most outrageous lies were often the most readily believed. 'Yes, lord,' he said, cowed.

'We travel to the land of the Scots,' Swithun said loftily, 'where we are commanded to consult with King Constantin in an attempt to bring peace to the island of Britain. Do you serve Constantin?'

'No, lord!'

'So we're not in Scotland yet?'

'No, lord, you must keep going north!'

'Then who is your lord?'

'The Bishop Ieremias, lord.'

'Ah!' Swithun sounded delighted, 'the Lady Æthelflaed said we might meet him! Is he here? Can we greet him?'

'He's not here, lord, he's,' Yngvild gestured north, 'he's at Gyruum, lord.' I felt a surge of relief and hoped Yngvild told the truth. I had feared that Ieremias might have gone to Bebbanburg, unlikely though that was if he was to conceal his treachery. 'He would send greetings, I'm sure,' Yngvild added hastily.

'Is he close?' Swithun asked. 'We have a gift for him!'

'A gift?' Yngvild sounded greedy.

'The Lady Æthelflaed is generous,' Swithun said, 'and has sent your lord bishop a gift, but we must hurry north!'

'I can take it!' Yngvild said eagerly.

'The gift must be given to Bishop Ieremias,' Swithun said sternly.

'Gyruum lies not far north, lord,' Yngvild said hastily, 'a short voyage, lord, very short. It lies in the next river mouth.'

'We may visit the place,' Swithun said carelessly, 'if we can spare the time. But do tell the Lord Bishop Ieremias that we are grateful for safe passage through his waters, and ask him to pray for the success of our mission. Boy!' He snapped his fingers and Rorik hurried to his side. 'Give me three pennies, boy.' Swithun took the coins and handed them to Yngvild, adding a silver shilling that bore the image of King Edward. 'A reward for your graciousness, father,' he said condescendingly, 'and a payment for your prayers.'

Yngvild bowed deeply as he backed across the deck. He remembered at the last moment to sketch the sign of the cross and to mutter a blessing on our ship, then he fled to shore in his small boat, but I knew that in the morning, as soon as it was light, a messenger would hurry across the hills to Gyruum. It was no distance by land, though we faced a journey of some hours, so Ieremias would have plenty of warning that three strange ships were off his coast. Ieremias might or might not believe that we were West Saxon envoys on our way to Scotland, but he would be assured that we were Christians and that, I hoped, should be enough. His worst fear, of course, would be that we were survivors of Einar's attack on Dumnoc who had somehow divined that Ieremias had scouted the harbour on the Norseman's behalf and had come for revenge, but why would we put into the Wiire and thus give him warning? That was not the only reason I had risked talking to Yngvild. We could easily have told him to sheer off and mind his own business, but I had taken the opportunity to discover whether Ieremias really was at Gyruum. I had carefully instructed Swithun not to ask any obvious questions such as how many men Ieremias commanded there or whether there were any fortifications at the Tinan's mouth. Ieremias would certainly want to know if we had asked such questions, and he would be reassured when he heard we had shown no curiosity. He would still be wary, but he would also be intrigued by the thought of a gift from distant Mercia.

'And perhaps,' I said to Finan and my son, who both joined me on the *Eadith* after sunset, 'I'm thinking too much. Being too clever.'

'He's clever though, isn't he?' my son asked. 'Ieremias, I mean.'

'He is,' I said, 'he's cunning clever, like a rat.'

'And mad?'

'Mad, cunning, sly, and dangerous,' I said.

'Sounds like Ethne in a bad mood,' Finan put in.

'What would he do if three strange ships just sailed into the Tinan?' my son asked.

'If he had any sense,' I said, 'he'd retreat to his fort.'

'He still might do that tomorrow,' my son said gloomily.

'All that matters,' I said, 'is that he's there, and Yngvild says he is. It's better if he isn't in his damned fort tomorrow, but if he is? So be it. We still get what we want.'

Tomorrow.

Gyruum's old Roman fort lay on the headland south of the Tinan's mouth. From the sea the fort hardly looked formidable, merely a bank of green grass on the headland's summit, but I had ridden that height and seen the ditch and bank, both much smoothed by rain and time, yet still dangerous to any attacker. As far as I could see Ieremias had not added a palisade, though I could only see the seaward face, and any attacker would almost certainly assault from the landward side.

It was mid morning as we rounded the headland. We had left the Wiire in the early dawn, rowing into a calm sea and windless air, and I had glimpsed a horseman riding north from the settlement and knew Ieremias would soon learn of our coming. He would also have sentries up on that high fort's green rampart watching to discover whether our three ships would keep going northwards or, instead, turn into the Tinan.

We turned. There was a fitful wind now, unable to decide whether it blew from the north or the west, but just enough to fret the sea. We rowed. We did not hurry. If we had been coming to attack Ieremias's settlement then we would be heaving on the oars, dragging the hulls through the sea as fast as we could. We would be wearing helmets and mail, and the bows of our ships would be crammed with men ready to leap ashore, but instead we came slowly, no one wore a helmet, and our three ships bore crosses instead of dragons on their prows. I kept looking up at the fort, and, as far as I could tell, it was not manned. No spears showed above the green bank. There were a couple of men up there, but only a couple.

227

Then we rounded the promontory into the river and I could see the southern bank and I felt a surge of relief because there, in front of me, tied to a newly built wharf that jutted across the marshland into the river, was Ieremias's ragged ship, the *Guds Moder*. A dozen smaller ships, all fishing craft, were tied to the pier, while two others, also fishing boats, were anchored offshore. Nearer was the beach where, years before, I had been freed from slavery when the red ship slammed into the shingle and my rescuers had leaped from the bows. It had been my uncle, my cousin's father, who had sold me into slavery, fully expecting me to die, but somehow I had lived, and I had met Finan, another slave, and there, on that shingle beach, our long road to revenge had begun. Now I prayed that road was almost over.

Ieremias had been alerted of our arrival by his look-outs, and some forty or fifty men and women were waiting on the beach, while still more were coming downhill from the old monastery that was Ieremias's hall. Swithun, wearing the fur-trimmed cloak again and with my gold chain bright at his neck, stood in the *Eadith*'s bows and waved a lordly greeting. I was at her stern where I turned and cupped my hands to call to my son who was steering the *Stiorra*. 'You know what to do?'

'I do!' he sounded cheerful.

'Do it slowly!'

He just grinned for answer, then gave an order that prompted his oarsmen to take the *Stiorra* slowly upstream. They did not row hard, just dipped the blades to pull their ship gently away from the *Eadith* and the *Hanna*, which were heading towards the shingle, using the oars to steady their hulls against the river's current and the ebbing tide. The *Stiorra* drifted back towards us for a moment, then the rowers pulled her upstream again, but still very lazily, as if she had no intention of putting men ashore, but was simply holding her position in the river until it was time for us all to go back to sea.

We were lingering off the beach because I was looking for Ieremias and could not see him among the men and women waiting on the shingle, but then an extraordinary procession appeared on the low hill where the monastery stood. Twelve men, I knew Ieremias called them his disciples, led the group, but these disciples were clad in mail, wore helmets, and carried spears and shields. Six small children followed, all robed in white and all holding leafy branches, which they waved from side to side as they sang. Ieremias followed them. The mad bishop was astride a diminutive ass, a beast so small that the mad bishop's feet dragged on the ground. He was again dressed in richly embroidered robes, carried his silver-hooked bishop's crozier, and wore a mitre crammed over his long white hair. Three women, all dressed as nuns in grey robes and grey cowls, followed. The six children's voices sounded clear and sweet above the sigh of the wind and the beat of the river's small waves breaking on the shingle beach. I gave Gerbruht the steering-oar. 'Hold her just offshore,' I told him. He was a good ship handler and I trusted him to keep the *Eadith* a few paces from the beach while I crouched in the belly of the boat where thirty of my men were also staying low, all of them in mail, but none of us had yet put on our helmets. Shields, swords, axes, and spears lay ready on the deck. The folk waiting ashore could see us, but would not see that we were ready for battle. I buckled Serpent-Breath around my waist. Rorik, grinning, was holding my helmet, the fine helmet with the silver wolf crouching on the crown.

'Who are you?' a voice shouted from the shingle bank. The man used the Saxon tongue, presumably because Yngvild's messenger had told Ieremias who we were. That message had evidently not caused any alarm because, though many of the men on the beach wore swords, only the twelve disciples were in mail.

'I am Æthelstan of Wessex,' Swithun called from the prow, 'and I bring you friendly greetings from my father, King Edward of Wessex, and from his sister, Æthelflaed of Mercia!'

'No closer!' the man called.

'The Lady Æthelflaed has sent your bishop a gift!' Swithun shouted, and held up a stinking jerkin we had wrapped in a piece of clean linen. 'They are the swaddling clothes worn by the infant John the Baptist! They are still stained with his holy piss!'

Rorik, crouching beside me, started to laugh. I hushed him.

'You can throw it to me!' the man called from the beach. He was being properly cautious.

'Wait! Wait!' It was Ieremias's high-pitched voice that interrupted. He had abandoned the tiny ass and was striding down the beach and shouting in his native Danish. 'Do not be so rude to our guests! A gift? It must be given properly. Lord Æthelstan!' I ducked out of sight as the bishop came near the water's edge.

'Lord Bishop?' Swithun responded.

'Come ashore!' Ieremias used the English tongue now.

'You want me to jump in the water?'

'I want you to walk on it, like our lord did! Can you walk on water?'

Swithun, taken aback by the question, hesitated. 'Of course not!' he finally shouted.

'You should practise!' Ieremias called reprovingly. 'You should practise! It just takes faith, nothing else, just faith! So come a little closer, just a little. And you may bring six men ashore, only six for now.'

'Do it clumsily!' I hissed at Gerbruht. The *Eadith* had drifted a little downstream, which is what I had wanted, and now Gerbruht called on the steerboard-side oarsmen to pull, which was the last thing he should have ordered if he was really trying to bring the *Eadith* gently into the shore because, instead of nosing slowly onto the shingle, the ship turned her head downstream and was carried seawards by the tide. Gerbruht appeared to panic by shouting at all the oarsmen to pull together. 'Now! Hard! Pull!' Then, as the *Eadith* surged, he dragged the steering-oar hard towards himself and I felt her turning towards the beach. 'Pull!' he bellowed. 'Hard now, pull!' He had done it beautifully.

At the same time Finan, or at least Berg who was Finan's helmsman, had let the *Hanna* go gently upstream, using nothing but lazy, slow oar strokes, just enough to carry her fifty or sixty paces away from us, and now he suddenly turned the long ship and also headed for the beach. 'Row!' I heard Berg shout. 'Row!'

'One more stroke!' Gerbruht bellowed. 'Now!'

The long oars bent with that final effort, and *Eadith*'s prow scraped on shingle, the boat jarred to a sudden stop, and mail-clad men erupted from her belly, scrambled past the oarsmen, and leaped ashore. Finan's men were jumping from the *Hanna*'s bows. What we had achieved by our apparently clumsy seamanship was to trap Ieremias and his men between our two forces, while my son, seeing us assault the beach, was suddenly rowing hard as he took the *Stiorra* fast towards the pier, which lay a good half-mile upstream.

'I want the bishop alive!' I shouted at my men. 'Alive!'

I was one of the last men off the boat. I stumbled in the shallow water and almost fell, but Vidarr Leifson, one of my Norse warriors, caught and steadied me. Rorik gave me the helmet. I carried no shield. I drew Serpent-Breath as I waded the last few feet, but I doubted I would need her. She would have her moment, and soon, but at this moment, on this beach, my men had done exactly what I had asked of them.

Finan's men were upstream of Ieremias's warriors, and mine were downstream, and together we outnumbered him. Ieremias, if he had had any sense, should have run the moment he saw what was happening. Most of his men had neither shields nor mail, and there were women and children among them who added to the panic by screaming, but Ieremias just gaped at us, then shrieked as he shook his crozier towards the clouds. 'Smite them, Lord! Smite them!' Three of his disciples mistook the prayer for an order and ran towards us, but my men were ready for battle, indeed were eager for it, they were starved of it, and there was a sudden clash on the shingle, a clangour of sword-blades, and each of Ieremias's men was facing at least two of mine, and I watched the sword-blades deflect the spear-thrusts, saw the sword-blades pierce bellies or hack into necks, and I heard the vicious roar of my men as they ruthlessly cut the three down and heard the shrieking from the women who saw their men dying on the beach.

A few folk, more sensible than those who had died, turned and fled towards the old monastery on the hill, but Finan's men simply scrambled up the grassy bank to block the inland path. It was all over in moments. Three men sprawled bloody on the beach, while the rest were being shepherded back to where Ieremias had dropped to his knees and was screaming to his god. 'Send Thy holy angels, Lord!' he pleaded. 'Defend Thy servants! Rip out the tongues of Thine enemies and blind their eyes! Avenge us, O Lord, avenge and save us!' Meanwhile his men were dropping their weapons. Some, like Ieremias, knelt, not in prayer as he was, but in submission.

I looked upstream and saw that my son had captured *Guds Moder*. I suspected that the capture of that ship was even more important than seizing Ieremias, who, knowing that he had been tricked, now called for heavenly reinforcements. 'Let worms consume their bowels, O Lord,' he screeched, 'and maggots feast on their bladders! They are loathsome in Thy sight, O Lord, so smite them with Thy mighty power! Send Thy bright angels to avenge us! Rot their flesh and shatter their bones! Lord, have mercy! Lord, have mercy!'

I walked up to him, my boots scrunching on the shingle. None of his men tried to stop me.

'Consume them with unquenchable fire, Lord! Drown them in the devil's stinking excrement!' His eyes were tight closed, turned up to the sky. 'Let Satan vomit down their throats, Lord, and feed their vile flesh to his dogs! Scourge them, Lord! Smite them! All this I ask in the name of the Father, and of the Son, and—'

'—and of the other one,' I finished for him, tapping Serpent-Breath's blade against his shoulder. 'Greetings, Ieremias.'

He opened his blue eyes, looked up at me, paused for a heartbeat, and then offered me a smile as sweet as any child's. 'Greetings, lord. How kind of you to visit me.'

'I came to have words with you.'

'You did!' he sounded delighted. 'I love words, lord! I love them! Do you love words, lord?'

'I do,' I said, and touched the sword-blade against his gaunt cheek. 'And my favourite word today is *banahogg*.' It meant a death-stroke, and I reinforced it by nudging his face with Serpent-Breath.

'That's a fine Norse word, lord,' he said earnestly, 'a very fine word indeed, but of all the Norse words I think I prefer *tilskipan*. Do you think we might come to a *tilskipan*?'

'That is why I'm here,' I told him, 'to come to an arrangement with you. Now on your feet.'

We would have words.

* * *

'No, lord, no! No! No!' Ieremias was crying. The tears ran from those very blue eyes and trickled down the deep furrows of his cheeks to disappear into his short beard. 'No! Please, no!' The last 'no' was a scream of despair. He was on his knees, hands clasped in supplication, gazing up at me, sobbing.

Fire flared bright in the night-time church. The flames leaped up, burned for a moment, then subsided.

'What did you say that was?' I asked.

'Jacob's spoon, lord.'

'It's ashes, now,' I said happily.

'Jacob stirred Esau's pottage with that spoon, lord,' Ieremias said between sobs.

The spoon, crudely carved from beechwood, was now white ash on the sea-coal fire that warmed and lit Ieremias's cathedral. More light came from candles on the altar, but beyond the windows it was dark, deep night. The building, he insisted on calling it a cathedral, was a stone church, built years ago, long before my grandfather's time, and it had once been an important place for Christians, but then the Danes had come, the monks had been killed, and the church and its monastery had fallen into ruin until Ieremias was given the place. He had been named Dagfinnr then, and had been a house-warrior to Ragnar the Younger, but one morning he had appeared naked in Dunholm's great hall and announced that he was now the son of the Christian god and had adopted the name Ieremias. He demanded that Ragnar, a pagan, should worship him. Brida, Ragnar's woman and a hater of Christians, insisted that Dagfinnr should be put to death, but Ragnar, pitying the man and mindful of his long service, had sent him and his family to the monastery ruins instead, doubtless thinking that the crazed fool would not live long. But Dagfinnr had survived, and landless men, outlaws, men without lords, found him and swore him fealty so that he was now the ruler of Gyruum and its lands. Rumour said that he had dug a well soon after arriving at the ruined monastery, but that instead of finding water he had discovered a hoard of silver buried by the old monks of Gyruum. I did not know whether that tale was true or not, but certainly he had prospered enough to buy *Guds Moder* and a fleet of smaller ships that trawled the sea beyond the river for herring, cod, haddock, salmon, ling, and whiting, which were smoked or salted on the foreshore before being traded up and down the coast. Brida, when she became the effective ruler of Northumbria after Ragnar's death, had left Ieremias alone, perhaps recognising in him an echo of her own madness or, more likely, amused that the real Christians were so outraged by Ieremias's absurd claims.

The old church, now repaired with a crude thatched roof, was crammed with small wooden boxes, each of which contained one of Ieremias's treasures. So far I had burned Jacob's spoon, a lock of hair from Elisha's beard, a piece of straw from the baby Jesus's crib, the fig leaf Eve used to cover her left tit, and a forked stick with which Saint Patrick had caught the last snake in Ireland. 'And what's this?' I asked, opening another box.

'No, lord, not that! Anything but that!'

I peered into the box and saw a shrivelled pig's ear. 'What is it?' I asked.

'The ear of the high priest's servant, lord,' Ieremias muttered between sobs. 'Saint Peter cut it off in the garden of Gethsemane.'

'It's a pig's ear, you fool!'

'No! It's the ear our Lord healed! Christ touched that ear! He put it back on the servant's head!'

'How did it end up here then? In this box?'

'It fell off again, lord.'

I held the dried ear close to the glowing brazier. 'You've lied to me, Ieremias.'

'No!' he wailed.

'You've lied to me,' I said. 'Lie after lie after lie. I saw you in Dumnoc.'

The sobbing stopped suddenly and a wicked grin crossed Ieremias's face. He was capable of sudden changes in mood, maybe because he was mad? 'I knew it was you, lord,' he said slyly.

'You said nothing when you saw me.'

'I saw your face, and at that moment I was not certain, and so I prayed, lord, and God took His time to answer me, but He did after a while, and when I told Lord Æthelhelm what God had said to me he thought I was moon-touched.'

'He still sent men to search for me,' I said angrily.

'He did?' Ieremias asked with apparent ignorance.

'Because you told him I was there,' I said, angry now. 'I'm your lord and you betrayed me!'

'I prayed to God to protect you.'

'You lying maggot!'

'God is my Father, He listens to me! I prayed!'

'I should slit your throat now,' I said, and he just made a whining noise. 'You told Æthelhelm your suspicions,' I said, 'to gain favour with him. True?'

'You're a pagan, lord! I thought I was doing my Father's will.'

'By betraying me.'

'Yes, lord,' he whispered. He frowned at me. 'You're a pagan, lord! I was just doing my Father's will.'

'And next day,' I said, 'I saw *Guds Moder* with Einar's ships. So whose side are you on?'

'I told you, lord, I am doing God's work by making peace! Blessed are the peacemakers for they shall be named the children of God! The archbishop told me that, lord, the archbishop himself! Hrothweard told me! No!' The last despairing word came as I dropped the dried ear into the

236

brazier's flames. There was a burst of fire, the smell of bacon, and Ieremias sobbed again. 'The archbishop said I must make peace!'

'Just kill the bastard,' Finan growled from the shadows.

'No!' Ieremias shuffled back towards the altar. 'No, no, no.'

'Lord Æthelhelm,' I said, 'who welcomed you in Dumnoc, is allied with my cousin. But Jarl Einar, who welcomed you and your ship when he sailed north from Dumnoc, now serves Constantin. Both think you are on their side.'

'Blessed are the peacemakers,' Ieremias muttered.

'I don't have much time,' I said, 'just this one night. But that's time enough to burn everything here.'

'No, lord!'

'Let me talk to him,' Finan growled.

Ieremias glanced at Finan and shuddered. 'I don't like that man, lord.'

'He's a Christian,' I said, 'you should like him.'

'Bless you, my son,' Ieremias made the sign of the cross towards Finan. 'I still don't like him, lord. Horrible man.'

'He is horrible,' I said, 'but perhaps he can get the truth from you?'

'I've told you, lord! Blessed are the peacemakers!'

I paused, watching him. Was he truly mad? Half the time he made perfect sense and half the time his mind wandered off into some airy place where only he and his god existed. His distress when I burned his baubles seemed real enough and his fear was no pretence, yet he still lied stubbornly. Finan wanted to beat the truth from him, but I suspected Ieremias would welcome some sort of martyrdom. And if you beat the truth out of a man you can never trust that it is the truth because a terrified man says what he thinks his tormentor wants to hear. I wanted to hear the truth, but what, I suddenly wondered, did Ieremias want? And why had he mentioned the archbishop? I remembered being told that he had travelled to Eoferwic and had talked with Hrothweard, the new archbishop, so perhaps there was some truth in his wild shrieks of peace?

I walked towards him, and he instinctively shrank away and began gulping air. 'I won't . . .' he began, but the words were overcome by a great sob.

'You won't what?' I asked.

'Tell you!' he said savagely. 'You're not a maker of peace! You're a pagan! You are Uhtredærwe!' It meant Uhtred the Wicked, a name Christians liked to give me. 'You worship idols and brazen images! You are an abomination to my Father in heaven! I would rather die than tell you!' He closed his eyes and raised his face to the roof where the brazier's smoke writhed slow about the rafters. 'Take me, O Lord,' he cried, 'take Thy suffering servant into Thy loving arms. Take me! Take me! Take me!'

I crouched opposite him, leaned forward, and whispered in his ear. 'Well done.'

He stopped his prayers abruptly, opened his eyes, and looked at me. For a moment he seemed almost more scared than when I had spoken harshly. 'Well done?' he repeated in a very small voice.

I still whispered. 'The archbishop wanted me to find out if you could keep a secret.'

'You spoke to . . .' he began, then went silent when I put a finger in front of my lips.

'Finan mustn't hear,' I whispered, 'he can't be trusted.'

Ieremias nodded vigorously. 'He looks treacherous, lord. You can't trust small men.'

'And he's Irish,' I said.

'Oh! Well! Yes, lord!'

'He must believe that I hate you,' I said, 'but I'm here for the archbishop! He promised he would replace everything I burned. He promised.'

'But,' he said, frowning, then looked down at the hammer that hung on its chain around my neck. 'You're not a Christian, lord!'

'Hush!' I said, holding my finger before my lips again. I stole a glance at Finan, then lowered my voice even more. 'Look!' I lifted Serpent-Breath's hilt, and there, in the pommel, was a silver cross. It had been given to me years before by Hild, whom I had loved and still did, though she lived now in a convent in Wintanceaster, yet for a time we had been lovers. I had placed the cross into the sword's hilt out of sentimentality, but now it served me well, as Ieremias stared at it. The silver caught and reflected the brazier's fire.

'But,' Ieremias began again.

'Sometimes Christ's work must be done in secret,' I whispered. 'Tell me, Ieremias, are the Christians winning the wars in Britain?'

'Yes, lord,' he said enthusiastically, 'God be thanked, the kingdom of God comes north year by year. The pagans are confounded! God's armies cleanse the land!'

'And who led those Christian armies?'

He gaped for a second, then, in a very low but surprised voice. 'You did, lord.'

'I did,' I said. And that was true, though I had led those armies only because of my oath to Æthelflaed. I hesitated a moment. My pretence was working, it was reassuring and comforting Ieremias, but now I had to make a guess, and if I was wrong then I could lose his trust. 'The archbishop,' I whispered, 'told me about Lindisfarena.'

'He did!' Ieremias was excited and I was relieved. The guess had been right.

'He wants it to be an island of prayer,' I said, recalling Hrothweard's words.

'That's what he told me!' Ieremias said.

'So he wants you to restore the monastery to its true glory,' I said.

'It must be done!' Ieremias said fiercely. 'It is a place of power, lord, far greater than Gyruum! A prayer said in Lindisfarena is heard by God! Not by the saints, lord, but by God Himself! With Lindisfarena I can work miracles!'

I hushed him again. It was time for the second guess, but this one was easier. 'My cousin,' I said, 'promised you the island?'

'He did, lord.'

I knew that Archbishop Hrothweard, who was a man of sense and duty, had never promised Lindisfarena to Ieremias. The island and its ruined monastery were sacred to Christians because it was there that Saint Cuthbert had lived and preached. My cousin had never restored the monastery even though it lay within sight of Bebbanburg's walls, probably because he feared that a new abbey and its buildings would attract Norse or Danish raiders. Yet now that he was under siege he needed ships to bring his beleaguered garrison food, and Ieremias's small fleet was harboured just south of Bebbanburg's land, so making a promise about Lindisfarena would have been an easy way to recruit the mad bishop's help. 'What did my cousin promise you?' I asked. 'That he would help you rebuild the monastery?'

'Yes, lord,' Ieremias said excitedly, 'he promised we shall make Lindisfarena more glorious than ever!'

I shook my head sadly. 'The archbishop has learned,' I whispered, 'that my cousin has also promised Lindisfarena to the black monks.'

'To the Benedictines!' Ieremias was horrified.

'Because they brought Christianity to the Saxons,' I explained, 'and he doesn't trust you because you're a Dane.'

'We're neither Dane nor Saxon in God's sight!' Ieremias protested.

'I know that,' I said, 'and you know that, but my cousin hates the Danes. He's using you. He wants you to bring him food, but then he will betray you! The black monks are waiting at Contwaraburg, and they will come north when the Scots are gone.'

'God won't allow that to happen!' Ieremias protested.

'Which is why he sent me,' I said.

He looked into my eyes and I looked back, not blinking, and I saw the doubt in his gaze. 'But Lord Æthelhelm . . .' he began.

'Has promised gold to the black monks,' I interrupted. 'I thought you knew that. I thought that was why you helped Einar attack him!'

He shook his head. 'The Lord Uhtred,' he meant my cousin, 'wanted food, lord, because there was a fire in his granaries. But he feared because Lord Æthelhelm is bringing so many men, he thinks Lord Æthelhelm means to keep the fortress.'

'I thought my cousin was going to marry Æthelhelm's daughter?'

'Oh, he is, lord.' He chuckled and his eyes opened wider. 'Very young and ripe, that one! A consolation for your cousin.'

Consolation for what, I wondered, for losing control of Bebbanburg to Æthelhelm's men? 'So Æthelhelm,' I said, 'would let my cousin keep Bebbanburg, but will insist on garrisoning it with his own men?'

'With a whole army, lord! Ready to smite the heathen!'

And that made sense. With Bebbanburg in Æthelhelm's grasp, Sigtryggr would find Saxon armies to his south and to his north. My cousin had cannily avoided becoming entangled in any of the wars between Saxons and Danes, but Æthelhelm's price for his rescue was that Bebbanburg was to be part of the crushing of Northumbria. 'And my cousin didn't want Æthelhelm's army in his fortress?' I asked.

'He doesn't want that! Some men, yes, an army? No!'

'So you said you'd weaken Lord Æthelhelm's fleet?'

He hesitated. I sensed he wanted to lie, so I growled slightly and he jerked as if surprised. 'The Scots were already planning to do that, lord,' he admitted hurriedly.

'You knew that?' I asked, and he just nodded. 'So what does God think of you talking to King Constantin?' I asked.

'Lord!' he protested. 'I didn't speak to him!'

'You did,' I accused him. 'How else could you arrange to guide their fleet to Dumnoc? You've been talking to both sides. To my cousin and to Constantin.'

'Not to King Constantin, lord. I swear it on the blessed virgin's womb.'

'You spoke to the Lord Domnall then.'

He paused, then nodded. 'I did,' he admitted in a low voice.

'You came to an arrangement,' I said, 'a *tilskipan.*'

'Yes, lord.'

'You wanted reassurance,' I said, speaking gently again. 'My cousin promised to let you have the monastery if you helped him, but what if he lost? That must have worried you.'

'It did, lord! I prayed!'

'And God told you to talk to the Scots?'

'Yes, lord!'

'And they promised to give you the monastery if you helped them?'

'Yes, lord.'

'And you scouted Dumnoc for them?'

He nodded again. 'Yes, lord.'

'But why didn't you join their attack? Why didn't you fight alongside Einar's men?'

He looked at me with wide eyes, 'I am a peacemaker, lord! Blessed are the peacemakers! I told Lord Domnall I could not carry a sword, I'm a bishop! I would help the Scots, lord, but not kill for them. God forbid!'

'And if you had fought alongside Einar's ships,' I suggested, 'then Lord Æthelhelm would know you had betrayed my cousin.'

'That is true, lord,' he said. If Ieremias was mad, I thought, then he was subtle mad, clever mad, sinuous as a serpent. He had convinced both the Scots and my cousin that he was on their side, all so he could build his new monastery on Lindisfarena regardless of which side won.

'Do you really believe,' I asked him, 'that my cousin will keep his promise? Or that the Scots will let you build a monastery on their land? Neither can be trusted!'

He looked at me with tears in his eyes. 'God wants me to build it, lord! He talks to me; He demands it; He expects it of me!'

'Then you must build it,' I said feelingly. 'And the archbishop understands that! Which is why he sent you a message.'

'A message?' he asked eagerly.

'He sends you his blessing and assures you he will be praying daily for your success. He promises he will support your work on Lindisfarena and send you treasures, such treasures! But only if you help me.' I took his hand and laid it on the silver cross in Serpent-Breath's hilt. 'I swear by my soul that this is true and I swear that when I am Lord of Bebbanburg you will be the abbot, the bishop, and the ruler of Lindisfarena.' I pressed his hand against the pommel. 'I swear that in the name of the Father—'

'My Father,' he interrupted hurriedly.

'In the name of your Father, and of your brother, and of—'

'And of the other one,' he interrupted again. 'You mustn't name the other one,' he told me anxiously, 'because it makes God jealous. He told me that.'

'Jealous?'

He nodded vigorously. 'You see it's the holy other one,' he said, stressing the word holy, 'while my Father and my brother should be holy, even holier, but they're not. And that's very wrong!'

'It is wrong,' I said soothingly.

'So Father asked me not to name the other one. Ever.'

'And your Father will also tell you to trust me,' I said.

I thought for a heartbeat that I had taken the pretence a step too far because Ieremias did not respond, but just frowned at me. Then he closed his eyes tight and muttered something under his breath. He paused, apparently listening, nodded, muttered again, and then opened his eyes and looked at me with unfeigned happiness. 'I just asked Him, lord, and He says I can trust you! Praise Him!'

'Praise Him indeed,' I said, still holding his hand. 'So now tell me everything I need to know.'

And in Gyruum's old church, in the smoke-haunted night, he did.

PART FOUR

The Return to Bebbanburg

ELEVEN

'You should have slit his god-damned throat,' Finan growled next morning, or rather later that night, because I had woken my men in the depths of darkness. The fires that smoked the fish flared up on the foreshore as my men fed them with driftwood, and by the light of the sudden flames they waded into the shallows and heaved armour and weapons into our ships. More fires showed on the hill above, surrounding the feast hall where I had imprisoned all of Ieremias's men, women, and children. Seven of my guards watched the hall, while two others stood watch over Ieremias who had begged to be allowed to spend the night in his relic-filled cathedral. 'I would pray, lord,' he had pleaded, 'I would pray for your success.'

'Pray!' Finan scoffed. 'You should have let me slit his god-damned throat.'

'He's mad, not evil.'

'He's cunning and sly, you said so yourself.'

'He believes in miracles,' I said. Somehow Dagfinnr the Dane had heard about Christian miracles and had convinced himself that the nailed god would give him the power to work them if only he collected enough relics, and so Ieremias had been born. He blamed his failure to turn water into mulberry ale or to cure blindness on the sad fact that he had been denied ownership of Lindisfarena. 'It's a place of power!' he had told me earnestly. 'Heaven touches the earth on that island! It is a holy place.'

'So,' I now told Finan, 'he wants to build a new cathedral on Lindisfarena and then he's going to rule all Britain.'

'King Ieremias?' Finan asked scornfully.

'Not King Ieremias,' I said, 'but Pope Ieremias, and he's going to call his realm the kingdom of heaven. Everyone will live in peace, there'll be no sickness, no poverty, and the harvest will never fail.' Ieremias, trusting me, had poured out his ambitions, his words running together in his excitement. 'There'll be no lords,' I went on, 'and no fortresses, the lion will lie down with the lamb, swords will be forged into ploughshares, there'll be no more stinging nettles, and a man can take as many wives as he wants.'

'Sweet Christ, is that all?'

'And god told him that the miracles will all start at Lindisfarena, so that's where he'll build his new Jerusalem. He wants to rename the island. It's going to be the Blessed Isle.'

'Bless my buttocks,' Finan said.

'And I'm to be Most Holy High Protector of the Blessed Isle.'

'Why does he need a protector if everyone will live in peace?'

'Because he says the devil will be roaming about like a roaring lion looking to devour folk.'

'I thought the lion was sleeping with the lamb? And anyway, what is a lion?'

'The devil in disguise.'

Finan laughed and shook his head. 'And you promised to give this idiot the monastery ruins?'

'I can't, they belong to the church, but I can give him land on the island. And if he takes the church land too? I won't stop him.'

'The church won't like that.'

'I don't give a rat's turd what the church likes or dislikes,' I said tartly, 'and Ieremias is harmless.'

'He'll betray you,' Finan said, 'like he's betrayed everyone else.' For some reason Finan had taken against Ieremias, a dislike that was mutual. I wondered if it was because Finan, a Christian, was offended by the mad bishop's delusions? I could imagine some Christians thinking that Ieremias mocked them, but I was not so sure. I thought he was sincere, even if he was mad, while Finan just wanted to cut his throat.

But I would not cut his throat, nor any other part of him. I had liked Ieremias. He was earnestly mad and he was passionately mistaken and he was also cunning, as he had proved by his dealings with Æthelhelm, with the Scots, and with my cousin, but all those lies and deceptions had been meant to bring about his miraculous kingdom. He believed the nailed god was on his side, and I was not willing to offend that god, nor any other, not on this day, which would bring the battle I had dreamed of all my life. So I had promised him land on Lindisfarena, then allowed him to offer me his blessing. His scrawny hands had pressed on my skull as he harangued the nailed god with a plea for my victory. He had even offered to come with us. 'I can summon my Father's angels to fight on your side,' he had promised me, but I had persuaded him his prayers would be just as effective if they were made in his own cathedral.

'You might let him live,' Finan said grudgingly, 'but don't just leave him here!'

'What can he do?'

'You'll just sail away and let him be?'

'What else?'

'I don't trust the bastard.'

'What can he do?' I asked again. 'He can't warn Bebbanburg that we're coming. He'd need a fast ship to do that, and he doesn't have any ships.'

'He's a miracle-worker. Perhaps he'll fly.'

'He's a poor, innocent idiot,' I said, then sent Swithun to recall all the guards who watched Ieremias and his folk in the old monastery. It was time to leave.

Ieremias was indeed a poor innocent idiot, but wasn't I just as foolish? I was taking a small band of men to capture the impregnable fortress where my cousin's men waited, where Einar the White waited, and where the Scots waited.

We sailed north.

Four ships. The *Eadith*, the *Hanna*, the *Stiorra*, and the *Guds Moder* left Gyruum in the darkness. I was in the *Guds Moder* now, leaving Gerbruht to helm the *Eadith*. We rowed down-river towards the sea, and the sound of our oar-blades striking the water was the loudest noise in that still night. Every dip of the oars stirred the black river to a myriad of twinkling lights, and each time the blades lifted they sprinkled a glitter of those lights that were the jewels of Ran the sea-goddess, and I took their sparkling to be a sign of her blessing. Small patches of mist clung to the river, but there was enough moonlight seeping through the thin clouds to show us the Tinan's dark banks.

We left on the slack water of low tide, but the flood began as we headed towards the sea. For the moment the current was against us, but once past the headlands we would turn north and the tide would help us. Later in the day we would fight the sea's currents, but I hoped by then a wind would be filling our sails.

But there was no wind as we left the river. There was just the silence of the night through which the four ships ghosted slow under their oar beats, and, as the clouds moved west, beneath a sky drenched with stars. There were stars above us and Ran's jewels below us and the sea was calm. She is never still, of course. A calm lake can look as smooth as ice, but the sea always moves. You see her breathing, see the slow rise and fall of the great waters, but I have rarely seen a sea as calm as on that starlit, silent night. It was as if the gods held their breath, and even my men were silent. Crews usually chant or sing as they row, or at the least they grumble, but that night no one spoke and no one sang and the *Guds Moder* seemed to glide through a dark void like *Skidblanir*, the ship of the gods, sailing noiselessly between the stars.

I looked back as the sea's hidden current carried us northwards. I was watching the headland of the Tinan for fire. I suspected Constantin, or at least Domnall, had posted men on the river's northern bank to watch Ieremias's ships. If there were Scottish scouts on that bank they could not ride to Bebbanburg faster than our ships could sail there, but they might light a warning beacon. I watched, but saw none. I hoped that any Scots who had occupied the southern parts of Bebbanburg's land would already have retreated, because Sigtryggr's forces should have crossed the wall by now. He had promised to lead at least a hundred and fifty men north, though he had warned me he was not willing to fight a pitched battle against Domnall. Such a battle would invite a slaughter, and Sigtryggr needed every sword for the Saxon onslaught he knew was coming.

There was no warning fire on the headland. The whole coast was dark. The four ships were alone, forging north with *Guds Moder* in the lead. She was the smallest and thus the slowest ship, and so the others matched our speed. It was not until the eastern horizon was edged with a sword-blade of grey light that the rowers began to sing. It began

251

on the *Stiorra*, the oarsmen singing the lay of Ida, a song I knew my son had chosen because it told how our ancestor, Ida the Flamebearer, had come across the cold sea to capture the fortress on the high rock. The song claimed that Ida and his men were hungry, they were desperate, and how they had flung themselves up the rock to be beaten back by a savage enemy. They were hurled back three times, the song claimed, and their dead lay thick on the slope as they huddled on the beach, taunted by their enemies. Night was falling and a storm was brewing offshore and Ida and his men were trapped between the fortress and the churning breakers, facing death by blade or death by sea, until Ida had shouted it would be death by fire. He had burned his ships, making flames by the water, and had seized a fiery length of wood and charged alone. He was wreathed in flame, sparks flew behind him, and he flung himself on the wall and thrust flame into his enemy's faces, and they ran, fearing this fire warrior who had come from a far land. My father had mocked the song, saying that one spear-thrust or a pail of water would have been enough to stop Ida, but it was undeniable that he had taken the fortress.

The singing grew stronger as the crews of the other three ships joined in, chanting the song of burning triumph in time to their oar strokes as we beat our way northwards along the Northumbrian coast. And as the sun touched the world's edge with the day's new fire a small wind ruffled the water, rippling it from the east.

I would have liked a southern wind, even a gale, or at least a blustery hard southern blow that might have penned Einar's ships in their narrow anchorage behind Lindisfarena, but the gods sent me a gentle east wind instead, and I touched my hammer and meekly thanked them that the wind was not northerly. Ieremias had confirmed that Einar the White's vessels were moored in the shallow anchorage behind the island, and a hard southern wind would have given them a long tiring passage to the harbour mouth at Bebbanburg. The east wind would still try to blow them back down the anchorage's entrance channel, but once beyond the shoals they could hoist their sails and race southerly with the wind on their bæcbord beam. 'And there's one Scottish ship there too, lord,' Ieremias had added.

'The *Trianaid*?'

'She's a lump of a boat, lord,' he had said. 'The Scots like to build their ships heavy so be careful she doesn't ram you. She's slow, but she can crush your strakes like a hammer falling on an eggshell.'

'How many crew?'

'Fifty at least, lord. She's a big brute.'

I had remembered seeing Waldhere, the commander of my cousin's household troops, at Dumnoc. 'Did you bring him out of Bebbanburg?' I had asked Ieremias.

'I did, lord,' he confessed, 'and two others before him.'

'How?' If the Scots had seen any of Ieremias's ships at the fortress then they would have known he was betraying them.

'Fog, lord,' he had told me. 'I took one of our smaller ships and laid up in the bay by Cocuedes till there was a deep fog.' Cocuedes was a small island just off the coast to the south of Bebbanburg.

'Who were the other two?'

'Both priests, lord,' he had sounded disapproving, presumably because the priests had not recognised his authority as a bishop. 'I picked them up a month ago and took them to Gyruum, and they found their own way south to negotiate with Lord Æthelhelm.'

Under my nose, I thought bitterly. 'They were sent to arrange the marriage?'

Ieremias had nodded. 'She brings a rich dowry, I hear!

Gold, lord! And she's a sweet little thing,' he had sighed wistfully, 'she's got tits like ripe little apples. I'd like to give her a thorough blessing.'

'You'd like what?' I asked, surprised.

'To lay my hands on her, lord,' he said in apparent innocence.

He was not entirely mad.

In mid morning, as the sun burnished a sea that was breaking into small waves, the wind freshened. We hoisted Ieremias's ragged sail that was decorated with a dark cross, and when it was sheeted home *Guds Moder* bent to the quickening breeze. We shipped the oars and let the wind take us northwards. The trailing ships did the same, loosing their great sails, and Æthelhelm's stag was there, pitch black against the pale woad-blue linen, blazoned across the *Hanna*'s bellying sail.

We were not yet halfway, but the wind was on our beam, the foam-flecked seas were breaking white at our prows, our wakes spread bright in the sun, and we were going to Bebbanburg.

When we are young we yearn for battle. In the firelit halls we listen to the songs of heroes; how they broke the foemen, splintered the shield wall, and soaked their swords in the blood of enemies. As youngsters we listen to the boasts of warriors, hear their laughter as they recall battle, and their bellows of pride when their lord reminds them of some hard-won victory. And those youngsters who have not fought, who have yet to hold their shield against a neighbour's shield in the wall, are despised and disparaged. So we practise. Day after day we practise, with spear, sword, and shield. We begin as children, learning blade-craft with wooden weapons, and hour after hour we hit and are hit. We fight against men who hurt us in order to teach us, we learn not to cry when the blood from a split skull sheets across the eyes, and slowly the skill of sword-craft builds.

Then the day comes when we are ordered to march with the men, not as children to hold the horses and to scavenge weapons after the battle, but as men. If we are lucky we have a battered old helmet and a leather jerkin, maybe even a coat of mail that hangs like a sack. We have a sword with a dented edge and a shield that is scored by enemy blades. We are almost men, not quite warriors, and on some fateful day we meet an enemy for the first time and we hear the chants of battle, the threatening clash of blades on shields, and we begin to learn that the poets are wrong and that the proud songs lie. Even before the shield walls meet, some men shit themselves. They shiver with fear. They drink mead and ale. Some boast, but most are quiet unless they join a chant of hate. Some men tell jokes, and the laughter is nervous. Others vomit. Our battle leaders harangue us, tell us of the deeds of our ancestors, of the filth that is the enemy, of the fate our women and children face unless we win, and between the shield walls the heroes strut, challenging us to single combat, and you look at the enemy's champions and they seem invincible. They are big men; grim-faced, gold-hung, shining in mail, confident, scornful, savage.

The shield wall reeks of shit, and all a man wants is to be home, to be anywhere but on this field that prepares for battle, but none of us will turn and run or else we will be despised for ever. We pretend we want to be there, and when the wall at last advances, step by step, and the heart is thumping fast as a bird's wing beating, the world seems unreal. Thought flies, fear rules, and then the order to quicken the charge is shouted, and you run, or stumble, but stay in your rank because this is the moment you have spent a lifetime preparing for, and then, for the first time, you hear the thunder of shield walls meeting, the clangour of battle swords, and the screaming begins.

It will never end.

Till the world ends in the chaos of Ragnarok, we will fight for our women, for our land, and for our homes. Some Christians speak of peace, of the evil of war, and who does not want peace? But then some crazed warrior comes screaming his god's filthy name into your face and his only ambitions are to kill you, to rape your wife, to enslave your daughters, and take your home, and so you must fight. Then you will see men die with their guts coiled in the mud, with their skulls opened, with their eyes missing, you will hear them choking, gasping, weeping, screaming. You will see your friends die, you will lose your balance as your foot slips in an enemy's spilt bowels, you will look into a man's face as you slide your blade into his belly, and if the three fates at the foot of Yggdrasil favour you, then you will know the ecstasy of battle, the joy of victory, and the relief of living. Then you will go home and the poets will compose a song of the battle and perhaps your name will be chanted and you will boast of your prowess and the youngsters will listen in envious awe and you will not tell them of the horror. You will not say how you are haunted by the faces of the men you killed, how in their last gasp of life they sought your pity and you had none. You will not speak of the boys who died screaming for their mothers while you twisted a blade in their guts and snarled your scorn into their ears. You will not confess that you wake in the night, covered in sweat, heart hammering, shrinking from the memories. You will not talk of that, because that is the horror, and the horror is held in the heart's hoard, a secret, and to admit it is to admit fear, and we are warriors.

We do not fear. We strut. We go to battle like heroes. We stink of shit.

But we endure the horror because we must protect our women, keep our children from slavery, and guard our homes. So the screaming will never end, not till time itself ends.

'Lord?' Swithun was forced to touch my arm to break my reverie, and I jumped, startled, to discover the wind blowing across our hull, the sail pulling well, my hand on the steering-oar, and our ship coursing straight and true. 'Lord?' Swithun sounded anxious. He must have thought I was in a trance.

'I was thinking of those blood-puddings that Finan's wife makes,' I said, but he still gazed at me with a worried expression. 'What is it?' I asked.

'Look, lord,' Swithun pointed over our stern.

I turned, and there on the southern horizon, faint against a heap of clouds that edged the world, were four ships. I could only see their sails, dirty and dark against the white clouds, but I would have wagered Serpent-Breath against a kitchen knife that I knew who they were. They were the remnants of Æthelhelm's fleet, the larger ships that had been moored on the wharf at Dumnoc, and which had escaped Einar's ravaging, and being big they would be faster than our four vessels. Not just faster, but with larger crews, and I did not doubt that Æthelhelm had at least two hundred and fifty men crammed into the long hulls that pursued us. For the moment, the four ships were a long way behind, but we still had a long way to go. It would be close.

My son hardened his sail so that the *Stiorra* quickened. He brought her close to our steerboard side and loosed the sheets so that he matched our speed. 'Is that Æthelhelm?' he shouted through cupped hands.

'Who else?'

He looked as if he was about to shout another question, then thought better of it. There was nothing we could do unless we wanted to abandon our voyage by turning into one of the few harbours on this coast, and my son knew I would not do that. He let the *Stiorra* fall back.

By early afternoon I could see the hulls of the pursuing vessels, among which the pale timbers of the *Ælfswon* showed clearly. The four ships were catching us, though I reckoned we would still reach Bebbanburg first, but beating them to the fortress would not be enough. I needed time before Æthelhelm interfered. Then the gods showed that they loved us because the wind must have dropped to our south and I saw their big sails sag, fill, then sag again. After a moment the sun reflected from oar-blades, then the long banks began to dip and rise, but no crew could row as fast as our ships were reaching on that friendly east wind. For a while the four West Saxon ships lost ground, but the patch of calmer wind did not last, and their sails filled once more, the oars were taken inboard, and they again began to close relentlessly. By now Æthelhelm would have recognised Ieremias's ragged ship, and he would guess the other three were mine. He would know I was ahead of him.

By mid afternoon I could see the Farne Islands breaking the horizon, and not long after the shape of Bebbanburg high on its rock. We were sailing fast, the wind was gusting high, the sails pulling us, and our cutwaters breaking the seas to send spray flying down our decks. My men pulled on mail coats, belted swords into place, touched their hammers or their crosses, and muttered prayers. Behind us the four West Saxon ships were near enough that I could see men aboard, could see the crosses on their prows, and see the criss-cross of ropes that stiffened their sails, but they had not quite closed enough. I would have a little time, enough time I hoped. I had pulled on a mail coat, my finest, its hems edged with gold, and Serpent-Breath now hung at my side. A glint of reflected sunlight showed where a man held a spear on Bebbanburg's ramparts. I could see the Scots too; a small group of horsemen was galloping north along the beach. They had seen our ships, and, like the sentinels on Bebbanburg's high walls, would have recognised the *Guds Moder*, and the riders were now hurrying the news to Domnall.

So four of us were making ready. My small fleet was closing on the fortress, the seas hissing down our wind-driven hulls. My cousin could see us coming, and his men would be going to the ramparts to watch our arrival. Domnall would be ordering Einar to take his ships to sea, while Æthelhelm was in desperate pursuit. The chaos was about to be unleashed, but for the chaos to give me victory I needed everyone to believe that what they saw was what they expected to see.

My cousin expected a relief fleet led by Ieremias. He had been worried that Æthelhelm, who was providing the men and most of the food, would bring too large a force and so usurp ownership of the fortress, but he would see four smaller ships, one of them *Guds Moder* with the dark cross on her sail and with her distinctive tangle of dishevelled rigging, and he would see the crudely painted leaping stag on the *Hanna*'s mainsail, and he would surely believe that Ieremias was bringing the promised relief, and he would reckon, from the size of the ships, that the force coming to his aid numbered fewer than two hundred men. A large force, certainly, but not sufficient to overpower his garrison. Behind us, and still some distance from the foam-fretted Farne Islands, were Æthelhelm's larger ships, and, so far as I could see, not one was flying a banner. My cousin might be puzzled by them, but he would surely have learned that I had purchased ships, and the easiest explanation for the trailing vessels was that they were mine, and that I was displaying crosses on their prows to mislead him. I had not reckoned on Æthelhelm taking any part in this day's confusion, but now I realised his presence could be of help if my cousin assumed his ships were mine.

The Scots, and their allies led by Einar, expected something wholly different. They too had been told that a relief fleet was sailing, but Ieremias had persuaded them that he would make Æthelhelm's fleet approach very slowly, under oars.

'To give Einar's ships time to intercept them?' I had asked Ieremias in Gyruum.

'Yes, lord.'

'But how would you have persuaded Æthelhelm to slow down?'

'I told him of the dangers,' he had said.

'What dangers?' I had asked.

'Rocks, lord! There are rocks between the Farnes and the mainland, you know that.'

'They're easily avoided,' I had said.

'You know that and I know that,' he had answered, 'but do the West Saxons? How many southerners have sailed that coast?' He had grinned. 'I've told them how many ships have been lost there, told them there are hidden rocks by the harbour entrance, told them they have to follow me very cautiously.'

That caution, and the creeping pace, would have given Einar's ships and the Scottish vessel time to block the relief fleet's approach. Æthelhelm would then have had a decision to make, either to fight his way through the enemy, or to refuse the offered sea battle and sail back down the coast. He still might have to make that decision, because, as we sailed between the islands and the fortress I could see Lindisfarena spreading across our bows and I could see Einar's ships rowing out of the anchorage. They were having a hard time of it, fighting against a blustering east wind, but if I had slowed, if I had dropped the sail and used the oars to creep cautiously as though I feared shoals and rocks, then Einar would still have had time to intercept me. But I did not slow. The water was seething and breaking at our bow and the wind was driving us hard towards the harbour's narrow channel. Soon, very soon, Domnall would know he had been deceived.

And what did I expect? I touched the hammer at my neck and then the cross on Serpent-Breath's pommel. I expected to be the Lord of Bebbanburg by nightfall.

Or dead.

But the whole madness depended on one thing, just one thing, that my cousin would open the gates of his fortress to me. I touched the hammer again and called to Swithun. 'Now,' I said, 'now.'

Swithun was wearing robes we had taken from Ieremias's hall, which, in turn, Ieremias had looted from some church back when he was called Dagfinnr and had served Ragnar the Younger. 'They're all so pretty, lord,' Ieremias had told me, lovingly fingering the embroidered hem of a chasuble. 'This one is woven from the finest lamb's wool. Try it, lord!'

I had not tried it, instead we chose the gaudiest of the vestments, and Swithun was now draped in a white cassock that fell to his ankles and was hemmed with golden crosses, in the shorter chasuble that was edged with scarlet cloth and decorated with red and yellow flames that Ieremias claimed were the fires of hell, and over it all a pallium, which was a broad scarf embroidered with black crosses. 'When I am Pope of the North,' Ieremias had confided in me, 'I shall wear nothing but golden robes. I shall shine, lord, like the sun.'

Swithun did not quite shine, but he certainly looked flamboyant, and now he pulled on a helmet that had a lining of wool. Eadith had taken the long grey horsehairs of the tail we had docked from Berg's stallion and sewn them to the lining's rim. Once Swithun had pulled the helmet down over his skull he looked like a wild thing with his long white hair catching the gusting wind. He went to the bows of *Guds Moder* and waved his arms frantically towards the fortress.

And the men waiting in Bebbanburg saw Ieremias coming to their aid, just as he had promised and just as they expected. They saw Æthelhelm's banner vast on the *Hanna*'s sail. They saw the crosses on our ships' prows. They saw relief coming fast on the strong east wind.

We were now sailing straight towards the entrance. The sun was low in the west, dazzling me, but I could see men waving from the high ramparts, and I ordered my men to wave back. I could see Scotsmen standing on the dunes north of the channel, just watching us because there was nothing they could do to stop us. Behind them I could see that Einar's ships had reached the open sea and were loosing their sails ready to turn south and intercept Æthelhelm's fleet. They were too late to stop us, but Æthelhelm's four ships were just reaching the islands. I prayed that they would strike the sunken rocks, but the east wind pushed them out of danger. I could see now that the *Ælfswon* was flying Æthelhelm's banner, but the east wind streamed the banner directly towards the fortress, meaning the men on the walls could not make out the stag that leaped upwards on the flag. The crews of Æthelhelm's ships were also waving to the fortress. If Æthelhelm had thought for a moment he would surely have realised that his best course was to run one of his ships aground on the beach beneath Bebbanburg's high ramparts and shout up at the defenders to warn them of what was happening, but instead he kept pursuing us, though he could not catch us now. We were running landwards in front of that east wind, our prows were splitting the seas, and our sails were strained taut. I could almost smell the land. I could see my

262

cousin's banner flying at Bebbanburg's summit. The sea floor shelved towards the beach, shortening the waves, and we drove into a patch of tumbling waters where wind and tide fought across the shallows, and still we ran, spray flying, and now Bebbanburg's ramparts were high above us, close enough that a man could throw a spear onto our deck, and I steered the ship into the channel's centre, and the gulls wheeled in the wind and screamed about our mast, and I thrust the steering-oar's loom hard away from me, and *Guds Moder* drove herself onto the sand just paces from the rock-cut steps that led up to Bebbanburg's Sea Gate.

Which was closed.

The *Stiorra* came next, grounding herself beside the *Guds Moder*, then came the *Hanna*, and *Eadith*, and all four ships were on the sand, blocking the harbour channel, and men were leaping from the bows with seal-hide ropes to hold the ships in place. Other men were hoisting empty barrels or sacks stuffed with straw, pretending to bring the promised supplies to replenish Bebbanburg's storerooms. The men carrying those burdens wore helmets and mail and had swords at their sides, but none carried a shield. To the defenders on the high ramparts it must not appear as if we came for battle. Half my men were still on the ships, oars in their hands, as if we were readying to row into the safer waters of the harbour.

Swithun was capering on the sand and screaming up at the ramparts. I was still on board *Guds Moder*, standing in her prow and watching the Sea Gate. If it stayed closed we were doomed. Over a hundred of my men were now ashore, carrying the barrels, crates, and sacks towards the stone archway. Berg climbed the steps to the gate and hammered on the solid wood with his sword hilt, while Finan came to the *Guds Moder* and looked up at me questioningly. 'No one has thrown a spear yet,' I said, looking up at the ramparts where I saw men gazing down at us. They were not throwing spears, but nor were they opening the gate, and I prayed that I had not utterly misjudged this day.

'Open the gate!' Swithun bellowed. Berg hammered again. A surge of waves crashed the stranded ships together. 'In the name of the living God!' Swithun shouted, 'in the name of the Father, the Son, and the other one! Open the gate!'

I jumped overboard, splashing into the shallows, and looked eastwards and saw all the pursuing ships, both Æthelhelm's and Einar's, surging towards us through the tangled breakers of the offshore shallows. Two of them collided and I saw men thrusting spears at each other, but though they fought each other we were the real enemy of both and in a few minutes we would be trapped against Bebbanburg's wall, we would be outnumbered and we would be slaughtered.

'The gate!' Swithun shouted up at the ramparts. 'I command you in the name of God to open the gate!'

Gerbruht picked up a massive stone and climbed the steps. He evidently planned to batter the gate's solid timbers into splinters, but even with his great strength we had no chance of entering the fortress before the enemy ships reached us. My son joined him, and, like Berg, beat on the closed gate with his sword's heavy pommel. Swithun was on his knees now, the long white horse-hair whipping about his face. 'Have pity, Christ!' he wailed. 'By Thy great mercy make these men open their gate!'

'For Christ's sake!' my son screamed desperately, 'open the god-damned gate!'

I was about to order my men to return to the ships, to retrieve their shields and so make a shield wall. If we were to die then we would die in a way that would make the poets marvel and forge a song that would be chanted in Valhalla's mead hall.

But then the gate opened.

TWELVE

Berg and my son were first through the Sea Gate. They did not rush. My son sheathed Raven-Beak and helped the defender drag one of the heavy doors fully open before walking calmly into the gate's tunnel. Berg kept his drawn sword low. There was a risk in sending a Norseman through the gate first, but Berg had borrowed a cross to wear over his mail, and presumably the guards merely thought he was a Christian who liked to wear his hair long like a Northman. I watched him vanish into the tunnel, closely followed by a group of men carrying sacks on their shoulders.

'They're in,' Finan muttered.

'Wait,' I said, not to him, but to reassure myself.

We had rehearsed this moment. We had to capture the Sea Gate without raising suspicion because, beyond it, and approachable only by a steep flight of rock-cut steps, was a higher gate that pierced the wooden palisade guarding the northern edge of the high rock. That higher gate was far less formidable than the big gate below, and it stood open now, but if the enemy shut that gate we would have a desperate struggle to capture it, a struggle that would probably fail. I could see three men standing in the entrance, watching what happened beneath them. None of them seemed alarmed. They slouched, one leaning against the gatepost.

The temptation was to rush that higher gate and hope that my leading men would reach it before the enemy understood what was happening, but the steps were high and steep, and deception had seemed the better tactic, except now I could see just how close our pursuers were to trapping us. The *Ælfswon* was closing on the harbour entrance. I could see red-cloaked spearmen in her bows, water suddenly hiding them as a wave shattered on the pale ship's prow. A mass of ships followed, all of them our enemies. I looked back to the high steps, but none of my men was in sight yet. 'Where are you?' I asked no one.

'Christ help us,' Finan prayed under his breath.

Then a man wearing a dark blue cloak and an expensive silver helmet appeared on the far steps. He was climbing, but was in no hurry. 'That's not one of our men, is it?' I asked Finan. I could usually recognise any of my men by their clothes or armour, but I had never seen the long blue cloak before.

'He's one of the *Stiorra*'s crew,' Finan said, 'Kettil, I think.'

'Been spending his money, hasn't he?' I asked sourly. Kettil was a young Dane with a love of flamboyant clothes. He was fastidious, almost dainty at times, and easily underestimated. He stopped now, turned, and spoke to someone behind him, then my son and Berg caught up with him and the three climbed to the upper gate together. 'Quick!' I urged them, and, as if he had heard me, Kettil suddenly drew his seax and leaped up the last three steps. I saw the short-sword ram into the belly of the man leaning against the gatepost, saw Kettil seize the man and haul him backwards before hurling him down the rocky slope. My son and Berg were through the gate, swords drawn now, and the men following them abandoned their straw-filled sacks and surged after them.

'Go!' I shouted to the men waiting outside the Sea Gate. 'Go! Go! Go!'

I ran up the beach. I was alarmed by a man suddenly appearing on the stone rampart above the Sea Gate's arch, but then saw it was Folcbald, one of my doughty Frisians. There had been no defenders on the fighting platform above that arch, and why should there have been? My cousin believed we were bringing food and reinforcements, and though he had sent men to this northern end of Bebbanburg's long rock, most of them had crowded at the seaward corner of the ramparts to watch the running fight between Einar's and Æthelhelm's ships. Those ships were almost in the harbour channel, and one of my cousin's men on the ramparts must have recognised the leaping stag banner flying from the *Ælfswon*'s masthead because I saw him cup his hands and shout towards the guards on the higher gate, but those guards were already dead. 'I was asking them where they wanted the supplies,' my son told me later, 'and by the time they realised we weren't friendly we were killing them.' The rest of my men were streaming through the Sea Gate's arch and pounding up the steps beyond. We had done it! We had captured a path through the outer ramparts, up the steep steps, through the inner palisade, and so into the heart of the fortress.

That makes it sound easy, but Bebbanburg is vast and we were few. My son, standing just inside the newly captured upper gate, could see a long open space rising in front of him to a tangle of small halls and storehouses built in the shadow of the high crag where the great hall and a church dominated the fortress. To his left, on the ramparts that faced the sea, there were scores of men and a few women, who had been watching the ships racing towards the harbour, and among them was one group who were distinctive because of the brilliance of their mail, and that finery made him think the group contained my cousin. A priest from among them was the first to run towards the captured gate, then he saw the sprawled corpses and the blood spilled on stone, and thought better of his impulse and turned back to the bright-mailed warriors. He was shouting a warning. More men were joining my son, making a line to defend the captured gate. 'Bring our shields!' my son called down to the Sea Gate. 'We need shields!'

On the beach, men were throwing down the empty barrels and straw-filled sacks and jostling through the Sea Gate's arch. The men who had stayed on board the ships, pretending to be ready to row to safety in the harbour, now came ashore carrying shields for the men already inside the fortress. Rorik struggled up the beach carrying our banner, my heavy shield, a thick cloak edged in bear fur, a horn, and my fine, wolf-crested helmet. I would fight in my war-glory. Bebbanburg deserved that, but before I could pull on the helmet or clasp the cloak at my throat, I needed to be inside the walls because the enemy's ships were now dangerously close. I glanced back and saw *Ælfswon*'s pale hull just entering the channel, while the big Scottish ship, *Trianaid*, was not far behind her. Gerbruht ran past me, going back to the ships, and I seized his arm. 'Get inside! Now!'

'We need more shields, lord!'

'Take them from the enemy. Now, inside!' I raised my voice. 'All of you, inside!'

The last of my men ran through the gate. The *Ælfswon* was close! I saw her sail fly crazily as the sheets were loosened and her prow turned towards the beach. Armed and mailed warriors were crowded at her bows, staring at me as I kicked an empty barrel out of the archway. I shouted at my men to shut the gate, and a dozen willing men dragged the ponderous doors closed. The weight of those doors was testimony to my cousin's fears, each was a hand's breadth thick with the inner face braced by long squared timbers, and both hung from massive hinges that squealed as the two gates were hauled shut. Gerbruht lifted the vast locking bar and dropped it into the brackets with a thunderous crash. Beyond the gate I heard the violent scrape of keel wood on sand, heard the *Ælfswon*'s bows splinter into the abandoned *Eadith*, and knew Æthelhelm's warriors were leaping onto the beach, but Æthelhelm's crew, like the three men who had guarded the higher gate, were too late.

I left Gerbruht and a dozen men to defend the Sea Gate. 'Stay up high,' I told them, pointing to where Folcbald stood alone on the fighting platform above the masonry arch, 'and drop rocks on any bastard trying to break in.'

'Big rocks!' Gerbruht responded with relish. He shouted at his men to start collecting stones, of which there were plenty, and to carry them up the steps. 'We turn their brains into pottage, lord,' he promised me, then turned as a second and even louder splintering noise sounded beyond the gates. I heard men shouting in anger, heard a blade hit another, and reckoned the heavy Scottish ship had rammed the *Ælfswon*. Let the bastards fight it out, I thought, and climbed the steep steps into Bebbanburg.

Into Bebbanburg. Into my home!

For a moment I was overwhelmed. I had dreamed of coming home for my whole life, and now, standing inside Bebbanburg's ramparts, it did seem like a dream. The sound of the fighting below, the cry of the gulls, the voices of my men faded. I just stared, scarcely daring to believe that I was home again.

It had changed. I knew that, of course, because I had seen the fortress from the hills, but it was still a surprise to see the unfamiliar buildings. At the fort's summit was a new great hall, twice the size of the one my father had inherited, while just this side of the hall was a church built of stone, its western gable surmounted by a tall wooden cross. There was a squat tower at the church's eastern end, and I could see a bell hanging in the roofed wooden frame on the tower's summit. Lower, on a rock ledge between the hall and the seaward ramparts, there was a burned-out building. All that was left were ashes and a few scorched pillars, and I supposed that must have been the granary that had caught fire. Other granaries, storehouses, and barracks, many of them new and all made of timber, filled the rest of the space between the great hall's high crag and the fortress's eastern walls. I heard more crashes as the boats piled up in the harbour channel, and glanced behind to see that two more of Æthelhelm's ships had joined the vicious fight that had broken out on the beach. Einar's ships were coming fast to support the Scots, who had overrun the *Ælfswon*, but who now faced West Saxon reinforcements. That fight was none of my business so long as Gerbruht and his men held the Sea Gate safe.

My business was to deal with my cousin's men inside the fortress, and, to my surprise, there were none to be seen. 'They ran away,' my son said scornfully. He pointed to the huddle of storehouses built beneath the crag on which the church and the great hall stood. 'They went to those build-ings.'

'They were on the ramparts?' I asked.

'About sixty of them,' he said, 'but only about a dozen were in mail.'

So they were not ready, and that was no surprise. Defending a fortress during a siege is a tedious business, mostly spent watching the encircling enemy, who, if they are attempting to starve the defending garrison, will do little except stare back. I had no doubt that my cousin had a large

270

force, all in mail and all heavily armed, guarding the Low Gate, and a similar smaller group at the High Gate, both of which were at the fortress's southern end, but what did he have to fear from the Sea Gate? It could only be approached from the ocean, or by men taking a long walk along the beach beneath the seaward ramparts, and the sentinels high above would have plenty of time to give warning if an enemy tried either approach. Those sentinels had thought we were friends. Now the first of them were dead.

'Father?' my son sounded anxious. I was gazing at the great hall, marvelling at its size, and amazed to find myself standing inside Bebbanburg's ramparts. 'Shouldn't we move?' my son prompted me. He was right, of course. We had surprised the enemy, who had withdrawn to leave all the northern part of Bebbanburg undefended, yet all I was doing was lingering at the gate.

'To the hall,' I said. I had decided we should take the fortress's highest point and so force my cousin's men to fight uphill in an attempt to dislodge us. I had put on my helmet, closing the cheek-pieces so that all an enemy would see were my shadowed eyes in the wolf-crested metal. I let Rorik tie the laces that held the cheek-pieces shut, then pulled the heavy cloak over my shoulders and clasped it with a gold brooch. I wore my arm rings, gold and silver, the trophies of battles past. I carried my heavy shield painted with the wolf's head of Bebbanburg, and I drew Serpent-Breath. 'To the hall,' I said again, louder. My men were carrying their shields now. They looked fierce and wild, their faces framed by helmets. They were my hard and savage warriors. 'To the hall!'

They raced past me, led by my son. 'Young legs,' I said to Finan, and just then the bell in the church tower began to sound. I could see the huge instrument swinging and see that the bell-rope was being pulled frantically because the bell was jerking wildly as it swung. The sound was harsh, loud, and panicked.

'Now they're awake,' Finan said drily.

The bell had woken the Scots too, at least those who had not already crowded onto the dunes to watch the ships approach. I could see men and women coming from the cottages on the harbour's far side to gather on the shore. Domnall would be wondering what caused the alarm, he would also be considering whether this was the moment to assault the Low Gate. My cousin would be wondering the same thing, and his fear of a Scottish attack would convince him to leave a strong force to guard the southern ramparts. Constantin, I thought with grim amusement, would not be happy if he knew how his men were making things easier for us. 'Hoist the banner,' I told Rorik. It was the same banner that flew above the great hall, the wolf's head banner of Bebbanburg.

I had taken a swift glance behind before following the younger men towards the great hall. The harbour channel was now blocked by my four ships, by Æthelhelm's four, by the *Trianaid*, and by Einar's vessels. Some of Æthelhelm's men had fled onto the northern beach and were being pursued by Norsemen, while others were waging a bitter battle on the ships' decks, but most of the fighting seemed to be on the beach immediately below the Sea Gate, which hid my view. I could see that Gerbruht and his men were merely watching the struggle, which told me that neither the West Saxons nor, so far, the Scots or Norsemen were attacking the gate. So my enemies fought each other, and the thought of that made me laugh aloud. 'What's funny?' Finan asked.

'I love it when our enemies fight each other.'

Finan chuckled. 'I almost feel sorry for Æthelhelm's boys. To come all this way to have a crew of furious Scotsmen up their arses? Welcome to Northumbria.'

Ahead of us was a rising stretch of bare rock, where, in my father's time, men had practised their battle skills and, on sunny days, women had laid clothing to dry. At the far end of the rocky stretch were storehouses, barracks, and stables, and on the right reared the crag of steeper rock where the hall and church were built. Those buildings were also approached by a crude stone ramp that followed the curve of the landward ramparts, and my son was leading our men up that ramp, which, in places, had been cut into steps. They went fast. I watched as the first of my warriors ran past the church and through a side door into the great hall. Almost immediately some women and children fled the hall through the bigger doors that faced the sea and overlooked the storehouses. They ran down the steep stairs, joined by some of my cousin's warriors, who, it seemed, were not inclined to fight for the crag's flat summit. Finan and I hurried, climbing a steep flight of wide stone stairs that led from the ramp to the church. The bell was still tolling, and I half thought of going into the stone building, finding whoever hauled on the bell-rope, and silencing the noise, but then decided the frantic sound was spreading panic, and panic was my friend in this late afternoon. A woman screamed from the church door when she saw us. I ignored her, following my warriors into the gloom of the hall. 'Uhtred!' I bellowed in search of my son.

'Father?'

'The front of the hall! Form a shield wall in front!'

He shouted orders and men followed him into the sunlight. There were four bodies among the tables on the hall's stone floor, the corpses of men caught inside and foolish enough to have offered a fight. A fire smouldered in the big central hearth, and oatcakes were baking on the ring of stones that bordered the fire. I climbed onto the dais and pushed open a door that led to a windowless chamber. There was no one in the room, which, I guessed, was where my cousin slept. There was a bed covered in furs, a tapestry on one wall, and three wooden chests. Their contents must wait. I went back into the hall, jumped from the dais and turned fast when I heard a snarl from my right, but it was only a hound-bitch under a table. She was protecting her puppies. My puppies now, I thought, and remembered days hunting in the hills behind the harbour, and suddenly it seemed as if the past unravelled and I could hear my father's voice echoing in the hall. It did not matter that the heavy rafters were twice as far overhead as they had been in his day, nor that the hall was longer and wider. This was Bebbanburg! It was home! 'Get a proper spear, you louse,' my father had snarled on the last day we had hunted boar together. Gytha, his new wife and my stepmother, had protested that a man's spear was too heavy for a nine-year-old. 'Then let him be gutted by a boar,' my father had said, 'it will do the world a favour and rid us of a louse.' My uncle had laughed. I should have heard the envy and hatred in that laugh, but now, a lifetime later, I had come to undo the wrong that my uncle had done.

I went through the big sea-facing door to find my men arrayed on the flat space beyond. We had captured Bebbanburg's summit, but that did not mean we had won the fortress. We still had to scour the rock of enemies, and they were gathering beneath us. Immediately below us, and reached by the steps down which the women and children had fled, was the wide patch of scorched stone, shadowed now by the great hall's gable and littered with charred beams which I supposed had been the granary that had burned. Beyond that were other storehouses or barracks, some with scorched walls, and my cousin's men, now properly armed with mail and shields, were filling the alleys between them.

And I realised I had made a mistake. I had thought that by capturing the great hall, the highest point of Bebbanburg, I would force my cousin's men to attack us, and men attacking up steep steps would die under our blades. But the men gathering in the alleys showed no sign of wanting to be killed. They waited, expecting us to attack, and I suddenly realised that if my cousin had the sense of a flea he would leave us on the summit while he recaptured the Sea Gate and admitted Æthelhelm's men. We had to dislodge my cousin's gathering forces, defeat them, and drive them out of Bebbanburg before he understood the opportunity, and the only way to do that was to go down into the tangle of smaller buildings and hunt them down. And I still did not know how many men my cousin led, though I did know that the sooner we started killing them then the sooner I could again call Bebbanburg home.

'Uhtred!' I shouted for my son, 'You'll stay here with twenty men. Watch our backs! The rest of you! Follow me!' I ran down the steps which were the great hall's main approach, and which led to the burned-out granary. 'Make a wall!' I shouted when I reached the foot of the stairs. 'A wall! Finan! Go left!'

Two alleyways faced us, both filling with enemies. Those enemies were still confused. They had not been expecting a fight on this summer's afternoon, and a man needs time to ready himself for the prospect of death. I could see they were nervous. They were not shouting insults, nor moving threateningly forward, but waiting behind their shields. I would not give them time. 'Now forward!'

And what did my cousin's men see? They saw confident warriors. By now they knew we were the dreaded enemy, the threat that had loomed over Bebbanburg for so many years. They saw warriors who came to the fight eagerly, and they knew what my men had achieved across the years.

In all Britain there were few bands of warriors as experienced as my men, who had a reputation as feral as my men, who were feared as much as my men. I sometimes called them my wolf pack, and the defenders who waited in the alleys feared they were about to be ripped apart with the savagery of wolves. Yet in one way those fearful men were wrong. We were not confident, we were desperate. My men knew as well as I did that speed would be everything this day. The fight must be finished quickly or we would be overwhelmed by enemies, who, at this moment, were still too confused to understand what was happening. We would live if we were fast and die if we were slow, and so my men charged with an eagerness that looked like confidence.

I led men into the right-hand alley. Three men could have made a shield wall to block that narrow passage, but instead of standing firm the enemy retreated. Swithun, still wearing his gaudy bishop's robes and the horsetail hung helmet, was on my right, and he carried a long heavy spear that he thrust hard into the men who were backing away. One of those men tried to block the spear-thrust with his shield, but instead of taking the blade in the shield's centre he used the edge, and the shield swung to one side with the violence of Swithun's blow and I lunged Serpent-Breath into the space he left, twisted her as the blade was buried in his guts, and then, as he bent over the sword in agony, I slammed my shield's iron rim onto the nape of his neck, and down he went.

Swithun was already attacking the man beyond as I kicked my man onto his back and tugged Serpent-Breath free of the clinging flesh. A blow struck my shield hard enough to drive the top rim back onto the iron strip that protected my nose. I thrust the shield away and saw a spear coming for my eyes, swayed to avoid it, rammed Serpent-Breath at the spearman, who was spitting insults, and glimpsed a movement to my left. The spearman knocked my thrust away with his shield as I saw a huge man in a dented helmet swinging an axe at my head. It had to be the same axe that had struck my shield so hard, and the big bastard was wielding it two-handed, and I was forced to raise my shield to cover my skull knowing that I invited a low thrust from the spear, but the spearman was also holding a shield, he was off balance, and I reckoned my mail could stop his one-handed lunge.

I instinctively stepped under the axe blow, using my shoulder to push the big man back against the alley's left-hand wall, and, at the same time, I rammed Serpent-Breath at the spearman. I should have been using Wasp-Sting, there was no space for a long blade in this struggle. The spearman had stepped back, the axe blow was wasted on my shield, but the brute let go of the weapon and tried to wrest my shield away instead. 'Kill him!' he was bellowing. 'Kill him!' I had brought Serpent-Breath back and managed to find the space to put her tip against his lower belly and heave. I felt her sharpened point break through mail and puncture leather, slide into flesh and grate on bone. The bellow turned to a gasp of pain, but still he kept hold of my shield, knowing that as long as he held it I was vulnerable to his comrades. The spearman had stabbed at my thigh, it hurt, but the pain vanished as Swithun skewered the man, bellowing curses as he drove the man backwards with his spear impaled in the man's chest. I pushed and twisted Serpent-Breath, then suddenly the big man's resistance ended as Vidarr and Beornoth, a Norseman and a Saxon who always fought side by side, pushed past me with Vidarr shrieking of Thor and Beornoth calling on Christ, and both turned on him with their swords. I felt blood spray on me and the whole alley seemed to be flooding with blood as the huge man collapsed. The spearman was gasping against the other wall and screaming for mercy as others of my wolf pack turned on him. They had no mercy. The rest of the enemy had fled.

'Are you hurt, lord?' Beornoth asked me.

'No! Keep going!'

The huge axeman had been wounded at least three times, but he still struggled to stand again, his face tight with pain or hate. Beornoth finished him by sawing his sword across the man's throat and more blood spattered me. Ulfar, a Dane, had broken his sword and stooped to pick up the axe. 'Keep going!' I bellowed. 'Keep going! Don't let them stand!'

The alley ended in an open space that bordered the stables beneath the sea-facing ramparts. Those ramparts were high, with a wide fighting platform of solid oak on which a dozen of my cousin's men stood. They seemed unsure what to do, though three carried spears that they hurled down at us, but we could see the flight of the weapons and so avoided them easily. The spears clattered uselessly on the stone. The men who had filled the right-hand alley had fled southwards, running to join the defenders of the High Gate that lay beyond a cluster of more storehouses, barns, and barracks. I was about to order my men to attack those buildings and so drive the defenders back to the High Gate, knowing that we could assault that formidable fortification along the rampart's wide fighting platform, but before I could give the orders Finan shouted a warning and I saw that many of the survivors of the brief fight in the alleyways, perhaps thirty or forty men in all, were running north towards the Sea Gate. They were the men who had defended the wider alley that Finan had cleared, and their route south had been blocked by my warriors, so now they fled for the safety of the Sea Gate's strong ramparts. The men who had been watching us from the high fighting platform also ran that way. 'After them!' I bellowed. 'Finan! After them!' He must have heard the despair in my voice because he immediately shouted at his men to run, and led them south.

And I was in despair. I was cursing myself for a fool.

I had left Gerbruht and a small force to defend the Sea Gate, but I should have left more. Gerbruht's dozen men could stave off any attack from the harbour channel by staying on the high fighting platform above the arch, but now they would be assaulted from within the fortress, by men who could unbar and open the gates to let a flood of enemies into Bebbanburg. Gerbruht was a formidable warrior, and his men were experienced, but they would have to leave the high platform and fight to defend the archway against three or four times their number, and I had no faith that Gerbruht would realise what needed to be done. I snatched at Swithun's arm. 'Tell my son to go to the Sea Gate. Fast!'

Swithun ran back through the alley and up the steps while I set off after Finan, still cursing myself. And I was puzzled too. There was something unreal about this day, as if it were a waking dream instead of the fight I had anticipated my entire life. My men were running through the fortress like a pack of aimless hounds, first chasing one stag, then another, without any huntsman to guide them. And that was my fault. I realised that I had spent hours planning how to get into Bebbanburg, but I had not thought what I should do once I was inside. Now the enemy was dictating the battle, and we had been forced to give up the high ground to protect our rear. I was in a daze and making a mess of the day.

And then the mess grew worse. Because I had forgotten about Waldhere.

Waldhere was the commander of my cousin's household troops, the man who had confronted me on the day Einar's ships had first arrived at Bebbanburg. I knew him to be a dangerous enemy, a warrior almost as experienced as I was myself. He had not fought in the great shield wall battles that had driven the Danes out of Wessex and harried them across Mercia, but he had spent years confronting the savage Scottish raiders who thought Bebbanburg's land was their larder. It takes a hard man to fight the Scots for so long and to survive, and there was many a widow in Constantin's country who cursed Waldhere's name. I had last seen him at Dumnoc, where, carried south by Ieremias, he had gone to escort Æthelhelm and Æthelhelm's daughter Ælswyth back to Bebbanburg. They had travelled north on the *Ælfswon*, the largest of the ealdorman's ships and the first of the West Saxon vessels to run ashore in Bebbanburg's harbour channel where she had been rammed and attacked by the Scottish *Trianaid*. Moments later more ships had piled up in the narrow channel, provoking a three-sided fight between Scots, Norsemen, and West Saxons. It had been chaos, and I had thought that chaos could only assist me.

But I had forgotten about Waldhere, and forgotten that he knew Bebbanburg much better than I did. I had only spent the first nine years of my childhood in the fortress, but Waldhere had lived here much longer, his life dedicated to keeping Bebbanburg safe from enemies. Safe from me.

As Waldhere approached the harbour he had seen what was about to happen, that the *Ælfswon* would be attacked by the big *Trianaid*, which, in turn would be assaulted by the ships that crowded behind, and, intent on avoiding that chaotic bloodletting, he had assembled Æthelhelm, Ælswyth, and her maids, with the best part of Æthelhelm's red-cloaked household troops on the *Ælfswon*'s prow. The *Trianaid* had rammed the *Ælfswon*, stoving in one side and crushing warriors beneath the heavy Scottish prow, then the struggle began as the Scots leaped onto the half-wrecked *Ælfswon*, and the savagery spread as more ships piled into the tangle and as the fighting extended onto both shores of the harbour channel. Waldhere ignored the whole struggle, instead leaping from the *Ælfswon*'s bows and leading his group first westwards, then southwards, taking them along the rocky beach under Bebbanburg's landward ramparts. Gerbruht saw them go. 'I thought they were running away,' he was to tell me.

But Waldhere knew Bebbanburg, and he knew that no attack was ever likely on those landward ramparts that were built on the slope of the crag where it rose from the harbour's water. Even if attackers landed from ships they would find the climb dauntingly steep, but all the same there was an entrance there. It was not a gate, there were no steps, just two massive oak trunks that looked exactly like the rest of the wooden palisade. That palisade was built on rock and was not buried in the ground like most ramparts, but instead the massive oak trunks rested directly on the crag's stone. The wall was old and needed constant repair. Those repairs were expensive because the great trunks had to be brought from deep inland, or else shipped from the south, and it was a week's work to replace even one of them. 'One day,' my father had said, 'we'll make the wall of stone. The whole wall! All the way around.' My cousin had started that work, but never finished it, and the west-facing ramparts above the harbour, which was the least likely place to be attacked, was where the two trunks stood. They were not pegged to the rest of the wall nor strengthened by lateral beams, which stiffened the rest of the ramparts, instead they were held in place by massive iron nails that were driven into the high fighting platform, but by seizing their lower parts the two trunks could be pulled outwards to make a small hole through which a man could crawl. The approach to the two oak trunks was steep and made even less inviting because the fortress's latrines were on the ramparts above. When the wind came from the west the stench was dreadful, but that same stench kept folk away from the secret entrance. A besieging enemy would watch Bebbanburg's gates, not knowing that the garrison had another place from which men could sally or, as on that day, infiltrate the fortress.

I knew of the old sallyport beneath the sea-facing ramparts. My father had made it, and I had considered the chances of sneaking into the fortress by climbing from the beach to that secret opening. That was how I had captured Dunholm, by ignoring the massive defences at the fort's entrance and slipping men through a small gate that gave the garrison access to a spring, a gate the defenders had thought too difficult to approach. But my father's old sallyport truly was too difficult. Reaching it meant a long and steep climb from the beach, almost impossible for a man in mail carrying a shield and weapons. Besides, once the fortress was under attack, it was a simple job to block the sallyport from the inside, and so I had dismissed the idea of even trying to use it.

But I did not know of the new entrance on the western side. I had no men spying for me inside Bebbanburg, no one to tell me of the new sallyport, or to tell me that the new one was even more dangerous than the old because, once through the gap, a man was hidden by the rock that climbed sharply inside the wall. So now, unknown to me, Waldhere dragged the trunks outwards and Æthelhelm and his red-cloaked warriors filed through. They gathered in the shadowed space beneath the fighting platform, close to the great hall, and we did not see them, smell them, hear them, or know they were there.

Because we were trying to clear up the first mess I had made. We were fighting to regain the Sea Gate.

Gerbruht had never impressed me as a clever man. He was huge, he was strong, he was loyal, and he was cheerful and there were very few men I would rather have beside me in a shield wall, but he was not a quick thinker like Finan, nor decisive like my son. I had left him to guard the Sea Gate because I had thought it a straightforward task, well suited to Gerbruht's stubborn, slow nature, and I had never anticipated that he would have to make a swift and crucial decision.

But he made it. And he made the right decision.

Neither Æthelhelm's men, nor the Scots with their Norse allies, had attempted to storm the Sea Gate. It would have been a massive task, though not impossible if they had used the ships' masts as makeshift ladders. That would have taken the rest of the day to organise, and they had no time, they were too busy fighting each other, and the few who had strayed up the rock steps had been met by more rocks hurled down by Gerbruht and his men high above.

Now, suddenly, Gerbruht saw my cousin's men streaming down from the higher gate and he understood the danger immediately. The panicked men could unbar the lower gate and let in a horde of enemy, and so Gerbruht abandoned his high platform and took his men down to make a shield wall in the archway.

My cousin's men had been bloodied in the alleyways where they had been torn apart by the sheer savagery of our assault, and now they were looking for refuge. They could not reach the great hall, I had barred their route to the southern gates, where, I suspected, my cousin was gathering his forces, and so they had fled northwards. The great stone fortifications of the Sea Gate promised them safety, and so they headed that way, and then they saw Gerbruht's wall forming. It was a small shield wall, but it filled the width of the gate's archway and it offered death to the first men brave enough to make an assault. The fugitives hesitated.

No one led them. No one told them what to do. The church bell was still ringing its panic, there were sounds of fighting beyond the Sea Gate, and so, leaderless and scared, they paused.

And Finan struck them from behind.

Finan, knowing better than anyone what slaughter would follow if the Sea Gate was opened, did not wait to form his men into a wall, instead he just fell on the enemy with Irish fury, keening his crazed battle song. He had the advantage of the high ground, he sensed the enemy's fear, and he gave them no time to understand the advantage they possessed. They had allies in Æthelhelm's hard-pressed survivors beyond the gate, and all they needed to do was overcome Gerbruht's dozen men, unbar the doors, and push them outwards, but instead they died. Finan's men, with the cruelty of warriors finding a terrified enemy at their mercy, showed none. They turned the rock steps into a flight of blood, and Gerbruht, seeing the slaughter, led his men out of the arch and attacked uphill. By the time I reached the upper gate my cousin's men were all either dead or captive. 'Do we want prisoners?' Finan shouted up to me. There were about thirty men kneeling, most holding out their hands to show they had no weapons. About half that many were dead or dying, cut down by Finan's ferocious attack. Not one of his men, so far as I could see, had even been wounded.

I did not want prisoners, but nor did I want to kill these men, some of whom were scarcely more than boys. Many were doubtless the sons of Bebbanburg's tenants, or the grandsons of folk I had known as a child. If I won this day then they would be my people, my tenants, even my warriors, but before I could shout an answer to Finan there was a hammering on the gate. 'Gerbruht!' I shouted. 'Get your men back on the fighting platform!'

'Yes, lord!'

'And Gerbruht! Well done!'

A voice shouted from outside the Sea Gate. 'For pity's sake! Let us in!' The man beat on the gate again. I suspected that he was a survivor from among those of Æthelhelm's men who had stayed to defend the ships and who had been cut down by the Scots and by Einar's Norsemen. I shared Finan's pity for them. They had been brought to this raw coast only to find themselves thrown into a merciless battle against savage northerners. It would have been a mercy to open the gate and let the last survivors inside, and some of those West Saxons might even have fought for me, but that was a risk I dared not take. The Sea Gate had to stay closed, and that meant Æthelhelm's men trapped outside the wall must die and that our prisoners had to remain inside the fortress. 'Finan,' I called, 'strip the prisoners naked! Throw their weapons over the wall!' I would have preferred to send the captives out of the fortress, but that would have condemned them. Stripping and disarming them would be enough. It would leave them helpless.

The hammering on the gate had stopped and I heard a bellow of rage as Gerbruht hurled a stone from the ramparts. A man shouted a curse in Norse, which told me that only Einar's men and the Scots, both of them my cousin's enemy, were now outside the Sea Gate. 'Guard it well!' I shouted to Gerbruht.

'They'll not get inside, lord!' he called back. I believed him.

'Father,' my son had pushed through the men crowded at the upper gate and touched my mailed arm, 'you'd better come.'

I followed him back through the upper gate to see that a shield wall had formed across the centre of the fortress. The wall began just beneath the high crag on which the church and the great hall were built and stretched all the way to the sea-facing ramparts. A banner flew at the line's centre, my banner of the wolf's head, and beneath it was my cousin who had at last assembled his forces. His men were clashing their swords against their shields and stamping their feet. There were still more men making a smaller shield wall by the church, and both walls were uphill of us. 'How many?' I asked.

'A hundred and eighty on the lower rock,' my son said, 'and thirty up by the church.'

'Just about equal numbers then,' I said.

'It's a good thing you can't count,' my son said, sounding more amused than he had any right to be, 'and there's more of the bastards,' he added as a large group of men pushed into the centre of my cousin's shield wall, which spread apart to make room for them. I guessed those men had been garrisoning the High Gate, and my cousin had summoned them, trusting the guards at the Low Gate to deter any assault by the Scots. I could see my cousin more clearly now. He had mounted a horse and was joined by three other riders, all of them behind the banner at the centre of the larger shield wall on the lower rock. 'He's become fat,' I said.

'Fat?'

'My cousin.' He looked heavy on his big horse. He was too far away for me to see his face framed by his helmet, but I could see he was just staring at us as his men clashed their blades against their shields. 'We'll take him first,' I said vengefully. 'We'll kill the bastard and see if his men have any fight left in them.'

My son said nothing for a heartbeat. Then I saw he was staring at Bebbanburg's summit. 'Oh, sweet galloping Christ,' he said.

Because the leaping stag had come to Bebbanburg.

'How in God's name did they get inside?' my son asked,

no amusement in his voice now, only astonishment, because Æthelhelm's red-cloaked men were appearing on the fortress's high crag. They were in mail, they made a new shield wall, and they cheered when they saw how few we were. Finan's men were still out of their sight, down the steps by the Sea Gate, and Æthelhelm's troops must have believed we numbered fewer than a hundred men. 'How in God's name did they get inside?' my son asked again.

I had no answer, so said nothing. Instead I counted the red-cloaked warriors and saw there were at least sixty men, and still more men were coming from the fortress's southern end to join my cousin's shield wall. My cousin, heartened by the arrival of his ally, was shouting at his men, as were two priests who harangued the thickening wall, doubtless telling them it was the nailed god's wish that we should all die. Above him, on the heights of the fortress, Æthelhelm stood tall in a dark cloak and bright mail. He too had a priest, who walked along the growing shield wall offering his god's blessing on the household warriors who were readying to kill us.

There were vengeful Norsemen waiting outside the gate, and death making two shield walls inside. I had fought badly so far, leading my men in wasteful attacks, and then been forced into a panicked retreat. Worse, I had given my enemy time to recover from his surprise and form his troops, but suddenly, as I saw that enemy ready and waiting, I felt alive. I had been wounded in the right thigh, stabbed by the spearman who had died screaming in the alley, and I touched my fingers to the wound and they came away bloody. I touched the blood to my cheek-pieces and then held the fingers to the sky. 'For you, Thor! For you!'

'You're wounded,' my son said.

'It's nothing,' I said, then laughed. I remember laughing at that moment, and I remember my son frowning at me in puzzlement. What I remember best of all, though, was the sudden certainty that the gods were with me, that they would fight for me, that my sword would be their sword. 'We're going to win,' I told my son. I felt as if Odin or Thor had touched me. I had never felt more alive and never felt more certain. I knew there would be no more mistakes and that this was no dream.

I had come to Bebbanburg and Bebbanburg would be mine.

'Rorik!' I called. 'You have your horn?'

'Yes, lord.'

I pushed through my men, going back through the upper gate. Finan had taken fifty men down the steps to rescue Gerbruht's small group, and those fifty were still there, hurling the prisoners' weapons, mail coats and clothing across the high stone wall.

And I realised that men often see what they want to see. My cousin could see about a hundred of us huddled by the northern gate, and it must have seemed to him that we had retreated and were now caught between his overpowering force and the vicious Norsemen outside. He saw victory.

Æthelhelm saw the same. He could count, and he could see that we were outnumbered and on the lower ground. He could see we were trapped, and as the sun sank towards the western hills he must have known the elation of imminent revenge.

Except I had woken from my unreal daze. Suddenly I knew how my wolves would fight for the rest of this day. 'Finan,' I called, 'keep your men out of sight till you hear the horn! Then leave six men to help Gerbruht and bring the rest to join us. You'll be a rearguard!' There was no need to explain further. Finan, when he led his men up out of the shadows, would see what I wanted him to do. He nodded, and just at that moment the church bell, which had been tolling ever since we broke into the fortress, stopped, and my cousin's men gave a loud cheer.

'What's happening?' Finan asked.

'Æthelhelm got in somehow. With maybe sixty or seventy men? We're outnumbered.'

'Badly?'

'Badly enough.'

Finan must have sensed my mood because he offered me a wide grin, or maybe he was just trying to encourage his men, who were all listening. 'So that bastard Æthelhelm is here,' he called up to me. 'We're outnumbered and they have the high ground. Does that mean we're attacking?'

'Of course it does!' I shouted back. 'Wait for two blasts of the horn, then come!'

'We'll be there!' he called, then turned away to hurry his men, who were shepherding naked prisoners into the gully between the rock and the outer wall.

A horn sounded. Not mine, but coming from the centre of the fortress. It sounded a long and mournful note and I thought my cousin must be advancing his wall, but when I went back through the upper gate I saw that it heralded a single horseman who approached us. The hooves of his big stallion sounded loud on the rock. He was still some distance away, walking the horse slowly, and his face was hidden by cheek-pieces. For a moment I hoped it was my cousin, but he was still with his shield wall, and I could see Æthelhelm among the dark red cloaks on the high ground. So the approaching warrior had to be a champion, sent to taunt us.

I turned my back on him and looked for my son. 'How many of our men have spears?' I asked him.

'Maybe ten? Not too many.'

I chided myself for not thinking of spears sooner, because

doubtless Finan's men had just hurled a few over the outer wall, but ten should be enough. 'When we attack,' I told my son, 'put those spearmen in the second rank. They won't need shields.' I did not wait for his response, but walked to meet the horseman.

It was Waldhere, who had arrived with Æthelhelm, but who must have joined my cousin as soon as he could. He curbed the horse some twenty paces from my shield wall and opened his cheek-pieces so that I could see his face. He wore the same bearskin cloak he had worn on the day of Einar's arrival. The heavy garment must have been hot, but it made him look huge, especially on horseback. His hard face was framed by his battle-scarred helmet that was crowned with an eagle's clawed foot, while his mail-clad forearms, like mine, were ringed with gold. He was a warrior in his glory and he watched as I approached, then picked something from his yellow teeth and flicked whatever he found towards me. 'Lord Uhtred,' he said, meaning my cousin, 'offers you the chance to surrender now.'

'He didn't dare come and tell me that himself?' I asked.

'Lord Uhtred doesn't talk to earslings.'

'He talks to you.'

For some reason that mild insult made him angry. I saw the grimace and heard the suppressed fury in his voice. 'You want me to kill you now?' he growled.

'Yes,' I said, 'please.'

He sneered at that and shook his head. 'I would kill you with pleasure,' he said, 'but Lord Uhtred and Lord Æthelhelm want you kept alive. Your death will be their entertainment in the hall tonight.'

'Get off your horse and fight me,' I responded, 'because your death will entertain my men.'

'If you surrender now,' he went on, ignoring my challenge, 'your death will be quick.'

I laughed at him. 'Too frightened to face me, Waldhere?'
He just spat at me for answer.

I turned my back on him. 'This is Waldhere,' I shouted
at my men, 'and he's too frightened to fight me! I've offered,
and he refused. He's a coward!'

'Then fight me instead!' My son walked out of the shield
wall.

In truth I did not want any of us to fight Waldhere, not
because I feared his skill, but because I wanted to attack the
enemy before they found their courage. The men who faced
us, who clashed their swords against their shields, were not
cowards, but men must summon the resolve to advance into
death's embrace. We all fear the shield wall, only a fool
would say otherwise, but my men were ready for the horror,
and my cousin's men were only just recovering from the
shock of realising they must fight for their lives in this late
afternoon. The church bell had jarred them into panic. They
had expected another dull evening, instead they faced death,
and it takes a man time to ready himself for that meeting.
Besides, they knew who I was, they knew my reputation.
Their priests and leaders were telling them they would win,
but their fears were telling them that I did not lose, and I
wanted to attack while those fears gnawed at their courage,
and fighting Waldhere delayed that attack. Which was why
he had ridden to us, of course. His demand that we surrender,
a demand he knew I would reject, was to give the defenders
time to summon their resolve. And his riding alone to
confront me showed those defenders he did not fear us. It
was all a part of the dance of death that always precedes
battle. 'And who,' he asked my son, 'are you?'

'Uhtred of Bebbanburg,' my son answered.

'I don't fight puppies,' he sneered. His horse, a fine grey,
suddenly tossed his head and skittered sideways on the rock.
Waldhere calmed the stallion. 'If you surrender,' he spoke

to me now, but loudly enough for my men to hear, 'then your warriors will live.' He raised his voice to make absolutely certain that all of my men could hear the offer repeated. 'Lay your weapons down! Lay your shields down, and you will live! You will be given safe passage south! Lay down your shields and live!'

There was a clatter behind me as a shield hit the rock. I turned, appalled, to see the tall man wearing the dark blue cloak and the fine silver helmet stride from the shield wall. He had his cheek-pieces closed, obscuring his face. He had thrown down his shield and now walked towards Waldhere. Finan had told me that this was Kettil, the young and fastidious Dane. 'Kettil!' I snarled.

'Yes, lord?' Kettil answered from behind me. I turned, frowning, to see Kettil in an iron helmet and wearing no cloak. 'Lord?' he asked, puzzled.

I looked back to the tall man. His helmet, I could see now, was chased with a pattern of interlocking Christian crosses, while another cross, forged from gold, hung at his breast. Kettil was a pagan and would never wear such things. I was about to demand that the coward pick up his damned shield and take his place back in the wall, but before I could speak he drew his long-sword and pointed it at Waldhere. 'This puppy,' the man said, 'would fight you.' He had not thrown down his shield as a sign of surrender, but because Waldhere carried no shield and he would offer the horseman a fair fight. 'If you have the courage to face me,' he went on, 'which I doubt.'

'No!' I shouted.

Waldhere glanced at me, puzzled and intrigued by my response to the tall man's offer to fight. 'Are you frightened I'll kill your puppy?' Waldhere sneered at me.

'Fight me!' I almost begged him. 'Fight me! Not him!'

He laughed at me. He did not know why I was suddenly

so agitated, but he had understood that I did not want him to fight the tall man who had defied him, and so, of course, he accepted the challenge. 'Come, puppy,' he said, then swung down from his saddle. He unhooked the cloak's clasp and let it fall so that its weight did not obstruct his sword arm.

I seized the tall man's arm. 'No! I forbid it!'

The dark eyes in the helmet's shadow looked at me calmly. 'I am your prince,' he said, 'you do not command me.'

'What are you doing here?' I demanded.

'I'm killing this impudent man,' Æthelstan said, 'of course.'

I heard the hiss as Waldhere drew his sword from its scabbard, and I tightened my grip on Æthelstan's arm. 'You can't do this!' I said.

He gently removed my hand. 'You command men, Lord Uhtred,' he said, 'and you command armies, but you do not command princes. I obey God and I obey my father and I no longer obey you. You should obey me, so now let me do my duty. You're in a hurry to win this battle, aren't you? So why waste time?' He pushed me gently away, then walked towards Waldhere. 'I am Æthelstan,' he said, 'Prince of Wessex, and you can lay down your sword and swear me loyalty.'

'I can gut you like the scrawny puppy you are,' Waldhere snarled, and, because Æthelstan was holding his sword low, Waldhere attacked fast, striking high, wanting the fight to be over in a heartbeat.

Waldhere was a big man, tall, broad-chested, solid, and muscled. Æthelstan matched his opponent's height, but he was thin like his grandfather Alfred. He looked frail beside Waldhere, though I knew that frailty was deceptive. He was sinewy and quick. Waldhere's opening stroke was a lunge at Æthelstan's throat, and it was fast. To those of us watching it seemed destined to slit Æthelstan's gullet, but he just swayed aside, almost contemptuously, and did not even bother to lift his blade as Waldhere's sword slid past his neck. It touched, but did not break his mail coif. 'Are you ready to begin yet?' he taunted Waldhere.

Waldhere's answer was a second attack. He wanted to use his weight to beat Æthelstan down. He had brought his blade back fast and still Æthelstan did not raise his sword, and Waldhere bellowed like a bull in heat and used both hands to ram the sword at Æthelstan's belly, charging at the same time, reckoning to skewer the prince and drive him to the ground where he could rip Æthelstan's guts to bloody shreds. He must have weighed twice what the younger man weighed, and he saw his blade going where he aimed it and the bellow turned into a shout of victory, then suddenly the blade was deflected as Æthelstan used his left hand to parry the lunge. That parry should have torn his hands bloody, even severed his fingers, but he wore a glove that had iron strips sewn into the leather. 'A trick,' he was to tell me, 'that Steapa taught me.' And as Waldhere's sword slid uselessly into air, Æthelstan punched his sword hilt into Waldhere's face. 'A trick,' he later said, 'that you taught me.'

He hit hard. I heard the blow and saw the blood from Waldhere's broken nose. I saw Waldhere stagger away, not because he had been beaten off balance, but because he could not see. The pommel of Æthelstan's sword had struck his left eye, destroying it, and the pain was confusing what was left of his vision. He turned, bringing his sword back, but the blow was weak, and Æthelstan swatted it aside and then shouted his own cry of victory as he made his one stroke of the fight. It was a back-handed swing and it crunched into Waldhere's neck and I saw Æthelstan grimace with the effort of dragging the blade back, sawing it as it broke through the mail coif, as it broke skin and muscle, as it severed the big blood vessels and so sliced to the big man's spine. There was a spray of blood that soaked Æthelstan's fine helmet, a red mist that the men watching the fight from the heart of the fortress could see plainly. And they could see their champion fall.

The sound of blades beating on shields had faltered, then stopped altogether as Waldhere staggered away from Æthelstan. The big man dropped his sword, put both hands to his neck, then collapsed to his knees. For a heartbeat he looked at Æthelstan with a puzzled expression, then fell forward and twitched his last beside his discarded cloak. My men were cheering as Æthelstan walked to the dead man's horse and hauled himself into the saddle. He rode a few paces towards the enemy, flaunting his victory, then cleaned his sword-blade on the grey stallion's mane.

'Now!' I shouted. 'Spearmen in the second rank! And follow me!'

We had wasted enough time. Now we had a battle to fight and a fortress to win and I knew just how to win it.

So we attacked.

There were two ways I could attack. One was to advance into the face of my cousin's shield wall, while the other was to use the long rugged ramp that led to the great hall, the route we had taken when we first entered the fortress. Once at the top of that ramp we would have to assault Æthelhelm's household warriors who waited at the head of the steep rock stairs. That would be a nasty business. Attacking uphill is always grim, and the steeper the climb, the nastier it is. The alternative was to charge my cousin's long wall. Most of that wall was two ranks, in places three, and a shield wall of two or three ranks is broken far more easily than a wall of four, five, or even six ranks. I wanted to advance with at least four ranks, so my wall would have no great width, and though I was confident my fierce wolves would smash their bloody way through the centre of my cousin's thinner wall, the sight of my short wall advancing would bring Æthelhelm's battle-hardened household warriors down from the fortress's summit. And while we were cutting though the centre, the wings of the enemy would wrap around us. All of the enemy's forces would be in the same place, surrounding us, and though that did not mean we would be defeated, it would be a bloody and prolonged fight and the casualties would be higher than in a short and savage attack, so there really was no choice. We had to do it the hard way.

We would attack Æthelhelm's men at the top of the ramp and face the prospect of fighting men who held the high ground, and who could beat axes and swords down on our heads. My cousin, seeing us use the ramp, could not readily reinforce Æthelhelm's troops because there simply was not enough room on the rock ledges outside the great hall and the church. What he would do, I reckoned, was follow me up the ramp. He would hurry his men to where we now stood and then assault our rear, and that is what I wanted because then I would have divided my enemy into two. And I would have two shield walls, one facing uphill to attack Æthelhelm, and my rearmost ranks facing downhill to beat off my cousin. And those ranks would fill the width of the ramp. We could not be outflanked.

The enemy had begun beating their swords against their shields again, though at first the sound was half-hearted and I heard men shouting at the troops to beat harder. Dogs were howling deeper in the fortress. The sun was almost touching the western skyline. I hefted my shield, then touched Serpent-Breath's hilt to my closed cheek-pieces. Be with me, I prayed to Thor. 'We're attacking Æthelhelm first,' I told my men, 'then we'll finish off the other bastards. Are you ready?'

They roared their assent. They were good, so good, like

hounds desperate to be unleashed, and now I led them to my right, to the ramp. 'Keep your ranks tight!' I shouted, though I had no need to give that command, because they already knew. We had nine ranks moving steadily up the ramp, a tight mass of men sheathed in mail; helmeted men, nervous, excited, confident, frightened, eager men. There was little I could teach them about the shield wall, we had been in too many, though on that evening we would do one thing differently. I turned to the second rank, who normally would have used their shields to protect the front rank, but this second rank had no shields. Instead they carried the long and heavy spears. 'Keep your spears low,' I told them, 'keep them hidden if you can.'

I saw that Æthelstan was still on horseback, riding just behind my rearmost rank. 'I suppose you brought him,' I accused my son, who was on my right. I knew he and Æthelstan were friends.

He grinned. 'He insisted.'

'And you hid him?'

'Not exactly, you just didn't look for him.'

'You're an idiot.'

'Men often tell me I'm like you, father.'

We climbed a short flight of three rock steps. Æthelhelm's men were chanting and beating blades. I could see a priest holding his hands high, calling on the nailed god to destroy us.

'You're an idiot,' I told my son again, 'but keep him alive and I'll forgive you.' I turned back again, 'Rorik!'

'Lord?'

'Sound the horn now! Two blasts!'

The sound of the first blast echoed back from the crag ahead as the second note sounded. Finan must have been waiting, poised, because his men appeared immediately, streaming from the upper gate towards the base of the ramp.

By now we were a hundred paces, perhaps slightly more, from the steep steps where Æthelhelm's men waited. His front rank was fifteen men, their shields overlapping, their faces masks of metal. That front rank was no longer beating swords against shields, though the men behind were. The priest turned and spat towards us and I saw it was Father Herefrith, my enemy from Hornecastre. His scarred face was twisted with anger and I could see a mail coat showing beneath the neckline of his priestly robe. He was brandishing a sword. So the church had not disciplined him, and he was here as one of Æthelhelm's sorcerers. He was shouting, but I could not hear what insults or curses he hurled, but nor did I care because the older gods were with me, and Herefrith was doomed.

I looked to my right and saw, in the shadow of the hills, a crowd, mostly women and children, watching from the harbour's far shore. Almost all were gazing towards us, which told me that Domnall had not made a move against the Low Gate. A few, very few, had walked northwards to see what happened at the Sea Gate, but even those folk were now staring to see what happened at the fortress's summit, so Gerbruht and his men were still secure, and the battle would be here, on the stony ramp that led to Bebbanburg's summit.

Æthelhelm's men held that summit. They appeared formidable, a wall of iron-rimmed willow and sharpened steel, but Waldhere's swift death must have shaken them. Yet Æthelhelm would have reason for confidence. We were attacking uphill, and the final stretch was a stairway of stone, as steep as the earthen bank of any fortress. Æthelhelm would be convinced I had made a mistake, that I was leading my warriors into a place of death, and he also knew that my cousin, seeing how few we were, was bringing his men to our rear. We would be fighting up a steep slope, assailed from the front and the back, and I glanced left and saw my cousin, still on horseback, urging his long shield wall forward.

Finan's men were hurrying to catch us now. By leaving the Sea Gate he opened it to my cousin's attack, but by now only my cousin's enemies waited outside that gate and to open it would be to invite a flood of Scots and Norsemen into the fortress. My cousin would not want the Sea Gate open, not till he had finished with me and felt confident enough to attack the men outside. So he would finish me first and wanted to finish me fast.

He must have thought the battle would be over quickly because men see what they want to see, and my cousin had seen how small my force was and that had encouraged him to advance his wall, but suddenly Finan and his men had appeared, and the sight of those reinforcements had made his shield wall hesitate. Finan was bellowing at his men to form ranks behind mine, and I heard my cousin shout at his men. 'Keep going! Keep going! God will give us victory!' His voice was shrill. Close to two hundred men were now hurrying to enter the ramp behind us. 'For Saint Oswald and for Bebbanburg!' my cousin shouted. I noticed he was not in the front rank, but far behind, towards the rear. He was still mounted, the only horseman now among the troops who came to assault our rear.

So I had the battle I wanted. Instead of hunting the garrison through the maze of Bebbanburg's buildings I had them concentrated in front of me and gathering behind me. All we had to do now was kill them. I turned to make certain that the spearmen were carrying their spears low. They were. 'Listen,' I called to them, but not nearly loud enough for the enemy waiting ahead to hear me, 'men fighting downhill don't hold their shields low. They'll fight as they always fight. They'll hold their shields to cover the bellies and balls, and that means you'll have a clear path to their legs. Thrust as high as you can. Go for their thighs and cripple the bastards. You cripple them and we'll kill them.'

'God and Saint Oswald!' a man shouted from my cousin's ranks. They were all behind us now, though a handful of my cousin's men had been sent to thicken Æthelhelm's ranks. I reckoned there were close to a hundred and fifty men at the top of the steps, forming a shield wall some five or six ranks deep in front of the church. There were more men than that behind us, but neither they nor the enemy above could outflank us, and now, with Finan's men added to mine, we had fifteen ranks. We were formidable. The enemy had seen their champion die and they knew they were fighting Uhtred of Bebbanburg. Many of the men in Æthelhelm's ranks had fought in armies that I had led. Those men knew me, and the last thing they wanted was to fight my wolf pack on a summer's evening.

Æthelhelm's red-cloaked warriors waited, their shields overlapping, and, as I had foreseen, they were holding those shields high. I could see their faces clearly now, could see them watching their death march closer. These men were experienced, like us they had fought in the long war to drive the Danes from Mercia and East Anglia, but we had fought more often and for longer. We were the wolf pack, we were the killers of Britain, we had fought from the south coast of Wessex to the northern wilds, from the ocean to the sea, and we had never been beaten, and these men knew it. They saw our war axes reflecting the lowering sun, saw the swords, saw how steadily we advanced. We were approaching that final flight of steps, keeping our shields overlapped, our blades low, and our pace slow but relentless. A man in Æthelhelm's front rank vomited and his shield wavered.

'Now!' I roared. 'Kill them!'

We charged.

Even in a nervous enemy there are always some men who welcome battle, who have no fear, who come alive in the horror. It was one of those who killed Swithun, who, like all of us in the leading rank, held his shield high and crouched beneath its shelter to receive the blow we knew was coming. Perhaps Swithun tripped on the steps, or else bent too far forward, because an axeman buried his blade in the base of Swithun's spine. I did not see it, though I heard Swithun wail. I was crouching, holding my shield above my head and keeping Wasp-Sting ready. Serpent-Breath was in her scabbard and would stay there until the shield wall ahead was broken. In the close business of killing men whose last breath you can smell there is no weapon as good as a seax, a short-sword.

We had taken the steps at a run, raised our shields, and the enemy had hammered those shields with a shout of rage and victory. Swithun died, as did Ulfar, a Dane, and poor Edric, who had once been my servant. A ringing blow struck my shield boss, but not hard enough to drive me down to my knees, and I reckoned it had to have been a sword that hit me. If Waldhere had lived, or if Æthelhelm had known his business, he would have packed the front rank with heavy, brutal war axes that would beat us down like cattle being slaughtered before the winter cold. Instead they mostly used swords, and a sword is not a beating weapon. It can slash or pierce, but to batter an enemy into a mess of broken bone, of blood and butchered flesh, there is nothing to rival a lead-weighted axe. Whoever struck at me had dented the iron boss of my willow shield, but it was the last stroke he gave on this earth. I was already pushing upwards and bringing Wasp-Sting up, feeling her pierce mail, feeling her break through the tough layer of muscle to reach the softness inside. I kept pushing with the shield and twisting the blade so it did not stick in the enemy's guts, and a spear came from behind me, lancing between me and my son to grind its blade in an enemy's upper thigh and I saw the blood run from the wound, and that man staggered, the man I was gouging with Wasp-Sting fell, and the ranks behind me were heaving forward, and I suppose, though I do not remember it, that we were roaring our battle shout.

I reached the top step. There were bodies obstructing me. Step over them. Another blow hit my shield hard enough to tilt it to one side, but Berg was on my left and his shield steadied mine. I rammed Wasp-Sting forward, felt her hit wood, brought her back and thrust her lower, this time feeling mail and flesh. A bearded man was screaming at me over the rim of my shield and his scream turned to open-mouthed agony as Berg's seax found his ribs. On my right my son was shrieking as he stabbed his seax between two enemy shields. The man Berg had wounded went down, and I stepped over him. The spearman behind me killed him then thrust the spear past me again, driving the blade into an enemy's groin. That man screamed horribly, dropped his shield, bent over the blood splashing on the stone, and I rammed Wasp-Sting down his back, raking his spine, and he fell. I stamped on his head, stepped over him. Two, maybe three ranks of the enemy were down. Step forward again, hold the shield steady. Peer over the top. Fear is screaming somewhere deep. Ignore it. You can smell the shit now. Shit and blood, the stench of glory. The enemy is more frightened. Kill them. Keep the shields steady. Kill.

A young man with a wispy beard swung at me with a sword. Thank you, I thought, because to swing he had to move his shield aside, and he died with Wasp-Sting in his chest. She drove through his mail like an augur piercing butter. Hours of practice went into that young man's death. My men were roaring. A sword struck my helmet, another hammered into my shield. Berg killed the man who had swung at my helmet. You do not swing in a shield wall, you stab. May the gods ever send me enemies who swing their blades. The man who stabbed at my shield was going backwards, his eyes huge with fear. I tripped on a body, went down to one knee and parried a spear-thrust from my right. It was a feeble thrust because the man was stepping backwards as he lunged. I stood and rammed Wasp-Sting towards the man who had struck my shield, then suddenly flicked her right to slice her blade across the spearman's eyes. Brought her back and drove her at the first man, who was shaking with terror. Wasp-Sting found his throat, drenched me with blood. I was shouting myself hoarse, hurling curses at an enemy who were discovering what it was to fight my wolves. I lowered my shield slightly and saw Æthelhelm wide-eyed against the wall of the church with his daughter, pale and frail, at his side. He had his arm around her. Cerdic thrust me aside. He had dropped his spear and found a war axe. He carried no shield. He just ran at the enemy, a big man filled with the battle rage, and the axe split a shield in two and he shook it off and thrust the blade into the face of the man behind. The blunt blow was so strong that the man's face was turned into a mess of blood. We stepped up to protect Cerdic. 'They're breaking!' my son said. Cerdic was screaming with anger, swinging the massive axe to beat men aside. One of his blows even hit my shield, but he was unstoppable that day. A red-cloaked man lunged at Cerdic with a sword, but Wasp-Sting slid into his open mouth and I twisted as I thrust it deeper. I was still screaming at the enemy, promising them death. I was Thor, I was Odin, I was the lord of battle.

Æthelstan had brought his horse to the foot of the corpse-littered steps. He had opened his cheek-pieces and stood in his stirrups with his blood-stained sword held high. 'I am your prince!' he shouted. 'Go into the church and you live!' Æthelhelm gaped at him. 'I am your prince!' Æthelstan shouted again and again. His grey horse was dappled red with blood. 'Go into the church and you live! Drop your weapons! Go into the church!'

Hrothard stepped in front of Æthelhelm. Hrothard! He was bellowing like me, his sword was reddened, his shield splintered with a sheet of blood spattered across the leaping stag. 'He's mine!' I shouted, but my son shouldered me aside and ran at the tall man, who rammed his shield forward and lunged his sword under the shield to strike my son's legs, but Uhtred lowered his shield fast, deflecting the blow, and slashed at Hrothard, who parried it, and the clash of swords was like a bell sounding. Hrothard was spitting curses, my son was smiling. The swords clashed again. Men were watching. Red-cloaked men had dropped their weapons, were holding their hands out to show they yielded, and they watched as the blades moved so fast it was impossible to count each stroke, two craftsmen at their work, then my son staggered. Hrothard saw the opening and lunged and Uhtred turned inside the lunge, the stagger a feint, and he was behind Hrothard now and his sword was at Hrothard's throat and it sliced. The air misted with blood and Hrothard fell.

Father Herefrith was shouting at Æthelhelm's men to fight on. 'God is with you! You cannot lose! Kill them! Kill the pagan! Christ is with you! Kill the pagan!' He meant me.

Æthelhelm and his daughter were gone. I did not see them run. A man made a feeble thrust at me with a spear and I swept it aside with my shield, stepped close and drove Wasp-Sting deep. He gasped into my face, sobbed, and I cursed him as I ripped the blade upwards, gutting him, and he made a mewing noise as he fell.

And Herefrith, seeing my seax trapped in the dying man's guts, charged me. My son stopped him, using his shield to throw the priest back against the church wall. My son was a Christian, or so he claimed, and to kill a priest would condemn his soul to eternal flames, so he was content just to thrust the big priest away, but I had no fear of the Christian hell. I let go of Wasp-Sting and picked up the spear that the dying man had thrust so feebly. 'Herefrith!' I shouted, 'meet your god!' And I ran at him, spear levelled, and his sword's parry did not deflect the blade by a hand's width and the spear went through his robe, through his mail, and into his belly and through his spine until the spear's point jarred and bent against the church's stone wall that was smeared, streaked, and running with his blood. I left him with the spear still inside him, left him there to die. 'They've broken!' My son was at my side. 'They've broken, father!'

'They're not beaten yet,' I snarled. I tugged Wasp-Sting from the corpse and looked back down the ramp to see my cousin was watching, not fighting. He saw Finan's shield wall waiting for his attack and he saw his ally's men broken and running. His men were halfway up the ramp, and they had seen our savagery, and the fear was beating in them like the wings of a captured bird. 'Lord Prince,' I said to Æthelstan, who was still at the foot of the steps behind Finan's men.

'Lord Uhtred?'

'Keep twenty men.' My voice was hoarse, my throat sore from shouting. 'Guard this place. And stay alive, damn you. Stay alive!'

And the battle-rage was in me. I had so nearly lost this fight. I had been careless at the opening, almost losing the Sea Gate, and I had been lucky. I gripped Wasp-Sting's hilt and thanked the gods for their favour, and now I would do what I had sworn to do so many years ago. I would kill the usurper. 'Finan!'

'Lord?'

'We're going to slaughter these bastards!' I strode to the top of the ramp, to the top step that was red with blood, just as the western sky was drenched with the scarlet of day's end. I was shouting so that my cousin's men could hear me. 'We are going to soak this rock with blood! I am Uhtred! I am the lord here. This is my rock!' I went down the steps, pushing through Finan's tight ranks. 'This is my rock!' I thrust Wasp-Sting at Rorik, and drew Serpent-Breath. I reckoned this last and bigger shield wall would not stand. From now it would be a slaughter, and Serpent-Breath was thirsty.

I stood beside Finan in what had been our rear rank and was now our front rank. My cousin was on horseback, some six or seven ranks behind his own leading men, and those men saw me smile. I had unlaced my cheek-pieces, let them see the blood on my face, see the blood on my mail, the blood on my hands. I was a man of gold and of blood. I was a lord of war and I was filled with the rage of battle. The enemy were ten paces away and I walked five of those paces so that I stood alone, facing them. 'This,' I snarled at them, 'is my rock.'

None moved. I could see the fear in them, smell it. 'Steady,' I heard Finan call, 'steady!' His men were edging forward, yearning to kill.

'I am Uhtred,' I told my enemy, 'Uhtred of Bebbanburg.' They knew who I was. My cousin had scorned me for years, but these men had heard the whispered stories of faraway battles. Now I was in their face, and I lifted Serpent-Breath to point her blade at my cousin. 'You and me,' I shouted.

He did not answer.

'You and me!' I called again. 'No one else needs die! Just you and me!'

He just stared at me. His helmet, I saw, had a wolf's tail hanging from the crown. There was gold at his neck and gold on his bridle. He was plump, the mail coat stretched tight over his belly. He might dress as a lord of war, but he was frightened now. He could not even open his mouth to order his men to attack.

So I ordered mine. 'Kill them!' I shouted, and we charged.

I tell my grandchildren that confidence wins battles. I do not wish them to fight, I would rather make Ieremias's world a reality and so live in harmony, but there is always some man, and it is usually a man, who looks with envy on our fields, who wants our home, who thinks his rancid god is better than ours, who will come with flame and sword and steel to take what we have built and make it his, and if we are not ready to fight, if we have not spent those tedious hours learning the craft of sword and shield and spear and seax, then that man will win and we will die. Our children will be slaves, our wives whores, and our cattle slaughtered. So we must fight, and the man who fights with confidence wins. A man called Ida had come to this shore almost four hundred years before. He had landed from the sea, leading ships full of cruel men, and he had taken the crude fortress built on this rock, he had slaughtered the defenders, used their wives for his pleasure, and made their children his slaves. I was Ida's descendant. His enemies, who were now the Welsh, called him Flamdwyn, the Flamebearer. Did he really burn his enemies off this rock? Perhaps, but whether the song of Ida tells true or not, one truth is certain, that Ida the Flamebearer came to this crag and had the confidence to make a new kingdom on an old island.

Now I trod in the Flamebearer's footsteps to drench the rock with blood again. I had been right. My cousin's men did not stand. They had no confidence. Some dropped their shields and swords, and those men stood a chance of living, but any who tried to fight was given his wish. I too had dropped my shield, not needing it because the enemy was giving way, retreating, some fleeing down the ramp. The bravest of my cousin's men formed a shield wall around his

307

horse, and we attacked it. I hacked at shields, forgetting that a sword will not beat down an enemy in a well made shield wall, but rage will. Serpent-Breath cut the iron rim of a shield and split the helmet of the man holding it. He sank to his knees. A man rammed a spear at me, it tore my mail, pierced my side, and Serpent-Breath took one of his eyes, and my son stepped past me to kill the man. Finan was coldly efficient, Berg was screaming in his native Norse, Cerdic was breaking shields with his axe. The rock steps were slippery with blood. My men were shrieking, howling, killing, carving their way through defeated men, and my cousin tried to push his horse back through his rear ranks, and Cerdic shattered one of the horse's back legs with the axe, and the screaming animal went onto its haunches, and Cerdic sliced the axe into its neck and dragged my cousin out of his fleece-lined saddle. Men were surrendering, or trying to surrender. A priest was screaming at me to stop. Women were screaming. My son grabbed a helmetless man by the hair and pulled him onto his seax and twisted the blade in his gut, tossed him aside and rammed the sword into another man's belly.

Then the horn sounded.

One long, clear note.

The sun had set, but the sky was still bright. It was red in the west, purpling in the east, and no stars showed yet. The horn sounded again to herald Æthelstan, who walked his horse down the long stone ramp. He had ordered Rorik to sound the horn, demanding an end to the killing. 'It's over, Lord Uhtred,' he called when he reached us, 'you've won.'

There were men on their knees. Men who had pissed themselves. Men who watched us in terror. Men weeping because they had met the horror, and it was us. We were the wolf pack of Bebbanburg and we had taken back what Ida the Flamebearer had first won.

'It's over,' Æthelstan said again, quieter now. Ravens were flying from the hills. On the summit behind us there were dogs lapping blood. It was over.

'Not quite over,' I said. My cousin still lived. He stood, shaking slightly, guarded by Cerdic. His sword had fallen on the rock, and I picked it up from beside the corpse of his horse and gave it to him, hilt-first. 'You and me,' I said.

He shook his head. His plump face was red, his eyes scared.

'You and me,' I said again, and again he shook his head.

So I killed him. I hacked him down with Serpent-Breath and went on hacking and no one tried to stop me, and I only stopped hacking when his body was a mess of blood, cloth, splintered bone, broken mail, and butchered flesh. I cleaned Serpent-Breath on his cloak. 'Cut off his head,' I ordered Rorik, 'and the dogs can eat the rest of him.'

I had come home.

Epilogue

Einar proved to be unfortunate. Along with the crew of the *Trianaid*, his men defeated what was left of Æthelhelm's force in front of the Sea Gate, but Einar took a spear in the belly and died that night. The Scots had wanted to assault the gate, but a few rocks hurled down by Gerbruht's men had dissuaded them, and Einar's men, after their lord was wounded, had no stomach for another fight. They plundered Æthelhelm's ships, took the golden dowry that had accompanied Ælswyth north, and that was victory enough for them.

The Scots did not attack the Low Gate. My cousin had left thirty men to hold that formidable bastion, and with thirty men I could hold that gate until chaos ends the world. In the morning I opened the gate and rode out with my son, with Finan, and with Æthelstan. The four of us waited on the narrow path where Einar had started to build a palisade, and finally Domnall came to meet us. He was an impressive man, dark-eyed, black-haired, broad in his shoulders, and elegant in the saddle of an impressive black stallion. He said nothing, just nodded a curt greeting. He came alone.

'Tell your master,' I said, 'that Uhtred of Bebbanburg is lord here now, and that the borders of my land are as they were in my father's time.'

He looked past me at the Low Gate that was decorated with skulls my cousin had put there as a warning to invaders. I had added two heads, the shattered and bloody remnants of my cousin's skull and the head of Waldhere. 'It doesn't matter who rules here,' Domnall spoke surprisingly mildly, but then he was a warlord who did not need insults to instil fear, 'we'll still besiege the place.' He looked back to me.

'No,' I said, 'you won't.' I shifted in the saddle to relieve the ache in my side. I had been wounded there, but the cut was not deep, nor was the slash in my thigh. 'I am not my cousin,' I told Domnall, 'I won't just sit behind these walls.'

'You terrify me,' he said drily.

'So give King Constantin my greetings,' I went on, 'and tell him to be content with the lands of his father, as I am content with my father's land.'

'And you may tell him something more,' Æthelstan had pushed his horse forward to stand beside mine. 'I am Æthelstan,' he said, 'Prince of Wessex, and this land is under my father's protection.' That was a bald claim and one I doubted King Edward would have agreed with, but Domnall did not argue. Besides, he knew that Sigtryggr was less than a half-day's march away with a large force of horsemen. I did not know that yet, but Domnall did, and he was no fool. He knew Bebbanburg had been reinforced, and knew that he would be badly outnumbered once Sigtryggr reached us.

So the Scots were gone by nightfall, taking their share of Æthelhelm's gold, all of Bebbanburg's cattle, and anything else they could carry with them. 'In two days' time,' I told my son, 'we'll take sixty horsemen north and ride our boundary. If we find any Scottish warriors on our land we kill them.' I would let Domnall and his master know that Uhtred of Bebbanburg was now lord here.

Sigtryggr kept his promise, just as I had kept mine. I had promised he would lose no men, because all I had asked of him was to bring an army into Bebbanburg's land that would threaten the Scots. Domnall had been forced to send men to watch that army, thus weakening the force that besieged

Bebbanburg. I doubted he would have ordered an assault, but Sigtryggr's threat had made such an assault even less likely, and that afternoon my son-in-law led more than a hundred and fifty men across the narrow isthmus, through the gate of skulls, and up into Bebbanburg.

Æthelhelm lived. He, like many of his men, had taken shelter in the church where they laid down their weapons and sent a priest to negotiate their surrender. I had wanted to kill him, but Æthelstan forbade it. He had spent a long time talking with the ealdorman, then came to me and decreed that Æthelhelm would live. 'You're a fool, lord Prince,' I told him, 'your father would kill him.'

'He will support my father,' Æthelstan said.

'He promised that? What makes you believe he'll keep the promise?'

'Because you're keeping his daughter as a hostage.'

That surprised me. 'I'm keeping Ælswyth?'

'You are,' Æthelstan said, then smiled, 'and your son will thank me for that.'

'Damn what my son wants,' I said, thinking what a sordid mess that relationship would cause, 'do you really think Æthelhelm wouldn't exchange a daughter for a kingdom?'

Æthelstan acknowledged the point by nodding. 'He's a powerful man,' he said, 'with powerful followers. Yes, he'll sacrifice Ælswyth for his ambitions, but if he dies then his eldest son will want revenge. You just exchange an ageing enemy for a younger one. This way Æthelhelm owes me.'

'Owes you?' I scoffed. 'You think he's grateful? He'll just hate you the more.'

'Probably. But you'll keep him here until he pays a ransom,' he smiled, 'to you. He's a rich man, and you, my friend, have spent much gold to take this rock. By the time he's paid the ransom he won't be a rich man any longer. That way we weaken him.'

I growled to hide my pleasure in that thought. 'One day I'll kill him,' I said, reluctantly conceding the argument.

'Probably you will, lord, but not today, and not till he has refilled your coffers with gold.'

And that night we had a feast. It was a poor feast, mostly fish, bread, and cheese, but there was plenty of ale, and that made it a feast. And those few of my cousin's men who we trusted, mostly the young ones, feasted with us. The rest we had pushed out to be masterless men in the hills. The survivors of Æthelhelm's red-cloaked guards were in the lower courtyard, between the Low and High Gates. I would send them south in the morning, letting one man in three carry a weapon to defend themselves on their long walk home. Æthelhelm himself sat at the high table as his rank deserved. He was as genial as ever, though his eyes looked haunted. I saw my son pouring ale for his daughter, so pretty and pale, and she laughed when my son leaned close and whispered in her ear. Æthelhelm heard the laughter and caught my eye. We stared at each other for a moment, enemies still, then a gust of cheering from the lower tables gave us both an excuse to look away. I missed Eadith, but one of Æthelhelm's ships was still seaworthy, and in the morning I would send Berg and a small crew south to bring our women and families to their new home.

My cousin's harpist played the song of Ida. My men sang. They danced. They boasted of their prowess, they told stories of their fight, and they did not confess to the horror. There were too many wounded men lying in a smaller hall. We had collected cobwebs and moss, torn up my cousin's banners to make bandages, and tried to staunch their wounds, but I saw one of my cousin's priests, a young man, giving the Christians his church's last rites. Others lay gripping a sword hilt or a seax. Some had the weapon tied to a hand, determined to meet me one day in Valhalla.

316

And that night I stood with Finan on the rock ledge outside the hall. The moon was long on the water. Its reflection made a shimmering path, the same path that Ida the Flamebearer had followed to make his new home on a strange coast. And there were tears in my eyes to blur that long bright path.

Because I was home.

HISTORICAL NOTE

The historical note is where I confess my sins by revealing what in a novel is invention or where I have egregiously changed history, yet *The Flame Bearer* contains so much invention that an historical note is almost nonsensical, because just about everything in the novel is fiction. There was no conference between Edward, Æthelflaed, and Sigtryggr, no confrontation at Hornecastre, and no Scottish invasion of Northumbria in AD 917.

That confession aside, the reader can at least have some confidence that many of the characters in the novel existed, and that the ambitions and actions I have given them are consistent with their known behaviour and policies. The one exception to that rather feeble defence concerns Ealdorman Æthelhelm. He did exist, and he was an extremely wealthy and powerful West Saxon noble, but he was probably dead before 917, and I have prolonged his life because he makes a useful opponent to Uhtred. He was King Edward's father-in-law, and it is a fair assumption that he wanted Æthelstan disowned and disinherited in favour of Edward's second son, Ælfweard, who, of course, was Æthelhelm's grandson. The rivalry between Æthelstan and Ælfweard will become important in time, but during the story told in *The Flame Bearer* it merely serves to give Æthelhelm his motives for causing trouble. Those folk, like Æthelhelm, who denied Æthelstan's legitimacy claimed that Edward had not married his mother, and that Æthelstan was therefore a bastard. The historical record is not entirely clear on the truth of that claim, and I have chosen in the novels to believe in Æthelstan's legitimacy. Edward apparently attempted to protect the young Æthelstan by sending him to his sister, Æthelflaed, who was the ruler of Mercia, and Æthelstan did find safety in that kingdom. This present novel also suggests that Edward was estranged from Ælflæd, Æthelhelm's daughter, and that too appears to have been likely.

The background story to the novels about Uhtred tells of the making of England, or Englaland, as it was called then. When the novels begin, back in the 870s, there was no England. Nor indeed was there a Wales or a Scotland. The island of Britain was divided into many kingdoms. Those kingdoms squabbled endlessly, but the Viking incursions and settlements provoked a response that will result in a united kingdom of England. A similar process happened in Wales, chiefly under Hywel Dda, and in Scotland under Constantin, both of them great kings who began the unifications of their realms. Although I have traduced Constantin by suggesting he made an unsuccessful invasion of Northumbria in 917, the idea is not altogether ridiculous; he was to make such an invasion later. He was wary of the growing Saxon power to his south, and, in time, attempted to break it.

When Uhtred was born the country that was to be called England was split into four kingdoms. The Danes conquered three of them and very nearly captured the last, Wessex, in the south. The story of England's making is a tale of how that southern kingdom of Wessex gradually recaptured all the lands to the north. The dream of a united England properly belongs to Alfred the Great, King of Wessex, who died in 899 and whose achievement was to secure Wessex itself, without which the process could never have happened. Alfred also adopted the system of burhs, or boroughs, which were fortified towns. The Danes, though fearsome warriors, were not equipped for siege warfare, and the existence of these strongly walled towns with their large garrisons frustrated them. The same tactic was used in Mercia, where Æthelflaed's husband ruled much of the southern part of that country. After his death, Æthelflaed, now recognised as Mercia's ruler, pushed her frontier northwards into Danish territory and secured what she had conquered by building more burhs. Her brother Edward was ruling in Wessex, and he was doing much the same in East Anglia, and so, by 917, the Danes had lost almost all of their territory except for Northumbria. The old kingdom of East Anglia was not revived, it was simply swallowed by Wessex, but Mercia still clung to its separate identity. The West Saxons undoubtedly wanted to integrate Mercia into their kingdom, but there was considerable Mercian resistance to the idea of becoming just another part of powerful Wessex, and Æthelflaed, despite her brother being the ruler of Wessex, encouraged Mercia to preserve its independence. Nevertheless, by 917, Mercia was certainly deeply indebted to and under the influence of the West Saxon monarchy. England is not yet born, but nor is the idea of a single country for all who spoke the English tongue the impossible dream it must have seemed in Alfred's lifetime. All that remains to be conquered is Northumbria, which was ruled by Sigtryggr, though I have written myself into an historical novelist's dilemma by marrying him to Stiorra, a fictional character.

The fortress of Bebbanburg existed. It still does, only now it is called Bamburgh Castle and is a magnificent and much-restored mediaeval stronghold built where the ancient fort once stood. An Angle called Ida, who his British enemies called Ida the Flamebearer, sailed from mainland Europe and captured the crag and its fort sometime around the middle of the sixth century AD. He established a small kingdom called Bernicia, encompassing much of what is now Northumberland and southern Scotland. I stubbornly call all the English-speaking tribes the Saxons, but of course there were Angles and Jutes among them, and, perversely, the English took the name of their country from the Angles rather than from the dominant southern Saxons. Ida's Anglish family remained the lords of Bebbanburg until the eleventh century, and many of them took the name Uhtred. My Uhtred is fictional, and his struggle for the possession of Bebbanburg (which was named for Queen Bebba of Bernicia, the wife of Ida's grandson) is equally fictional. What is remarkable, perhaps, is that the family remained in possession of the great fortress throughout the period of Danish rule, preserving it as a Saxon and a Christian enclave in a Viking and pagan country. I suspect they collaborated, but we do not know, and certainly the fortress they built was formidable, one of the great citadels of pre-Norman Britain. Visitors to today's castle might wonder where the harbour and harbour channel are, but that shallow anchorage and its entrance have silted up over the centuries and no longer exist. The family that used the name Uhtred does still exist, and still uses a variant of that name as their surname, though they no longer live at Bamburgh. I am a descendant of theirs, which persuades me that I can take liberties with their distinguished history.

So, in my fictional world, Uhtred is again the rightful lord and owner of Bebbanburg. His great ambition of regaining his father's fortress is fulfilled, but the greater ambition, that of one country for all who spoke the English tongue, remains unfinished. Which means, whatever Uhtred might think, that his story is also unfinished.

Also by Bernard Cornwell

The LAST KINGDOM Series
(formerly The WARRIOR Chronicles)
The Last Kingdom
The Pale Horseman
The Lords of the North
Sword Song
The Burning Land
Death of Kings
The Pagan Lord
The Empty Throne
Warriors of the Storm

Azincourt

The GRAIL QUEST Series
Harlequin
Vagabond
Heretic

1356

Gallows Thief

Stonehenge

The Fort

The STARBUCK Chronicles
Rebel
Copperhead
Battle Flag
The Bloody Ground

The WARLORD Chronicles
The Winter King
The Enemy of God
Excalibur

By Bernard Cornwell and Susannah Kells

A Crowning Mercy
Fallen Angels

Non-Fiction

Waterloo: The History of Four Days, Three Armies and
Three Battles

The SHARPE series
(in chronological order)